DEADLY TIES

Jaycee Clark

Romantic Suspense

New Concepts   Georgia

Be sure to check out our website for the very best in fiction at fantastic prices!

When you visit our webpage, you can:

* Read excerpts of currently available books
* View cover art of upcoming books and current releases
* Find out more about the talented artists who capture the magic of the writer's imagination on the covers
* Order books from our backlist
* Find out the latest NCP and author news--including any upcoming book signings by your favorite NCP author
* Read author bios and reviews of our books
* Get NCP submission guidelines
* And so much more!

We offer a 20% discount on all new ebook releases!
(Sorry, but short stories are not included in this offer.)

We also have contests and sales regularly, so be sure to visit our webpage to find the best deals in ebooks and paperbacks! To find out about our new releases as soon as they are available, please be sure to sign up for our newsletter (http://www.newconceptspublishing.com/newsletter.htm) or join our reader group (http://groups.yahoo.com/group/new_concepts_pub/join) !

The newsletter is available by double opt in only and our customer information is *never* shared!

Visit our webpage at:
www.newconceptspublishing.com

DEADLY TIES

Deadly Ties is an original publication of NCP. This work has never before appeared in book form. This work is a novel. Any similarity to actual persons or events is purely coincidental.

New Concepts Publishing
5202 Humphreys Rd.
Lake Park, GA 31636

ISBN 1-58608-703-7
© copyright 2004, Jaycee Clark
Cover art by Eliza Black, © copyright 2004

All rights reserved, which includes the right to reproduce this book or portions thereof in any form whatsoever except as provided by the U.S. Copyright Law.

If you purchased this book without a cover you should be aware this book is stolen property.

NCP books are available at special quantity discounts for bulk purchases for sales promotions, premiums, fund raising, or educational use. For details, write, email, or phone New Concepts Publishing, 5202Humphreys Rd., Lake Park, GA 31636, ncp@newconceptspublishing.com, Ph. 229-257-0367, Fax 229-219-1097.

First NCP Paperback Printing: 2005

Printed in the United States of America

Acknowledgments for Deadly Ties

The critique gang, you know who you are.

A huge thanks to J., for answering questions she'd probably rather not have. George for the same, and Aunt T., thanks for answering all the medical and ER questions.

I'd like to thank Officer Kenny Bryson of the Metro Police Department for patiently answering my long list of questions.

This is for family, for teaching me that blood is never everything and love heals all.

PROLOGUE

Travis County Correctional Center, Austin, Texas, December

How dare they! Who in the hell did that bitch Shepard think she was? Nina Fisher would make them all pay.

"The appeal to reinstate parental rights has been denied. Ruling stands," the lawyer said sitting across from her.

No! They couldn't do this to her. He was hers, damn it. Ryan was her flesh and blood. It wasn't Nina's fault the eight-year-old kid didn't listen. The little shit had never listened. It was her right to discipline him any way she saw fit. Ryan was to blame for this mess. If he'd only behaved she wouldn't have had to hurt him. And what was the big deal? Nina still didn't know why they had charged her with Ryan's attempted murder. He'd lived hadn't he? So he'd spent a while in the hospital and had a broken arm and some bruises. What was the fuss about?

Damn, what she wouldn't give for a fix. Just one quick fix. A bump, yeah, a bump would be great to get over this freekin' jonesing.

"Ms. Fisher, did you hear what I said?" the slick lawyer--she had forgotten his name--asked. Probably fresh out of law school.

Nina stared at the brick behind Mr. I'm-cool-because-I'm-a-lawyer's head.

DEADLY TIES

"Yeah, I heard you."

She shifted and stared at the man across from her with his perfectly groomed blond hair, starched shirt and neatly knotted tie. Probably never worried about things like paying for childcare or whatever the hell.

"I bet you drive an SUV. Or no, one of those perfect law firm cars in either gray or black, like a Lexus or maybe a BMW? No, you're too new. Like gourmet coffee don'tcha?" Anger rose up in her, clawing to get out.

The lawyer ignored her.

Just one fix. She leaned up, tapping her fingers, bouncing her legs on the balls of her feet. "Ryan's mine."

The lawyer sighed. "Ms. Fisher, it's over. You lost. I have to say, I warned you. Going in with the attempted murder charge against you, we really didn't have a chance to win."

"And I bet you just tried your ever living damnedest, didn't you, sport?"

He stiffened. Then stuffed the file into his briefcase and clicked it shut.

"No judge was going to give you your rights back after you nearly killed your son."

She slapped her hands on the tabletop. "That's right! Mine! My son! Not that social worker, Taylor Shepard, bitch."

He took a deep breath. "As far as the courts are concerned, you have no child and Ryan Shepard's mother is Taylor Shepard."

Nina wanted to tear the idiot to shreds. She lunged across the table, grabbing the man's tie and jerking him over the edge of the table to her. "Never. I'll never let him go. He's mine. Mine! A piece of paper doesn't make him anyone else's. My blood flows through his veins."

The guard jerked her back, muttering to the lawyer to leave.

"He's mine!" she screamed. Another guard pinned her to the table.

"Good day, Ms. Fisher." The door clicked shut behind him.

Prison sentence or no, Nina would find a way to take what was hers. Attempted murder, my ass.

Thinking of Ryan with Mrs. Shepard stormed rage through her veins. "I'll make you pay, bitch. Before long you'll wish you never heard of me. I'll make your life hell," she whispered.

"Come on Fisher," one guard said, jerking her up and slapping the cuffs on her.

She walked out, the guard, a large ebony skinned man twice her size, pushed her down the hall.

Her chest heaved up and down with emotion, and she stumbled along the corridor. All this because Ryan had fallen through a plate glass window. She really hadn't meant to throw him *that* hard. If he'd only listened, she never would have thrown him in the first place. Stupid brat.

"You're gonna have fun where you're going, Fisher." The other guard was a woman with pale blonde hair, who looked too much like a doll to be sporting a uniform.

"Go to hell," she spat back.

"No, I'll wait and let you tell me what it's like," answered the guard. "Most inmates don't look well on those who hurt kids, especially their own. It's lower than low. In the pen, it's almost as bad as being a cop. Yeah, you're gonna have lots of fun."

Nina opted for silence. The rage boiled and rolled through her, a strong black cloud eating everything in its path. Time. She needed time. Time to think, to calm down, to plan. Damn it, if she only had some goods, she could focus enough to figure out what the hell to do next. Her laceless shoes squeaked on the linoleum. She'd have plenty of time for that once she reached Gatesville. Nothing like a maximum security prison for lots of thinking time.

Damn Ryan and his do-gooder savior.

It might take her awhile, but she'd figure out a plan. She always did. Always.

And when she did, those who wronged her, paid. They paid dearly.

CHAPTER ONE

Washington, D.C., June

Bllleeeeeepppppp. The high-pitched whine of the flatlined EKG echoed against the confines of the operating room.

Gavin's latex covered hands gripped the paddles again, blood smearing on the handles. The metal plates slid smoothly together. "Clear."

The medical team stepped back from the table.

Just for a moment the EKG graphed a slight fibrillation as the heart muscles attempted to once again live. The heart beat again, but then flatlined. It was useless. Shit.

"Dr. Kinncaid?" asked one of the surgical nurses.

"Damn it." He handed the paddles to another assistant. He hated calling time of death. He wiped his forehead with his arm before he looked at the large black and white clock. "Asystole. 12:32 p.m."

Hell-fire and bloody damnation. Gavin could only look down at the young, beaten face lying relaxed and lifeless on the operating table. Bruised and swollen it pleaded for help. Help that never came. Or when it had, it had been too damn late. Clear tubes ran out of her. IV's hung suspended from metal hooks. The black plastic of the ventilator stood still and silent now, no longer pumping air into her lungs.

DEADLY TIES

He fisted his hands on his hips. Pointless. It was all so damned pointless. Everything about this situation could have been prevented. Everything from the teen being pregnant in the first place, to her abuse, to her death. If only someone had taken the time to run an ultrasound down in the ER, they would have seen the internal bleeding. Someone might have caught onto the fact that the young girl was hemorrhaging to death. And by the time he had discovered the mistake up in the maternity ward, it had been too late.

His sigh heated his face against the clinical mask he wore. People shuffled quietly around him. The coppery scent of blood mingled with the stringent smells of antiseptic and disinfectants.

"Dr. Kinncaid?" He glanced up to see the anesthesiologist, Dr. Rita Farganio, holding the door. Most of the others had filed out.

"I'll be along in a moment."

The door swooshed behind her as it swung closed.

Gavin gently laid his hand on the girl's forehead. "I'm sorry, honey. I'm so damn sorry."

On another sigh, he turned, jerking off his bloodied surgical uniform and left the OR. He didn't care what others thought. Distance was all well and good, and a necessary part of the job. But, sometimes certain cases and certain patients grabbed you by the throat.

Cold water gushed over his hands, the fruity scent of the antibacterial soap tingled his nose. Was there even anyone to notify? The girl's parents? He'd learned they were in custody, since the father was the one who'd beaten his pregnant daughter. And who would notify them? Him? Their lawyer? Or the cops?

Gavin tried to remember if he'd ever been in such a situation before and couldn't think of a single one. The closest he'd come was when he'd been called in to help with a molestation case and needed the parent's permission to do the exam, only to find out the father was the bastard behind it.

The excess water sprinkled on the stainless steel as he turned off the faucet and reached for a paper towel. He tossed the towel angrily into the trash bin.

"Dr. Kinncaid?" asked a gray haired nurse in the maternity ward's pastel uniforms.

What now? He turned. "Yes?"

"There is a woman inquiring about Miss Gibbons. I just heard what happened. She's been pacing the floor for the last hour or so. She said she was the girl's social worker."

Hell, the social worker. Great. Wonderful. "Thank you, Bess. I'll take care of it."

He held open the door for Bess and stepped into the hall.

"I didn't think you were on call today, doc," she said briskly.

"I wasn't. But they called me in for this. I was supposed to help my brother move into his new house today, and the whole family is having some lawn party or something at the place. I need to get up there."

"You look like you need some sleep."

He grinned. "That too."

"Well, doctors need their rest too." She opened the nurse's station door and disappeared inside.

His most hated part of the job. The pale green walls did not soothe him. Pastel colors on the maternity floor seemed to mock him. There was nothing he hated more than losing a patient, mother or child, except having to explain it to family or friends, to shatter worlds. Well, putting it off wasn't going to make it the least bit easier. Gavin walked down the hallway towards the waiting room.

At the double doors, he looked through the window. Yes, indeed. There she was pacing down the distance to the doors opposite him that lead to the recovery rooms.

The waiting room, along with the nurses' station and nursery--set between the recovery rooms on one side and labor/delivery and the OR's on his side--appeared mostly empty, save for a few people clustered around the glass wall of the nursery. Miss Social Worker turned just short of the group and started back towards him. Her jeans and tee shirt, with white sneakers and a pony tail, made her look like an undergrad. What kind of social worker was she? Wasn't her job to protect those children in her care? She looked too young to be a social worker with her reddish blonde hair pulled back. On a resigned sigh, he pushed through the door.

She looked up and her gaze locked with his. He saw the question in her light brown eyes.

"Miss...?" What was her name? Had she told him?

Her stride stopped a few feet from him.

"Dr. Kinncaid, isn't it? How's Amy?" Her voice was soft, gentle.

Her expectant expression pulled his attention back to her question. He gestured to the chairs beside them, lining the wall. She looked so fresh, so full of life, so young. Anger at what had happened to the young girl in the OR simmered over.

"Why don't you have a seat?"

Her head shook back and forth. "No. I don't need to sit down. Just tell me. How is Amy Gibbons?" Her eyes narrowed on his.

Gavin ran a hand over his face.

"Let's sit down anyway," he said, sharper than he intended, but after what had just happened and right on the back of the night he'd had, he was too tired to care if he hurt her feelings. He firmly took hold of her elbow and led her to a chair.

"I'm sorry, I've forgotten your name," he said.

Her russet brows pulled down over her eyes. "Reese. Taylor Reese."

Taylor, that was different. "Well, Ms. Reese, I'm sorry to tell you this." He took a deep breath. He really *hated* this, even if he did wonder at her professional competency. "We lost Amy and the baby."

DEADLY TIES

Her brown eyes never left his. In fact, she never moved a muscle. "What do you mean, you lost her?"

"They didn't make it through the operation."

For a single moment, she said nothing, didn't move.

"We did everything we could."

"What happened?" she asked.

"Complications arose and --"

She raised a hand, palm out and halted his words.

"I've been around hospitals before, Dr. Kinncaid. I've seen kids die because parents shook them, hit them, beat them, starved them. Now tell me exactly what happened to Amy Gibbons. It'll all come out in court anyway, and the district attorney's office will need a copy of all her medical records and charts." Her voice might be soft, but there was steel in it, sharpening her tone.

Gavin sighed. "Once she arrived up here, I performed an ultrasound. There was a complication and apparently Amy had been and was still hemorrhaging," he told her frankly. Some liked explanations and others didn't. Ms. Reese was right. In this instance it was all going to come out in the end anyway.

"And no one noticed this before?" her own soft voice sharpened.

The hospital would be lucky if they didn't get a lawsuit out of this, or him a malpractice suit.

"I would have to assume, no. When I arrived in the ER, Miss Gibbons wasn't dilated at all, though I suspected she was in labor, which is why I immediately moved her up here to maternity and for general observation. Why she was not moved up here before that, I do not know, but I will find out." Someone was going to discover incompetence was a fault that cost lives. "However, once I had her up here and after an ultrasound, we discovered the blood was leaking into her uterus." Gavin watched as her eyes narrowed.

"What kind of hospital is this? I told that nurse downstairs hours and hours ago Amy needed an ultrasound."

He leaned forward, resting his elbows on his knees, ignoring her outburst, he continued. "After the sonogram, I immediately had her prepped for the OR." He knew going into the operating room that the baby was lost, it flatlined before they'd reached the end of the hall. Since the baby wasn't far enough along for delivery, there had been no way it could have survived, but he tried all the same. No need to tell Ms. Reese this though.

He cleared his throat and continued. "We did everything we could." Didn't they? "I am sorry. Is there someone I need to notify? Normally, I wouldn't even be telling you this, but would be telling her family. However, you told me earlier that her family was in police custody."

She looked away from him. He blinked and continued to stare at her, waiting for her answer. Gavin couldn't help but notice her perfect classic profile. Creamy skin, high cheekbones, though flushed, a straight patrician nose, and a straight, almost stubborn jaw. Her face was devoid of makeup with a dusting of freckles scattered across the bridge of her nose. He noticed then her hair was more red than blonde. Finally, she looked back at him. Her eyes glistened with cold acceptance.

"Yes, I suppose under normal circumstance one would tell a family these things." Her chest rose as she took a deep breath. "Don't worry, I'll tell who needs to be told." She shook her head.

"You said you were her social worker?" Gavin had no idea why he asked, but he did.

"Yes."

"What happened to her?"

"Her father beat her because he didn't like the fact she was pregnant." Her brows, the same reddish color of her hair, rose. "What do you think happened to her?"

"Was hers normally an abusive home?" he asked.

Her frown said she thought that a stupid question. She shook her head again. "Did it *look* to you like hers wasn't?"

Color flamed high in her pale cheeks.

Anger at what had happened to that girl, at the uselessness of it all, came crashing down in his tired brain, loosening his control. "Well, I can't help but wonder, Ms. Reese, what the girl was doing in that home to begin with."

She drew back as if someone jerked her from behind, her plain white tee shirt, pulling back across her chest and trim torso. "Are you questioning my professionalism?"

Gavin rubbed a hand over his face and took a deep breath. "I'm sorry for your loss." This was where he had been taught to walk away. But her eyes held him. They were filled with pain, anger, and tears. And he'd always been a sucker for female tears. Damn it.

"I'm sorry, too," she said. One lone tear trickled over lashes the color of her hair. Her forefinger, long and delicate, reached up and swiped it away. "I am too. And I have to wonder where the hell you were while that girl laid downstairs bleeding to death."

She was questioning him?

"Excuse me?"

Ms. Reese stood, looking down at him. "Look, you have your questions about me, fine. I have mine about you." She sniffed. "We'll call it even."

Gavin stood. "Now wait just a minute."

"What, don't like it when the tables are turned?" She crossed her arms over her chest.

Gavin closed his eyes and counted. It really didn't help. "As you said, we both have questions. I am sorry for your loss, and I'm sure you're doing your job."

She tried for a smile and he noticed her dimples winking at him. "I

DEADLY TIES

11

don't know if I should waste my energy to even bother with that insult." Her head shook ruefully. "I should let you go. After all, I'd hate to keep such an important doctor." Her gaze scanned him from the top of his scrubs, where her eyebrows arched at his alien do-rag, to the tips of his shoes. "Of course, one does wonder."

He shouldn't. He knew he shouldn't. "Wonder what?"

She only smiled, a thin, straight one, but still her dimples caught him off guard. "Thank you for informing me, Dr. Kinncaid. Social Services will be contacting you for details and what not. And I'm quite certain you can expect some questions from the Gibbonses' lawyer and probably someone from the district attorney's office." She reached down to grab her purse and he noticed her hands shook. Gavin caught of whiff of flowers--honeysuckle.

Whether or not she did her job, she did care. He could see that in her tears, angry or otherwise, the tremble of her hands.

He sighed. "I'm sorry for insulting you. I'm certain you did everything you could. I hate to lose a patient, any patient, and especially young ones."

She straightened. "Then I suppose we have even more in common than questioning the other. I guess we'll find out if we both did our jobs, won't we?"

Ms. Reese slug the brown leather strap of her purse over her shoulder. "Good afternoon, Dr. Kinncaid." She walked to the elevators and jabbed the down button repeatedly.

"Good afternoon, Ms. Reese." He started to say 'have a nice day'.

Yeah, that'd be good. What in the hell was with him? Gavin stood there with his hands on hips, watching the woman step into the elevator and the doors quietly swishing shut.

Damn woman. So much for his apology. He frowned for a minute. What the hell was the matter with him? He was a doctor. It wasn't exactly standard procedure to come out, inform someone of fatal news then grill them about job proficiency. And she'd questioned *his* competency. Gavin wasn't a braggart, but he knew he was one of the most successful doctors in his field for his age. He glared at the shut elevator doors, wondering at what had just happened and his total lack of tact, lack of control.

And if Gavin Kinncaid was anything, it was in control.

It was only then, he realized she talked like Jesslyn, his sister-in-law. Ms. Taylor Reese smiled her vowels. Maybe she was from Texas. On that absurd thought came another, more pressing one.

Social Services and lawyers. He shook his head as he turned and shoved the door back open through which he'd entered the waiting room. Hell. He needed to call the Chief of Staff and let her know what was going on.

Still cursing, he walked back up the hallway. The battered face of a young dark haired girl haunted him.

So much for his day off.

* * * *

Journal Entry

I know I said I thought this journaling stuff was stupid, but I've kinda gotten used to it. Dr. Petropolis was right. It helps to write things out sometimes, so I guess I'll keep doing it.

Today is hot here in D.C. I really like that Taylor and I moved here. I didn't like Austin. I hate Austin.

I'm at the neighbor's house. Jeremy Webster and I are friends. He has two brothers. They're really cool. And his mom and dad are neat too. I hope Jeremy and I get to be in the same class when school starts.

Taylor got a call this morning to go to the hospital. We were supposed to go to the Smithsonian again. I love the Smithsonian, but a call came about one of the kids she tries to help.

She said I could go with her, but I don't like hospitals. They bring back all those bad things I wanna forget. They remind me of Austin, and of HER. Nina. Dr. Petropolis said I don't have to call her mom if I don't want to and I DON'T WANT TO. So I won't. Dr. Petropolis is nice and she understands stuff, but I still don't like talking about all that stuff she wants to know about. At least I like her better than Dr. Siel, my shrink in Austin. I'm not supposed to call them shrinks, but shrinks binks, it's what they are.

So, that's why I begged Taylor if I could stay with Jeremy. I didn't want to go to the hospital. And I'm glad I didn't.

Sometimes I know things, like that time I couldn't find my bow to my violin and then I just knew. Like that. But today it was worse. Bad. And I don't really like when I see things. I get all cold and I can't hear things around me. It's kinda like when I sit on the bottom of the pool when we go swimming and I can hear other kids yelling and splashing but it's muffled.

At least Jeremy was in the house or he might think I'm a freak and not want to be my friend anymore. I was up in his tree fort when I got all cold and stuff and I just knew. Just knew that the girl Taylor was trying to help wasn't going to make it.

She's dead. I think a blue eyed doctor with black hair told Taylor. I 'saw' them arguing, but he's nice, I think. Maybe not. Just cause someone looks nice doesn't mean they are.

Lots of times people are just mean, no matter what they look like. Some people just like to hurt others. I wish I knew why. O.K. gotta go. Mrs. Webster has snacks ready and is calling us.

* * * *

Taylor thrummed her fingers on the steering wheel as she sat in late Saturday traffic.

The knowledge that Amy was dead still hadn't sunk in, she knew that. It was vague, in the background. It had to be, because if she dwelled on it, she knew there wasn't a damn thing she could do about it

DEADLY TIES

and the failure would consume her. The entire situation had all been so pointless, so preventable.

Dr. Kinncaid's words echoed in her and made her question herself. *Had* she done enough? Could she have done more? Was there anyway she could have prevented this tragedy?

No answers came. And stupid, proud anger still shimmered through her at that arrogant doctor. Were all med school grads given classes in self-assurance? Every last doctor she'd ever met were the most self-assured people, arrogant and usually rude.

Rude or not, those blue, blue eyes of his kept interrupting her thoughts. They reminded her of the shade of the Northern Atlantic. And the rest of him hadn't been bad either, in a rugged, six-foot-four-or-five-kind-of-pro-football-player way. His sharp nose was ridged and his square jaw had bunched when she'd questioned his doing his job properly. She'd been surprised when she'd met him in the ER before the surgery. He'd thought she was Amy's sister because he'd said she was too young to be the girl's mother. When she'd told him she was the social worker, he thought she was too young for that too.

Figures. Even insulted her then. Though it hadn't sounded like an insult. For a man as large as he was, he all but swallowed up the space in a room, it seemed he'd have a loud booming voice. Instead, his voice was soft, like distant thunder, faintly echoing.

But enough about Mr. Doctor.

Taylor held a hand to her cheek. She'd just left the meeting at the city jail with her boss, the prosecutor from the D.A.'s office and the Gibbonses. Mr. Gibbons had taken exception to a remark Taylor had made and before anyone could stop him, he'd decked her clean out of her chair. The man had hard fists, but then, were there soft ones? Maybe he had scrambled something in her brains after all.

The prosecutor had all but danced with glee at the new charge against Mr. Gibbons. Glad she could be of assistance.

Carefully, she moved her jaw out and in, back and forth. It felt like her eye was about to pop out of its socket.

Taylor held the baggie of crushed ice to her face as she waited on the light to turn green.

She checked her watch--five o'clock. Great. Ryan was probably wondering where in the world she was. She'd dropped him off to play at the neighbors when the call came in about Amy earlier this morning. What a weekend.

She pulled the visor down. The little lighted mirror reflected off her cheek.

Good God, it was going to look really bad tomorrow. Her cheek was already bruising. Wonderful. This was just what she needed.

On a sigh, she flipped the visor back up and moved along with the rest of the traffic as they crawled through the D.C. streets.

She was ready to go home, where things were normal, and figure out where she and Ryan were going, or if they still had time to go somewhere for the weekend. She needed to make today up to him because today was supposed to be their day. Instead he'd been playing at the neighbors', Mr. and Mrs. Webster, who had three boys. She'd been gone since almost noon, though she'd called and checked in with Mrs. Webster before the meeting in the police station. Ryan was fine. The boys had spent the afternoon up in the tree fort.

Taylor shook her head. At least Ryan was making some friends.

What to do to make up today to him?

Maybe they would head up Montgomery County and see some of the sites. She'd heard the countryside was scattered with bed and breakfast stops. They could stay at one tonight and catch some of the tourist traps tomorrow. Having moved here under a month ago from Texas, both she and her son were still finding their way around, in more ways than one.

Her cheek throbbed and she gently touched it. Some ibuprofen would be great right about now. Then again, it seemed she and Ryan had always had to find a new path in some hostile situation. Maybe one day things would go smoothly for them.

CHAPTER TWO

That day was not today. Taylor took a deep breath and tried to see through the rain blanketing down from the night sky.

Ryan, headphones stretched across his light brown hair, hummed some classical piece from the back seat of her older Mercedes, one of the few things she got out of the settlement with Charles Shepard.

She slowed down again and flicked her lights as an oncoming car barreled towards her.

Taylor hated to drive in weather like this. She wanted to pull over, but there wasn't really a shoulder. She'd taken a wrong damn turn at some point.

"Are we getting close? I don't see any lights, Taylor," Ryan commented from the back seat.

She sighed. "No, neither do I. I need to turn around somewhere." Though she had no idea where.

"We could just spend the night at that last little town in a motel. It's okay. We don't have to stay in some historical bed and breakfast."

Taylor's head hurt, the ibuprofen doing little to take the throb out of the left side of her face.

Finally the rain lessened and she saw the road sign. She grabbed the map and tried to find it while slowly maneuvering the narrow winding road.

DEADLY TIES

Hell.

She tossed the map aside. "I think I'll just go a little further up this road, whatever this road is, and find a spot to turn around."

"Okay." He started humming again. Ryan was always humming. He was gifted in music, thank goodness. She discovered his talent by accident, but he'd become more than proficient in playing the violin in an amazingly short amount of time. She often wondered if it was God's way of bringing something wonderful and beautiful into his otherwise darkened life.

Taylor listened to his humming, Beethoven. Figured. The boy loved Beethoven and Handel and she had no idea what else.

The wet black pavement gleamed in her headlights. As she rounded a curve, the steering wheel jerked in her hand. The tires swooshed over the large puddle of water.

Her heart slammed in her chest.

She grabbed the wheel and realized they were heading across the yellow center line. Hydroplane.

"Oh, God."

She jerked on the wheel and the car spun out of control.

"Taylor!" Ryan yelled from the back seat.

"Hang on!"

The car rocked over the opposite non-existent shoulder and nose-dived into the steep bar ditch on the opposite side of the road. It slammed to a bone jarring halt against a tree. The airbag exploded from the steering wheel.

For a moment, she sat absolutely still. Then she punched the already deflating airbag out of the way. Tired of fighting it, she reached down and leaned the seat back.

Her heart slammed against her ribs. Lightning flashed outside, thunder ripped the air apart. Oh, God. Oh, God. Oh, God.

She licked her lips. "R-Ryan?"

Oh, God.

"Yeah?" he whispered.

The seatbelt. Her fingers fumbled with the latch, and she shook her head. When it snapped open, she turned in her seat.

"Ryan?"

She could see his ashen face in the dim lights. She reached over the seat, her hands running over him.

"I'm okay. I'm fine, Taylor. Are you okay?" he asked, letting her fluster over him.

"Taylor, you're crying. Are you hurt?" It was the fear lacing his words that stopped her.

A deep breath. She just had to breathe. For one moment, they stared at each other. Ryan's sky blue eyes and freckles clear in the low light against his pale cheeks, his scar a pink contrast.

He was okay. he said he was okay. "You're sure you're not hurt?"

she asked, her voice trembling.

"I'm okay. Really. You can stop crying."

She grinned and wiped a hand over her cheeks.

"What happened?" he asked her.

She thought, then shrugged. "I think we hydroplaned."

"What's that?"

What was a little accident when it afforded an eight-year-old such questions?

Taylor sighed and sat back, still facing the back seat. "It's when water comes between the tires and the pavement and you glide instead of stay on the road," she simplified.

She closed her eyes and reached for her phone.

Damn it! No. She whirled around in the seat, looked in the console. "No. No. No."

Where was it?

"The phone is charging at home," Ryan told her.

And a lot of good it did her there. Damn it. Why hadn't she grabbed it?

Rain pelted down from the heavens again and lightning strobed the outside world.

This was *not* happening.

What the hell could she do? It was miles back to the town and she could hardly walk in the rain with Ryan and she wasn't irresponsible or stupid enough to leave him here. Someone could come along and....

"Taylor, there are lights over there."

She jerked around. Sure enough. Headlights winked through the trees.

"Thank you, God." She reached under her seat and pulled out the umbrella. "Stay in the car."

"Be careful. The policeman on the Discovery Channel said how you shouldn't flag cars down and--"

"Yes, and he's right. But right now, I have little choice." She opened the door. "Ryan, stay. In. The. Car."

His huff floated on the air. "Yes, ma'am."

She shut her door. The sweet smell of rain, musty wet ground, and earthy leaves and mud assailed her. Taylor could barely hear the sound of the car coming. She needed to hurry, or it would pass them by and God only knew when the next one would come.

The slope of the ditch wasn't easy to climb in her slick soled shoes, but she reached the top. Huffing, she waited for the car to come around the corner. Already soaked, she cursed the umbrella and tried to keep the rain off.

* * * *

Gavin was almost there. Three more miles and he'd be at his brother's new house, and several miles past that, was his parents' estate. Why his brother wanted to live this close to home was beyond

DEADLY TIES 17

him. He loved his parents, really Gavin did, but the thought of living only a few miles from them was just too much. Oh well, Aiden was different. The party was now probably indoors thanks to the summer thunderstorm.

He'd dealt with the Chief of Staff, filled out all the paper work, talked to the lawyers, and still he was pissed.

Gavin hated to brood. Life was too short to brood.

And he was brooding because --.

"What the hell!"

He slammed on his breaks, his Lincoln Navigator sliding until the tires caught the pavement again.

A woman stood in the middle of the damn road holding an umbrella. In the glare of his headlights he saw very little, other than she was wet. She stayed in his lights for a moment more, before she hurried over to his side of the car. He noticed then the car in the ditch.

He rolled his window down and yelled. "Let me get off the road." Checking the rearview mirror, then the other lane, he drove across the yellow line and pulled his SUV off the road, setting the hazards and brake. His headlights shone on the back of a dark Mercedes sedan.

Gavin jumped out of the vehicle and hurried down the small shoulder of the country road. The woman backed up and something niggled his memory at the sight of her jeans and plastered white tee shirt.

"Are you hurt?" he asked.

"Can you help us?" she asked.

"Ma'am?" he calmed his voice. "Are you hurt? Is anyone hurt?" He pulled out his phone and punched nine-one-one.

"No," she said. "No. I don't think so. We just need some help. I left my phone at home--stupid I know, and we flew off the road and I was scared Ryan was hurt, but I don't think he is and...." she trailed off.

That voice. He knew that voice.

"Ms. Reese?" he asked.

"What? How do you know me?" she backed up.

How bad could this day get? He was cursed. God hated him.

"Dr. Kinncaid."

"You," she groaned.

A moment passed, the rain pelted his hair to his head, thrummed off the top of her nylon umbrella.

"You are the most idiotic woman I have ever had the misfortune to meet."

"Me? You're still the arrogant ass you were this afternoon."

"Arrogant? Well, I'd rather be arrogant, than ignorant."

"Ignorant?" she gasped.

"You were standing in the middle of the road in the rain in the dark." He walked towards her, and she no longer backed up. "I could have killed you."

She huffed and muttered, but he didn't catch it. Finally, she turned and started back down the hill to the car that sat at an odd angle in the bottom of the ditch, the front right fender hissing against a small oak tree.

"Of all the guys, in all the cars, on all the roads," she said, loud enough for him to hear.

"I could say the same of you," he said, skidding down the embankment after her.

From the interior, a shadow moved. A small someone.

"Are you certain no one was hurt?" he asked again.

He wasn't surprised when she ignored him and kept going to the car. "Ms. Reese."

She stopped and turned. "What?"

He strode up to her, ignoring the rain that fell down in buckets. "Are. You. Hurt?"

Her sigh huffed out. "We're fine, I think." She looked in the backseat. "Oh God, he could have been … I could have … What if…."

She took a deep breath and dropped the umbrella.

Gavin picked it up and hit the send button on his phone. While he talked to the dispatcher, he handed her the umbrella back and reached for the woman's wrist. He didn't let go, even when she tried to pull away. "I'm a doctor. I'm going to take your vitals whether you like it or not."

"Check Ryan first."

Fine. He opened the driver's door and motioned her to at least sit down. Quickly and concisely he relayed pertinent information to the dispatcher. Then he opened the backdoor. The kid stayed in the far corner.

"Hey," Gavin said, leaning down. "I'm Dr. Kinncaid. Are you hurt?"

The boy looked from him to the front seat. "Taylor?"

"It's okay. He is a doctor. Are you all right, Ryan?"

The boy nodded. "Yeah, nothing hurts, 'cept my shoulder where the seatbelt is."

Gavin sat in the backseat with the boy and reached over to take his pulse. A little fast, but considering the excitement it was normal. Didn't appear to be in shock at least.

"Let's all go up and sit in my car. It's warm and dry and we'll wait on the cops and EMT's up there."

After some grumbling from the front seat and silence from the back, they made their way back up the incline to his Navigator.

Once inside he checked both their vitals, and Ryan's shoulder. Good rotation, didn't seem dislocated and the boy didn't complain of any pain when moving it. Now here, he saw the boy was slightly pale and looked little like Ms. Reese other than the coloring of hair. The boy's was a dark red-brown color. He had freckles like his mom. A large pink scar cut a jagged mark down the left side of his face, over his eye. As a doctor, Gavin wondered what happened, but he didn't ask.

DEADLY TIES

Instead, he said, "You'll probably be bruised tomorrow, but I don't think any damage was done."

Taylor's snort drew his attention to her. He didn't say a word, just reached over and took her wrist again, noticing how delicate the bones were. Her hand shook.

"You're fingers are like ice."

She, on the other hand, could be in shock.

He reached over and flicked on the heater even though it was a good seventy degrees outside. The faint whiff of flowers floated to him across the seats.

Sirens wailed through the night. "Cavalry is coming."

"This is a day from hell," she said.

He tried to get her to look at him, but she always kept part of her face adverted.

"Ms. Reese--"

"Oh, call me Taylor," she snapped.

Gavin couldn't help but chuckle. "All right, Taylor, if you call me Gavin. Are you certain you didn't hurt your neck?" He reached up to touch the nape, but she jerked away.

"I said I was fine."

The woman was touchy and had 'keep back' plastered all over her.

"Oh-kay." He relaxed in his seat and picked his phone up. He needed to call Aiden. When the county sheriff's car and ambulance pulled up, he got out and walked to them.

"Yeah?" his brother asked through the phone.

"It's me. Sorry, but it doesn't look like I'm going to make it. Something came up, but I am heading to Mom and Dad's."

"Thanks for helping me move," Aiden said.

Though he knew his brother was joking, he was not remotely in the mood. "Look, I'm sorry. I'll make it up. There are things that I can't control, you know."

"Yeah, those women in your life are a real nuisance."

Gavin ignored the jab and continued. "Like babies, and abusive parents, and dying teenagers." The cops got out of their car and Gavin held his hand up hoping they'd give him a minute. "Car accidents."

"Car accidents?" Aiden asked sharply. "Where the hell are you? Are you okay?"

Gavin felt like cursing. "I'm about a mile from your turn off and it's not me, so yeah, I'm okay."

"I'll be there in a--"

"Everything is fine. Just tell Mom I'll be late." He looked back at his car. Did they have a place to stay tonight? It was almost ten at night. "And I might be bringing someone."

No one answered him. Well, damn Aiden anyway.

Gavin spoke to the EMTs on his quick assessment of the two people in his car. He followed the cops down the embankment and told them

20   *Jaycee Clark*

what he knew of the accident, which was really very little.

Red and blue lights flashed in the night.

"Gavin!"

Gavin sighed and looked up the slope of the ditch to see his brother's silhouette. Well, had he really expected Aiden Kinncaid to sit quietly at home after he mentioned an accident?

He nodded to the sheriff's deputy and walked to where his brother stood frowning. Aiden was shorter, even if he was the oldest Kinncaid brother. Though, truth be known, they were all over six feet. And like Gavin, Aiden inherited their father's jet-black hair and cobalt eyes. But that's where the similarities ended. Aiden was a complete family man. Must be the oldest-sibling thing. He ran the family hotel business and though the others had some say in it all, Gavin couldn't have cared less except that he had shares and he had a trust fund. His passion was medicine.

"What the hell happened?" Aiden asked.

"That woman ran off the road," Gavin said, pointing to his car, where he saw Taylor sat half in, half out of the open passenger door talking to one of the uniformed officers.

"*That* woman?" Aiden drawled, a grin hinting.

"Yeah, and the idiot then decided to wave a car down in the middle of the damn road." The more he thought about it, the madder he was getting again. At her.

"And may I ask what *that* woman's name is?" Aiden crossed his arms over his chest.

"Taylor. Taylor Reese. Contrary, incompetent, and annoying."

Gavin stood staring as the medic turned Ryan's arm one way, then lifted it higher, holding the shoulder. Another EMT moved the officer away and checked Taylor. He was turning Taylor's face one way, then the other.

"Interesting," Aiden drawled again.

Gavin ignored him and walked to the car.

"I don't know what happened. We were going about fifty, probably closer to forty-five because I'd just slowed down to a crawl to look at the map. Anyway, we took the curve and the next thing I knew, I couldn't control the car and it was just flying off the road," Taylor said.

He saw then the shadow darkening the left side of her face. Had she hit the steering wheel? The window? Why the hell hadn't he noticed it before?

"I thought you said you were fine," he barked, all but shoving the medic out of the way.

One eyebrow cocked.

He reached out, but she pulled back, her brown eyes reminding him of fox in the low light, the freckles on her face standing out.

Taylor leaned away from his hand, awareness tingling through her at his nearness.

DEADLY TIES

"I am fine," she told him, tired.

"You look it, too."

She glanced at his left hand, and saw there was no ring.

"You're not married, are you?" she asked. "No wife could put up with your do-as-I-say attitude."

His eyes left the side of her face and zeroed in on hers. "What a subtle come on."

Taylor snorted. "That wasn't a come on. You are the most arrogant man I have ever had the misfortune to meet."

He tsked. "You've already told me that." He held up a finger. "Watch my finger."

"Is it going somewhere?" She huffed out a breath. The man was impossible. "The medic has already done that, thank you very much. I don't have a concussion or anything else, so just stop being all … all…."

"My finger."

She rolled her eyes and took a deep breath. This close to him, his scent, some expensive outdoor cologne and rain, wafted between them.

Deciding it took more energy to fight the man than give in on this, she watched as his long, blunt-tipped finger went one way then the other.

"Anything else, Doc?" she asked.

"Yeah, how did you get this?" His brows furrowed as his fingers grazed her cheek. She pulled away, startled at the shock his touch sent through her. Just like earlier when he'd felt her wrist for her pulse. It was like a low electrical hum.

Taylor stared at him, saw the way the soft rain glistened on his dark hair in the lights of the other cars. His square jaw was shadowed with stubble, sprinkled with moisture. For some absurd reason she actually wanted to reach out and touch his cheek.

Which was stupid and just went to show that she must have hit her head, or that Mr. Gibbons had scrambled her brains.

"What happened?" he asked quietly, his voice low and deep like beckoning thunder.

"N-nothing."

One brow cocked. "It looks like nothing."

His finger touched it, pressed.

"Ouch."

"What happened? Looks like someone punched you."

"Someone did," Ryan said, standing beside Gavin.

Both black brows rose, then immediately beetled on a frown.

"Who?" Gavin asked her.

Taylor rolled her eyes and glared at her son. "It's nothing."

"Who hit your mom?" Gavin asked, partially turning to Ryan.

"A man."

"What man?"

She was seriously going to have to talk to her son about loyalty. He liked new words, she'd have to teach him that one.

"Mr. Gibbons," she all but sighed out. "It was Mr. Gibbons."

Gavin turned back to her, his head cocked. "The father of the girl who died?"

"Yep," Ryan said. "Knocked her right out of the chair."

Gavin's eyes narrowed, the blue hardened, iced. "Out of your chair?" he asked quietly.

Taylor looked to her son. "How do you know that?"

"I heard you talking on the phone to Mrs. Jenkins before we left. You said, 'Well, yeah, when the man knocks you out of the chair, it tends to hurt'." Her son's small shoulders shrugged.

"Look up eavesdropping when we find a dictionary," she said.

The two males, one who must be in his thirties and the other eight, were not related, but the angry expressions, fierce eyes and tense jaws were identical. She couldn't help it, she laughed.

"I'm fine you two. Quit frowning." To her son, she said, "You know it sometimes happens with what I do."

His set expression didn't change. "That doesn't mean I can't get mad about it."

True.

"What were you doing with the man?" Gavin asked.

She sighed. "Is it really that important?"

"Humor me," he muttered, while his fingers pressed around her eye, felt her cheekbone.

Trying not to wince, let alone shove his hand away, she said, "It was a legal meeting. Social Services, lawyers. The cop was outside the door." She shrugged. "Man just moved really quick."

Gavin grunted.

What did that mean? Her stomach tensed when his fingertip grazed her hairline near her ear.

"Did you have this checked out? X-rayed?"

The man was a doctor, and a bossy one at that, even if he did smell good.

Taylor made to stand, but he didn't move.

"Did you?" he asked again.

She glared at him. "I. Am. Fine. It's only a bruise. They go away."

He pulled back a fraction and simply stared at her with such an intense expression, she shifted.

"What?" she asked.

"They go away?" He stood, shoved a hand through his damp hair.

What was with this guy? One minute he was snapping at her and the next he seemed upset because she had a bruise.

He shook his head.

Taylor looked past him to the man standing on the other side of the open door leaning against the front fender. He was grinning. A single

DEADLY TIES

23

dimple winking at her from his right cheek. He was one of the most handsome men she'd ever seen; short black hair, swept off a high forehead, the same eyes as Gavin, but where Gavin's features were blunted, rough, this man was polished. He looked like he'd just stepped out of *GQ*. Perfectly put together in a "handsome aristocratic businessman" type of way.

He offered her his hand. "Aiden Kinncaid. I'm Gavin's brother."

She took his hand. "Taylor Reese. My son, Ryan."

"Looks like you had quite a night."

"You have no idea."

"Do you need to call someone?" he asked.

This man was nice. She looked back at Gavin, noticing the way his wet tee shirt sculpted over the muscles of his arms and chest. She sighed. The damp jeans fit him perfectly. He cocked a brow and she realized she was staring. Lord, he'd think her simple-minded before long. "Why is it that your brother has all the manners?"

Aiden chuckled. "Ah, but Gavin here got all the charm."

She snorted. "Yeah, right."

Aiden's smile slid away, and he tilted his head, studying her. Finally, he turned back to his brother. "You could bring them up to the house."

One of the officers came up. "We need to take a statement, and ask some more questions."

She nodded to Deputy Ainsworth. Then to Aiden said, "Thank you for the offer, but--"

"You have some place else to go?" Gavin interrupted.

Who did the man think he was?

"See?" she said it his brother. "No manners."

* * * *

Ryan dug his journal out of his backpack. He was sitting in the back of the doctor's Navigator, the smell of leather filled the car.

Taylor and Gavin were still talking to the cops. The other Kinncaid guy had left earlier.

They were staying with this doctor and his family for the night. Taylor was stressing, she was running her hands through her hair a lot. And she only did that when she was worrying about stuff.

Taylor worried about stuff a lot. Not that she'd want anyone to know, but she did. He liked the doctor. The guy was nice and he didn't like Taylor's bruise any more than Ryan did.

That meant he was a good man. Men who didn't like bruises on women wouldn't hurt them.

And Ryan knew all about people hurting other people.

Sometimes adults were just mean.

Ryan's stomach growled. He was hungry. Pizza sounded good. Or maybe some ice cream. If they were at home, he'd have asked Taylor if he could have had some of that Chunky Monkey kind that was in the freezer.

He shrugged and pulled his pen out, turning on the little interior light on above his head. At least he had his journal.

We're out in the middle of nowhere. Taylor wrecked the car. Charles is going to be mad I bet. Or maybe she can fix it without him knowing. Probably not, since he pays the payments and insurance and stuff on it. I heard them arguing about it during the divorce.

I met this doctor. He's nice. And big. I bet no one messes with him. I bet people move out of his way. And he's a good guy. Or seems to be. He was mad at Taylor's bruise. Plus, he's a doctor and I don't think doctors hurt people.

I wish we hadn't wrecked, then we'd be in a hotel somewhere and doing stuff tomorrow. But now we're spending the night at this doctor's house. Or his family or something. But he said there was a pool and I like swimming. Maybe it'll be okay.

Taylor's not happy about it. But he told her to quit arguing. How was she going to get back to town to stay somewhere, he wanted to know. She started to say something, but then the doctor's brother--his name is Aiden--he said his mom wanted us to stay with them. So I guess we are.

I wonder if the doctor still lives with his mom. That seems kinda weird. Guess we'll find out.

I'm kinda tired. I wish we could go already. Wonder what we'll do tomorrow.

CHAPTER THREE

Taylor opened her eyes as sunlight streamed through the windows, warming her. Making her way to the bathroom, she gently touched her throbbing cheek and wished she didn't have a headache. Last night the bossy doctor had brought her and Ryan here after the cops were done asking their questions. This house was huge, more along the lines of a mansion she'd see on some special show on cable. Set a couple miles back off the road, a security gate around the property--or rather estate-- clearly screamed upper class.

These people were wealthy. She had no idea what his family did, thinking it probably rude to ask. There were more rooms than she could count in this mansion. And it was that, a large, gray stoned mansion full of antiques and priceless heirlooms. It hushed with an air of family wealth.

Her room alone was a hotel suite. A large queen, sleigh bed, the sitting area where Ryan slept, and a bathroom that any woman would envy with its large jet tub, multi-headed shower and lots of light.

She stopped to the sink, closed her eyes then opened them.

"Mother of God." The entire left side of her face was purple from her

DEADLY TIES

ear to almost her nose. Her eye was swollen and black. "Wonder if Mary Kay will cover this?"

Half an hour later both she and Ryan descended the stairs. Her sundress floated around her ankles. At the bottom of the stairs she wondered which way to go. She couldn't believe people actually lived here. No wonder Dr. Kinncaid was so arrogant and self-assured.

"It's like a museum, isn't it?" Ryan whispered.

"Shh," she told him, listening. Finally, she heard a clink of a utensil on a dish. Breakfast.

Following the sound, she ran a hand over her vintage beige dress, walked through double doors and into a large dining room.

Gavin sat behind a newspaper.

Taylor stopped in the door.

"Oh." A woman, the same height as Taylor hurried from the sideboard over to them, her shoulder length red curls bouncing around her face. "Hello, I'm Kaitlyn Kinncaid, Gavin's mother."

The newspaper rustled.

Taylor offered her hand. "Hello. I'm Taylor Reese and this is my son Ryan."

Mrs. Kinncaid looked perfectly groomed. If her other son last night looked like he had stepped out of *GQ*, she looked like she'd walked off the pages of *Nordstrom*. Taylor shifted, wishing she'd had other clothes. One of her few quirks were vintage clothing, circa 1920's and 30's. Flapper dresses, tank dresses out of filmy material and lace. The one she had on now had set her back a bit, but the beige georgette overlay had caught her fancy. Now though, they probably looked like Goodwill rags, as Charles had often called them.

After a silent moment, Mrs. Kinncaid asked, "Are you in pain? I thought Gavin said no one was hurt in the accident."

Her face. Though she'd tried, makeup could only do so much. She gently touched the side of her face. "I'm okay. And it wasn't the accident."

The woman tilted her head. "Did you take anything for it? Your face looks like it hurts."

Taylor shifted and sighed. "Some ibuprofen."

Mrs. Kinncaid frowned. "Come on. Load up your plates. Becky, our housekeeper-cook-general, cooked too much this morning."

Taylor dared a glance at Gavin. He'd lowered his paper and stared at her. Frowning as always.

"Do you ever smile?" she blurted.

His gaze narrowed. "Not before noon and never when looking at a bruised woman."

She rolled her eyes. His mother laughed as he flipped the newspaper back up.

Taylor and Ryan loaded their plates with eggs, waffles, and fruit.

"Gavin tells me you work in Social Services," Mrs. Kinncaid offered after everyone was seated.

Taylor nodded. "Yes, I do."

Mrs. Kinncaid shook her head. "I was a pediatric surgeon for years. It is a shame, a horrible shame what some parents do to their own children."

"I know."

Ryan shifted next to her. He looked up, his eyes shadowed with memories she knew she'd never be able to erase. Looking to Mrs. Kinncaid, he said, "Some people are just mean."

The woman cocked her head to the side and for a moment she said nothing, then, "Yes, yes sometimes they are."

From under her lids, she caught Gavin's study of them.

"Are you married?" Mrs. Kinncaid asked her.

Taylor almost dropped her fork. She could feel Gavin's eyes on her. "No, divorced."

The woman smiled, a single dimple winking in her cheek. Just like the other son, Aiden, Taylor had met last night.

"And your name is Ryan?" she asked.

Ryan nodded, not looking up.

"Well, if I can talk my son here into staying a bit longer, you might meet Tori, my granddaughter. She and her father live here, but they've been gone. Should be back this afternoon."

"Mother, we can't stay."

Since the man was driving her back to town, Taylor said, "If you want to see your brother, I can wait."

He shook his head. "No, I'll see Bray later. We've got to call a wrecker to take your car to the nearest Mercedes dealer. There's one in D.C."

She sighed. The insurance would now be going up, which meant that Charles would have something else to complain about. Hell, the man hardly paid child support, he wouldn't like the fact the car insurance went up. But, she wasn't going to think about Charles Shepard right now.

"I feel bad for ruining your weekend," she admitted. And she did. Doctors were as busy as she often was, probably more so. People got hurt and needed medical assistance at all times of the day and night, and babies came when they wanted. This man probably liked his time off.

Gavin shrugged. "It's fine. Stop worrying."

His mother frowned from him to her. "You know, you're more than welcome to stay. Your father and I have hardly seen you in a month. The kids could play and Taylor could rest."

Gavin smiled at his mom and Taylor swallowed. *My God.* The man could give a woman all kinds of fantasies with that wicked smile alone. Straight and quick, perfect white teeth, it completely transformed him from grumpy into … devastatingly charming. The corner of his eyes

DEADLY TIES

even crinkled. But charming handsome men were last on her to-do list. She'd tried that before and look where she was now. Dumped, relocated and begging for child support from the tight ass while he pampered the new Mrs. Shepard with all she wanted.

Taylor shook off the brooding thoughts.

"An entire month, Mom? And just think, there used to be days you'd wonder if the house would ever be quiet."

Mrs. Kinncaid smiled back. "Yes, every parent's wish, only to realize years later that they'd love the noise again. That is why grandchildren are so wonderful. Don't you think?"

Gavin shook his head. "Don't even *think* it."

"Do you like children, Taylor?" The woman waved a hand. "Dumb question. You help kids, have one of your own. Of course you do."

"Mom, we're leaving. I told you there are things we need to do."

Taylor was having trouble following the conversation. Gavin picked up his coffee cup and quickly took a drink.

She cleared her throat. "You're right, Gavin, I need to call a tow service. Do you know of any? And then there is the issue of another vehicle." She sighed.

He turned and looked at her, the smile slipping slowly away. "Exactly." Back to his mom, "See, we need to go. Especially before Dad or Bray get home, then we'll never get out of here."

For some reason, Taylor got the impression he simply didn't want her here.

She speared the waffle with her fork and shoved it in her mouth, quickly taking another bite.

"Where is Dad anyway?" Gavin asked.

"The Club."

Of course the dad would be at the country club. Would a residing patriarch of this mansion be anywhere else?

Taylor closed her eyes. Her head still ached and when she was tired and hurt, she got cranky. Mr. Kinncaid was probably as nice as Mrs. Kinncaid.

"Taylor?" his voice didn't frown, it caressed. Maybe if she didn't open her eyes she wouldn't have to see his frown.

"Yes?" Sure enough, there was that frown.

The vague thought that she'd like to see him smile at her the way he had at his mom floated stupidly through her tired brain.

Sleep. She just needed some sleep.

"Are you all right?"

"Dandy." She got another bite and decided she was no longer hungry. Looking over, she saw Ryan had all but licked the syrup from his plate, scarfed the eggs, but left the fruit. Well, life could hardly be perfect. Fruit and vegetables were often asking a lot.

She tried to ignore him, but her eyes kept drifting to Gavin. This morning he was dressed in a black polo and chinos. She sighed.

Picking up her coffee, she tried to hide her yawn behind the cup, but halfway through pain pierced her cheek. She closed her eyes and waited for it to go away.

"You okay?" he asked again, softly.

She swallowed and nodded. "Yeah. If you'll give me a few minutes, I'll go get our stuff together and we'll be ready." To Mrs. Kinncaid, she said, "Thank you so much for your hospitality. You have an extraordinary home."

The woman laughed and waved a hand. "It was our pleasure. Maybe you'll come to visit sometime. And I suppose extraordinary is one way to describe it."

"Museum is a better description," Gavin muttered.

Ryan chuckled.

She smiled at him, and turned back to Gavin.

Gavin caught his breath at her grin. Two dimples deepened her cheeks. That floral scent he'd detected last night and the day before at the hospital had floated into the room the moment she'd walked in. And it teased him from across the table now. Her eyes were a soft brown color, like the color of whisky. Though he thought maybe they lightened when she was angry, or he seemed to remember them being more amber yesterday when they were insulting each other in the maternity ward.

Taylor shifted and answered something his mother said. Early morning sunlight shot red fire off her hair, which she'd pulled back into a braid.

The dress she had on was something else. It was made out of some filmy material and seemed to glide over her skin. Hell, every time she'd picked up her fork and moved forward, he'd watch it bunch and pull over her chest. The sleeveless dress showed off pale shoulders with a smatter of freckles.

"Is that okay with you, Doc?" she asked, drawing his attention.

Gavin shook his head. "What?"

"Leave in half an hour? You're mother wants to show me something."

Great, now Mom was showing her things. He knew what his mother was thinking earlier with all the divorce questions and children. Lord, ever since Aiden and Jesslyn were married and had the twins, he was expected to go next.

Marriage? No. Too big, too long term, too much commitment on both sides.

Hell, he couldn't get enough time to eat most of the time, let alone sleep. What would he do with a wife?

His ex dating partner--he didn't think of them as his girlfriends until after several dates--had yelled at him last night and dumped him because she was pissed he couldn't spend more time with her.

His family might joke about all his women, but he was lucky to date

DEADLY TIES

the same woman four or five times without work getting in the way. And women seemed to be funny about that. Wanted hearth, home, and leashes. It was fine for a pregnant woman to want him to deliver her baby at four a.m. But if she was the doctor's lover, let alone wife, she might have something to say about it.

"Hel-leewww," Taylor said.

Gavin shook off his thoughts again, wondering why in the world he'd thought of marriage in the first damn place.

Leave, half an hour. "Yeah. Yeah, that's fine. Sorry, I was thinking of something."

He watched as the other three left the room. What about her rubbed him wrong? Ever since he met the woman, they'd bickered. And he generally got along with women.

Gavin gave up trying to figure it out and went to get his stuff.

* * * *

Gavin grinned as he drove through the streets to Taylor's house. Lunch had been entertaining and informative. They'd left later than he'd planned and Gavin decided to take them to lunch. Taylor had, of course, declined. Was the woman always so contrary? Though after he'd talked her into lunch, a sort of truce seemed to reign. He'd noticed several things as Ryan wolfed his burger and Taylor ate her salad. He picked up on the fact that Ryan wasn't Taylor's biological child, more from what wasn't said than what was, but he had yet to figure out the dynamics. Ryan was exuberant, full of factoids, and liked to hum classical music, yet the boy was often guarded. Sometimes he seemed hesitant to do things and Gavin caught him either asking or looking to Taylor for permission. He wondered at that. Was it simply shyness or was it more? Gavin was curious about Ryan, but he didn't know how to broach a subject that he had no business delving into.

Taylor, herself, fascinated him. She talked and laughed through the lunch. Amazingly enough, they'd actually gotten along. He learned she was the more health food type. She liked water and salads. He'd asked where in Texas they were from, telling them he'd been to the Austin area for the last year off and on while his brother's family lived there. A conversation started up about Texas places to see and things to do. He'd enjoyed himself more than he thought he would.

"Have you always lived here?" she asked him as they pulled up to her house, a brownstone with a low fat porch that had geraniums in little pots on it.

"All my life."

"It's different here." Her hands lay calmly in her lap, long tapered fingers on elegant hands, short buffered nails. Taylor was built like a dancer he'd once dated, long and lithe, her movements graceful.

"I would imagine it would be," he said.

"Thank you again for lunch. I wanted to treat you to lunch. After all you've done for us."

Gavin smiled at her disgruntled voice. "Call me old fashioned, but my father taught me to be a gentleman. You open doors for ladies and you pay for their food."

Her dimples deepened as she smiled fully at him. "Even ones who set your teeth on edge? I feel privileged and I'm sorry you inherited us for the day."

He wasn't. "Don't worry about it."

Gavin helped them get their bags and walked them to their house.

She opened the door and let Ryan rush in. "Would you like to come in for something to drink? I don't have a clue what we have. Probably Koolaid and who knows." She smiled. Those dimples.

He'd never thought of himself as a dimple man, but maybe he was.

"I better get going and let you get your stuff squared away," he said.

A moment of silence hung between them. She reached up and touched her cheek and the small movement had the anger shifting in him again. Gavin bit down at the sight of her bruised face. His fist bunched in his pocket. It looked swollen even with her shades. And he could see the shadow of it beneath her makeup. He wondered how many different colors it was. He could see the dark purple and blue hue of battered skin. What if her jaw had been cracked, or her cheekbone? Gavin started to reach out and touch her, but instead, he curved his palm around the edge of the door.

He had been taught to cherish and protect both women and children. As a child, these were values his parents instilled in him, and later as a doctor in his field he came to believe it even more. Her lips were moving, but he hadn't heard a word she said.

"What?"

She tilted her head. "Do you tune out all women or is it just my charm?"

He smiled. "It's just you."

Her sigh was enough that he felt it brush his face. "I wanted to thank you for all of this. Again."

"You've already thanked me."

Silence stretched between them and he watched as she licked her lip, and rubbed one bare arm, the movement causing that filmy material to stretch and glide over her torso.

"I did, didn't I?"

On impulse, he said, "How about lunch later this week?"

She tilted her head. "Call me and I'll let you know."

* * * *

Ryan stood upstairs in his room looking out the window as Gavin Kinncaid pulled away.

Gavin was pretty cool. He often seemed almost rude to Taylor, but then she was rude back to him and Taylor was never rude. Even with that jerk she'd been married to, Charles. She'd always been nice to that man.

DEADLY TIES

Adults were strange sometimes.

Ryan looked around his room, saw his space posters, and his violin.

He ran a finger down the wooden body, huffing out a sigh. He was glad to be back home with his stuff, especially his violin.

A honk from below drew his attention back. Ryan waved and wondered if they'd see Dr. Kinncaid again. The man was cool and had this deep rumbly voice and his family was neat, living in that great big house that had the pool. They hadn't had a big tour because Mrs. Kinncaid and Taylor started talking about plants. Who wanted to talk about plants?

Gavin and his mom got along great. Maybe when he was that old, he and Taylor would still get along. Taylor was great. Not like that other one. No, he wasn't going to think of *her*.

His stomach churned and tightened.

Shaking his head, he picked up his violin and found a piece of music he wanted to practice. The notes flowed from the instrument, through his arm and chin, connecting at his heart and flowing back out. That's how he liked to think of it anyway.

Music was the best.

CHAPTER FOUR

Taylor walked out of the office and onto the sidewalk.

"Taylor," his quiet voice had her turning. Gavin stood still and silent, leaning against the wall.

He was dressed in a dark button down shirt and slacks, those wicked eyes hid behind black shades. A sigh slipped out of her. *Idiot.*

"Lunch?" he asked.

"Funny, I don't recall my phone ringing." She dug her keys out of her purse. Her heart did a little skitter as he stepped closer to her.

"I like spontaneity. Women tend to get irate when something planned gets cancelled due to say, labor, or complications."

Women, plural. "You would know, I'm sure."

"Jealous?"

She ignored him and shook her head.

"Okay. Truce. I'm hungry and you're off for lunch I presume, so let's go eat."

Taylor figured she should say no, but she was hungry and knew no one. "Fine, since you asked so nicely, how's a girl to refuse?"

"Did you get a rental?" he asked.

"Yes." Taylor pointed and they walked to her gray compact car. Gavin took her elbow and her blood hummed at the simple contact, even as she stiffened for a moment. She cleared her throat. "At least the dealership loaned me a car while mine is in the shop."

"Well, I'm right over here."

She started to jerk away, but the slight shiver from his touch, made her pause. Plus, she had to admit, she liked the feel of his hand, warm on her arm. It had been a long time since a man had not only walked her to a car, but had been a gentleman about it. Which, considering who this was, it seemed almost odd. She was used to his rude, sometimes condescending behavior. Though yesterday he had been nice enough. And here he was today to take her to lunch.

And she was reading more into this than she should be. *Idiot.*

He looked to her car and said, "I'll admit, for some reason, I didn't expect you to drive a Mercedes. Social workers make more than I thought. At least you have another to drive."

Taylor only smiled at him. She didn't want to tell him how she had all but blackmailed Charles for the damn car, and then had to give him the money to let her keep it. Should have just let her ex have the stupid thing and bought a new one. She did have money from a comfortable inheritance, from her parents and a distant aunt, but it was the principle of the thing. And it was hers. And now it was in the shop.

"I never asked, are you busy today? I just assumed you were going to lunch."

"Yes, I was … going to lunch that is. Actually, someone else asked and I lied and said I already had a lunch appointment." She smiled. "And you fell nicely into place."

He leaned closer to her, backing her against the door of the car. "Did I now? Sort of like being used, isn't it?"

She licked her lips. "Um…. No, not really, because I didn't know you'd be here and…."

He was so close she could see his eyes behind his shades, smell that cologne he used, or maybe it was his aftershave.

"Oh, but being used has its advantages," he continued with a wicked grin and a wiggle of brows.

What did that mean?

If she leaned a little closer she could kiss him. Taylor blinked, cleared her throat.

Finally, she took the bait. "Dare I even ask what those advantages are?"

For a moment he only have her his almost-smile, and tilted his head down so that he stared at her over the rims of his shades. His eyes twinkled, catching up at the corners.

Gavin Kinncaid could be dangerous, no doubt about it. His full charming smile caught her breath.

"Do you really want to know?" he asked, his voice low and deep.

Yes. No. Probably. Taylor sighed.

This time a laugh rumbled out before he tapped her nose. "Yes. No. Probably?"

DEADLY TIES

Oh, God, did she say that out loud?

Again his chuckle vibrated the air between them. "You're cute when you're flustered."

It was from spending too much time with him yesterday, that's what all this was about.

A man. He was just a man.

And she knew most men were pigs, jerks, or worse. Friends. Yeah, they could just be friends--even if she did have fantasies about him.

Taylor wasn't up for anything else. Was she? No. She had Ryan, her new job, and…. And that's all she needed. His cologne assaulted her. It was.

Then why did she wonder if there was more out there for her or if she'd already had her chance on the love merry-go-round and blew it?

That was a depressing thought. Charles, her one and only? No, don't think so.

But right now, she needed to concentrate on her job, getting Ryan settled, and starting life over. And that's what she would do. Concentrate on Ryan and her work. But this dark-headed doctor kept intruding. Thoughts of the man had kept her up half the night. Either she had it really bad for some guy she'd just met--okay that was probably a given--or she'd been too long without sex. Probably another given.

Sex with her ex had just been sex. But with Gavin?

Where had that thought come from?

"Hello?" Gavin said loudly in her face, his expression questioning.

Taylor shook her head. Lord, he'd think she was an idiot.

"Um. Sorry," she muttered.

"I'd dearly love to know what you were thinking about," he said in that soft, rumble of voice.

She just bet her would. She could feel her face flaming.

"Nothing."

His expression, one brow cocked, one lowered, said he was trying to figure her out. "And just where were you going to meet me?" he asked.

"Meet you?"

He poked his tongue in his cheek before saying. "Lunch? You said you lied and told someone you had a lunch appointment, and I fell nicely into place."

"Oh!" God help her! "I haven't a clue," she admitted. "Maybe you have an idea. Though I'm telling you now, I'm paying." She held up her hand. "And spare me your gentleman's speech."

Another crooked smile, this one devastating charm, and she felt nerves dance at the flash of teeth.

"Fine. I get to drive though, and we're taking my car." A hand was held out to her, and she simply stared at it. His sigh filled the air between them. "Don't tell me, besides no one taking your elbow, no one ever offered you their hand either. What's wrong with those Texas cowboys?"

Taylor rolled her eyes and reached for his hand. Her breath caught in her throat. Such a simple thing, a glance of fingers on palm, but it felt like her entire being had suddenly awakened. Nerves no longer danced--they reeled as blood pumped through her veins. She blinked, staring at her long pale fingers still lying on his tanned large palm.

"They must be too busy with their horses," he continued as his fingers closed over hers.

By the grace of God, she didn't stumble along after him. Even managed to remember to lock her car. Talk about humiliating. Did he not feel it? Amazingly enough, her mind still functioned within the context of his dumb remark.

"Not all men in Texas are cowboys. Not all of them go to rodeos, know how to saddle a horse, or own cattle contrary to popular belief. You couldn't have caught Charles or any of his cronies dead in a pair of boots or a hat if you had all but paid them." *Great! Just great. Can I say anything more idiotic than bringing up my ex?*

They walked in silence to his SUV.

Gavin held her hand in his, and like the day before, he opened the door for her, making certain she was in before he shut it. Hopefully, he wouldn't pick up on her mention of Charles. He'd leave it alone. She could have been talking about anyone. And why should he care? He wouldn't. Leather groaned and sighed as he slid into the driver's seat.

"Charles?" he casually asked as they pulled out of the parking lot.

But she caught the slight tension in his voice, noticed he wasn't exactly smiling now.

Instead of answering him, she just shook her head and grinned. "Where are we going to eat?"

"Charles?" He was stubborn.

Two could play this game. "I was sorta thinking Mexican or maybe one of those bar and grill places with great salads."

* * * *

"Here we are," Gavin said, ushering her through the door of a brownstone. The glass and wooden door opened and the inner air wrapped its cool arms around them, welcoming and inviting from the heat outside. Dark woods and leathers greeted, multicolored glass lamps dulled the light on the wooden tables. The noise here was muted and quiet, an old jazz tune played on the air.

"Hope this is all right. Lots of choices and it's not too far from where we were."

Taylor smiled at him. "It's fine. Perfect."

The hostess grabbed a couple of menus and led them to a table. Gavin's hand dropped from her elbow to the small of her back, almost possessive, and the breath caught in the back of her throat. What was this? A friendly lunch? Or a date?

Gavin felt her slight tension when his hand went to her back. He

DEADLY TIES

hadn't meant to do that, it just seemed like the most natural thing. Hadn't even thought about it, to tell the truth. They stopped at a walled in booth and Taylor slid into one side, he in the other. A slight furrow between her brows wasn't lost on him.

Nothing was lost on him, when it concerned Taylor.

He'd noticed the edginess when he'd first called her name, replaced by a smile. He also noticed her almost nervousness, not to mention she'd ignored his question about Charles. Who the hell was Charles? Some guy from Texas, obviously.

And *why* did he care? It wasn't like he and Taylor were even dating, for God's sake.

But where Taylor was concerned, Gavin found himself not only thinking about her, but also wondering how she was, what she was doing. Hell, the woman kept him up half the damn night. Thoughts of her dancing through his head. Maybe that was where this protectiveness was stemming from. Yeah, friendship. They were friends, of sorts. Weren't they? Did he want to be friends with her? She kept him on his toes, aggravated him half the time. So where did that leave him?

Who was Charles?

"Today's salad sounds great. What are you getting?" she asked him.

Today's salad? What? Gavin shook off his thoughts.

"I have no idea, probably what I always get when I'm here." He popped his menu open, stared at the all the letters, prices and words, and didn't comprehend a damn thing.

Taylor ordered the coconut shrimp salad and since that actually sounded good to him, he got one too.

He watched the muscles move in the long column of her white throat as she swallowed the cool drink of her tea. And thoughts of kissing that pale skin just below her chin flashed into his brain.

Friends? Yeah, right.

She leaned her bare elbows up on the table. The white sleeveless shirt buttoned down the front, and as the top two buttons of her shirt were undone, he couldn't help but get a glimpse of white lace as she shifted. Damn.

"So tell me about your family, Gavin."

He cleared his throat. "You met Mom. And Aiden"

"Hmm. What does your brother do?"

"Aiden? He runs the hotels." Gavin didn't want to talk about his family. "You know lots about me, and I know very little about you. Seems kind of one-sided to me."

"Is that right?" Cinnamon brows rose above those dark eyes of hers. "And how do you figure that?"

"Well, you know what I do, what I drive."

"For all I know you could be engaged to an intern or some socialite woman from the country club."

"Jealous?"

She leveled him a look.

"No and no. There was Scarlett but I was about to dump her when she dumped me."

Taylor tilted her head. "Aw. Poor baby. That kicks the pride doesn't it?"

He ran his tongue around his teeth. "You been dumped?"

"Been there and done that. Scarlett? As in O'Hara? Oh my," she breathed in a heavy Southern accent. "Why Rhett, did she find her long lost Ashley?"

"I hated that movie."

She straightened. "It was actually a book first, but so did I, the heroine was too tedious. So what was Miss Scarlett's problem with you? I have to ask, is she from Georgia?"

Her grin was contagious. "Oh yeah. Her state representative daddy plays golf with mine. Same functions whatever. But she had a problem with my responsibilities."

Taylor shook her head. "High maintenance. Never took you as the type who would go for that."

"We're off subject."

"Was there one?"

"The fact you know more about me, than I do of you. You even know about my lack of relationship success with a Georgia woman, and you know about my family." The glass of tea cooled his palms. "Now you, I know you're new here and that you're a caring social worker and you have a son named Ryan. That's it." Well, maybe he knew a bit more, but not compared to what she knew of him, and he found himself wanting to know more.

"You know I let my job get to me sometimes," she said with a smile.

"True, but I don't know why." There it was that slight tensing of her again, an almost indiscernible pull of brows. "Besides," he added, "that has to do with work."

Her sigh settled between them. "What do you want to know? Though I get to answer only the questions I can or want to and get to ask one in turn."

Gavin nodded. "Fine."

He shifted his weight in the seat, stretching his legs out a bit more, and felt his pant's leg graze along her skirt. He cleared his throat and asked. "What are you doing in D.C.? And don't tell me working. I mean, what made you move from Austin to here."

Her eyes looked away from him and back towards the door, then settled back on the glass that sat in front of her. "It seemed the best for all concerned after the divorce."

"Ah. Methinks me found a tale."

Gavin wanted to understand Taylor and he had absolutely no idea why. Normally, he just went after the chase, spent some enjoyable

DEADLY TIES

evenings and times with women, but nothing serious. None of his previous relationships had ever plagued his mind like this one woman whom he knew very little about, and wasn't even sleeping with.

"Look," he told her, "you don't have to tell me anything you don't want to."

"No, that's okay. I don't know why I make such a big deal out of it anyway." Her shoulders lifted in a small shrug. Finally, her eyes lifted back up to his. "Charles and I were married for almost eight years. Got married in college."

Ah, the elusive Charles. "What happened?"

A rueful smile frowned her mouth. "Oh the normal I guess."

"Normal?"

"I don't know, exactly. We were both busy in work. I thought we should start working on starting a family, and he kept putting me off...." Her voice trailed off as her finger slid through the condensation on the side of the glass. Just before she looked away he saw the pain flash into her gaze. "But anyway, between both our jobs, we didn't. Ryan came along and we adopted him. Then, the divorce was finalized and a few months later Ryan and I moved here. That's it."

"I doubt that. What was wrong with the guy?" *This is none of your business.* "Sorry."

"No, it's okay. I actually never told anyone. Just let everyone think what they wanted to, or rather what he led them to believe." She said the last part almost to herself. "It didn't matter then. Doesn't matter now. The adoption was finalized and Ryan was all I cared about."

Gavin opted to just stay silent. The more she talked, the more questions arose.

Her voice continued, but it no longer sounded like a gentle summer breeze. There was no emotion there, nothing. "But, looking back, it was for the best I think. Charles didn't want a family and I did."

"Then why did you adopt Ryan?"

The more he learned of her, the more questions he needed answered. Like yesterday. The more time he spent with Taylor and Ryan, the more he found he *liked* spending time with them. Yesterday evening and last night they'd stolen his thoughts. Ryan was a cute and intelligent kid and Taylor.... Taylor fascinated him. She was gentle and caring, not his usual ilk of women. He went for the fun-time type. Classy and polished usually, like Scarlett. None that he would consider anything serious with.

Then what exactly was he doing with Taylor?

Gavin guessed the conversation was over since she hadn't answered him yet.

"I adopted Ryan because I had to," she whispered, finally answering his question. A watery laugh and a wipe under her eyes gave him another glimpse into her as did her words. "I can't go into what happened to him, not now. Not today. But when I saw him, the more time I spent with him... Well, I fell in love with him. I know that makes no sense. None at all. I never could get Charles to understand it. And then I just quit trying. He waited on the divorce until after the adoption and that was all I wanted. Time enough for Ryan to become mine. Then, as far as I was concerned, Mr. Charles Shepard could do whatever the hell he wanted."

Anger and a bit of resentment there. "He hurt you."

She started to shake her head, then stopped. "Yeah, a bit. Or maybe I let myself get hurt. It's more the hindsight thing, if you know what I mean. Charles is Charles and always will be. Now, I don't know if I'm angrier at him or myself."

Gavin took a chance. "There is more to this story than you're telling."

Again, Taylor shifted. "Probably. Suffice it to say, I have a hard time getting over infidelity."

He ran his tongue over his smooth teeth. "Idiot guy."

"Oh, but Rhonda doesn't think so." A sugary smile deepened her dimples.

"Rhonda?"

"The newer model. You know, buxom, curvaceous, without a cluttering thought in her head. Perfect for Charles, actually."

"So you divorced the two-timer." He made it a statement not a question. "Can't say as I blame you there, the divorce and moving and all. I have a problem with infidelity myself. Guess I'm either old fashioned or just selfish. But what is mine stays mine." He looked straight into her brown eyes. "I don't share."

Fidelity was at the top of his list. He figured if a woman cheated on him, he didn't need her. If he hadn't meant enough to her for her to remain faithful, then she wasn't worth his time. Then again most women would see his occupation as his mistress; colleagues of his had warned him.

"Neither do I, but he wanted to file long before I walked in on his side show. He filed a month after the adoption was final, and as soon as the divorce was stamped, sealed and notarized, he flew to Mexico and married Rhonda."

Gavin knew there was even more here than she was telling, but the waitress chose that moment to bring them their food.

Taylor picked up her fork. "So what happened with Miss Scarlett?"

Gavin speared himself a golden fried shrimp. "I told her from the beginning that I wasn't looking for a serious relationship right now. And after canceling plans again on Saturday in lieu of family obligations.... Well, Scarlett had enough." Though she had called him last night to gripe at him some more for being more interested in his job and family than sex with her. No, Scarlett was no longer a problem.

"Wow, a free man. You must be so happy."

His next forkful stopped midway to his mouth. "You have no idea."

Her dimples winked at him before she took another bite.

DEADLY TIES

The rest of the lunch seemed to fly by. On the way back to her car he asked if they could swap phone numbers. Why he asked was beyond him.

"Hmmm."

He pulled up behind her car.

Gavin got out a business card and scrawled his home number and mobil on the back. Ignoring her comment, he said, "If you ever need anything, just give me a call. I'm not promising that I'll be able to get to you right away, tend to get called away sometimes, but...." He took a deep breath.

Her shades hid her eyes from him. She reached up and grabbed his card, glanced at it, flipping it over to look at the back.

"Anything?"

When he'd met her, she was all spit and fire, and the other night she'd been annoying and snappy. But now, Taylor was such a composed woman, that he couldn't help but be intrigued. He wondered if he preferred this soft, composed side of her, or the angry, insulting woman he'd met on Saturday.

"Of course," he answered.

"Well, then." She riffled through her purse and came out with a card of her own, scrawling her numbers on the back. Handing it to him, she said, "I guess you can call me sometime too. I'm usually home during the evenings, but I too, tend to get called out or away sometimes. But I'll tell you right now, I think you're arrogant--"

"I know."

"--and rude--"

"Got that already."

"I have neither the time, nor the inclination for a relationship of any kind."

"Not even a long night of sweaty sex?"

Her eyes rounded.

He laughed. "My feelings are really hurt, Taylor."

"You're impossible."

"I try to be, but it's good to know where the other stands, so I should be honest and say I'm not looking for anything either. I just split from one clingy woman who couldn't respect what I do. I'm in no hurry to tangle with another one."

Her grin flashed. "But I think that might depend on the tangle. Does sweaty sex count as tangling?" Her eyes narrowed on his. "And just for the record, I have *never* been clingy, nor would I be with men like you."

"Men like me?" he asked as she started to get out.

"Rude, self-absorbed men who know their appeal to the opposite sex."

He grinned. "Find me appealing do you?"

She ignored his remark. "Thanks for dropping by today."

"You're welcome." He stared at her and wished he could clearly see her eyes. "Just for my side of the record, I enjoyed today."

Taylor opened the door and hot air sweltered in. He was already rolling down her window, leaning over the console into the passenger seat. Her door shut with a soft click.

"Try not to provoke anyone today, Taylor."

Her laugh danced out. "I know. You don't count towards my daily goal."

She started to straighten, but then leaned back into the window giving him a glance down her shirt. "By the way, I enjoyed today with you too."

Before he could compute that, Taylor was already at her car and behind the wheel.

Gavin smiled all the way to his office.

CHAPTER FIVE

Texas was hot in June. Hotter than hell. In fact, it was rumored through the prisons that Satan made Texas as a vacation spot. Apparently, the devil decided even he didn't care for the place, leaving the land to its prickly pears and rattlesnakes, scorpions and other assortments of lovely things. Nice load of bullshit, but Nina Fisher didn't care either way.

Large, circulating fans swirled the hot sticky air at Valleyview State Penitentiary near Gatesville, Texas. The female population contained some really bad bitches. A few were even on death row. Nina didn't care to think about them. If Ryan ever remembered everything that went on that last night, she might be one of them.

Damn Jonny Hayes. That bastard was still out on parole. He'd left out the window when he'd heard the sirens the night Ryan fell through the damn glass. Nina really wanted to nail Jonny's ass for killing that narc agent--which in her opinion started the entire nightmare--but it was hard to do that without nailing her own. No, she'd bide her time. He was another one that she owed. Jonny, Ryan, the judge and of course that social worker slut and her husband. Yeah, one day she'd get them all.

"Fisher."

Her name jerked her attention back. The guard, Rod, held a package up. All of the packages were sniffed and x-rayed before the inmates got them to make certain nothing was in them. That was all well and good, but once the package was past the checkpoint was when you could get the goods.

A book. Hot damn. She hurried through the melee of bodies.

DEADLY TIES

"Fisher's got a boyfriend on the outside," someone said.

"Wonder what the idiot sent the bitch."

Nina ignored the comments of the other inmates and walked on. Just as she grabbed the book, she caught the slight wink Rod gave her. Thank God! She was starting to wonder. She looked at the title and tried not to laugh out loud. *Living With Addiction: Making a Life from the Hollows.*

Yeah, right.

Nina hurried over to a window set high and narrow in the wall. No bars, but that didn't matter, couldn't get out if she wanted to. The light outside was a dull gray color tinged with a murky green. Thunder occasionally disturbed the sultry air. Maybe a freaking tornado would come and blow the damn building away.

Prison life sucked. It sucked big. Who in their right fucking mind got up at three-thirty in the morning, every morning? Inmates, that's who. Breakfast at four, and work started at six. They had three hours a day for "personal" time. Basically, the hour for recreational activity, weights, walk around, exercise, and the two hours for classes. Nina was enrolled in Substance Abuse Education and Spiritual Growth. Both were a complete joke. Just about every damn person in her Sub class was either stoned or jonesing when they got there. Everyone knew how to score a hit, to get a bump, regardless of whatever rules and regulations there were. Money and other things were available. This was a woman's prison, so if there wasn't money, other 'favors' could be given.

And Nina was currently working on that. Rod would be her ticket out of here. She was sure of it, but she'd have to be careful. It was frowned upon for the guards to fraternize with their female inmates. 'Course most of the guards and workers here were female, but a good many of them were males. Thank, God.

Again she looked out the window. Why in the hell was it called Valleyview? Was there a single damn valley in sight? Not that she could remember from her trip here, or from what she could see once she'd gotten inside.

There wasn't much about the trip from Austin to here that she did remember, save for the blinding rage she'd felt. But she'd quickly learned to hide that after she'd gotten here. It had only taken a few 'cell times' for her to live for the recreation hour. The weights gave her focus on something other than her shitty luck and whose fault that was. The classes were earned through good behavior. Cell time restricted all an inmate's time to the cell. You even had to eat in the damn thing.

Course it could have been worse, she could have gotten solitary that time after she'd gotten in the fight, but thank God she didn't. God and Rod. Yeah.

Nina laughed at that little rhyme.

Later that night as she lay alone in her small cell. The walls were so close she could have touched them both at the same time if she'd so desired, which she did not. Nina held the book under her pillow waiting for lights out.

After the noises died down, and turned into those of nightly prison life, Nina got the book out. Someone, probably a newbie, cried out in their sleep, or maybe they weren't sleeping after all.

The spine ripped away, and she could feel the small plastic bag in her hand. As quietly as possible, she opened it up and sniffed it in the pale light.

This was good, she would bet it was. Please let it be. That was all she needed, some cut meth. Yeah, nothing like snorting laundry detergent or horse tranques, or God knows what else. Nina hoped to hell Rod knew his contact and that this was legit shit.

The tear of several pages ripped the air. She rolled one up and used the others to straighten her carefully measured line. She'd have to save the rest. Who knew when Rod would come through again.

Anticipation raced through her as she leaned down and snorted the powder up the make-do tube. It hit her nose, burning until the numbness set it. With her head tilted back she waited for gravity to help. Finally she felt the shit drop, the back of her throat burned like it was on fire. Sweet pain.

Ahh…. A moan sighed out. About damn time. On a contented, almost sated sigh, she leaned back and enjoyed her well-earned bump. Her world was as it should be again.

Well, almost. The meth straightened her head, giving her clarity, so that her plans and ideas solidified within her mind.

No, it wouldn't be long now. While her high lasted, she plotted, planned and thought up and discarded half a dozen scenarios.

Stick close to the truth, yeah. She'd win Rod over that way. Cry and plead and he'd probably buy it. No doubt he would. Then, she'd get him to help her figure out how in the hell to get out of this place. Maybe if she was really good she could apply for one of the other classes, those in the fields. Might work. She'd have to get closer to Rod first, figure out exactly how things played. No way she was leaving all the planning up to a dick. No, she did that already and look where it got her. The trick was to play him, play on his weaknesses, drop little ideas, plan most of it and make him think he was doing a great thing. Righting a wrong.

A soft chuckle escaped. Righting a wrong.

Oh she couldn't wait to start 'righting'.

CHAPTER SIX

DEADLY TIES

43

"I'm going to go practice my music while dinner cooks." Ryan said as he started down the hallway. They'd just finished setting the table.

"Okay." Taylor ruffled his hair. "What are you playing?"

He shrugged. "Ms. Johnson gave me an Irish reel. It's really fast and neat and I've already got it mostly figured out." Ryan stopped, cupping the newel post with both hands.

"Goodness. You got it today and have it mostly figured out?"

Again he shrugged, then turned and raced up the stairs.

That boy never ceased to amaze her.

Taylor watched him go, heard the click of his door. She turned to the entry table to check the mail and realized she hadn't gotten it yet. Swinging the door open, she almost stepped into the raised fist. Taylor swallowed the yelp.

"Good evening." Gavin Kinncaid stood on the porch, lowering his hand back to his side.

"Umm...." Would he always take her completely off guard? She hated that. Well, mostly. What was he doing here? "Hi."

His smile tugged a flutter from her stomach. "I probably should have called, but I was wondering if you wanted to, or if you could, go out tonight."

He wanted to go out with her? As in a date? "What happened to no time for us clingy, stupid women?"

"Never said you were stupid."

Stepping back, she gestured for him to come in. "Good answer. Well, I do thank you for the offer, but I've already started dinner. In fact, it's in the oven."

"Oh," he said.

He walked past her and she couldn't help but admire the way his dark trousers fit against his behind before falling down those long legs. She wondered if he was a boxer or brief kind of guy. Jerking her eyes up, she decided it didn't matter and shook her head at herself. She caught his speculative reflection in the mirror studying her with a quirk of brow and smirk. Her cheeks flamed. Taylor started to shut the door before she remembered the mail. The man made her forget her own head half the time. And why was that? Had absolutely *nothing* to do with those muscles or the perfect body or that wicked smile or the eyes ...oh God, those eyes. She needed help. Lots and lots of help. She reached around grabbed the mail out of the slot. One letter got hung on the metal mail slot, and she heard it tear as she ripped it free.

As she shut the door, a quick glance at him showed her the single Gerber daisy he carried. Pumpkin orange petals surrounded the yellow face. He bought her a flower? Her stomach did another roll.

Taylor licked her lips.

"I should have called. Sorry." He jerked his hand and a single petal fell to the floor as he held the blossom out to her. Something inside her smiled as deeply as she knew the dimples creased the sides of her mouth.

"Thank you and what do you want?" She reached for the flower and her fingers brushed his, sending a little jolt through her system. Her eyes flew up to meet the dark blue of his. God she could get lost in those cobalt depths, just lost and lost. A moment passed and then another and all she could think about was how incredible his eyes were, how his gaze could capture hers with the least bit of effort, or how the slightest meeting of touches made butterflies dance in her middle. A soft sigh escaped as he gave a small smile.

"You're welcome and to ask you to dinner."

Music drifted down the stairwell, notes and scales stringed through the air, muted, yet still discernible. His gaze rose to the ceiling. The moment was broken.

"I take it the young musician is practicing?" His hands went to his pockets and he rocked slightly back onto his heels. The movement made him seem nervous, but she knew that wasn't right. Men like Gavin oozed charm and confidence and girls tended to stutter and stare. Not her. But she *might* if she fell for the charming, sort--which she didn't.

"Umm.… Yes, as a matter of fact, he is. Wanted to polish up an Irish reel he learned today."

"Cool. I bet Mom has some reels, if he's into that. Mom's from Ireland."

Another silence stretched. She was so damn out of practice at this. And what was *this*? She'd had friends to dinner before. Herbs wafted and scented the air. Dinner!

"I know you asked to go out, and thanks for that, but would you like to stay for dinner?" He just stared at her. Without taking a breath, she hurried on. "It's nothing fancy, just baked chicken, rice and salad. But, you're more than welcome to join us if you'd like." Deep breath.

There was his smile, full and charming and completely disconcerting. Damn the man, what was he up to? "I'd love to."

Taylor tossed the mail on the entry table. One letter fluttered to the floor and they both leaned down to pick it up. Gavin reached it first, then handed it to her. She almost didn't look at it, but gave a quick glance anyway.

The pleasantness popped.

For a moment all she could do was stare at that letter with her son's name printed neatly on the outside with the exception of the last name. This letter was addressed to Ryan Fisher. The return address was Valleyview, Gatesville, Texas. Damn the woman!

Rage rolled through her. That Nina would even try to send another letter. Why couldn't she just leave them the hell alone? But then, the fear slithered in. Had she found them? Would the phone calls be next?

Taylor stood, the flower forgotten, as was Gavin. All she saw was that letter and her mind simply froze on it. She closed her eyes.

DEADLY TIES

"Taylor?"

When she opened them, the first thing that registered was the little black, stamped-hand with the forefinger pointing to: *forward.*

Forward. Relief huffed out on a whoosh.

"Damn, Charles, too," she mumbled.

"Are you all right? You're kind of pale." Gavin's voice pulled her back to where she was and what was going on.

"Oh, uh--yeah. I'm--I'm fine," she lied. Another sigh had her running her hand through her hair. She tried a small smile. "Sorry."

His look was rueful. "Don't apologize. Come on, you look like you could use a drink of something, or sit down."

"My tea's in the kitchen. I'll get you a glass, too." She walked down the hallway and into the kitchen. A look back showed her Gavin carried her flower. Had she handed it to him? No, probably dropped it.

"Do you like your tea sweet?" she asked, as he stepped into the kitchen.

"That's fine." He held the flower out to her. "You dropped this."

She took it. "I'll put it in some water. Please, have a seat."

Wood scraped on wood as he pulled a chair out and sat in it. He moved with remarkable ease for such a large man. She carefully put the flower in a blue vase with water and set it in the windowsill by her herbs.

Finally, she gave him a glass of tea. The letter was lying between them on the table. She lowered herself into the chair thinking they could talk about something, but her gaze magnetized to the white envelope.

"Are you going to give it to him?" Gavin asked.

It was an impertinent question, but she didn't care. She needed someone to talk to, and Gavin was the nearest thing she had to a friend. Nearest thing? He was her *only* friend. Over the few weeks or so they had talked just about every night on the phone. Sometimes just for a few minutes and other times they could talk for hours. Yes, he was her friend, and the niggling suspicion that he was becoming something more kept creeping upon her. Whichever, it didn't matter. She just wanted someone who cared to talk to, someone to listen. And she already knew Gavin listened to her, though he often aggravated the hell out of her.

Leaning up on her elbows, she shook her head, then reached for the offensive correspondence. "No. I don't even want to read it, but I will later to see what sort of poison the woman is spewing."

"It is addressed to him. Though what's with the last name?"

"What's with the questions?" Taylor closed her eyes. With half an ear she still heard the notes descending from above. "I'm sorry," she whispered, opening her eyes back up.

"I'm prying," he stated. "You just looked like you could use someone to talk to."

46   *Jaycee Clark*

Taylor *could* use someone to talk to, but she wasn't used to sharing *this* sort of thing with a guy. Charles had never wanted to know, and then he was gone, and never cared, so it didn't matter. Taylor had dealt with Nina's threats and harassment alone.

Alone. Sometimes she got tired of handling things alone. Single parenting was not, by any means, easy. She and Gavin already talked about work, dreams and Ryan. So, why in the world couldn't she share this with him, too? Taking a deep breath and a chance, Taylor followed her gut. "Fisher is his biological name. Nina, his biological mother, is in prison for the attempted murder of her son, several counts of child neglect and abuse, kidnapping and possession of narcotics with the intent on distribution."

Heavy silence settled between them. His eyes, always dark, lightened around the edges, and even as that fascinating fact registered, so did the muscle bunching in his jaw. "No wonder you went pale."

"Yeah, well. For months we got letters in Austin. A few times, phone calls. Then, after we moved out and Charles moved back into the house, I asked him not to forward anything but bills." Her mouth settled in a frown. "I see he listened," she said more to herself than to Gavin.

"You going to tell Ryan?"

She vehemently shook her head. Music, fast and flighty danced from Ryan's room. Still, Taylor softened her voice to almost a whisper. "Do you have any idea what the simple sight of this would do to him?"

Gavin stared at her.

Taylor continued, "He still has nightmares. I know he had one last night, but he doesn't talk about it. He never talks about any of it. Dr. Petropolis tells me to be patient, that he's writing about it, which is better than completely bottling it up, and he's talked to her some." Taylor jabbed a finger at the tabletop. "But no, I'm not going to tell Ryan that she wrote him another letter, let alone let him read the thing. You have no idea what kind of woman she is. The obscene things she says, or the threats she issues. Absolutely not. No, he will never know."

Gavin still sat, staring at her, as though he expected her to say something else. "Dr. Petropolis is his child psychologist?"

"Yes."

His gaze was starting to unnerve her.

"What?" she asked. "You think that's harsh of me? Cruel of me? To deny a mother her son?" Damn it. Why was she doing this? Just because Charles had said those very words didn't mean Gavin thought that way. Why was she taking this out on him? On another silent curse, Taylor got up. They needed another plate didn't they? he said he'd stay for dinner.

She grabbed a plate, silverware, and a napkin. After she placed it all in front of him, slightly eschewed and jumbled, her mind on at least the menial task of his place setting, she turned to walk back to the counter.

DEADLY TIES

His hand shot out and grabbed her wrist.

"Taylor," his voice was still gentle, just as his fingers were. Yet, she caught the edge to both. "Sit down."

Too flustered and upset to argue she sat.

"Do you think you're being harsh?" He withdrew his hand from her wrist.

"No," she immediately answered. "That woman is no mother to him. She never was. She's scarred him and hurt him too many times to count. Damn near killed him the last time." Her voice was shaking and so were her hands. Taylor fisted them and put them in her lap, took a deep breath and tried to rein in on her emotions. "I'm sorry. I really am. I swiped at you. I shouldn't have."

"You always swipe at me. I'm getting used to it."

She just looked at him.

"It's okay. Better to get out than to leave it bottled up. Can I ask you a question though?" It was his turn to lean up on his elbows.

"If you're certain you want to hear the answer. Or dare another swipe."

One eyebrow cocked. "Why did you ask me if I thought you were harsh or cruel? I'd never think that of you. A hard ass maybe. Driven, definitely and sometimes narrow minded."

Taylor licked her lips. How to answer the man? "You know how to compliment, don't you?"

Both brows rose at that. "I keep in practice. So ... back to the topic at hand. The reason you asked me?"

Taylor sighed. "Charles."

"What do I have to do with the ex?"

"Charles told me that when I asked him not to forward her mail, or let her know where we'd moved to."

The downturn of the corner of his mouth and the narrowing of his gaze told her before his words what he thought of that. "You know, I really don't think I like your ex at all, and find I like even less being lumped in any form or fashion with him."

"But you both have so much in common."

His eyes hardened. "Really?"

"Hmm...." She took a drink. "Both handsome, charming and successful men."

"Those are usually sought after qualities."

"You mean a beautiful, successful, charming woman like Miss O'Hara is fine with you?"

He took a deep breath. "You make my head spin."

"Aww...."

"Like when I have a hangover."

She smiled. "There you go with those compliments again."

He shifted closer to her, his voice lowering, his gaze trapping her. "Not all men are the same."

48 *Jaycee Clark*

"Maybe not." She shrugged.

For one long moment, he stared at her, a faint frown between his brows, the corner of his mouth pulled tight. Very quietly, he said, "The man was an idiot to let you and Ryan go."

What did she say to that? Taylor swallowed. Clearing her throat, she picked at the tabletop with her fingernail. "Glad you noticed." She raised her eyes back to him. "I'm sorry. You're really nothing like Charles."

Silence stretched, then, "Are you going to open the letter?"

The envelope lay there, pulling at her, begging to be opened. She shook her head. "No, I'll just throw it away. Or read it later."

Gavin tsked, and gave her a small half-smile. "Neither of those is smart. One because she might have mentioned something in there that could lead to her getting into trouble when pointed out to the correct authorities. And two, I hate to think of you reading something the mere sight of upsets you alone. Why read it and brood by yourself when you can read and unload on me, then get a good night's sleep?"

She could read it. What he said made sense. Well, the first part anyway. She wasn't exactly sure how to take the second half.

Taylor sighed and ripped the letter open.

Dear Ryan,

How is your new life? Must be nice to get to choose a new family, a new mom. Though, you should know that no one can be a mother to you like I can. Only I know the real you. No one else does. No one. I try not to think of you too often with Mrs. Shepard. Nope, don't like to go there. I only get mad. And you know what happens when I'm mad.

I'm in a class for my drug addiction and to help me control my anger. I'm finding a new me. That's what we're supposed to do anyway. New me. New you. Who knows what the future holds. When I get out, we'll be together again.

I hope your arm has healed up real good. Hate for you to be deformed or something. That would suck if you looked weird. How's the cut on your face? You know, you can't really blame me for that. That little spill was your fault. If you hadn't jerked away none of it would have happened. Better yet, if you hadn't been listening to what you shouldn't have, none of it would have happened. Did it leave a scar? I hope so. That way you will always remember to mind to your mother.

You know I'll be up for parole in a few years. After I get a job, you can live with me. They took you away and I promise, if it's the last thing I ever do, I'll get you back. You are mine.

Well, it's lights out in a few minutes, I hope you get this. You can write me back if you want. You should write your mother, you know. I haven't heard from you yet, and I'm hoping that's HER fault and not yours. Would love to hear from you, just don't talk to me about that Shepard bitch. Don't wanna hear about that. And remember no matter

DEADLY TIES

where you go, no matter what you do. You'll always be mine. As that old saying goes, blood is thicker than water, or in your case—ink. Ha ha.

Love, Mom

No way in hell was Ryan going to read this. Taylor could only shake her head as the words stared back up at her, reminding her of the woman in the courtroom screaming obscenities. Of the monitors bleeping in the hospital. Of Ryan screaming out in the night or flinching away from offered love because he didn't know that love didn't hurt. Not real love.

"You okay?" Gavin's deep voice pulled her back.

Deep breath. Anger pumped through her. "Yeah, I am." She looked up into his dark eyes filled with concern. Whatever was between them was easy and comfortable, in a strange complex way.

Well, most of the time. Gavin could be patient and soothing, something, she admitted that was all too foreign to her. Yet, he also pushed all her buttons and made her want to either strangle him or kiss him. Another foreign thing.

Maybe she didn't know as much about love as she thought. She had loved her parents, but that was so long ago she couldn't remember exactly how that was. But she knew what love with Ryan felt like. She wondered how mutual love between man and woman would be like. Between friends. What difference did it make? Love is love is love.

"Tell me what you're thinking," he said.

Taylor laid the letter back on the table, caught his quick glance at it before he looked back up to her. His hand came up and grasped hers. She liked this, sitting here talking about things that bothered her with her hand clasped in his. The smells of dinner mixed with his spicy cologne. It felt right, and that worried her.

"Talk to me." His quiet voice was cajoling and persuading, no impatience, no teasing jibe.

"Why?" What if Charles had been right and she simply wasn't made to be a wife? No. She was *not* going to give that man credit for anything. Wife? Where had that thought come from and what difference did it make?

A cocky grin danced up to crinkle the corners his eyes. "Because you can't resist me?"

Taylor only shook her head at him. "You don't want to know." With barely a moment's hesitation, she handed the letter out to him. "Want to read it?"

Did he want to read it?

Hell yeah, but then again he wanted to know what Taylor had been thinking just a moment ago. There had been a look in her eyes that he thought he read wrong. Surely he must have, pain and confusion, mixed with hope. Gavin didn't know what to think. He'd come over to ask Taylor out for dinner or drinks, but was sitting here at her table in this cozy blue and yellow kitchen.

"Do you want me to?" Gavin didn't want to pry, he just wanted to understand.

"Doesn't matter to me."

Still looking in her light brown eyes, Gavin reached out and picked up the letter. He saw her glance towards the oven.

"I should finish dinner." Taylor stood up and went to the counter.

Before he started the letter, he asked, "What can I do?"

"Nothing." She turned and gave him a smile, though her dimples were faint and it didn't come close to reaching her eyes.

Gavin scanned through the letter. Disbelief, bafflement, and rage mixed his emotions.

"What does she mean by his arm healing and a scar?" Gavin had a sinking feeling. He'd noticed the shiny pink scar marring the upper left portion of Ryan's face. He glanced up at Taylor, momentarily lost in her simple grace. She moved fluidly, and she was only dumping broccoli into a steamer. For some reason, that Gavin didn't care to contemplate on right now, he could just sit and watch her do the ordinary or the extraordinary. Taylor dusted off her hands on a dishtowel.

"That…." Her mouth frowned, and still her dimples winked at him.

Those damn dimples would be the end of him.

"Well, that would be why she's in prison basically. The shortened version is that the adoption was halted two days short of completion and then a judge gave her one last chance. Nina took off with Ryan." She leaned against the counter and gave the towel she was twisting her undivided attention.

"For how long?" he asked.

"I didn't see or hear from him for almost three days. Those were the worst days I've ever had. Then the hospital called at three a.m. Seems something had happened, though no one knows exactly what. Ryan's arm was broken, his shoulder dislocated, two cracked ribs and his face was lashed open where he either fell or was thrown through a plate glass window. Nina was tripping really well. Apparently had spent days on speed, to the point the police said she was hallucinating."

"God." Gavin couldn't imagine.

"Yeah." She turned and tossed the towel on the counter top. Steam rose from a pot on the stove and she dumped the rice in.

"Were you alone? Had the divorce gone through yet?" And why did he care? Like that would make it any easier.

Taylor looked back at him over her shoulder. "No, it hadn't. Though for the first question, I might as well have been. Charles couldn't have cared less. Trash and riffraff was what he considered Ryan and Nina and I guess me, too. I don't know, don't really care. He stuck with me long enough for the adoption to be finalized and then another month after that before the divorce. He couldn't wait to get on with that

DEADLY TIES
51

curvaceous secretary of his. Of course the rumor was that who could blame him? What man would want a wife who…." She stopped. "Well, somehow it got placed all at my feet."

Damned bastard. "As I said, I don't care for your ex."

"That makes two of us, honey."

Honey? She called him honey? Gavin smiled, he caught the slight pause of her movements as she mixed the pot after what she said must have hit home. He wouldn't mention it, let it slide. Honey. He liked that. And it was said with smiling vowels. Hunee.

Gavin took a drink of his tea. What else had she been about to say? *What man would want a wife who*? Who what? What man wouldn't want a woman like her?

Where in hell had that thought come from?

Didn't matter. It wasn't like he was thinking of Taylor as *his* woman. Just someone's wife. Anyone's woman. Though, he didn't really like that thought either. Damn.

"Hope you reamed the son of a bitch really good in the settlement."

She shook her head and it caught the lights in the kitchen, reflecting red and gold.

He wanted to feel those strands, wanted to run his hands through those locks. They had to be as soft and silky as they looked. Had to.

Gavin grinned to himself, glancing back at the table and saw the letter. "Poor kid. At least he has you." With a silent curse at people who would hurt their own children, he folded the notebook page and stuffed it back in the envelope.

"Thank you," she said, turning back to the counter.

Feet pounded down the hallway and sneakers squeaked near the doorway. Taylor whirled, probably to grab the letter, but Gavin stuffed it into his pocket just as Ryan came bursting through the doorway. Her eyes reflected her relief.

"Is dinner ready yet?" Ryan asked from the doorway. "Oh." Ryan stopped and stared. "Hi, Gavin. What are you doing here?"

"Hi," Gavin answered him. Taylor's face told him she'd seen him get the letter and the stark fear he'd seen there for that split second bothered the hell out of him.

Ryan shuffled into the kitchen and Gavin stood, offering his hand to the boy. Ryan stared at it for several moments before he finally grasped it. He caught the slight hesitation. However, now that he understood some of Ryan's past, the distance between them wasn't that surprising either, even if they had talked several times on the phone.

The table remained between them.

"Hmm." Ryan looked at the table, then at Gavin. "I take it you're staying for dinner."

Was that a question or a statement? The flat words held no emotion, so there was no way for Gavin to tell if Ryan was happy about the addition or not. "Yeah, your mom invited me. I hope that is okay. I stopped by to ask her to dinner, or rather both of you to dinner since it was last minute, but she said dinner was in the oven."

Ryan studied him for a minute, obviously weighing something. "I think you wanted to take Taylor out by yourself. Otherwise you wouldn't have called so much lately."

Smart kid. Gavin gave him a smile. "Okay, you've got me. I was going to see if I could take your mom out, but now looking back, that wouldn't have been exactly right. Maybe I should've called and seen if you wanted to have a guys' night out. Catch a movie, or go to the arcade or something." What in the hell was he thinking? Arcade? He'd taken Tori, his niece, and one of her friends to an arcade once and vowed to never, ever do that again. It was exhausting keeping up with kids.

Ryan's smile lit his entire face, the blue eyes dancing with delight. "I bet that would be lots of fun. Can Taylor come?"

Looking at Taylor, he saw a soft smile playing on her face as she studied both him and Ryan.

"All right. I suppose we can have a girl tag along. But one day it will just be us guys. Pizza, burgers, fries. Lots of root beer and junk food."

"Cool." Ryan plopped down in the chair beside Gavin's. "That sounds great."

Taylor laughed again as she removed pans from the stove, drained the contents and bowled them before setting the dishes on the table. She the fridge and grabbed a salad and dressing. Gavin, red-blooded male that he was, could do nothing but admire the way her jeans molded to her cute little derrière. With a booted foot, she kicked it closed.

Watch her all day indeed. Maybe all night too. There was a thought. More like a fantasy, one that had plagued him night and day since one Saturday evening when the waters of fate delivered her into his hands. Time to think other thoughts.

"What are the two of you doing tomorrow afternoon? Say three-thirty or four?" Gavin asked, mentally calculating his last appointment, which was the one-thirty. Then, he had to check a couple of patients at a couple of hospitals before he was going to head up to his parent's place this weekend. Spend some time with everyone. But he could leave later for Seneca, spend some time with Taylor and Ryan. Maybe visit a museum or something, grab a quick dinner.

Taylor looked at Ryan as she set down. Gavin didn't miss Ryan's small nod.

Smiling at Ryan and then at Gavin, Taylor said, "Well, I'm off tomorrow afternoon. And after two, we're free. We could meet you somewhere around three-forty five. I think we're planning on a stop at the bookstore. That ought to give us plenty of time."

Topics moved and shifted, flowed and danced through dinner. Smiles and laughter mixed with the sounds of dinner, clinks and chinks, brass and bluesy tunes from the stereo graced the meal. Gavin watched these

DEADLY TIES

two, wondered at their past, what he knew and what he didn't. And while he wondered about their past, he steered himself away from their future. Or tried to.

Dinner was great. He had more fun than he could remember having in a long time. Dinners for him, were more frequently, alone, unless they were with his family. Though dinners used to be either business or pleasure. The latter of which had been his usual forte of getting acquainted with the sole purpose of seducing the woman with whom he dined. Of course, the women he went after and chased usually knew the rules of his game, for the most part. They recognized the signs and went mutually along.

Most, being the women they were, had to at least try to make the relationship between them more serious. After all, his name was Kinncaid wasn't it? Of Kinncaid Enterprises? Didn't matter he only invested his earnings, and had little to do with his part of the family hotel business. That was more his brothers' area. Gavin was the healer.

With Taylor, things were shifting. He just wanted to spend time with her, just…. Well, he wasn't exactly sure why, just because. And half the time she acted like she didn't like him and he knew she could careless what his last name was.

Ryan started up a conversation about places to see in D.C., things he'd read about. Which, from what Gavin was learning about the boy, didn't surprise him in the least. With Ryan it was music and books and any knowledge he could gain with the two. The kid knew more about music than he did, and Gavin always thought himself rather fairly knowledgeable in that area.

Taylor was … Taylor.

She captivated him. Gavin hardly tasted the food he put in his mouth, though he did know it was good. Her voice, her smile, her laughter all waltzed around him, and it wasn't just him. He saw how Ryan held onto Taylor's every word.

After dinner, Ryan excused himself and headed upstairs. He offered to help clean the kitchen, but Taylor told him to go on and practice his reel.

* * * *

Journal Entry June 29,

Sometimes I don't like to sleep. Sometimes I have nightmares, really bad nightmares about that night in Austin. I don't remember all of it, and I don't think I want to. When I wake up, I can't quit shaking. I don't sleep over at Jeremy's, he'd probably think I was a baby because I like to sleep with a light on. Just in case. Just in case I have a bad dream about HER, and when I wake up, I want to see that I'm not with her anymore.

Sometimes I forget. Right when I wake up, it's like I'm still in that dirty little apartment and I can feel my arm hurting where it broke. I do remember that. My arm felt like it was on fire. And sometimes when I wake up, my scar on my face will hurt. Just for a minute I expect Nina to come screaming at me. But then, I see my room with the posters Taylor and I have put up and I know where I am.

I had a nightmare last night, and even after I woke up and knew where I was, I still shook and cried. I wanted to go get in bed with Taylor, and she wouldn't have cared, or I don't think she would have, but I didn't.

I'm not a baby, even though sometimes I feel like one. Last night, I pulled the covers up tight around me--like that would help. Why do we do that? Grab blankets to us or over our heads? Like the material is magic or something. Like a shield that will keep the monsters away?

It doesn't work. I know. Monsters just rip the blanket away or shred through the puny shield.

But back to last night, I had the bad dream and then stared at the model planes and space shuttle we hung from my ceiling, and the poster of the galaxies and nebulas.

The posters on my wall show places I want to see. There's Stonehenge in England, rhinos and lions in the Kalahari, this old temple on the Isle of Crete--that's like in that story Taylor told me about and that we read a little of about Troy and Mycenae. The last poster is one of the Great Pyramids of Egypt. There are lots of places I want to see. The pictures take my mind off my nightmares.

The light helps, but the shadows seem to whisper words from that time, that place. Things I don't want to hear or see. So, I look at my posters instead. I try to pretend I'm in those places. Sorta like a game. What's the weather like, what the smells are, what sounds I hear. Most of the time it works, but sometimes it doesn't. Last night it took a long time to work.

I don't like talking about my dreams because then I have to talk about her *and all that stuff that happened. Dr. Petropolis thinks that maybe I should start talking about it a bit more. Nothing big, just a little here and there.*

Then, when I have bad dreams I can talk about them and just the words won't scare me or hurt me. It all sounds really good, but I'm not ready. Not yet.

At least, I'm writing about it. That's good, right? Like you can answer me. Sometimes this journalling thing seems dumb, but I still like it.

Taylor knew this morning that something was wrong. She just took one look at me and asked if it was a bad night and why didn't I come wake her up?

I love it when she talks to me like that, but it confuses me too. Taylor is worried about me and work. Taylor worries a lot, about a lot of things. Work, her cases, life.

Gavin called last night and they talked for a while. I answered the phone and got to talk to him for just a bit. I like Gavin and I think he

DEADLY TIES

likes Taylor--well he seems to, and he called. Isn't that what guys do? I don't know if Taylor likes him or not. I think she probably does, but after Charles, she probably won't admit she likes Gavin unless you point it out. I really don't like Charles, but that's another story. I do like Gavin. He's funny and nice. Yeah, I like Gavin.

He came for dinner tonight. It was fun. We're supposed to go with him tomorrow after I see Dr. Petropolis and we go to the bookstore. Gavin seemed to know lots of cool and neat places to see and visit. I want to go to the Holocaust Museum, and the Mint. Taylor wants to see some of the country. I don't know about that, but we'll see.

Today after Taylor got home, we just messed around the house and fixed stuff up in the yard. I wish it were a bigger yard so we could get a puppy. I've always wanted a puppy, but I know we can't here. Maybe one day.

Oh, and I finished A Wrinkle In Time. *That was a great book. Taylor said there are others, that it's kinda like a series. So, if nothing else, maybe I can get another one when we can go to the bookstore tomorrow*

Okay, I'm gonna practice my new Irish reel that Ms. Johnson found for me. I just got it today, but I've finally got the tempo down. I just miss a few notes, but I'll get it.

* * * *

Gavin and Taylor cleaned the kitchen, talking, joking, laughing. Having her this close, it was damn hard not to kiss her. With most women he wouldn't have cared, but Taylor was different. She was as likely to bite or shove him as kiss him.

With Taylor, Gavin just wanted to know things about her, what she was thinking or doing. There was also Ryan. Gavin kept thinking about how the boy had stated he was going up to practice before taking a shower.

Very self-sufficient kid, but then he would have needed to be, wouldn't he? Gavin remembered he, and probably all of his brothers, balking at the thought of bedtime, let alone a shower. But then again, he and his brothers never had a mother who scarred them either.

Gavin leaned against the doorway watching as Taylor rifled through a cabinet. That same familiar reel from earlier danced down the stairs.

"Is he always like that?" he asked her.

Taylor lit a candle set in a tin can, vanilla from the scent of it. "Yes. Very helpful. Never arguing. Something I want to talk to Dr. Petropolis about. I never really noticed it before. What I wouldn't give for a good 'I don't want to,' or a simple, 'no'. But, Ryan never does that."

"You have yourself a little adult." Gavin held his hand out to her as she made her way to him.

She took it, and just like before, like all the other times their skin had met, lightning seemed to jump-start his system. Blood raced and all he wanted to do was kiss her. Just one quick kiss to see how she tasted--or how she reacted.

God knew she smelled like honeysuckle, and Gavin wondered if she tasted as sweet as he remembered the nectar of those flowers tasting. Probably. Instead of pulling her to him as he badly wanted to do, he simply held her hand, studying the paleness of hers fingers held snugly in his tanned palm. A gentle hand. Taylor was grace, a slow sort of grace that seemed absent from other women he dated. It was in the way she moved, as easy as water over stones. It simply was. But the steel was there too. That driven determination to make things better.

Clearing his throat, he said, "I should probably go. I've got an early morning." Though, right now he couldn't have cared less if he had a dawn surgery scheduled. "Thanks for dinner. I had a great time."

Their footfalls echoed down the hallway, past the stairwell to the door. He noticed the comforting feel of her place before, but it hit him again standing here in her entry, looking into her living room. The walls were a warm red, not bright, or over-bearing, but muted and dusted so that the whitewashed woodwork stood out against the walls. Pictures hung on the walls. In the living room, the walls were the same. The furniture there wasn't for show or pretenses, but for use. Deep denim couches, their cushions plush, sat facing each other. Red pillows were tossed haphazardly in the corners. He liked her taste in things.

"Great place, too, by the way."

"Thank you," she answered. "I'm glad you could stay. I'm sorry you have to go so early. Are you sure you wouldn't like a cup of coffee or something?"

Her tea was strong enough he wouldn't need any coffee any time soon. He only smiled. "No, thank you. I really should get going. I had a wonderful time."

The sultry night air was alive with sounds only noticed when darkness settled. Electrical lines hummed with a slight buzz. Dogs barked somewhere down the street and a cat hissed and howled as Gavin stepped out onto the porch, humidity lapping against him. He heard Taylor flip the light switch but nothing happened.

"Sorry, I guess it's out."

"You have a bulb?" He could change it before he left.

Taylor shook her head, her dimples causing his blood to almost boil. Her hand was still in his. "No. I need to get some."

The darkness surrounded them, the only light from the entry window and what spilled through the door.

He circled the back of her hand with his thumb and felt her shiver. What the hell.

"Just as well," he whispered, pulling her slowly to him. In the dim light her eyes looked darker. "You're contrary and sometimes I don't think you like me very much. For some masochistic reason, I like that about you. I like you, Taylor. Have I mentioned that?"

"Uh.... No." Her voice, when she whispered reminded him of silk

DEADLY TIES

stockings being removed in the dark, sexy as hell, almost dangerous.

"No? Well, that's something I need to clear up then." Just one taste. One simple taste.

He leaned in and set his lips to hers. Her lips were warm and smooth beneath his. Soft as satin. Honeysuckle, there it was again.

A simple taste would not suffice. She was shorter than he, considerably, but then most women were. She must have stood on tiptoe but he could feel all of her against him. She tightened her hold on his hand, and wound her other arm around his neck, a sigh from her mingled on the edge of his mouth, moist and heated.

Gavin licked the corner of her mouth with his tongue even as his other arm wound around her back and he lost his hand in all that long silky hair.

She sighed again and he angled his head to deepen the kiss. He had to taste more of her. Honey and salt, fire and ice. Taylor was a delicious dessert made with contrasting flavors. Their tongues danced and mingled as they both held the other on her darkened porch to the music of a practicing fiddle.

Something … some unidentifiable feeling swirled in his gut. It was like nothing he'd ever experienced and nothing he wanted to forget.

Finally, he pulled away, rested his forehead against hers. "I should go."

"Hmm.…"

Her response had him smiling. She seemed so in control all the time that when she wasn't, he found it cute and wonderful. "Are we still on for tomorrow?" he asked her.

"Tomorrow?"

This time his grin allowed a chuckle out. Definitely not in control now, was she.

"Tomorrow afternoon. Ryan. You." He glanced at her lips. "Me."

"Oh." Her lips held that vowel out, and he wanted to kiss her again. "Yes. If you're sure." Her words whispered against his lips made him long for another taste.

Just one.

"I'm sure." Then he dove again. There was nothing gentle about this kiss, both wanted it, both gave into it and both took from it. Her arms tightened around him as his did around her. He backed her up against the door facing, leaning into her warm, pliant body. He reacted instantly to their waists contacting, to the feel of her soft breasts crushed against his chest. He licked the roof of her mouth, felt her shiver and let his hands roam up and down her back, feather light. She arched, sighing into his mouth. He could feel the ridge of her backbone and as he dipped into the base of her spine, the thought of one day kissing her right there shot through his brain. When they pulled back both were panting.

"God, woman."

Her laugh, husky with passion swirled between them.

He'd wanted to explore those dimples, but that would have to wait, or neither of them would be leaving this porch. "Next time."

"Next time? What?" she asked him.

"Dimples." On a resigned sigh, he disentangled them. Her confused look was completely adorable. That pull of brows that left the faintest frown between them.

"Good night, Gorgeous." He tapped her chin with his finger before he turned and walked down the steps. The promise of rain tinged the air.

"Good night, Gavin." At his car, he looked back, opening the driver's door. He couldn't see her, not really, just her outline against the light shining through the open door.

"Taylor?"

"Yeah?"

"She's not his mother, you are. One thing runs deeper than blood. Love. Those ties are a hell of a lot stronger." With that, he slid into the seat and started the car.

He couldn't wait till tomorrow.

CHAPTER SEVEN

"Taylor, it's Gavin. I'm sorry, but I'm going to have to cancel our afternoon...."

His message on her voicemail kept interrupting her thoughts. She'd gotten it while she and Ryan were at the bookstore. And like some lovesick teenager, she'd listened to it twice. Okay, maybe three times. Friends. What the hell happened to friends and neither of them wanting or needing a relationship?

It was that soothing, calm baritone voice of his.

She tried, she really did, not to think of the kiss they'd shared, but then she'd tried--quite unsuccessfully--to forget that all day.

The man was a distraction even when he wasn't around. But what a kiss it had been, nothing like what she and Charles had ever shared. No with Gavin....

With Gavin, Taylor could stand for them to simply kiss all night. Well, she admitted honestly, that was highly doubtful, especially if he did what followed as well as kissing. And with a man like Gavin Kinncaid, Taylor knew, just knew down to her bones, that a night with him would be far more distracting than some kiss. And *why* was she even *thinking* about a night with him for God's sake? Kissing was one thing. Sex another.

"I wish Gavin could have come with us," Ryan's voice jerked her back.

DEADLY TIES   59

"I do too, but you know a doctor's life is very demanding. He has to be there for his patients." Taylor pulled Ryan close to her side. "Gavin said to tell you he was sorry."

Blue, clear as the June sky, peeked at her beneath lashes most women would kill for. Ryan had such wonderful eyes. Summer blue framed with long, slightly curled, light brown lashes.

Was that hopefulness she caught in his voice? She'd noticed he had taken to Gavin, for the most part at ease around the man, but Ryan would always have that look about him: a studying, observant look, a consideration in the eyes that weighed situations and people in seconds.

Thankfully, Ryan hadn't looked at her that way lately, but she noticed when Gavin was around, that sharpness would come into her son's eyes and her heart would squeeze. Regardless of his hesitancy, Ryan seemed to genuinely like Gavin. Last night at dinner and the day they'd gone to eat, just listening to Ryan's half of the phone conversations when Gavin called, was enough to tell her Ryan felt more comfortable around Gavin than he ever had around Charles.

Charles. Taylor shook her head and stared out the cab window. Rain grayed the world outside and water sprayed on the taxi as another car passed them.

She wasn't going to think about her ex husband, his betrayal, or his cold attitude towards both her and Ryan, even if she had had all but a cussing fit on the phone with him this morning.

Taylor sighed and focused back on Ryan. "Did you get enough pizza? I thought when we got home, I'd make some brownies and we could watch a movie. How does that sound?"

"Brownies with icing?" Ryan asked.

She smiled. "Is there any other way?"

His grin made his freckles look happy.

Rain sheeted down as they rode home. Ryan looked out the window and hummed his Irish reel, which she had yet to learn the title of, but recognized the tune.

Gavin.

She'd laid awake half the night, wondering if she'd imagined those feelings Gavin evoked, if it was one-sided and if it wasn't, what she wanted to do about that. She knew this attraction wasn't one-sided, but she didn't know if she wanted anything other than friendship. Okay, friendship and this great wonderful attraction *might* work.

Of course, the kiss was very persuasive. So, did that mean they were now more than friends? Taylor worried. Gavin was a smooth talker, no doubt about it, and she didn't necessarily think he kissed all his friends the way he kissed her last night.

At the same time, she didn't want to go jumping to the conclusion there was some sort of tangible relationship between them if he wasn't thinking that. Maybe it just sort of happened last night and that was it.

Did she want that to be it?

There was the question. Did she want just friendship between them or something more?

Yesterday she would have said friendship with Gavin Kinncaid would have been enough, and probably could have convinced her self of it. Now, after that mind-numbing kiss, she had to be honest. She enjoyed Gavin's company and the talks they had, and that kiss had awakened something in her that she was honest enough to want to explore.

So, it was no wonder that even with her understanding of Gavin's job that she was disappointed at not being able to spend the afternoon with him. That would have been really nice, probably more than nice.

It was after five when the cab pulled up to the curb at their house. Rain poured down, pounding the roof of the car in an unforgiving rhythm. Of course, she'd never thought about grabbing an umbrella earlier.

Taylor shoved the fare into the driver's hand and told him to keep the change as she slid out of the door behind Ryan. Both of them raced to the porch, he with his books tucked securely against his chest and she with her purse held by her side.

Thunder boomed.

Taylor didn't want to mess with digging in her purse. She grabbed the extra key out from behind the geraniums.

Something was wrong. The key wouldn't turn in the door. Taylor tried the knob. It turned easily in her hand. Hadn't she locked it? The door swung inward. Overcast skies shadowed the entryway. Her breath caught in her lungs.

Her arm shot out as Ryan tried to pass her.

"No. Stay here."

Pictures hung crookedly from the wall and a potted fern was lying on its side, the dirt scattered across the floor. She vaguely remembered one didn't enter a house after a breaking and entering for fear of the perpetrator still being there.

From her right, a shadow moved towards her.

"Taylor!" Ryan yelled.

"Home wrecking bitch." The person hissed, swinging out.

Taylor ducked shoving Ryan to the side. Wood splintered against the doorframe. She kicked out with her foot. The masked man stumbled, dropping a tire iron. He leapt over her, off the porch and raced around the next house.

Taylor stayed crouched on the porch, panting.

"Taylor? Taylor?"

She turned and saw Ryan's pale face. "I'm okay. Are you?"

He swallowed and nodded.

Taylor turned and sat down on the porch, digging in her purse for her phone. Finally. She called nine-one-one.

Who would break into their home? Who the hell was that? Fear

DEADLY TIES 61

slithered across her damp skin as she remembered Nina's letter. Taylor reached out and grabbed Ryan's hand, giving it a squeeze.

Her hold on Ryan tightened as she gave off her address and emergency to the dispatcher.

"Who was that?" Ryan asked her, shaking off her hand after she punched end.

Her eyes adjusted to the fading light and shadows and obviously so had Ryan's. His eyes shone fiercely as he looked up at her. She noticed he had a death grip on his books.

"I don't know. A burglar. Though I didn't see him carry anything." Taylor stood and helped Ryan to his feet. Both of them backed away from the door and sat on the short brick wall that enclosed the porch area. Water gushed off the eaves and splashed loudly onto the wet ground below.

Minutes stretched as they waited for the police in silence. She turned to tell Ryan that maybe he could wait at the Websters, but even then, she noticed the house down the street was dark.

"My violin!" Ryan jumped up, his book slapping to the porch. Before Taylor could grab him, he raced into the house.

"Ryan! Come back here!"

His feet pounded up the stairs, mixing with the wails of sirens from outside.

Taylor quickly followed her son. "Ryan, we're not supposed to be in here. You don't go into a house someone's broken into. Ryan!"

A sound, between a growl and a cry came from Ryan's room. Taylor tore around the corner to see him standing in the middle of his room staring down at the floor. Everywhere was destruction. Posters were ripped, the sheets and blankets were torn off his bed, clothes laid scattered around everything, but at his feet was the worst of all.

Ryan knelt down at what remained of his violin, broken and smashed.

"Police!" a male voice shouted up the stairwell.

"We're up here." Taylor leaned out the doorway and flipped on the light switch. A man hurried up the stairs, a gun pointed to the floor and his badge pinned to his belt.

"Ma'am?"

"Sorry, I'm Taylor Reese. I know we're supposed to wait outside, and we were, but Ryan.…" she trailed off. He still sat on the floor staring at his most prized possession. The policeman came up to stand beside her and looked into the room. "He thought of his violin and dashed inside before I could stop him."

Ryan turned to her and rage and heartache warred in his shining eyes.

"I understand. I'm Lieutenant Morris." More shouts from the outside and feet on the floors below. "We're here," he told someone coming in. "Lieutenant Morris."

"Sergeant Bachall, sir. That's my partner Diamonds." A uniformed officer stood on the stairs still holding his gun. "What are you doing on a B&E?"

"Driving a couple of streets over and thought I'd drop by," Morris answered.

Bachall looked at his partner. "Yeah, right. Let's check the rest of the house."

"Yes, sir."

"Ma'am, could you come downstairs with me please?" the man asked her. The lieutenant was average in height with the look of a hardened man about him. He was dressed neatly, brown hair buzzed short. A lantern jaw gave him a no nonsense appearance, as did dark, sharp eyes.

"Let me get Ryan." She turned back to the room, and went inside. The detective stayed in the hallway, but didn't leave the doorway.

"Ryan? Honey?"

Her son picked the pieces up and held them to him. A quick hand darted out to wipe the tears away before he looked up at her. "Why did he break my violin?"

Freckles stood out almost harshly against his skin. She reached out to run her hand over his head, but he jerked back. Taylor sighed inwardly.

"I don't know, baby. I don't know. Come on, we need to go downstairs so that the police can look through everything."

* * * *

"Ms. Reese?"

Taylor turned at the sound of her name. She and Ryan were downstairs, back out on the porch. First they had gone to the kitchen but it seemed to be in the worst shape, so they were led back out onto the porch.

"Yes?" she answered the lieutenant. Morris.

"Sergeant Bachall would like to speak to you."

She turned to Ryan who sat in the corner of the porch, his books forgotten beside him. In his lap lay his violin, or what was left of it. On top of it was his journal which he'd gone back upstairs to get, having forgotten it in his night stand drawer. He sat scribbling away in it. So far he hadn't said another word to her. Taylor sighed.

"I'll watch him."

"Thank you." She frowned. "Are you in charge of this? Doesn't a lieutenant outrank a sergeant?"

He grinned. "I'm actually with the special crimes division. I was bored and on my way home. This falls under the sergeant's collar."

He sounded sincere, but there was something about the words that didn't ring exactly true. Now she frowned. "Glad I could offer you some entertainment, Lieutenant."

With that, she turned and walked inside. The heels of her small ankle boots clicked on the floor, the sound echoed, yet muffled in an eerie sort of way. The mess was beyond her comprehension. Spray paint on

DEADLY TIES
63

her walls, things ripped, broken and shattered material things. That's all it was. Material things. Then why was she more upset about these than the man who swung at her?

"Ms. Reese?" The sergeant stood in her living room. "You need to look through and see if anything is missing."

Her gaze ran over the destruction. She only cocked an eyebrow at him.

His smile was wry. "We'll leave you some forms to fill out."

"He wasn't carrying anything that I could see though." She sighed. "I guess that's it?" She knew it was. But something needed to be done.

His head shook. "I'm afraid so. There's just no way to thoroughly check out ever B&E in this town. We don't have the money or the manpower, regardless of what people see in the movies. We'll ask around and see if any of your neighbors saw anything and then we'll see if this matches any M.O.'s in the past. Though the tire iron is assault with a deadly so…." He shrugged. "Lab might get a print off it."

Taylor noticed a painting she'd managed to keep in the divorce was ripped, not stolen. It wasn't priceless, but it was worth about a grand. Her television was still intact and sitting on the entertainment center along with the stereo and c.d.'s. Her mother's silver candlesticks were still on the shelf. Why hadn't they stolen that?

Because he didn't want your stuff, idiot. He wanted to scare you.

Home breaker was written in black spray paint on the walls.

"Have many enemies? I would hazard a guess that this was a bit personal and had nothing to do with theft."

"You moved up quickly didn't you?" Taylor regretted her smart reply as soon as it was out of her mouth. His gaze weighed on her. "Sorry," she said with a wave of her hand in his direction. "I don't care about all this, not really. It's just Ryan." Another sigh.

"Any ideas who would do this?" he asked again.

Taylor answered with a chuckle. "I'm every family's favorite person, Sergeant. I'm a social worker."

He jotted something down in his little notebook. "Angered anyone off lately?" he asked.

Taylor liked this guy. He was friendly in his own straight-faced, hard-edged sort of way. "I make enemies daily. The largest lately would be Gibbons, but he's in jail, so it's probably not him." Though he could be out.

"Ever heard of bail?" He was a smart-ass, too. "Why do you say Gibbons?"

"Oh, just that he decked me, swore revenge. Your normal day at the office." She needed a cleaning service, she thought, crossing her arms over her chest. "The guy could've been him, but I'm not certain."

Taylor gave Sergeant Bachall the information he needed.

"The worst of the destruction was in the kitchen, seems almost feminine." His gaze was studying, and Taylor felt the blood drain from her face and a chill race up her spine. Nina. Could she be out? No. No.

"Something you wish to share?"

The phone rang. Taylor held his stare a moment before the second ring moved her. Where was the damn phone? Normally on the entry table. Quickly, before the machine picked up, she found the cordless under papers and the over turned table.

"Hello?"

"Hi ya, Gorgeous."

Gavin. Her relief whooshed out. Just the sound of those three words settled her frazzled nerves.

"Hi."

"I just left the hospital and I'm already late for my parents' dinner, so I thought maybe we could still all go out and grab a pizza or something." A horn blared in the background.

What to tell him? "Um. Well, actually, we--um--we already grabbed a pizza." A uniform leaned back into the front door.

"Sergeant? You need to see this." His voice wasn't quiet, and she tried to cover the mouthpiece, but obviously didn't cover it enough.

"Sergeant?" Gavin asked. "What are you watching?"

Chaos? "Not a thing."

"What's wrong?"

Nothing. Everything. Taylor only sighed as Morris gave her a look as she crossed the porch following Bachall.

"Taylor?"

She licked her lips. "I don't suppose you know any cleaning services do you?"

"Why?" His voice hardened, all but daring her not to tell him.

She walked down the steps, absently noting that the rain fell softly now and the policemen stood to the side of the house looking at her car. Her eyes narrowed as she walked towards them, heedless of the drizzle.

"Taylor?" Gavin asked again in her ear.

"Ms. Reese." Morris turned to her. How had she missed this? Her windshield was spider-webbed, the tires were flat, or the two she could see were. Across the hood *bitch* was cut into the paint.

"Taylor!"

"What?"

Gavin wouldn't be put off. She had to tell him something. "I uh--I." This was *not* his problem. It was hers. "Someone broke into our house," she whispered.

"I'll be there in five minutes."

"You don't have to...." Taylor trailed off. He didn't have to but he would. "Gavin?"

No answer. Did he hang up on her?

"Gavin?"

So much for arguing with him. Taylor glared at the phone as though

DEADLY TIES

65

that would do a single thing and then hit the OFF button.

"I'm sorry, Ms. Reese." Bachall pulled her attention back to the matter at hand. Her car. No the dealership's car. Mercedes was *not* going to like this.

She turned back to the porch. Ryan sat staring out into the rain, Morris sitting beside him. It could have been worse. What if they had been home? Cars, paintings, couches, and walls. All that could be replaced or restored. That's what insurance was for.

"You have anything else to add?" Bachall asked her.

Yes, but not now. Taylor could only shake her head, then turned and walked back to her son. She'd need a cleaning service and a garage.

Ryan hadn't said a word since he'd asked her why they'd broken his violin. Maybe they could just rent a car and go away for the weekend. That would be nice.

* * * *

Gavin turned onto Taylor's street. He wasn't going to think how her voice shook when she'd whispered about the break-in.

Were she and Ryan all right? His pulse raced at thoughts he wouldn't allow to continue. If only he'd been with them this afternoon. Trees dripped with rain that his wipers shoved off the windshield. There. Cop cars were parked at the curb. Lights were shining in the windows.

The tires screeched to a halt and Gavin all but jumped from the Navigator.

"Taylor!" He hurried across the small yard. "Ryan!"

"We're fine." Taylor stood on the porch. "We're fine."

His long legs took all three steps at once and wrapped her in a hug.

Gavin sighed. Honeysuckle soothed him. Her scent wrapped around him even as her arms circled his waist. She was all right. She was all right.

Taylor pulled back and with reluctance, he let her go. "Ryan?" he asked her, tucking a strand of hair behind her ear.

She looked to the side and he followed her line of vision. In the corner of the porch sat the normally smiling boy. Now there was no smile. Giving her shoulder a squeeze, Gavin walked over to Ryan and squatted down on his haunches beside him.

"Hey, champ." Gavin noticed the shattered and ruined violin. The belly had been split and two of the four wires were sticking out in lazy spirals where they had been stretched and broken. The other two were all that held the instrument together.

Gavin sighed even as anger raced through him. "I'm glad you and your mom are okay."

Nothing, not a word or a single movement to let him know that Ryan heard a word he said. He wanted to reach out and ruffle the boy's hair, if for no other reason than to reassure him self that Ryan was okay. But, he knew now wasn't the time. Ryan was withdrawn and too quiet.

He just sat staring out into the rain. Shock, maybe?

"Ryan?" he tried again.

Nothing. Carefully, he reached out and placed his fingers on Ryan's wrist. The boy started to pull away, but then stilled. His pulse was normal. Gavin withdrew his hand.

"I guess you don't want to talk. Don't blame you there. Things here are pretty hectic right now." Gavin sighed and decided on another approach. "I am sorry about your instrument."

Was there a slight narrowing of his eyes? It was hard to tell in this damn light. Evening was falling and the overcast skies dulled everything to gray. "We'll find you a new one tomorrow."

A long moment passed, but finally, that small freckled face turned to him. Gavin's breath caught at the look in the blue eyes. So much emotion was boiling in their depths. A shrug, and Ryan looked back out to the rain. For all the world, Ryan appeared quiet and almost nonchalant, but his eyes told the truth. The control the child obviously had on his own emotions surprised Gavin.

Out of the corner of his eye, he saw a man standing in the doorway with a badge clipped to his belt and a shoulder holster strapped to his back.

"Gavin, this is Lieutenant Morris," Taylor introduced.

Gavin stood up and walked to the door, his hand out stretched. "I'm Dr. Gavin Kinncaid."

The cop's eyes were like many Gavin had seen. Hard, sharp, eyes. Shark eyes. Another policeman came down the stairs and brought Gavin's attention to the interior of the house.

"Holy Hell." He pushed by Morris and strode into the house. Everything was trashed. Those comfortable denim couches were slashed. Pictures and paintings were ripped, or broken. Things were over turned and spray-paint graffitied the wall. A cleaning service?

Gavin turned and studied Taylor in the light. A worried frown creased her brow and her braided hair was mussed, probably from running her hands over it as she did right then.

"I'm sorry, Taylor."

She only nodded at him. "So am I."

"What's going to be done?" he asked the cop.

Morris raised dark brows. "Done? We've done all we can do Dr. Kinncaid."

"And that is?"

A heavy sigh wafted on the air, but the other cop answered.

"And you are?" Gavin asked.

"Sergeant Bachall. Look. I feel badly for Ms. Reese and her son. The truth of the matter is that this was a breaking and entering, and vandalism. Though we've got him on assault with a deadly if we find him."

Gavin stilled. "Excuse me?"

The cop looked to Taylor, then back to him. Shrugging, he said, "The

DEADLY TIES 67

perpetrator took a swing at Ms. Reese with a tire iron." He pointed to dented, chipped wood on the door frame.

Christ. Gavin swung his gaze to Taylor.

Bachall continued. "We'll dust for prints and if we get lucky, we'll lift one."

What the man said, made sense, but Gavin didn't care.

Bachall shut his little notebook, tapping his pen on it. His attention shifted to Taylor. "You have a number where I can reach you?"

Taylor nodded and rattled off her mobile number as Bachall wrote it down. Lieutenant Morris leaned over and said, "Are you with the Kinncaids that own the hotels?"

Gavin as watching Taylor. "Yeah." He turned to Morris. "What of it?"

"I hear your dad and Commander Newart play golf together."

"So?"

"You could push this, you know."

"I'm not one that uses my family that way." Gavin turned his attention back to Taylor and Bachall.

"I will run a check and see if any matching incidents fit this," Bachall stated

"Fine." Gavin grabbed his own phone, then looked to Taylor. "You still want a cleaning service?"

Her eyes were weary. "Yeah."

He punched in the numbers he'd recently learned. Of course, Aiden wasn't home. Aiden, like Gavin's other brothers were at their parents'. So, he quickly dialed that number.

Becky, the housekeeper for the last thirty years, answered the phone.

"Hi, Beck. This is Gavin. I really need to speak with Aiden."

"And why isn't yourself seated at the family table this evening? Broke your poor muther's heart, ye did." Rebecca Murphy's voice still danced with Ireland. Her County Waterford accent got heavier the madder she got, or if she was trying to guilt trip. Gavin figured it was the latter.

"I know, I know. Tell, them I'm sorry. I'll be there in a couple of hours. Something came up at the hospital."

He could picture the rotund woman standing by the phone as she tsked him. "Excuses, excuses. Ye work too hard. Now who was it ye wanted to talk at?"

"Aiden." Becky knew damn well whom he wanted to talk to.

"Something wrong, boyo?"

"Becky, I really need to talk to Aiden now. I'll fill you in when I get home."

A hmph echoed through his phone before Aiden finally got on.

"Kinncaid." His brother's voice said.

"You're not the only one with that name you know. Others are also graced, or cursed with it." Gavin noticed Morris was talking to Taylor and she shook her head before taking the man's arm and leading him away from the front door and the window. They walked more into the living room, which he stood to the side of. He half-heard Gatesville and prison.

"What do you want?" Aiden asked him.

"Hang on," Gavin answered. He looked to Taylor, and tried to cover the mouthpiece on his phone. "Taylor, did you show him the letter?"

Her eyes narrowed on him. "Finish your call and then you might join this conversation."

Her tart reply released the bands around his chest. His gaze shifted to the front door. A damn tire iron?

"Hello?" Aiden said. "I don't have anything better to do than sit here and listen to your muffled voice."

"What?" he asked his brother. "Oh, sorry. Listen, I need a favor."

"Anything."

"I need a cleaning crew. Can I get one?"

"What? Did your latest orgy party leave your house trashed?"

It might be the running joke in the family that he was a ladies' man, but the joke was getting old. So, he went out on a few dates, he didn't have time for anything else. And it really bothered the hell out of him, that his own brothers believed the crap.

Gavin sighed.

"Can I get a crew or not?" He didn't quite keep the bite out of his words.

"Sorry, just kidding." Aiden's voice shifted, lowered. "What's up? What's wrong?"

"I'll explain later."

Without another joke or hesitation, Aiden agreed. "Yeah, I'll call the hotel with your address and get a crew out there."

"It's not my address, but...." What was Taylor? For his family's sake, she was his friend. "A friend's."

"Hmm."

Gavin chose to ignore that comment. Taylor and the cops were still talking in lowered voices and Morris was now writing in his notebook. Gavin looked back out towards the open front door to the darkness beyond.

"Do you know any places around Seneca that sell violins?"

Aiden's chuckle was deep. "Dare I inquire as to why you're looking for a musical instrument?"

"Because he broke Ryan's."

"Who is he, and who is Ryan?"

Gavin was getting ahead of himself. He crammed his hand into his pocket and leaned against the wall. "*He* is the question in everyone's mind and Ryan is Taylor's son, remember?"

A silent moment passed. "Oh, yeah. And Taylor would be the friend? Nice lady."

DEADLY TIES   69

Hell. "Yes."

"I'm intrigued. This is interesting coming from you."

Gavin listened with half an ear to his brother's amused statement. Instead, he heard Taylor say something about staying at a hotel probably.

Over his dead body. They'd argue about it later.

"Aiden?"

"Yeah?"

"Tell Mom I'm bringing a couple of guests out for the weekend."

Aiden's laughter echoed through the phone before the line went dead. God only knew what Aiden would tell them all. Gavin didn't have time to think about it. He had a woman to persuade. And he had the suspicion she could be stubborn.

* * * *

I'm writing again today. I've made lots of entries today in this journal, huh?

The break-in sucks. I know I'm not suppose to say that word, but I don't care. It's not that bad, not compared to some other words I know. I try not to use them though. They're not nice and make you sound mean. I don't want to be mean.

I'm worried about staying away for the weekend. Taylor's not happy about it either, but then again, she wasn't exactly in the best mood when Gavin showed up.

I do remember when he came. He seemed worried about us. I saw him hug Taylor close to him and close his eyes real tight, like he never wanted to let her go. For just a second, I wished he would hug me that way, but then I got scared that he would, so I'm glad he didn't.

But I wonder what it's like, to be held that tightly and know everything's gonna be all right, even if someone doesn't tell you that.

But maybe it's all lies anyway. I don't think anything is ever okay, no matter what anyone says. I was starting to believe that it could be, but now I don't know. I don't know why someone tried to hurt Taylor or why someone ruined our new house. He ripped all my posters and my....

Well, you already know all that. I've written four pages already. I should probably stop writing and start talking to Taylor, but I just don't want to talk. She'll only tell me that everything will be okay, but she can't promise that. It's only a hope for her, like it always has been for me. Hope--smote. Whatever.

If that man hadn't ruined my violin, I would play something as soon as I could, but now I can't. Gavin's talked about how tomorrow we'll go look for a new violin, but I don't know. Maybe I shouldn't want another one so soon. It seems almost wrong to just go out and get a new one. The old one was special and part of me. I can't explain that to Taylor or Gavin. They'd think I was weird.

And I'm already weird enough.

I knew something was wrong when we got home. But I didn't 'see' my violin until we were sitting on the porch. Then I knew. I just knew.

I wonder what other musicians do when one of their instruments die. That's what it feels like. My violin died and I don't know what to do. Maybe I will talk to Taylor, but when she's alone. She loves me, so even if she thinks I'm weird, she'll still help me.

And I shouldn't worry about my violin anyway. The guy could've hurt Taylor. I don't know what I'd do without her. Where I'd go.

Maybe I'll give her a hug when we get there. She tried to hug me back at the house, but I wouldn't let her, and I know that hurt her. I am sorry about that. I just wasn't ready, but now I am.

I still wonder what it's like to be hugged the way Gavin hugged Taylor. He likes her, and she likes him. But before they can have the light, they'll pass through darkness. That scares me, very bad. I can't tell Taylor that. She doesn't know that sometimes I just know things, and right now I don't really know anything.

Last night when I came into the kitchen and saw Gavin sitting there, I just sort of knew. All I saw was that they were happy and laughing and it was bright and behind them was darkness and crying. I didn't like that vision. I'm hoping it's one of my flukes. Not everything I 'see' or 'know' happens, but some do.

Well, we're slowing down and I see that BIG house--what do they call them? Oh yeah, mansions--up ahead. I'll write you later and let you know what all of Gavin's family is like. His mom was nice, guess we'll see about the others.

CHAPTER EIGHT

Lights shone from several windows on three levels of the enormous house. She knew the grounds were immense, landscaped, and beautiful. The headlights glistened off the wet stones of the mansion. Gavin pulled the car up to the front steps of the graveled drive.

What was she doing here? She had argued, pleaded and talked until she was blue in the face. Gavin had a way of steamrolling over any obstacle. He didn't quite ignore her arguments, reasons, or in his terms, excuses. No, he just turned it all around so that the only *logical* thing to do was to come stay the weekend at his parents' house.

That in and of itself was simply imposing on this family and it felt awkward. She'd done this once already a couple of weeks ago. Obviously she and Gavin were more than friends and at the same time, not yet lovers. So, where did that leave them? Taylor had no idea. What would his family think of the additions for the weekend?

Taylor turned to look again at Ryan in the back seat. He hadn't said a

DEADLY TIES

word all evening. She noticed Gavin repeatedly looking in his rearview mirror, concern for her son evident.

What a day.

At least nothing had been stolen, not that she immediately found anyway. She had talked to Lieutenant Morris about Nina and gave him all the pertinent facts she could. He promised he would place a call to the prison tonight and get back with her. She had yet to hear from him and that worried her. She'd also learned he'd actually stopped by because he was investigating some murder that was tied into a burglary. Actually, she'd only overheard that part. But it made her wonder all the more.

Gavin put the vehicle in park, turning her attention back to the house. "Are you certain this is all right? It just doesn't seem right, dropping in uninvited and...."

Normally, Gavin's eyes held a trace of mischief, of amusement. Now, they were serious, almost coldly so. Instead of answering her, he turned in his seat and looked at Ryan.

"Hey champ. We're here. I forgot to warn you, Tori, my niece, is here. She's about your age. She'll probably run you ragged with questions and talk your ears off, but she's nice. And I promise not to let her talk you into any tea parties or doll-salons."

Taylor didn't turn around, but caught Gavin's grin before he said, "Thought that would get a smile out of you. Now, you met Mom, but everyone will wonder who you are, and who your mother is. I thought I'd tell them you both came from another planet and landed in my office this afternoon, kidnapping me and making me late because you wanted to see all the tourists' sites."

This time an ever so small giggle whispered on the air. Taylor didn't move.

"But then they might not like you because you made me miss dinner with the family, and it was a lie too, and my mother wouldn't want me to lie. So, I figured I'd tell them the truth. Taylor is a very special friend and you are her son and my sightseeing partner. What do you think? Will that work?"

How did he do it? As easy as that, it seemed all problems could be solved. Taylor dared a glance back over her shoulder, catching Gavin's eye for just split second before she looked at Ryan.

Ryan nodded his head, and she was glad to see that he was indeed smiling. Patience, patience, she reminded herself.

"We can come back and get our stuff later," Gavin told them. "Let's just go in, say hi to everyone and get the introductions over."

Their doors shut in a trio of clicks. The air was still damp and sweet with the evening's rain and hinted with jasmine. Taylor looked down at Ryan who quietly came up to her side and slid his hand in hers.

A soft sigh slipped past her lips as it did within her heart. Her hand squeezed his. She knelt down on one knee in front of him, the lights from the house allowing her to see his face.

"Hey, it's going to be okay."

Would it really, his eyes questioned.

"Please talk to me, Ryan. Just one word." Her other hand came up as she ran her fingers through his short, soft hair. He didn't pull away from her, but leaned into her palm. Taylor could have cried from that simple action. "Please?"

Without any warning, he threw his arms around her neck as though she were a lifeline in a stormy sea. Barely keeping her balance, Taylor held onto him as tightly as he was she.

"I love you, Ryan." She didn't expect him to answer her, he never did. But she knew he cared for her. She wanted to make life perfect for him and felt like she failed, miserably. This son of hers who had known little of love and security deserved to have it now. "I promise it's going to be okay. I'll make it that way, I promise."

His arms tightened even more as she heard him whisper, "I love you, too."

This time she did cry. Silent tears. *I love you, too.* Those were the sweetest words she'd ever heard. Taylor wasn't aware of how much time passed and she didn't care. Right now was all that mattered, here in the arms of her child.

Finally, she pulled back, and with a small whispered laugh swiped a hand under her eyes.

"You make me so proud and happy," she told him.

His grin was sheepish, and she caught the slightest blush beneath his freckles.

"Are you going to talk to me now?"

"I guess so." The toe of his sneaker made a circle in the gravel. "I just needed to think things through, I guess. But I still don't understand any of it." His sigh breezed against her face.

"I know."

"Are you okay?" he asked.

She nodded. "I'm fine, honey."

"That kick thing you did on that guy was cool," he said on a smile.

She laughed.

Gavin cleared his throat and she looked up at him. He wasn't but a couple of feet away to her right.

"Thank you," she told him, as she stood.

"What was that?" His voice held so much disbelief she knew he was teasing her.

Ryan giggled. "I wondered if she'd ever say that. Thanks, Gavin. I'm glad we came." His freckled nose scrunched up. "I know you've told us a dozen times it's okay that we came, but is it really?"

"More like a hundred. And yes, it's okay. And you're welcome." Gavin turned back to her. "Both of you."

He held his arm out to her, "Shall we?"

DEADLY TIES

This time she smiled at him as she placed her hand on his arm and held Ryan's hand with her other one. They walked up the curving cobbled walk lined with little lights. The whole place still reminded her of something out of a movie from Colonial times, or the Civil War. Complete with Doric columns rising to the third story, giving her the feeling she was entering a palace or something.

Now things were settled to a degree with Ryan, her nervousness about meeting Gavin's family started eating at her stomach. Stupid, they were just people, like any others and Mrs. Kinncaid and his brother had seemed nice. And with her job, Taylor was used to meeting people. So, why the sudden nervousness?

It had absolutely nothing to do with the fact that this was Gavin's family. Nothing at all.

"What did you mean about Kinncaid Enterprises and global resorts?" she blurted her question out as they reached the porch.

She knew his brother, Aiden, did something with hotels and Gavin was a doctor. He had other brothers, but he'd never told her much about them. She'd just assumed they were rich businessmen from the way he talked.

Gavin sighed. "Hoped that would slip by you." They were standing under the light and his expression was one she'd never seen before. It was guarded, almost nervous. No, it had been a long day and she was simply reading things wrong. Gavin nervous? Like that would ever happen.

"Are you two ready?" Gavin asked.

Were they ready? No. No. No. Could she stall anymore?

A grin danced in his eyes and at the corner of his mouth. "You met Mom and got along. You know Aiden. None of them bite, I promise. Well, except for Dad, but he's all bluster, so just ignore his barks."

Before she could think of all that, he was pressing the latch on the door. Had she expected him to knock at his own home? Taylor shook off her scattered and jittery thoughts. She was going to make a fool of herself if she didn't pull it together.

Taylor grabbed Ryan's hand and they walked into the entrance. Their entry was quiet. No one was in sight, a blessing in her opinion.

Dark, planked floors echoed their footfalls

"Hello? Where is everybody?" Gavin hollered at the top of his lungs.

His voice jolted her and apparently Ryan as well, since he'd tightened his hold on her hand. Ryan's eyes were big and round, absorbing everything he saw.

"There you are," stated a deep voice from in front of them. The man walked forwards with a bowl of popcorn. The buttery smell tickled Taylor's nose. Aiden. He popped a piece in his mouth before dusting his hand on his trousers. "We'd almost given up on you."

He was as handsome as she remembered--same coloring as Gavin and maybe same striking cobalt eyes, and maybe the same straight nose.

"Yeah," Gavin said, "we got sidetracked shopping."

"Really? Now I was just saying to Jessie, I bet Gavin and his cohorts got lost in the mall. Not a thing to worry about."

Gavin only shook his head. "Taylor, Ryan, you remember Aiden. He lives just down the road, and will hopefully be going home very soon."

A single-dimpled smile answered, before he turned his attention to them.

Gavin took her hand off his arm and held it. The touch that still sent the butterflies dancing, managed to also calm her somewhat. "Aiden, you remember Taylor Reese, and her son, Ryan."

Aiden's gaze studied her before it shifted to Ryan. "Yes. How could I forget? Nice to see you again." He held the bowl with one arm and held out his hand to her.

"Where is that popcorn?" A woman with honey-blonde hair and a baby on her shoulder came from the opposite direction from which Aiden had emerged.

"Here, I was on my way." Aiden rolled his eyes.

"Oh." The woman smiled at Gavin, before propping a hand on her hip. She was clad in jeans and boots. Something Taylor hadn't seen since she moved from Austin. And this wasn't commercial western wear with fringe and pointed-toed, hot-pink, snake skin boots. This woman wore denim jeans and brown lace-up ropers.

Of course, the sister-in-law from Texas. Aiden's wife.... Jennifer? Jessica? She knew it started with a 'J'. Taylor smiled at the familiar clothing before the woman turned dark brown eyes on her in an intense weighing gaze.

"Hi. I'm Jesslyn Kinncaid. If you're stuck with Gavin, I feel for you." It was said in such a straight-faced, no-nonsense tone, Taylor wasn't certain if the woman was joking or not.

"Thanks, but I cut him a break tonight," Taylor said.

Aiden put his arm around his wife's shoulders. Jesslyn said, "He's a smart-a ... aleck. You are a brave woman." Her smile was full of amusement.

Well that was the truth. "He's not quite that bad," Taylor tried.

Gavin turned a dramatic expression on her. "Not that bad?" He shook his head and looked back at Jesslyn. "I must be losing my touch. Good thing I came here so I could brush up on my repartee with you, Jess."

A husky laugh from Jesslyn mixed with a full rumble from Aiden.

"Behaving yourself with this one, are you, Gav?" Jesslyn asked him.

"This is Taylor, honey," Aiden said, leaning down. "The one I told you about."

Jesslyn's brows rose. "Ooohhhh."

And just what did that mean?

Gavin only shook his head before turning back to Taylor. "Ignore them."

DEADLY TIES 75

"She talks like we do," Ryan said, pulling on her hand.

Gavin obviously heard him, as did everyone else, but it was Gavin who answered. "Indeed. It's those smiling vowels."

"They get you every time, don't they?" Aiden asked with a dance of black brows at his brother.

Taylor had no idea what they were talking about, and Ryan's furrowed brow said the same thing.

"Our accents," Jesslyn clarified.

"Oh." Smiling vowels? She'd taken theater in high school, and had been involved in one-act play competitions. There had been a judge who'd said something about smiling vowels. There was another name for it. Oh, she hated when she had a question, she knew she knew the answer to, but couldn't think of. Of course, that was years and years ago and why the thought suddenly seemed important was completely beyond her.

"So, Taylor, how did you get stuck with this guy for the weekend?" Jesslyn asked.

Straightforward indeed.

"Sorry," the woman added on a wave. "Don't mind me. I tend to be curious and just ask questions." Jesslyn Kinncaid was an open woman, easily so. Taylor envied her.

"It's a long story."

"The best kind," Aiden said.

Jesslyn hunched down so that she was eye level with Ryan. "Hi, do you like popcorn?"

Ryan nodded.

"How about Koolaid?"

Again he nodded. At least he was answering questions, which was more than they'd had an hour ago.

"Board games?"

This time, a shrug.

"Well," Jesslyn said, rubbing the baby's back, "Tori's playing with her grandmother, something with ladders or maybe that game called, *Sorry*." She shrugged. "I don't know. If you want to play, I bet they would love to have you join them."

Ryan's gaze, Taylor noted, was drawn to the baby. Jesslyn obviously noticed, too. "Would you like to hold Alec here? Have you ever held a baby?"

Ryan shook his head back and forth. "No. Could I just ... touch him? Or is it a she?" Curiosity often overcame childhood shyness. Taylor didn't care what it was as long as he was talking.

Jesslyn smiled. "He's a boy, and yes you can touch him. His name is Alec."

Hesitating for a moment, Ryan reached his hand out and gently ran his fingers over the baby's dark hair, and down the side of his chubby cheek. Big blue eyes looked up at her. "Wow, he's so soft."

"Yes, he is," Jesslyn stood and placed a kiss on the baby's small head. "And so is his brother, Ian, so if you want to hold one of them, just let me know."

"Okay."

Everyone started down a hallway. Taylor didn't pay much attention to her surroundings. She was too worried about meeting the rest of his family.

"I won that round fair and square," said a woman in the enormous room where they stopped.

"Please, that was so easy," came a deep voice from a replica of Gavin. Ahhh … the twin.

"If it was so easy, Brayden, why didn't you win?" The brunette woman glared at the man who was smirking at her.

Gavin leaned down and whispered in her ear, "That's Christian and Brayden. Brayden's my twin brother, in case you couldn't tell. Christian is like a sister to us. She's helped raise Brayden's daughter, Tori."

"Your twin? Never would have guessed it."

A shrill whistle from Aiden cut the air. "Hey, everybody, the lost finally found his way home along with two strays."

Taylor saw Gavin jab his brother in the ribs, even as Aiden only smiled in return.

"Well," came a booming voice from a deep chair. "It's about damn time." The man, with white hair streaked with gray, stood and started to make his way to them.

"He sounds mad," Ryan whispered.

Taylor caught both Gavin and Aiden turning to her son. Ryan didn't like angry people and she couldn't blame him, not after what he'd lived through.

"I don't think he's mad, sweetie, just worried about what was keeping Gavin for so long," she tried. Ryan's look said he wasn't buying that. "Well, even when you're as old as Gavin, I'm going to worry about you."

Gavin turned so that he was more in front of her and Ryan. "Oh, don't worry about, Dad. Jock's like an old dog, he barks a lot."

Her son looked up at the older man who approached them, and softly said, "Even old dogs can bite."

Taylor sighed, and looked to Gavin.

Even as Taylor put her arm around Ryan's shoulders, Gavin squatted down on his haunches. "Ryan?" he asked.

Ryan kept looking up at Mr. Kinncaid.

"Ryan," Gavin tried again. Finally, her son looked at him and Gavin said, "No one here will hurt you. Or your mom." His mouth tightened. Ryan continued to stare at Gavin, the apprehension plain on his face and in his eyes. "Do you think I'd bring you to a place where you'd get hurt?"

DEADLY TIES 77

Ryan shook his head.

Gavin smiled. "Well, glad to see you trust me that much. Dad is just loud. He really likes little kids, just ask Tori. Neither he nor anyone here will hurt either you or your mom. Why do you think I brought you here?"

The last was a question Taylor would like answered herself, but had yet to get one from him, other than it was the *logical* thing to do.

Ryan looked from Gavin up to her. Taylor didn't know what to tell her son, or Gavin, or Mr. Kinncaid.

"What's this?" Mr. Kinncaid asked. "Surely the boy doesn't think I'd hurt him." True shock resounded in his thundering voice as his eyes turned to question his sons and her.

"Dad...." Gavin looked up and over his shoulder before he stood, keeping himself between Ryan and his father. "Not now, okay? I'll explain later."

Mr. Kinncaid's brows pulled down in a familiar frown. "Look son," he said to Ryan on a shrug. "I'm just a grumpy old man most of the time, ask anyone. Didn't mean to frighten you."

Ryan just looked at him.

A strained moment passed and clearly no one knew exactly what to do.

Finally, Jesslyn snorted. Mr. Kinncaid turned a glare on her.

"I'm sorry, but I agree with Ryan." The woman winked at Taylor's son. "The first time I met him, he scared me too. Thought I was.... Never mind. I'm still not sure if he likes me or just tolerates me because I gave him two grandsons to dote on and play with."

Taylor caught Ryan's almost-smile.

"I don't think you're helping matters, Jessie girl," Aiden whispered to his wife.

The old man hmphed and walked off a few feet, mumbling under his breath, before he stopped and turned back to the group.

Gavin watched his father's confusion mirrored in everyone else's expressions. How to smooth the rest of the introductions? He hadn't thought of this.

Turning, he saw Ryan still studied his father. Taylor--well, Taylor's thoughts he couldn't read. It was obvious she didn't exactly want to be here, but then he hadn't really given her a choice.

"Taylor, Ryan, the retreating bear is my father, Jock Kinncaid." His mother walked up then and put her arm through Jock's. "The woman by him, as you both know, is my mother, Kaitlyn. The two who were arguing are Brayden, my brother, and Christian, who is basically, our sister."

"Everyone," he said, turning back and taking Taylor's hand, "This is my friend, Taylor Reese and her son, Ryan. Sorry, we're late."

His mom came forward. "Don't worry about it."

Gavin leaned down and let his mother kiss his cheek.

78   *Jaycee Clark*

Kaitlyn waved a hand absently towards Jock, before she said to Ryan, "Ignore that old man. I've always told him he roars too loud."

"I do not roar." Jock sniffed. "I'm not that bad."

Gavin couldn't believe his father said that.

His mother replied, in her perfectly modulated voice, "Yes dear, you are and can, unfortunately, be even worse. However, we've all learned to tolerate you."

"Kaitie lass," his father's voice held a slight burr. "Don't take that high road with me."

"Bosh!" His mother ignored her husband and turned to Taylor, leaning in to hug her. "I'm so glad Gavin brought you both back to join us this weekend. I hope you enjoy yourselves while you're here."

"I'm certain we will, Mrs. Kinncaid," Taylor answered. "Thank you for your hospitality. I really hope we're not...."

"Imposing," Gavin finished for her on a sigh. Lord, the woman was always worried about imposing.

His mother chuckled. "Oh, my no. It's no imposition, none at all."

Gavin noticed Jess and Aiden heading towards the couches in front of the big screen television. Ryan seemed a bit less wary, but not yet relaxed. Taylor was still wound tight as a bow. He caught her fingers fidgeting on her thigh.

"We were about to start a movie. It's an old black and white, *Notorious.* But, have you eaten?"

Gavin hadn't. Had Taylor? "Have you eaten? Ryan?" Both gave nods. "Actually, Mom, I haven't. Things got hectic and I didn't get time to grab a bite. I'll just get a sandwich later, don't worry about it."

She arched a perfect red brow. "Mothers will always worry about their children eating." She turned then to Taylor and Ryan. "Would you two like anything to eat or drink? Tori is having Koolaid, but we have everything." After she found out what everyone wanted, she said, "I'll be right back."

The three of them started walking to the couches. His father raised a questioning look at him and he mouthed, "Later."

Brayden and Christian were still bickering about some stupid game. Gavin started to ask Ryan a question when a laughing girl came hurling into the room in a storm of giggles, squeaks and shuffles.

"Uncle Gavin!" Tori yelled and launched her self at him. "Where have you been? What took you so long? Uncle Aiden said you were bringing someone."

The questions were fired so quickly and jumbled that he felt like he was in a whirlwind. He squeezed her until squeals of protest sounded and then he set his niece on the floor.

"Now, you little hoyden, be quiet so I can introduce you to someone." He turned and noticed Ryan standing by Taylor just behind him. He stepped to the side. "Tori, this is my friend, Taylor Reese, and her son Ryan. I hope you can show him how friendly we Kinncaids are and

DEADLY TIES   79

how much fun we can have over the weekend."

"Pops was right," Tori said on a sigh.

Gavin didn't even ask.

"Probably a woman," his niece finished.

The four at the couches tried to unsuccessfully hide their snickers. Gavin merely raised a brow at his father who was staring out darkened window that was at least ten feet away. Gavin rested his gaze on Taylor. Both her brows rose in question, even as he caught the slight narrow of her eyes.

"Yeah, well, Pops was almost right," Gavin clarified.

"Hi, Ryan," Tori's dark bob bounced as she walked to the new kid. "I'm Tori, well Victoria, but no one calls me that unless I'm in trouble. Brayden's my dad." She pointed out which person in the room she belonged to. "I was playing in the music room."

Ryan's eyes widened before he asked, "Music room? I don't remember seeing that before."

"Yes. It's a room filled with instruments. I was practicing the piano."

"You play the piano?" Ryan asked.

"Yes. I've taken lessons for years."

"How old are you?" Ryan wanted to know.

Gavin saw the other adults were as interested in this child conversation as he was.

"Seven, almost eight. Why?" Tori's tilt of head, reminded him of his mother's when she wasn't certain if she would like the answer.

Ryan shrugged. "I just wondered. I play the violin."

It was Tori's turn to look wide-eyed. "You do? I was practicing a piece I want to play for my recital. How long have you played the violin?"

"Not long."

"What piece is that, Tori Bori?" Gavin asked her.

"Beethoven's *Moonlight Sonata*."

That sounded hard for her age, but he knew better than voice such a thought. Kinncaids were proud people regardless of sex or age. "Hmmm. Why that one?"

Her small shoulders shrugged. "I heard Grams playing it and wanted to learn and I did. Well, mostly. I still have some things to work out."

"I played that in Austin," Ryan confided.

"Cool. Did you bring your violin? We could play it together if you remember. Put on our own show." Tori's smile was like her grandmother's, with a single dimple in her right cheek.

Ryan shook his head and didn't say anything else.

"That's okay. There are a couple of violins in there. No one plays them though, so I don't know if they work very well. Would you know?"

The boy lifted one shoulder. "Probably."

"Well, come on then." Tori pulled him towards the door. "Maybe we can put on a show or something. I bet...."

His niece's voice faded, and Gavin noticed not once did Ryan look back. Progress often came from unexpected places. He shook his head even as Taylor came up to stand with him.

"Is that all right? Him playing one of the instruments?" she asked.

"Of course. Why wouldn't it be?"

"I don't know. I just didn't want...."

Gavin put his finger against her lips. "Hush. I know whatever you say will only insult me or my family and I don't want to hear it. Imposition, uninvited, rude--whatever word you were going to use. Just don't."

Her brown eyes lightened with emotion, turning an amber color rich and golden with specks of moss. The shift in their depths made him want to kiss her, replace his finger resting against her mouth with his own lips. But he figured the fire burning in her eyes was not for the same reason. She'd been pissed at him all evening. Not that he cared. Stay at a hotel--absolutely not. Instead, he leaned forward and kissed her forehead.

"You're still mad at me."

She shook her head and he moved his hand.

"Yeah, you are."

"Can you blame me? There I was telling Sergeant Bachal and Morris where we'd stay and you come charging in like ... like...."

"Gallahad?" he supplied.

Her droll look only made him keep on.

"Lancelot?" he tried again.

This time she rolled her eyes.

"Cu Chullian?" He lilted his 'l's like he'd heard since childhood.

"Cu--what?"

"Cu Chullian." Gavin sounded it out for her. *Ku cull-in.* "He was an Irish warrior, rode in a chariot."

Taylor shook her head, and as he'd hoped, her dimples peaked out. "You're impossible. Irish warriors? Please."

Something shifted again in her eyes, and he saw the worry and tension in them. "Hey, it's going to be okay. Are you certain you're all right?" A damn tire iron. He couldn't get past that.

She pulled her lower lip in, he noticed she did that quite a bit this evening. Must be a worry habit.

"He hasn't called, Gavin," she told him.

"Who?" Gavin asked, leading her to one of the chairs by the couch.

"Bachall, or Morris either for that matter. he said, he'd check with Gatesville and call me back." Taylor sat in the chair and he sat on the arm beside her. "Why hasn't he called yet? How long can it take to see if she's there? Either, she's there, or she's not. God, what if she's not?"

"I'm sure everything's fine." He'd make certain it was.

Her look wanted to know how he knew that.

"So," Brayden asked, "what took so long? You called almost three

DEADLY TIES 81

hours ago." He grabbed a hand full of popcorn and shoved it in his mouth.

Gavin looked to Taylor. He'd rile her some more. "I was busy rescuing damsels in distress."

That got a reaction out of her.

"I would like to make it clear I am *not*, nor have I ever been, anyone's damsel to rescue or otherwise." Her eyes flashed at him even though her voice remained calm.

"Oooo," Aiden laughed out. Brayden followed with a whining sound of a downing airplane before he rumbled, what Gavin assumed to be, an explosion.

Someone, Jess, he figured, murmured, "Crashed and burned."

Gavin ignored them and leaned down so that his arm rested on the back of the chair, letting his fingers play with strands of her hair. "Now, Taylor, come on, tell the truth. You were happy to see me."

Smiling herself, she retorted, "At that point I would have been happy to see Charles."

That wasn't funny, not one damn bit.

"Who's Charles?" Christian asked.

"Never mind," Gavin answered.

"Wow, I sense a tangled story here," Jesslyn said. "Maybe this will be more entertaining than *Notorious*."

"God, we can hope," Aiden said.

All the men agreed, as they didn't exactly care for chick-flicks, let alone some old sappy black and white.

An argument started up about movies and what wager the men had lost. Insults were thrown and tossed along with popcorn. Gavin was starving. Taylor, he noticed was quiet, but tentatively joined the conversation.

"Here you are, laddy." Gavin turned at the sound of Becky's Irish voice. She carried a tray piled high with food.

"Becky, why won't you marry me?" he asked the plump, gray-haired housekeeper while he made his way to her. Taking the tray with one hand, he gave her a one-arm hug. The little woman barely reached his chest.

Smells rose up from the selections on the tray: sandwiches, fruit, salad, cheese, and cookies. The last made him want to forget the rest. "Cookies? You made cookies? You have to put me out of my misery, Becky, and be mine."

"Ah, be off with ye. Scoundrel that ye are." Her rosy cheeks plumped when she smiled.

He looked at her then. "I'm sorry for being so short and rude on the phone earlier."

She waved him off. "What with the break-in and all there's no apologizing necessary, but I appreciate the gesture all the same. Right proud I am of ye."

"Break-in?" Jock barked. "Becky, what are you talking about?"

Becky and his father had a love-hate relationship. Each went out of their way to rub, jab, or barb the other, and both loved every minute. The housekeeper simply huffed a sigh, ignored Jock and looked back to Gavin. He caught everyone staring at them out of the corner of his eye.

"The young ones were prattling on about it to your mum. Poor little tyke. Bastard. Pardon me, but they are. Killed his violin, he said and could have bashed your head in too," she said to Taylor. "Shame it is, what the world has come to. A shame." Shaking her head, she turned to Taylor then. "I assume you're Taylor? The little lad's mum?" Becky was already nodding to her own question. "Ye just don't worry about a thing. We'll take right good care of ye, we will. Won't we, Gavin, me boy?" The last was asked to him with a twinkle in her eye as she introduced herself to Taylor.

Bless Becky's heart. "Indeed, Becky, we will."

"Are ye all right?" she asked Taylor.

"Yes, thank you," Taylor said with a small smile.

"Did they really kill his violin?" Becky asked, directing her question to him instead of Taylor.

Gavin was aware they had everyone's undivided attention. There was no privacy in this family. Everyone knew everything sooner or later. He sighed and rubbed his chin. "Yeah, they or rather, he did. Busted and broke it up, along with all the rest of Taylor's house."

Becky tsked, and patted Taylor's arm. "Not to worry, dearie. Things'll work out. They always do. Shame though." She turned to leave. "Kaitie'll be along in a minute. She's in the music room tuning on the fiddles."

Becky left and Gavin placed the tray on the coffee table before he plopped down on the floor, leaning back against Taylor's chair. He tore into his food, eating what he wanted and leaving the rest.

On a sigh, he draped an arm over Taylor's crossed legs and finished answering the questions bombarding from everyone in the room. Some Taylor answered, several he did.

At last the story was told and Gavin learned where they needed to go tomorrow to find Ryan a new violin. Brayden said he and Tori might go with them, and since Brayden knew where the music store was, Gavin agreed.

Earlier he hadn't noticed what Taylor was wearing, too much had happened, too many thoughts and emotions running high, but now he couldn't help but notice. Her pants were soft, pale beige linen. Just as her foot kept tapping, his fingers kept up their lazy patterns on her calf. Strange, he hadn't even noticed he was doing that until his finger ran low at one point and her foot stilled. Then he'd noticed.

The others decided to start the movie and he craned his head back when Taylor tapped high on his shoulder.

DEADLY TIES

What would her fingers feel like on his neck? Last night when they'd kissed, she'd wrapped her arm around him, but he wondered what her fingers playing on his skin would feel like. There was a thought.

The woman kissed like a siren, or what he imagined one would kiss like. Gavin had thought of her kiss all damn day long, and it was one long day. Her mouth, soft and warm, her tongue, quick and tantalizing, her taste, ahhh....

"I think I should go check on Ryan," she told him in that calm, soft voice of hers.

"Hmmm...." Here he was thinking of kissing the woman, and she was, understandably, thinking of other things.

Music floated down the hall and into the family room. Gavin smiled, bent his elbow, curving his forearm back up her leg so that his hand cupped her knee.

"I think things are fine," he told her, tracing a slow circle with his thumb on the inside of her knee. Her light brown eyes deepened just a bit, or maybe it was a play of light. But then she shivered. Gavin winked at her, then turned around as *Notorious* started.

Though several of the notes were enharmonic and stilted, two fiddles danced slowly down the hallway in a familiar Irish reel.

CHAPTER NINE

Taylor cut through the warm, dark water, smooth and silent. At the end of the pool, she slicked her hair back from her face before propping her elbows on the ledge. Her chin rested on her stacked hands and she watched the nightlife around her. The rain had finally stopped. Clouds still blanketed the moon before skirting into the midnight sky.

The Kinncaids were an incredible family. She had yet to pin everyone down. Aiden and Jesslyn and their twins were happy and funny, the newness of their lives together was lost in the ease she noticed between them. Brayden was quiet and reserved, as was Christian. Taylor got the impression from their bantering that something might be going on between the two of them.

Tori and Ryan seemed to have clicked, which surprised her. The little girl and her son spent the rest of the evening in the music room practicing various pieces of music.

Water splashed as she flicked an ankle out behind her. Pushing off from the side, she floated on her back, letting her gaze travel the inky velvet of the clouded sky.

So whom did that leave? There were two brothers she had yet to meet. Quinlan, who was labeled the workaholic. And another brother that she could have sworn Gavin had mentioned before, but who hadn't been mentioned tonight.

Then, there were the parents. Jock and Kaitlyn were an interesting couple. Jock was, as Gavin described him, all bluster.

After the movie held no one's attention, everyone just sort of migrated down to the music room and Mr. Kinncaid's true colors had shown as he'd held one of the twin babies and teased Tori. Seeing him play so openly and easily with the kids had warmed her over and had eased Ryan somewhat. Though, to be honest, Ryan wasn't exactly at ease with anything.

Kaitlyn was the show runner. That much Taylor figured out. The mistress of the house had given Taylor's son a temporary fiddle to borrow until he found another one. Then she'd dug out all of her 'old fiddlin' tunes' as she'd called them and played a few for everyone.

Taylor couldn't remember an evening spent, in the form of family time with more than two people, in.... Well, since her parents had died. What a depressing thought. Here she was almost thirty and had no husband, no extended family, and no hope for one.

But, she had an amazing son.

An incredible, musically gifted son, if tonight was any indication. He and Kaitlyn had really gotten into some of those Irish music pieces. Taylor smiled to herself.

Ryan was all the family she needed.

Earlier, after she'd known he was asleep, she'd walked out on the balcony to see the pool below. Kaitlyn and Gavin had told her to make herself at home. That didn't really sound plausible to her, but the pool had been entirely too inviting. As a child and a young girl, she'd loved to swim after a rain had cooled the air and water off.

She'd given in to the temptation and pulled out the swimsuit Gavin had said she'd need for the weekend and quickly donned it. Not wanting to wake anyone, she'd left all the lights off. Besides, she didn't know where the switches were anyway. The slight nervous feeling that she shouldn't be out here kept her from truly enjoying her swim, and she tried to push the thought away. She knew what Gavin would say to that, if he said anything after rolling his eyes.

Gavin. There was a thought. Taylor had no idea where they had been heading before. That they were more than friends had to be clearly evident to the blind--which none of his family were. If his arm-over-her-legs didn't shout that little fact to his family and to her, then in the music room would have answered any doubts they might have had left. The man had kissed her there in front of God and everyone. Not a kiss like they'd shared the night before, granted. A simple kiss that had still managed to make her stomach riot, as he'd wrapped his arms around her and pulled her back against him while the music had danced on the air.

But still a kiss.

Of course, everyone had to pop off some smart-assed comment then.

DEADLY TIES

Well, Aiden and Jess did. Brayden and Christian only shook their heads, and Jock…. Well, Taylor knew now where Gavin inherited his supercilious lift of brow. Kaitlyn only smiled, a single dimpled smile at her.

Taylor moved her arms, keeping afloat. Water caressed her bare stomach.

The sky shifted, allowing the moon to periodically peek out on the world below. She turned back over to swim a bit more before heading in.

Four laps later, she sensed someone was watching her. Taylor dipped under the water and heard the splash as someone else joined her in the pool. Surfacing, Taylor wiped the water out of her eyes. Her feet didn't touch the bottom.

"Hello?" No one had surfaced yet, and the water absorbed the night so that only the shadows of the shifting waves were visible.

A tingle ran up her spine. She thought of the masked man earlier and shivered again. Someone jerked her ankle, and water rushed in her mouth as her yell was cut off before it even started.

Taylor came up sputtering and coughing to hear his deep chuckle behind her.

She whirled, angry at being frightened.

"That was *not* funny." Taylor glared at him and swam to the side, where she gripped the edge and pulled herself out to sit on the lip. Now she could kick him.

Gavin swam up to her. His face was shadowed, but she'd been out here long enough for her eyes to adjust to the dim light. White teeth flashed in his crooked grin. Damn the man. Her heartbeat would never be the same.

"You scared the tar out of me."

His elbow grazed and stayed against her thigh as he rested them on the lip.

"I got that." His voice was made for the night.

"Did you now?" she asked. The only sound was the soft lap of water. "The idea of the masked man with the tire iron flew through my brain."

"Sorry." A silent moment stretched between them. "I've been watching you for a while," he said, lowering his voice. Definitely for the night. His voice could tempt a nun to sin.

Taylor licked her lips.

"Thought I might join you," he continued. His hand lay on top of hers. "But you got out. Sorry, I scared you."

Taylor could only sigh. The low light made him seem even more rugged, shadowing his jaw line, the hollows of his eyes, highlighting his strong, straight nose.

His hand tightened atop hers. "Don't you want to join me? It's cold out there."

Circles on the inside of her wrist sent another shiver down her spine, just as a breeze, cool from the earlier rains, blew across her wet skin. Cold. Yes, it was cold, and hot, and....

"Come on."

A voice like that should be banned.

Taylor thought about it for less than a second. "Don't scare me like that ever again. I *hate* that. Absolutely hate it."

A smile flashed again. "Promise."

This was probably a mistake.

Taylor grasped the edge of the pool and lowered herself back down into the water. Gavin didn't move. Her leg brushed his chest, his stomach, then his thigh. One of his hands remained on the side of the pool. The other went from her hand, up her arm to slide over to her waist.

Another sighing shiver as the water closed back over her. Taylor started to tread water, but Gavin was too close. She reached out and put her hand on the hard curve of his muscular shoulder.

If the man's voice did wicked things to her, well, his body.... His body would make an artist long for a way to capture that essence of pure male. The man had to work out regularly. His sculpted shoulders and chest were visible to her above the water, making her want to run her hands down the taut, chiseled planes. If the water would allow her, which unfortunately it did not, she would probably be able to see a washboard stomach.

"Better?" he asked.

Her tongue darted out to lick the top of her lip. "Umm...."

Umm, indeed.

This time she couldn't keep the sigh to herself.

Gavin watched her and wondered....

Her breath breezed against his face, warm and almost moaning. Almost. Gavin wished she had.

Her bathing suit should be illegal. When Gavin had told her to grab a suit, he never banked on this. Black was still the sexiest color. And bikinis were man's best friend, or worst enemy. Taylor's suit was all of the above. The midnight material stood out against her skin, reminding him of females of old compared to alabaster.

Taylor in some old-time dress caught his fancy, made his head turn. In jeans or trousers, she brought fantasies storming through his brain. But, Taylor, in what was basically three triangles of black spandex, wet and slick, felled him to his knees.

Her stomach curved beneath his palm, smooth, flat and soft as petals. His fingers flexed on her side, catching the breath in the back of her throat. Slowly, so as not to startle her, Gavin pulled her closer and closer to him, until she was a mere inch away.

The moon chose that moment to peek out of its cocoon, and he could see the light reflected in her eyes. Taylor's top teeth grazed over her lower lip.

DEADLY TIES

Gavin closed the rest of the distance between them, stopping just shy of kissing her. Their breaths mixed and sighed against the other. Taylor's lids slid down over her eyes.

He smiled as his lips closed over hers, soft and gentle. Fruit. Taylor tasted like fruit. His tongue skimmed the edge of her mouth. Nibbled, until her lips parted, allowing him access. He knew she expected him to dive in and taste her all at once like he had the night before. Hell, he wanted to. But, he wouldn't.

As if he had all the time in the world, his tongue meandered along the curve of her smile, the edge of her teeth, the ridged roof of her mouth. Her quick in drawn breath and grin against his mouth seemed to jolt her out of her passiveness.

With something between a moan and a purr, Taylor's arms wrapped around his neck as her tongue parried and forayed with his. She half floated, half hung onto him, her body buoyant in the water, feather light against him. Up and down.

Gavin slanted his mouth over hers, deepening the kiss. Her naked stomach slid against his, her breasts brushed against his chest making him want more. On that thought, he broke their joined mouths, before he returned to place a chaste peck on her lips. "I've thought of that all day today. All last night too."

"As you can see, kissing you never crossed my mind." Her words whispered out.

"Didn't think so." He cleared his throat. Taylor's arms were stilled twined around his neck, his one hand holding the edge all that had probably kept them from going under. Madness. Taylor was a madness to his well-ordered life. Gavin started to inch his hand back a few feet towards the shallow end, or at least where his feet could touch the bottom.

"What are you doing out here?" he asked her, paddling with his other hand to help keep them afloat. Her arms remained around his neck.

Dimples shadowed her cheeks in the low light. "Swimming."

"Hmm…." Gavin searched her eyes, saw the tiredness, the anxiety, the worry. "Why?"

He'd managed to get his feet under him, and jerked her legs around his waist as he kept up his backward trek.

"What are you doing?" she asked, ignoring his question.

Gavin chose not to answer her. Pulling her with him, they made it to the deep steps set into a small cove in the side of the pool. He sat on one, and pulled Taylor across his lap. It wasn't lost on him that she straddled him. Nor, from her wide-eyed, and probably flushed, expression was it lost on her.

"I can sit beside you," she said in a voice made for the night.

Gavin draped his arms over her shoulders. "You could."

Taylor didn't move. Finally, she shrugged and relaxed.

The water lapped around and between them. Wet hair slicked back from her face accenting her classic beauty. High cheekbones and her patrician nose were highlighted in the shifting moonlight. Her neck was long and smooth. The moonlight glistened off pearl-drops of water clinging to her skin. He wanted to kiss them all off.

"So," he said, letting his gaze roam back up to her face, and asking instead, "why are you out here in the middle of the night swimming?"

Again she shrugged, looked away. "I don't know."

"Taylor." He brought his hand up to cup her chin and turn her face back to him.

After a moment, she answered him. "I just needed to think and the pool seemed like a great place to work off some worry."

Made sense. "Particular worries, or just your general worries?"

"Both."

"That's lots of worry there, Gorgeous. Care to share it?" he asked.

A silent moment passed between them. Crickets and cicadas sang in the night, and Gavin caught the throaty sound of frogs down by the creek.

Apparently the woman didn't like sharing troubles, but he already knew that about her.

"I don't understand you sometimes," she whispered to him.

That wasn't what he was expecting to hear. "What's not to understand?"

"Everything." Taylor waved one hand by his head. "One minute I think one thing about you, and the next, another. I just can't peg you down."

"And I need to be pegged?"

Taylor shook her wet head. "Yes. For my peace of mind. I don't know. I just--I don't know."

"What are you worried about?"

When all else failed, Gavin had learned to go back to the starting question.

"Everything."

"Another everything? Taylor, you can't worry about everything. Most things work themselves out." One long, wet lock fell forward and he tucked it behind her ear. She shivered as he traced the small shell shape with his finger.

"He didn't call, Gavin. I tried Lieutenant Morris earlier, but he wasn't in."

Ahhh. "I'm certain things are fine, or he would have called by now."

"Maybe." She ran a hand absently through her hair.

He didn't like her worrying like this. Gavin was mad as hell at the fact someone had broken into her house and vandalized her private living space. That Ryan hadn't talked for almost three hours still infuriated him. But raw fury and yeah, fear, crawled through him at the thought of what could have happened to Taylor. However, there was little Gavin could do about any of it, at present, other than take their

DEADLY TIES

minds off of it all.

"You swim like an eel," he told her, slipping his hands from her shoulders down her back, his forefingers on each side of her spine.

She bowed up, bring her breasts even closer to him. His gaze dropped to the barely hidden nipples. Not exactly hidden. She was obviously cold as he could easily see the points of her breasts through the thin, black material.

"Exactly how long were you watching?" Her head cocked to the side.

He didn't raise his gaze, wondered what she'd do if he just leaned in and kissed one. "That's for me to know."

"You don't think I knew you were there?" Taylor wiggled slightly, shifting her position on his lap, and what little blood he had managed to control thus far went racing to his groin.

Gavin grunted and placed his hands on the curve of her waist to keep her still. She hadn't known he was there, in the shadows watching her slice through the water as though she'd been born in the blue depths. Taylor had remained oblivious for almost fifteen minutes. He knew the moment she felt him watching her. Her strokes had stopped and she jerked up in the water. No, she hadn't been aware of him, but he had damn sure been aware of her.

"You know, you're even more sexy all wet," she murmured, one hand lifting to streak through his hair while the other slid over his shoulder and down to his chest, her nails slightly scraping .

"You think I'm sexy?" Gavin couldn't keep the smile out of his voice. "Funny. I was thinking the same thing about you." He pulled her even closer. Her long legs bent on either side of him as he leaned back against the edge of the pool.

Her smile…. God he loved her smile. Those dimples just tugged at him and made him want to kiss her until neither of them could think.

She pulled her lower lip between her teeth. On a whisper came, "I'm glad you called when you did." Her head shook and she leaned into him until their chests were almost touching. "I'd thought of you all day long, even though I tried not to. I was really looking forward to our little afternoon." Her sigh breezed against his mouth. "I'm sorry if I seemed ungrateful earlier, I just--it's been…."

When Taylor stopped, he supplied, brushing a thumb across her bottom lip. "A bad day?"

Her tinkling laugh flirted between them. "Not the worst, granted, but it still ranks among them."

"I have a prescription for a bad day."

Her dimples were driving him mad. Russet brows rose in mock fascination. "Oh, doctor, please tell."

"Have I told you, I like it when you get all sassy?" White teeth flashed at him and the corners of her eyes narrowed on her smile. Gavin continued, "Why don't I show you my cure for bad days?"

He leaned into her closing the distance between them. Their lips met, parted, and tongues tangoed, first meeting in a gentle dance, only to duel in furious abandon. Her breasts grazed his chest. Just three little swatches of cloth separated him from all what he wanted.

Gavin moved his hand, traveling up her stomach, over the triangle of spandex covering one breast. Taylor sucked in a quick breath. His hand continued on to that long smooth column of throat, where he wrapped his fingers around to caress her nape. Her shiver brought a smile to his lips.

Gavin gentled the kiss, drawing it out. He stretched his hand across her waist, rubbing her hipbone until she squirmed against him. She tilted her head to the side and Gavin kissed the pulse, felt it beating beneath her jaw. Dimples. He kissed back to the side of her mouth, where his tongue delved and tasted those curious little dents.

Her whispered giggle had him pulling back.

"No one's ever kissed my dimples before," she told him, in that lowered voice made for seducing.

"This is first for me too. Virgin Dimple Kissing."

Her chest vibrated against his as her laughter filled the air.

"Shhh," he warned her. His parents' bedroom was directly above the pool. He might be over thirty, but he still didn't relish the thought of his mother looking down on him making out in the pool with a girl. Some things were better for parents not to see, in his opinion.

"Sorry," she whispered against his mouth before her lips lowered to his.

Gavin was so taken back that she kissed him, he sat frozen for a moment. Her tongue explored the edge of his lips, before dipping down the side of his neck. At the base, near his collarbone, she gently suckled and Gavin almost came up off the step.

Grabbing her head in his hands, his fingers lost in her hairline, he kissed her as he wanted to all evening. His wasn't a gentle kiss, or a longing kiss, but one of possessiveness, of expectations, of want, and Taylor returned it stroke for stroke and caress for caress.

Their hands glided over wet, slick skin. Gavin cradled the side of her face in his hand as he kissed her jaw line, the length of her neck and her chest, tasting all those little water droplets. His hands followed his mouth to cradle the sides of her breasts. She wasn't overly endowed, but he didn't care. She was made perfectly to fit in the palm of his hands. His thumbs flicked out and rubbed their centers, bringing a low moan from Taylor. The sound filled the night air around them.

He no longer cared who looked out a damn window. He leaned close and pulled one nipple into his mouth through the material. She arched, pressing her breast against him as her hips shifted on his.

"You are beautiful," he whispered.

Her fingers splayed against his head, urging him on. In one deft movement, he untied the string holding up her top and let it fall, the ribbons floating in the water like lazy black snakes. He left the back

DEADLY TIES

strap buckled. He'd get to it later, after all, he uncovered what he wanted to see. The moon had banished most of the clouds and he could see the creamy paleness of her breasts against the pink softness of their centers.

"Beautiful." Gavin lowered his head to kiss the valley between her breasts before giving them equal attention with his hands, his mouth, his tongue. He twirled his tongue around her nipple before pulling it into his mouth. Taylor moaned against the back of her throat. He followed the moan up her neck, to catch it in his mouth.

His fingers rippled over her ribs down to her hipbone, and up the curve of her legs to her knees where he drew circles on them. She shifted on him again, still astride him, her knees bent on either side of his torso, she leaned down and blazed a hot wet trail down his neck, his chest. When her teeth scraped his nipple, he couldn't remain quiet.

"Taylor."

He moved his hands down her legs to curve around her muscled calves. Their mouths met again in a hungry dance of passion.

Gavin had to touch her. His fingers trailed up the inside of her legs, over the bony cartilage of her knees to the soft, supple skin of her inner thighs. Her breath shuddered into his mouth.

Teasing her he trailed a single finger on both sides of the edge of her bikini bottoms. Taylor's breath hitched. Slowly, so very slowly, he slipped his thumbs beneath the elastic. Taylor whimpered into his mouth as he touched her heated core, gently pressing in, then retreating.

"Easy," he calmed her.

God, he wanted to be inside her. Now. He was so hard, he hurt.

His thumb flicked over the tiny bundle of nerves that he knew could send her over. He slipped another finger under the barrier between them and then another, promising what could come. Taylor's breath went ragged as she kissed him with as much passion and want as was coursing through him.

When his finger filled her, Taylor arched against him sighing out his name. "Gavin…"

She was hot and tight. He worked another digit into her, working his fingers deep, his thumb flicking back and forth over her clitoris. With his other hand, he reached behind her and caressed her bottom, watching her as her head fell back and the moonlight bathed her in its pale glory.

Her hips rocked against his hand, her chest panted in the moonlight and Gavin just watched the beauty take hold.

He pressed and circled his thumb.

"Oh God, Gavin…." When he felt her tighten around his fingers, he pulled her head up to look in her eyes. As the climax ripped through her, she vised around him, and her eyelids slid down.

Gavin pulled her to him and ravaged her mouth.

"I want you out of this damn thing now," he said into her mouth.

Her throaty chuckle answered him. "I might need some help there."

Gavin was already working on the drawstring of his swim trunks. Taylor's arms slid from his shoulder to unhook the back of her bikini top. As she leaned up to remove the rest of her suit, a light from the upstairs window glared down and caught them in its illumination.

Both jerked their heads around, though Taylor was off his lap and now neck deep in the water looking for her top, no doubt.

Damn.

Just before the light went back out, Gavin thought he saw a man standing at the balcony doors, behind sheer curtains, directly above the pool.

Well, hell.

"Oh God," Taylor said, mortification clear in her voice. "Oh. My. God."

He turned and gave her his attention. She was quickly working herself back into her bikini top. The evening had effectively been doused.

"That was your father!" Her furious whisper was not lost on him. "Oh my God!"

Gavin swam to her, but she ducked out of the way, tying the ribbons back behind her neck. "Taylor."

"I am almost thirty years old and I will never be able to look either one of your parents in the eye again. *Never!*" Her voice was so incensed he couldn't help but laugh.

"You think this is funny?" she fired at him.

"No, actually, I don't." He still wanted her, so much he ached, and it was obvious to him that wasn't going to be happening tonight.

"I have not been this.... I can't believe.... What if they *saw* us?" Taylor flustered was a sight he had yet to see. This was a new side of her. She swam to the side of the pool and started to get out, but Gavin followed her and gripped an ankle.

"I already forgave you once for that tonight," she said, turning to him.

Gavin shook his head. "Come here."

"No."

"Why not?" Three heartbeats later and he was wondering what she was going to come up with.

"I'm going to bed that's why."

"At least one of us can," he muttered. Had there not been an interference she might be going to sleep in his bed--okay, maybe not to sleep--but Gavin was smart enough to know this was not the time to voice such a thought.

"What?"

"Nothing." Gavin pulled her to him. "Don't I even get a good night kiss?"

Her heavy sigh filled the air. "No."

"Come on," he coaxed.

DEADLY TIES 93

She muttered to herself. Something about lack of passion and cold fingers.

"What?" he asked.

She huffed. "Nothing." She tried to wiggle out of his hold, but stopped. "What are we doing?" she asked him,

He thought it wise not to answer.

"I've never been in this situation before. I mean your parents … and all the … all the.…" She waved a hand. "Rest."

"The rest?" Gavin wondered what she was talking about now.

Taylor looked away. "You know…. The rest."

Gavin had to bite the insides of his cheeks to keep from laughing. "By the rest, you mean me driving you crazy with lust?"

Taylor tried to jerk away from him, but he was having none of that.

"Will you let me go?" she asked him.

"No." He pinned her against the side of the pool, rocked against her so she could feel his erection. She gasped. "Answer the question."

She shook her head at him. "Yes, that's what I mean. I'm not good at it."

"Not good at what?" Now he was lost.

"The whole sex, lust, passion, love thing."

He did not hear her right. "Excuse me?"

"You heard me. Can I go now?" She tried again to wiggle away.

Thank, God they were still in the shallow end. He still had his feet under him. "No. What do you mean, you're not any good at it?" If the woman was any better, she'd kill him. And he hadn't even had her yet.

"I'm just … not."

"Where," he said getting angry, "did you get such a stupid idea?" The moment he asked the question, he knew.

He wanted to let her go, but instead he jerked her closer and plundered her mouth in a hard, savage kiss, grinding against her from their lips to their tangled legs. When he pulled back, he released her, and swam to the other side. Gavin waited until she got out and was wrapped in her robe. "I told you before I don't like to be lumped in any form or fashion with your ex. When you realize that, you know where I am."

Her wet hair slapped as she whirled around to face him.

"That's not.…" she trailed off. "I didn't mean.…"

Her sigh reached him and he thought about going to her, but he wouldn't. Not yet. No, she had to come to him.

"Maybe I did," she admitted. Her head lifted and across the night, their eyes met. It was too dark for him to see the exact expression, but he could see enough to know she was tired. "I'm sorry. But I don't have anything or anyone else to compare anything to."

Gavin treaded the water, too charged and frustrated to think about going in just yet. "I don't have to be compared to anyone or anything. Go to bed, Taylor."

She stood there, seemingly undecided for a moment. Then she mumbled a good night and walked to the outside steps and up to the upper balcony. He watched until she slipped back into her room before he cursed and started to swim laps.

No way in hell was it now a good night. Twenty laps later, he stopped and looked up at his parents' French doors. Just how much had they seen?

* * * *

"The boy's still out there swimming."

"Jock, come to bed, and leave them alone." His wife's voice mumbled from the covers, throaty from sleep.

With one last look out the window through the sheers, he shook his head, walked back to bed and climbed in with his wife. "It's not like I saw anything. They were only kissing."

Kaitlyn leaned up on her elbow. "I have a feeling you would have seen more than that if I hadn't intervened."

Jock hmphed. "You could have left the damn light off, Kaitie lass."

She settled in the crook of his arm, the same place she'd settled for the last forty years, and it calmed him as it always had. He wanted this for all his children. This happiness and contentment that he'd found in Kaitlyn O'Rieley.

"I could have, but I didn't." The smile was evident in her voice.

He would never understand how her mind worked, he had tried for over half his life and it had given him nothing but a headache.

"Why not?" he asked her.

Her sigh wafted in their darkened room. "I don't want them to rush things. She's a lovely girl, and I like her."

Then what the hell was the problem? Jock was smart enough not to voice the question. Instead, he waited her out. Finally, she complied with his silent request to continue.

"If they hurry things along too quickly, the magic, the wonder of it all might ruin things because it's no longer an unknown."

Jock had seen the way his son looked at Taylor and he had an idea where these two were concerned. One that he'd keep to himself lest his wife think he was meddling. Rush things. He bit down on the laugh that threatened to erupt.

Kaitie could be so ... blind? No, that wasn't right. How could she not see the way Gavin looked at the girl, and how, like some silent bird, Taylor had stayed practically glued to his side all evening.

Rush? Jock knew his son wouldn't see it as rushing things. And if he were right about the way the wind blew, Gavin would only want that-- what had Kaitie called it--magic, wonder even more after he tasted its power.

Hell, he never tired of it, not with Kaitie. Never with her. Jock grinned as his wife huffed a sigh and said, "Gavin needs someone like Taylor in his life."

DEADLY TIES 95

"Gavin needs to settle down," Jock muttered in full agreement.

Kaitie shook her head. "That's not what I meant. No, he needs to loosen up. Regardless of what rumors abound, Gavin is just as much a workaholic as Quinlan. He needs someone to make him see that there is more to life than work or social functions."

If his wife wanted to be naive about their son's social life, Jock wasn't going to disillusion her. He only hummed his comment.

"Perhaps," he allowed. Kaitlyn settled again beside him and he squeezed her tight. "I love you, Kaitie lass."

He felt her grin against his chest. "I love you too, Jock, me boy."

His chest rumbled with the laughter that he was trying to contain. "If the lad would get out of the damn pool, we could go have our own swim."

She tilted her head up and kissed him. "Who said we needed a pool?"

God, he loved this woman.

* * * *

"You should get the one you really like," Tori told him.

Ryan looked at Taylor, they were at the music shop.

"I think the Roma will work." The Roma was the one he liked. It was really a neat instrument, hand crafted in Romania, or so the pamphlet read. The shiny maple wood almost seemed to call out to him. Pirastro, whom Ryan knew was the world's largest string manufacturer, made the steel strings. The bow and rosin were Brazilian wood and Mongolian horsehair.

Ryan studied the violin, but he was more interested in mastering the instrument itself than knowing which woods made better sounds. However, now that he thought about it, Ryan realized he *wanted* to know those things. He'd have to talk to Taylor about researching different woods, and strings, and different materials used for all of violin making.

"Is that the one you want?" Gavin asked him.

Ryan studied Gavin. Something was up between Gavin and Taylor. Ryan didn't know exactly what it was, but both of them were too quiet, and frowning too much. And he caught them looking at each other when the other wasn't aware. Adults confused him. Ryan noticed Christian and Brayden were the same way.

Mr. and Mrs. Kinncaid decided to tag along. This whole family thing was something Ryan was trying to figure out.

Tori tugged on his sleeve. "Don't you want to play it again before you decide? I mean it's your instrument, you shouldn't rush."

Ryan smiled, he didn't know why, but he liked this girl. "I guess I could play it again." Though he really didn't like to play in front of people, but that was something he was starting to overcome.

The salesman tried to show him how to tune the thing, but Ryan brushed off his attempts. "I know, but thank you."

"He's very talented," Tori said to the man.

Ryan shook his head at her. Thinking, he decided on a variation of scales.

He fitted the ½ size violin under his chin and positioned his fingers on the ebony fingerboard. Closing his eyes, Ryan started to play. The notes and sounds vibrated through his arm, into his neck and head, filling him with harmony. When that was completed, he changed keys and started another set of scales. After going through several keys, rhythms, and octaves, Ryan lowered the instrument to see them all staring at him.

Quickly he ducked his head.

"That was great!" Tori told him, helping him pack the instrument back in its case.

Ryan shrugged. "It was just scales."

"Well, I can't play the scales on the violin. I can on the piano, but how do you know where to put your fingers?"

Ryan looked at her. "You just learn, same way you did the piano."

"I guess so," she agreed, scrunching her nose up.

"This is the one you want?" Taylor asked him.

Ryan nodded to her. "Yes, it is."

"I like it, too," Taylor agreed.

He saw her dig out her credit card and hand it to the salesman. "All right, this one it is then."

The violin was purchased and they stopped by their vehicles to drop off what everyone had bought so far.

"I want some coffee," Mrs. Kinncaid said. "Would anyone else like some? Kids? How about a pastry or donut?"

That sounded good to Ryan, but he looked to Taylor first who nodded to him. Tori was already telling her grandmother what she wanted, while also trying to tell him what was the *very best* to get. Tori was hard to keep up with sometimes.

"Why don't you guys go on ahead. Taylor saw an antique shop she wanted to check out," Gavin told them, draping his arm over Taylor's shoulders.

"Maybe I'll go with you two," Ryan said, looking at Taylor. She seemed tired, or down or something. Both she and Gavin were acting weird.

Taylor smiled down at him. "No, it's okay, Ryan. Go have one of those raspberry-cream-cheese pastries for me. I'll be along after I see if the shop has anything I like."

"Come on, Ryan!" Tori pulled him along with her and her grandparents. He noticed Christian and Brayden were already going into the antique store.

What was so great about old clothes and furniture anyway?

Ryan and Tori walked in front of her grandparents. Mrs. Kinncaid was a nice, sweet lady, but he still wasn't sure about Mr. Kinncaid.

They all ordered and sat down out on the sidewalk under green

DEADLY TIES

umbrellas. The tables were little square wooden ones and there were trees planted in great big pots.

"Are you just going to sit there looking at everything or ya gonna try your pastry?" Tori asked around a mouthful of whatever it was she had ordered. There was a smudge of red stuff at the corner of her mouth.

"Tori darlin' don't talk with your mouthful," her grandfather said.

"Yes, Pops."

Ryan tried his, and found he liked it. It was sweet and flaky and the icing was his favorite part. This was really good.

"So, Ryan," Mr. Kinncaid said, "you like your selection?"

Ryan swallowed his bite. "Yes, sir."

"They are good, but don't beat my Kaitie's here." One large finger waggled in the direction of Mrs. Kinncaid. "Now this woman can make a pastry that would simply melt in your mouth."

He didn't know what to say so he nodded.

After several moments, the old man cleared his throat. "You know Ryan, I didn't apologize for scaring you last night, or if I did, I don't remember."

Ryan shrugged. "It's okay, Mr. Kinncaid."

The man's eyes were like Gavin's but different. Ryan hadn't noticed before, but Mr. Kinncaid's eyes were sharp and wise, and made him feel like they saw all the way down inside him to that part Ryan wanted to forget.

"I don't think it is, son," Mr. Kinncaid said softly.

Ryan squirmed in his chair.

"Wow," Tori suddenly said. "What happened to your face? Did you scratch it on something?"

Ryan reached up and felt his face. What was she talking about? And then he knew. Turning back to her, he shook his head.

"My scar?" he asked her. Nah, surely she wasn't that blind.

"Is that what it is? No, you must have scratched it. If it was a scar, I would have seen it before now."

Ryan rolled his eyes and shook his head. Normally, he got mad when people asked about his scar, but with Tori, he didn't. He could only stare at her. Was she kidding? No, that tilted head and pull of her black brows gave her face a seriousness that he had yet to see from her.

She really hadn't noticed? Weird.

"It's a scar," he told her and picked up his pastry.

"You don't have to lie," she said, sitting up in her chair.

"I'm not. You saw it last night, and this morning."

"No, I didn't," she insisted.

Ryan put his pastry back down and looked straight into those Kinncaid eyes. Everyone had them, except Mrs. Kinncaid.

"How in the world could you miss it?" He couldn't believe she was serious. Ryan smiled. She hadn't noticed his scar. Everyone noticed.

Finally, she turned to her grandfather. "Was that there last night?"

Gray brows rose as Mr. Kinncaid lowered his coffee cup. "I'm afraid so."

"I must be going blind." Her voice sounded almost like a whine on the end. "Oh no! What if I have to get glasses?"

That sounded like the worst thing in the whole entire world. Tori was funny.

"You will look just the same in glasses, dear," Mrs. Kinncaid said.

Ryan poked her in the arm. "No you won't. You'll look brainier."

For just a second she glared at him, her eyes narrowing.

"I look brainy?" Her smile made one dimple stand out in her cheek like her grandmother's.

"Yeah."

"Cool."

They both ate the rest of their pastries in silence.

"How did you get it?" Tori asked him.

He'd only met the girl last night, but Tori was easy to get to know, easy to read. Ryan hoped she wouldn't ask, he should have known better.

He saw the look that the Kinncaids exchanged. Did they know? He shrugged and looked back at Tori.

How did you tell someone like her about what happened to him? "You wouldn't understand."

Tori didn't like that. She sat straight up in her chair. "What do you mean I won't understand? I'm brainy, you just said so."

"It has nothing to do with being smart, Tori." Ryan took a drink of his water.

"Then what?"

Ryan sighed. "You wouldn't understand because you are who you are."

Her hands propped on her hips, even though she was sitting down. "What is that suppose to mean?"

She reminded him of the birds he'd seen at the zoo. "It's not a bad thing, Tori. It just is. Trust me, this you could never understand, and I'm glad."

Her blue eyes narrowed on him. Then, she hopped off her chair. "Grams, I need to go to the restroom please."

Mrs. Kinncaid rose and patted him on the shoulder as she passed him, heading to the restroom with Tori.

He looked back to see Mr. Kinncaid smiling at him. "You're a good boy, and one day will be a good man, I think."

This time Ryan smiled at him. "I don't know about that."

Mr. Kinncaid leaned up on his elbows. "Sure you do, Ryan. Otherwise, you would have told Tori what happened to you. I figure it's not a pretty picture, and you spared her that. Thank you, son." He held his large hand out. Gavin had hands like that.

After thinking about it for a minute, Ryan reached out and shook the old man's hand.

"You're welcome, Mr. Kinncaid."

"I should warn you though, Tori is like her grandmother. Let me give you some advice before those two get back...."

CHAPTER TEN

Valleyview, Gatesville, Texas

One month from now. One more whole, entire month to spend in this shit hole. But she wouldn't bitch about it. One month is a hell of a lot better than the ten to twenty she was suppose to serve.

Sweat dripped in Nina's eyes as she hefted the weights up again and started another rep. She was better than this life. Much better. The sky wouldn't seem blue enough when she got out. Rod had come through for her yet again and he should for what she was putting out for him.

Someone shoved her from behind and Nina had to fight to keep her balance. Whirling, she dropped one of the weights.

B.J. Bitch was one big woman, close to six feet if not a couple of inches over and weighed, probably two hundred pounds of tight, street hardened muscle. None of the other inmates messed with her. It was a glutton for punishment if someone tried. A signed, sealed and delivered death certificate.

B.J. Bitch was not her real name, just a shortened version of her earned nickname.

Nina held her stare. The air was sweltering, ripe with body odor, in the cement block they called home.

She tried for a smile. "Hi, B.J. How's tricks?" B.J. was her name after all.

"Think you're smart don't you, slut? I should ask you that question." B.J. took a step towards her. Nina held her ground. Scrapes and clangs filled the air as weights dropped and people either moved closer or back. The smarter ones moved back.

If a fight broke out, it was solitary. Rules and regulations were followed above all else. In that moment, Nina made her decision. She dropped the other dumbbell she held.

No way in hell was she going to be accused of starting some freaking fight.

"Why's that?" Nina asked, holding the flat gray stare of the other woman.

"Rod...." The word hung on the air heavy with judgment.

And this was the blowjob queen talking?

Nina only raised a brow.

"Think you're so much better than the rest of us don't you?" B.J.'s breath reeked.

"I don't know, you've got it all figured out B.J. Why don't you tell me?"

She saw the fist coming, but she didn't do a thing to stop it. The Bitch had one hell of an upper cut. Nina felt as if her jaw exploded as the lights dimmed around her and her feet flew out from under her.

Her head rapped hard against the concrete.

"Fight! Fight! Fight!" The words chanted in a chorus like some movie. The kick to her ribs had her gagging.

"HEY!" Feet pounded on the floor as the guards rushed forwards. "Break it up. Break it up!"

Nina moaned. If she was lucky, she'd get the infirmary. Please, let her be lucky.

Shuffles and curses pounded the air as the guards wrestled The Bitch to the floor and cuffed her.

"It's solitary this time for you, B.J.," one of the guards said.

"Fucking slut started it."

"Yeah, Fisher started it."

Nina moaned again, the world was gray and fuzzy. Her head must have hit the floor harder than she thought. Damn.

"No, she didn't," said a voice she didn't recognize.

"Yeah, Rose is right. The Bitch started picking on Fisher. She didn't even say anything. Then, B.J. decked her."

Nina didn't know who all was standing up for her, but hopefully, the guards believed them.

"Fisher?" Someone squatted down next to her. "Fisher?"

Nina opened her eyes. There wasn't any need to pretend pain; it sliced through her skull. Please don't let her vomit all over the place. She swallowed the nausea and tried to focus on the two guards swerving above her.

"She prob'ly has one of them concussions or whatever the hell they're called. Whacked her melon good. Bam! Like a damn ball."

Nina had no idea who was doing all the talking. Holy shit, her head hurt.

"Fisher, how many fingers am I holding up?"

"Which one of you?" she asked before the world went dark.

* * * *

When she woke up it was to the stringent smells of ammonia and disinfectant. It still felt like a mob of jonesing bag brides wanting their hits stomped through her head in three inch spiked heels.

A small dim light over a desk drew her attention.

She tried to move her hand, but nothing happened. Damn, restraints. So much for a bump. Here she was in the prison's treasure trove of drugs and she couldn't even get off her ass to get a capsule of Tylenol.

Oh well, she'd been without before. She wasn't an addict. She would

DEADLY TIES

101

just rather be high than not. There was a hierarchy to things, even addictions, in her opinion.

Nina spent the rest of the night looking at the gray rectangled ceiling, darkened florescent lights marched down the center of the room in a perfect line.

One more month. Rod had to come through for her. He simply had to. And she knew he would. He bought her story, hook, line and sinker. Felt sorry for her too. 'Bout time somebody did.

She'd have to be careful. No way could she afford to have any of her privileges taken away or to have any of the guards, and certainly not the warden, watching her. The next month was important. Clean bill. No more drugs sneaked in, too risky. No fighting. The last had been all too close a call. It was a wonder anyone stood up for her, and if they hadn't, she could easily have been in solitary or cell time, either one was not an option. Time to be the perfect inmate.

Nina gave a harsh laugh and noticed another bedridden prisoner watching her. This woman had black hair, stark against the pillow and her cadaver complexion. Not wanting another confrontation, Nina turned her head to the side and thought about the first thing she'd do when she got out.

She'd head towards San Antonio, get Rod to make a pit stop at that rundown place outside of Brownwood and get some rocks. If she could swing it, she'd try to get him to buy a bit more that they could sell to make some extra cash. That would take care of some money problems. Nina would just have to get Rod to shell out the dough.

That shouldn't be too hard with what she was giving him. Rod had cursed at one point during their last encounter that she should be nicknamed B.J. and not The Bitch. Yeah, Rod would give her whatever she wanted. 'Course, she'd also contact some old dealers. And once she got back into the swing of things, she'd track down Johnny and the Shepards and her lawyer.

Now what she would do to them, once she'd found them, was another story. Rod was a still a problem she was working on. He would be useful no doubt, but Johnny could and probably would help her more when the going got tough. But, Rod would stick with her when they were too far in because he wouldn't know how to get himself out of a mess. Johnny on the other hand would leave at the first sign of real trouble from the SPOC. SPOC--COPS... either or. Didn't matter.

In her world, Johnny's world, one was the same as the other.

So as far as Johnny, she didn't really know, he was a great lay. A much better fuck than Rod, but needs wants when the devil drives.

The Shepards would have to die.

As far as Ryan--well, Nina had yet to come up with what she would do with the little bastard when she got her hands on him. He was her flesh and blood, so it did seem wrong to kill him, but she still had to make certain that he never squealed about that night in Austin. No way

102 *Jaycee Clark*

was she ever going down for killing a cop.

The questions and problems that she would face after she got out of this hellhole plagued her until the window pinkened with the oncoming dawn.

Nina sighed and dreamed of revenge.

CHAPTER ELEVEN

Fourth of July

Taylor stood at the entrance of the massive room and surveyed these people in this atmosphere. It had been awhile since she'd gotten all dressed up for a party. And she had to admit, though she was nervous, she was having fun.

The ballroom, overlooking the long sculpted lawn leading down to the Potomac, was in full swing. The party, held in the honor of the nation's independence and Jock's birthday, was by invitation only.

Several couples twirled to Sinatra on the dance floor, the brassy band jazzing out tune after tune. More food than could be consumed that evening had been piled high on tables in shapes of animals, forests of vegetables, meats, fruits and decadent desserts.

The last few days had strained her nerves and she still didn't know if they were more settled or more frazzled. Morris had finally called her to let her know Nina was where she was supposed to be, and a print was lifted from her house belonging to one Mr. Gibbons. Case of the burglar solved. He was back in custody and looking at more charges against him than what he already had. After the night in the pool, Gavin kept up his assault on her, very subtly of course. A smoldering look here, a daring I-know-how-you-feel-look there, maybe it was a brush of fingers against her palm, or the way his arm draped around the back of her chair.

All these little things and he had yet to touch her, yet to kiss her again.

The man had warned her, and she was learning he was stubborn. They had yet to get past the tension that swirled around them every time they were together. Taylor still wasn't certain she wanted it to end. There was a great deal of excitement simply knowing he wanted her and she had the power in upping the ante in her refusal.

A deep rumbling laugh made her turn to see Gavin talking with some people across the dance floor. Lord, he made her heart skip. Gavin was handsome, too handsome truth be known. But dressed in his black tuxedo he was breathtaking.

She wished he'd smile at her again. Not like he was smiling now, but one of those, cocky, sexy smiles he'd used on her since they met. One

DEADLY TIES

she had only seen rarely since their swim in the pool.

The day after that had been a tense one. Taylor had cleaning crews to talk to, and to top the day off, her ex had called pissed because the Austin Police Department had the audacity to ask him if he held a grudge against her, enough to trash her new home. Yeah, Charles had been slightly put out. Taylor had shrugged off his temper and words, as she had for years. Ryan and Gavin had not been so easily forgetful. Unfortunately, both had been with her in the car when Charles had called, and both had clearly been infuriated, both for the same and different reasons.

The house she came home to Sunday night was one with new locks, fresh paint, some new furniture and a state-of-the-art security system. The last was her favorite and most calming out of the new purchases-- though she didn't remember ordering one. Gavin had told her not to ask so many questions and that she was 'welcome'.

After that, the half-week flew by. Gavin, or rather, his entire family, had informed her and Ryan that they simply *must* come to the party. Taylor still had no idea how she'd gotten talked into this.

She scanned the room again from her place in the doorway and saw Ryan chatting with Tori and Aiden, both he and her son held the baby boys. Anna Lopez, the twin's nanny, sat smiling at the same table. Taylor wondered where Jess had gotten off too.

"There you are," came the soft Texas drawl.

"We've been looking all over for you," said Christian.

Both women stood just to the side and behind her. The two were complimenting in their attire. Jesslyn wore a black silk pants suit. Christian was dressed in a deep crimson gown that flowed down her long figure.

"Sorry, I was powdering my nose," she explained to them. She liked these two and had made friends with them over the weekend.

"There's no reason to be nervous," Christian told her.

"Oh, I'm not." Then Taylor tilted her head in agreement. "Okay, maybe I am, but it's from being out of practice from these gatherings." The hair on her nape shifted and she turned, looked and locked eyes with Gavin across the floor. The flutter in her stomach had nothing to do with nervousness or lack there of. No, it was an aware tingle of what could be--what probably would be--if she'd go to him. After all, she 'knew where to find him.' Taylor swept her eyes down him and back up to meet his. Feeling wicked, she slowly smiled at him and gave him a wink, before turning her attention back to the ladies at her side.

"What, is going on between the two of you?" Jesslyn asked point blank, taking two flutes of champagne off a tray from a passing waiter, then handed them off to both Taylor and Christian while asking for a bottle of water.

Taylor took a sip, the crisp almost fruity wine tingled on her tongue. How to answer that one? "What do you mean."

Christian and Jesslyn's laughter mixed together.

"Come on, Taylor, spill it," Christian said. "There is something from the looks of things, and everything else."

"What are you talking about?"

"Well," Christian said, leaning against the wall beside Taylor. "He brought you out to the house for the weekend. He's never done that before, at least not as long as I've been here. And the looks he sends you...." Christian shook her head. "I've always wondered if the rumors about him were true."

"What rumors?"

Jesslyn leaned close, a one sided grin on her face as her eyebrows wiggled. "*Those* rumors that supposedly make any woman fall at his feet because of how good he is."

Taylor hadn't heard any of those rumors, but she could well imagine them. She didn't know a thing about women falling at his feet, but that thought made her smile.

"He's used to women falling all over him is he?" *You know where to find me....* So, if she went to him, then she'd be just like all the women he was used to. That made her wonder who could outlast whom. Which of them would give in first and if the wait would be worth it.

"So the rumors say," Jesslyn admitted.

"Though I often wondered how true they are. He's always working, always at the hospital, always on call." Christian shrugged. "Seems to me he does little more than work, eat and sleep--less of the latter two and more of the first. Then again he's a Kinncaid, so the women fall all over him regardless of whether or not he has time for them."

Taylor had no idea what to make of the conversation.

The two women looked at her then back out to another woman who was walking up to Gavin.

"I never knew what he saw in that one," Jesslyn muttered.

"I think it was the 'dahrlin' Gavin' whispered in her breathy over - done Southern belle routine," Christian retorted.

"Is that Scarlett?" Taylor asked.

Both of her friends turned and gave her questioning looks. "How do you know about Scarlett?" they both asked.

"he told me," Taylor shrugged. "Why?"

Christian leaned towards her. "Jock liked her, though God only knows why. I heard him tell the other boys and Mrs. K. he hoped they stayed together." Christian grinned. "Mrs. K. told him to please mind his own business, he meddled too much."

"Aiden told him if that was the case then she was the wrong woman because whoever Jock picked was a disaster," Jesslyn added.

"What do you mean?"

Jess waved an absent hand. "Long story. Suffice it to say that Jock's idea of perfect wives for his sons rarely corresponds with theirs. Personally, we've all met Scarlett and can't stand her. Thank God, you

DEADLY TIES

came along."

Wives? What did she say to that? Taylor took a big drink of champagne and choked.

"You all right?" Jesslyn thumped her on the back.

"Fine," she coughed out. Wives? "Uhm.... Gavin and I are just friends." Yeah, just friends.

Jesslyn stuck her tongue in her cheek and nodded.

Christian cleared her throat. "You just keep telling yourself that."

A brassy blues tune came from the band and Gavin and Scarlett joined in with the other dancers on the floor.

"By the way, I love that dress," Christian told her.

"Thank you," she said smoothing her hand down the side of her sleeveless dress. She'd found this one in a consignment shop just the other day. The Georgette material was sheer with gold and crimson stitching woven into various shapes of dancing paisleys. It overlaid the underlying material of peacock blue. The dress, a 1933's original, shoved a dent into her budget, and she loved it.

"Hi, would you like to dance?"

Taylor jerked around and wondered who the man was talking to. Handsome devil, whoever he was, about her height with gray eyes.

"Who are you talking to, Robbie?" Christian asked.

His eyes raked down her. "This lovely new lady, I've yet to meet."

Christian laughed. "This is Taylor Reese."

"Hi, Taylor. I'm Robbie Trelington."

She held her hand out expecting to shake his hand, but he held hers up and kissed it, old fashioned. She grinned. He was a flirter.

"There you are."

Taylor blinked as Gavin slid his arm possessively around her shoulders and hauled up against him, effectively pulling her hand away from Robbie's. "Why didn't any of you save me?" he asked them. "I swear that woman does not understand the meaning of the word no."

He glanced down at her. "Where have you been? We haven't even danced yet and I still have another surprise to show you. Hi, Robbie. Excuse us."

Gavin's arm felt like a weight on her shoulders, and she could feel his eyes boring into the top of her head as he led her a few feet away.

Looks like he came to her first.

Taylor licked her lips, her side warm and tingly where it touched his. Finally, she craned her head back to look at him. She couldn't exactly pinpoint the expression in his narrowed eyes.

"What?" she asked him.

"Have I told you how great you look tonight?"

She first thought he was only being his regular charming, flirting self, but though he smiled, it was a small, almost serious one. Turning, she hesitantly put her hand to his chest, smoothing it along the pristine white shirt, though Taylor kept her eyes on him. What she saw in them made her heart slowly roll over as her stomach skittered. They were still that deep almost, midnight blue, but the depths were a turbulent sea. They reminded her of the night in the pool; passion mixed with ... with.... That was the part that worried her, the part she couldn't figure out. Was it caring? Protectiveness?

Taylor licked her lips. "I can't remember if you have or not. I know I haven't told you that you look very dashing and handsome in your sharp lined tux. Very you."

His arm from her shoulder had shifted to rest around the small of her back and she couldn't help but smile.

Ebony brows danced above those spine-tingling eyes while his other hand brushed along her cheekbone.

Spine tingling indeed.

Gavin noticed her deep intake of breath as he smoothed the back of his hand along her cheek. So soft. She was so damn soft. When he'd seen Robbie saddle up to her, he'd left Scarlett in the middle of some sentence and stalked over to Taylor. He found he didn't like the prick ogling Taylor.

"Well, since you can't remember," he told her, "let me say that you...." He started to say look lovely. Instead, he leaned down and whispered in her ear, "Make me want to take you upstairs and slowly see how lovely you look without anything on."

Her sigh made him grin.

Another slow song started. Before she could do more than shiver-- and he knew it wasn't from the cold--he laced his fingers through hers and led her to the dance floor. Her eyes had gone almost amber. Fascinating.

With their fingers linked and his hand on the curve of the bottom of her back, they swayed to the slow song of love. Her cheek rested against his chest and his against the silky curls piled high atop her head. He saw his mother and father dancing just as he and Taylor were, saw his father tilt his mother's face up by the chin and lean down to kiss her. They broke apart laughing. Something about that scene, and the woman in his arms, opened a longing within him that he hadn't known had existed--or he *had*, he just hadn't focused on the search of it.

Until now.

Shaking off the thoughts, he turned his attention back to Taylor.

"Guess you didn't like my idea, huh?" he asked her, rubbing small circles in the bottom of her back on the sheer material of her dress. When she'd bought it over the weekend at one of the antique stores they'd gone into, he'd wondered what it would look like on her, as he didn't know many--or any--that went around in eighty-year-old clothes. It was called a flapper dress, she informed him. He didn't care what the hell it was called. The bright blue color contrasted with the red and gold stitching and made her hair stand out like burnished copper. He kept circling the small of her back, the sheer overlay material sliding

DEADLY TIES

sensually over the blue silk underdress.

He wanted her and she still hadn't answered his question.

"You're used to women falling at your feet."

Gavin pulled back a bit from her. "I never asked them to."

Taylor's eyes narrowed. She was serious. Damn some stupid rumors and his reputation.

He shook his head. "I don't care if an entire harem resides in my damn condo, woman." Bringing their joined hands up, he followed his father's lead and tilted Taylor's chin until he could lean down and kiss her. Instead, he stopped a hair's breath away and said, "I don't want you falling at my feet. I just want you."

....*falling at my feet*. Well, to be perfectly honest, that wouldn't be such a bad thing, but he doubted she wanted to hear that right now. Not to mention the mere thought of her on her knees before him.... No! He could not, would not go there. Talk about causing tongues to wag. He was already so aroused he just wanted to leave--with Taylor.

Taylor's brows pulled down to that slight frown he found so adorable. "You have a harem?"

He kissed her, just a quick peck, but a kiss none the less. Granted not the kind he wanted to give her, but he if kissed her like he'd wanted to since he'd seen her walk in the damn door, they would be going upstairs. Or maybe just to the elevator....

"Doesn't everyone? If I want someone falling prostrate in front of me, I'll just go visit one of them."

"Them, being the ladies stashed at your condo. Shall I call you Hugh? Or Heffner? Or just Sheik Al bin Gavin?"

Her dimples winked, but he still saw the serious pensiveness in her eyes. This was not something he wanted to joke about with her. He knew what had happened to her because of Charles--the bastard--and he didn't even really want to tease her about infidelity.

After he'd cooled off after their pool scene, he'd understood where she came from. Sort of, but that didn't rub him any less for the fact that she had a tendency to compare her previous relationship with what they had now. They'd already spent the last few days too damn apart for his tastes. She'd pushed him away because of her fears. Or maybe he'd pushed her so she could get a grasp on the situation.

Gavin sighed and cupped her face in his palm, letting go of her hand. "Taylor, I care about you. I love listening to you talk...."

"It's just my West Texas diphthong," she interrupted putting both her arms around his waist, beneath his jacket. That simple movement had him sidetracked.

"And...." He stopped. "West Texas what?"

Her shoulders--which as far as he could tell was the only thing holding up her dress--shrugged. "Diphthong. That was the word I'd been trying to remember. Jesslyn and I have what, in theater, is called the West Texas Diphthong. It's the smiling vowels thing. Or that's how a certain theater director termed it."

He had no idea what the hell she was talking about. He knew about thongs, though not her West Texas dipping one. Fascinating thought though it was, he tried to continue, "I like spending time with you. I love to hear you laugh, though I must say I don't get to hear it enough. And the way you frown when you're trying to figure something out, or the way your head tilts to side." Like it was doing right now. "Hell, I even like you when you're moody and snapping at me. And I think you feel the same way. I want to know you, all of you, all about you."

Her eyes never left his and Gavin caught the wink of a dimple. "Perhaps," she conceded.

Their bodies swaying together, her scent of honeysuckle wrapping around the both of them, the slide of her dress between them, under his hand. All this had him praying she wouldn't turn from him this evening.

"You and Ryan are staying the night here at the hotel, aren't you? You both have a suite, though I heard Tori tell Ryan he had to stay in their suite so they could watch movies and practice." Please let her say yes. If not, he'd just have to persuade her.

Her tongue darted out wetting her lips and he could have groaned.

"I don't know."

He rested his forehead against hers. "Say yes."

She knew what he was asking. He could see it in her eyes, in the way her breath quickened.

"I—I...."

Gavin rested his lips on hers again, this time not caring that they were in the middle of a dance floor. His tongue traced the line of her mouth, felt it part under his and he smiled against her, nipping her bottom lip softly as he pulled away. "Say yes."

"What about the cutting of the cake?"

He didn't give a damn about any of the cake. "Say yes," he repeated.

Her head tilted to the left and she scanned the crowd.

"After the cake? I don't want you to miss your father's big moment."

Gavin felt the corners of his mouth lift.

"I don't want any cake." Not unless he was eating it alone with her. Or off of her.

Her eyes twinkled at him and the edges lifted when she smiled. "Say yes."

Gavin couldn't help it, he laughed. "Minx."

Both of them swayed to the next song.

Apparently the woman wanted cake. He'd give her cake. "All right. Yes, we can stay for the cake thing." Plus it would give him a minute to ask Brayden if it would be all right if Ryan stayed with them till morning. But, he didn't want to let go of her yet. "If we can keep dancing."

"Fine, we'll dance," she answered.

DEADLY TIES
109

"*You* never said yes."

God he loved her dimples, and that collarbone where he could see her pulse pounding just above it. He wanted to kiss that little indention, suck on the creamy pale skin and feel her blood rushing, pumping against his tongue, knowing it was him that caused her heart to race.

"Yes," she whispered.

Gavin didn't know if he was relieved or wound tighter.

A fast song started and by mutual agreement they both moved to the side of the dance floor. They headed over to the table where most of the family was congregated. Becky was bouncing one baby while Anna made goofy faces to it. Aiden's arm was draped around his wife's shoulders. Brayden and Christian oohed and ahhed over the other twin. Gavin still couldn't tell them apart.

"You two have fun?" Jess asked.

Christian looked up from the baby and shared a wicked grin with Jesslyn.

What were these two up to?

"Yeah, poor Robbie, just kept looking over at you the entire dance. Really bruised my ego. What's a girl to think?" Christian said to Taylor

Taylor groaned.

"Robbie," he muttered.

Jesslyn chuckled. "Yeah, he was checking out Taylor. You have competition."

Gavin cocked a single brow and turned to stare at Taylor. "Competition?"

She started to shake her head, then stopping she sassed, "What? You're not the only one with a harem. Robbie looks like he might know a thing or two." At his shocked look, she laughed. "Do you honestly think you are God's single gift to Woman?"

"If that woman is you? Damn straight." This time he spun her into his arms, dipped her over his arm and kissed her full on the mouth, not a sweet chaste kiss, but one born of possessiveness and passion.

Someone cleared his or her throat.

"We are in a hotel. Might seem a given, but I'm quite certain there are rooms available," Aiden drawled.

Gavin pulled back, straightened them both and saw her eyes were still closed. When his thumb touched her lip, the lids slowly rose.

"Or the elevator," Brayden quipped.

His twin knew him too well.

"The elevator?" Jesslyn asked. "That's one I haven't tried."

"You should all be ashamed of yourselves," Anna Lopez admonished.

"Small ears and not a whit of refrain from any of you," Becky lilted, adding her two cents in.

"Sorry," echoed around the group.

"Taylor?" Ryan asked clearly excited. "Are we staying here tonight?"

Taylor seemed to finally realize where they were and everything around them, her eyes narrowed on him with irritation and he perversely smiled. She turned to her son and said, "I don't know yet."

What? Gavin closed his arms around her from behind and swayed to the beat of the Armstrong music pumping through the room. "What she means to say is yes."

Ryan looked from him to his mother back to him and then to Tori, to whom he told, "See, told you. They're still at it."

"At what?" Taylor asked.

The kids rolled their eyes. "Not getting along."

A moment passed in complete silence as the adults sat staring just as expectantly as the kids.

"No, we're getting along fine, Ryan," Taylor said. "I just haven't decided yet. Gavin thinks since it's getting late, we should stay. But I don't want to...."

"Impose...." chorused from around the table.

Taylor's blush crept up her cheeks and she shook her head.

Aiden said. "Trust me, dear, you and Ryan will be no imposition at all. In fact there is currently a two bedroom suite with your name on it."

She wavered.

Gavin leaned down and whispered in her ear, pulling her tight back against him. "You already said yes. Are you going to welch on me?"

"I suppose we could stay," she finally conceded.

"All right!" Tori said. "After Pops cuts the cake, we can go upstairs and watch movies and eat popcorn."

"Cake and popcorn, definitely. I wanted to be up all night," Brayden mumbled.

While everyone waited for the cake to be cut, Gavin slipped away. There were a few things he needed to do. Arrangements to make, surprises to bring to about.

Cake with lots of icing, fruit, fondue, chocolate, strawberries. The list got longer. He hoped she would like his surprise and not be offended. Knowing Taylor she would be a little irritated at his assumptions, but he'd talk her around it, or kiss her around it.

He made a mental note to tell Bray they'd have to call his suite and not Taylor's if a problem came up. His suite was bigger and he wanted everything to be perfect.

* * * *

The private elevator slid smoothly to the top floor on the north side of the hotel. Soft music filtered through the air around them. Ice blazed in her stomach. Taylor didn't know if she wanted to laugh, sigh, scream-- just to relieve some tension--or turn and kiss the man whose arms she was in.

As soon as the cake had been cut and Mr. Kinncaid gave the first pieces to his granddaughter and Ryan, Gavin pulled her out of the room and down a dim hallway. Now he was leaning against the darkened

DEADLY TIES

mirrored wall of the elevator with his arms around her, pulling her back against him.

"You could relax you know. I promise not to gobble you up." His deep voice tugged at her, low and smooth it reminded her of the promise of storms.

She tilted her head to the side of his shoulder and looked back up at him. "I know."

"Then why are you so nervous?"

The man had to ask? All Taylor could do was sigh.

His arm snaked up and around her middle to tip her chin up before his knuckles brushed along her neck. "We won't do anything you don't want to do, you know."

No, he wouldn't do anything she didn't like, or want. Part of her, the woman who had been criticized and demeaned by a selfish man was scared.

"What are you fearing so much?" he asked, reading her thoughts.

She could lie, but she wouldn't. "That I'll disappoint you."

There was that grin, she'd waited all night for that grin with the devilish light twinkling in his eyes. "That's not possible," he whispered. His breath warmed the side of her face. Taylor shivered again, and goosebumps danced along her arms.

The elevator stopped and they got off. He kept his arm around her shoulders as he steered her down a hallway to a door where he slipped the key in and opened it.

Music played here softly, too. The interior of the room was elegant, or what she could see of it. There was a living room, a dining table that sat eight and a kitchen. Plush rugs sporadically covered hardwood floors.

"I think we need to go shopping again," Gavin said as he shut the door, leaning against the wall. He tossed the plastic key onto the entry table.

What?

"I love that dress on you." He pushed away from the wall and stalked towards her. Her heart began to race, her blood humming from the hungry look in his eyes.

His fingers dove into her hair as he pulled her against him, his mouth crushed down over hers stealing her breath, her thoughts. His waist was hard and chiseled where her hands rested on it beneath the jacket. He was warm against her palms, his shirt crisp. His scent, male, spicy with a hint of the outdoors, tickled her senses. She could only hold onto him or be completely conquered.

Before she could even participate in the kiss, he pulled away, skimming one hand down her neck, over her collarbone, down over her chest to rest on the curve of her waist as his mouth planted kisses along her jaw. His tongue was warm against the lobe of her ear, causing her breath to catch.

"I'm used to seeing every curve," he murmured. "Dresses that leave little to the imagination. I had no idea this could be so sexy. Every time your arm moved I would get aroused just by catching a glimpse of the edge of your breast. Right here." His fingers danced up her ribs to the deep side cuts of the sleeveless dress. One slipped under the silk underdress to caress the side of her breast. She only wore a silk camisole under the layered dress.

"This skin right here, called to me all night." The tip of his finger circled on the soft edge of her breast, just as his tongue circled her ear.

"Hmmm...." Taylor realized she had never felt more cherished.

"I want you Taylor." His teeth scraped over the sensitive skin just behind her ear.

She shivered. "Oh...."

He leaned back, his other hand joining the first so that two of his fingers, barely even touching her, ignited her nerves.

"Do you want me?" he asked her.

"Do I...." Taylor could only blink at him. He didn't know? With a burst of brazenness she didn't know she had in her, Taylor reached up, grabbed fists full of his hair and pulled him down to her. She kissed him as he had her. Hard. Hot. Passionate, wanting him to know the fire that burned inside her. Her tongue explored the inner cavern of his mouth, dueling and dancing with his.

Gavin swept her up in his arms, never breaking the kiss. She loosened the hold on his hair and spread her fingers along his scalp.

The kiss lasted down the hallway and into the bedroom, not even breaking when he sat her on her feet. Something tickled her nose.... Honeysuckle. Taylor pulled back and turned to see where the smell was coming from. The king-size bed, already turned down, was covered in the blooms; white, gold and pale pink scattered along the white sheets. Candles burned around the room and she saw the champagne chilling in an ice bucket beside the bed. But it was the honeysuckle on the bed that brought her up short.

She looked at him, standing there before her. Like a blinding light, Taylor realized she didn't want this to just be sex, to just be lust. And where had that come from?

Honeysuckle.

"They remind me of you," he whispered, taking her in his arms. "I know it was probably presumptuous of me to...."

Taylor laid her finger on his lips. No one had ever cared like this, this stupid little thing.

She leaned up on her toes and kissed him, soft and gentle. Trailing her tongue along his lips until he parted his beneath hers. Her hands moved up to twine around his neck. She let her nails scrape gently along his nape, the hair tickling her knuckles.

He moved his mouth to take control of the kiss. His hands trailed along her waist to her chest, back and forth. The silk and chiffon

DEADLY TIES

material sliding over each other with fluid ease. Cradling the sides of her breasts through the dress, his thumbs flicked out and circled the centers until her nipples peaked and she moaned.

Then his hands went down to her waist, and she felt the material slowly bunching, felt the hem shifting over her knees, sliding over her thighs. Stepping back, she reached down and helped him lift it up over her head. Gavin tossed it to the chair and stood looking at her.

Good God. There she stood, her breasts begging for attention under the camisole. Her long, lithe legs sported garters, hose. Pantalets. Had he ever known a woman who wore pantalets? Forget the thongs. Gavin took a deep breath.

"You are beautiful."

Her dimples winked at him. Holding back away from her, he gently removed her camisole. She kicked off her heels. Gavin pushed her gently onto the bed.

The smell of honeysuckle filled the air as they crushed beneath her.

"I don't think, in all my fantasies, I ever could have imagined you wearing such a fascinating outfit." he told her, standing between her legs hanging over the side of the bed, slowly unclipping a garter. With deliberate ease he rolled her stocking down, scraping his nails gently on her inner thigh, skimming his fingers under her knee, making her squirm. He cupped her calf, wrapped his fingers around her ankle before tossing the silk to the floor and repeating the process with the other hose.

One arm was flung out above her head, the other across her smooth alabaster stomach. Her breasts lay soft and inviting.

Gavin slowly caressed his way up her legs, to that sexy little underwear.

He cupped her, felt her heat and dampness through the ivory lace. Grinning and watching her, he grazed his finger along the length of her. His gut clenching when he realized how wet she already was. Still watching her, he pressed, once, twice a bit deeper and she moaned. Carefully, so as not to rip the lace, as he'd really have loved to do, he rolled the underwear down her long legs.

He stood there, between her bent knees, looking down at her. Finally, she was naked. There wasn't a stitch of clothing to keep any of her from him.

"You're staring," she told him, moving her hands to cover herself.

"I know," he told her, grabbing her hands. "And I could simply stare all night."

Her bottom lip pouted out. "Simply stare all night? And here I had such high hopes for us."

"There's that sass again. High hopes? Well, all right, maybe we'll do more than stare. After all," he told her leaning into her. "We don't want those high hopes to waste do we?"

Her smile warmed him.

"It's not fair."

"What?" he asked, leaning down to kiss her, his hand lying across her stomach.

"I can't stare at you?" One of her brows arched. "Not that you're not breath-stealing in that tux, honey, but I'd rather you were out of it." Her finger ran down the front of his white shirt.

Gavin laughed, as they both fumbled to get his clothes off. Her hands were everywhere at the same time and seemingly nowhere at all.

The flowers bedded the area around her with a soft dreamy feel. While Gavin kicked his pants and boxers off, she picked up a handful, held them above her and let the flowers fall.

In a blink, Gavin joined her on the bed. Skin touched skin, charging both them and the air around them. Smooth and gentle met hard and angled.

Gavin looked into her eyes. Beautiful, she was so damn beautiful. He kissed the edge of her mouth, turning up into a dimpled smile, traced the corner with his tongue. Her breath wafted against him as she sighed. They were soon lost in each other's kisses. Hands skimmed along bodies, exploring, learning, caressing, building the feelings within her.

Gavin propped up on his elbow beside her. She watched him just watching her. What was it with this man that he simply liked to look at her? She couldn't really get her mind around that.

His tan hand reached out and cupped her breast, one blunt tipped finger circled the edge of the breast, then moved closer and closer to the center, until finally he plucked her nipple. The quick shot of nerves electrocuted straight through her belly.

Still those dark blue eyes bore into hers, as if were studying what she liked, what she didn't, without even asking.

His hand moved from her breast to her navel, a long, lazy figure eight.

He leaned down and kissed her, robbing her of thought. His fingers trailed a fire from her heart to her core. Up and down, up and down, until she just wanted him to touch her.

Her hands came up to spread across his torso, her fingers twirling in the patch of dark hair veeing across his wide chest. She leaned up, kissed his flat nipple.

She heard his intake of breath just as she she found her with his fingers. This time it was her turn to gasp as he started the magic.

"Gavin…."

He loved the sound of his name on her lips. Gavin trailed his fingers over her, along the wet, slickness of her, circling her center begging for him to touch the small point of passion.

"Gavin…."

"Taylor," he told her on a grin. He leaned down to kiss her as he finally flicked over her sensitive bundle of nerves, at he same time

DEADLY TIES

slipping a finger inside her.

"Ohhhh…."

She was so tight, so hot, so ready.

But he wanted more….

He leaned closer, kissed her as he dipped one finger even lower and had her arching off the bed.

Gavin worked her to the point of shattering before backing off. He kept up the torture, until she was begging him, until her eyes lightened to the color of perfect aged Scotch.

He settled between her thighs.

Taylor held her breath, waiting. If he didn't come into her now, she didn't know what she'd do.

He kissed her thigh, drew a figure eight on it with his warm tongue.

Taylor pulsed with need.

Slowly, so damn slowly, he pushed her thighs wider. She looked down, her eyes locking with his wild blue ones. He leaned closer, paused, his fingers coming up to play just as he leaned in and covered her with his mouth. His tongue laved and promised, flicking lightning rods to every nerve in her body. Taylor arched, tried to hold it. Not yet. Not without him…. Just as she reached the edge of the precipice, he stopped. Then suckled hard on her clitoris while his fingers danced wickedly.

She screamed and came in a blind furious bolt.

"Gavin … please." She locked her legs around him as her hand reached down to find him.

Wrapping him in her fist, she looked into his eyes. They were the color of the sky near dawn, a pure, deep blue, the color of a lapis lazuli stone.

He wanted in her now. Now. But something…. Reason….

"I need a condom," he managed.

"No, you don't. It's fine." She tried to pull him down for a kiss.

"You sure?" he asked her.

Her hand tightened and he closed his eyes. "You don't have to worry about me getting pregnant, or that I have some STD. I'm clean."

"Fine." Gavin grabbed her hand and with one single thrust entered her. She gloved him in heat. "Oh, God."

Exquisite. She was absolutely exquisite. He leaned up on his elbows and looked down at her, kissing her gently.

"Taylor," he whispered against her mouth, nudging the side of her nose with his own. "Open your eyes."

Amber darkened as passion danced in her eyes. They shifted together, the age-old movement as simple and beautiful as the ebb and flow of waves on a shore.

With each measured stroke he slowly built her back up until she was nearing the peak, only to change rhythms and prolong this joining. He didn't want this to end too soon, the pleasure over too quickly. Slow and deep, fast and shallow, rotating, thrusting, until she thrashed her head to the side.

"Oh God.… Gavin.…"

When they were both glistening with moisture, when Taylor was all but begging him, Gavin reached down between them and found her again. She crested, vising around him, yelling his name.

"Gavin!"

Pulling him over the edge with her.

Gavin poured himself into her, losing his mind, his thoughts, all reason and more of himself than he ever had before as her muscles squeezed everything from him.

They both lay gasping for breath. Gavin knew she was alive because her heart pounded beneath him, and her breath puffed against the side of his face. And he must be alive if he felt those things.

Gavin rolled to the side, and brought her with him so that she lay tucked up beside him.

Minutes passed in silence. His fingers trailed over her arm and hip. Hers skimmed over his chest.

"I never knew…" she whispered, her head on his chest.

"Never knew what?" he asked her, tucking his chin in and looking down at her.

"I didn't know it could be like that," she admitted.

Gavin thought about that for a minute. "You mean you've never…?"

Her head shook back and forth, the hair sliding over his arm and chest. "Yes, I've had an orgasm, oh great one. Just not like.… I didn't understand what the big deal was.…"

Grabbing her against him, he pulled her atop him.

"Not that big a deal?" he asked her. "Poor Taylor, so deprived."

Her dimples calmed him. "Deprived?"

It was stupid, juvenile even, but primitive, too. He had pleased her, opened this world of passion for her. He felt invincible.

Her back was as soft as the blooms scattered all around them and over them. Gavin picked several of them out of her hair. He loved those coppery strands in his hands, sliding like silky water through his fingers.

Her head turned to lie on his chest.

"What's the champagne and cake for?" she asked.

"Oh." He'd meant to drink some before, but had gotten side tracked.

Gavin sat up and Taylor moved away from him, tucking the sheet up beneath her arms, sitting cross-legged. One knee stuck out of the sheet. He opened the bottle of the hotel's best champagne. The pop of the cork preceded the dry scent of the wine as a cloud swirled out of the mouth of the bottle. Bubbling gold sloshed into two flutes. He handed one to her.

"To us," he said.

She tilted her head, studying him, and he thought she'd never looked

DEADLY TIES

more beautiful. Her pale cheeks were rosy from lovemaking. Fiery strands of hair tasseled down around her shoulders and breasts. Lips full and pouty from his kisses gently smiled. He wondered at the question he saw in her eyes. Finally, she clinked her glass to his. "To us."

Instead of taking a drink like he, she looked down into the glass.

Gavin reached out and titled her face up. "What is it?"

"I don't know how to explain," she said.

"Try."

Her teeth scraped over her bottom lip. Taking a small sip, she shrugged, then said, "Thank you."

"For?" He didn't want her damn gratitude. "For making love to you?"

She shook her head, a small smile playing at the edge of her mouth. "No, even though that was amazing too."

She took a deep breath. "For everything. For listening to me, for wanting to listen, for the flowers." Her hand waved out over the bed. "For wanting me. This will probably sound dumb, but it's the little things that matter most to me. A phone call, a smile across the room, just when you reach for my hand."

She looked over the bed then back to him. "How did you know this was my favorite flower?"

"You smell like honeysuckle." He leaned over and pulled her towards him until they were sitting side by side. "Besides, roses are generic."

Her laugh tinkled around him. "You make me laugh, Gavin. I like being with you. You make me feel foolish and stupid and special."

He tilted his head. "You are special, Taylor."

Her gaze went back to her glass and she took a drink. Gavin reached out and held her hand over her flute. "You are special."

"I don't know about that, but you believe it, and that's enough to make me smile, to make me believe it too."

Gavin took her flute, set it on the nightstand beside his. He started to roll them over and show her just how special she was to him.

Her slow smile and wiggling brows stayed him. Taylor's small hand pushed against his chest. He obligingly laid back. "It's my turn now."

"Are you're hands always cold?" he asked her, as she straddled him.

"Pretty much. Why?"

"Just wondered."

"Hmmm…" Taylor leaned down and kissed him. And it was unlike any kiss they'd ever shared. This was no easy, gentle kiss. It was as if all her feelings, all her emotions, all her everything was in that single mating of tongues.

"I want to kiss all of you," she said into his mouth. "Can I kiss all of you?"

Gavin smiled. "If you want."

"Close your eyes."

What was this? Gavin looked at her.

"Please?" she asked him. "I promise not to do anything you don't like." That she'd turned his words back on him was not lost.

With a sigh, Gavin closed his eyes. "Can I peek?"

"No." He kept his hands on her waist, felt her shift her weight and reach over him, her breasts brushed his chest and his breath caught.

"Here you need some cake." Her finger skimmed his mouth and he reached out, licked it. The creamy icing sweet on his tongue. He pulled the digit into his mouth before he released it.

"I like cake." He wiggled under her. "Can I have some more?"

"In a minute." He could hear the smile in her voice. The clink of flutes hinted only a moment that she had the champagne before he felt the chilled liquid drizzle over his chest, around and into his mouth. More clink and the tinkle of ice as she set them back apparently in the ice bucket.

Her mouth was warm against his as she kissed him. Her hot tongue licked the wine from the corner of his mouth, from his chest.

Taylor moved down him reveling in the fact that he was hers for the night. She kissed the hardened contours of his chest, twirled her tongue around his flat nipples, down his sculpted muscled stomach.

Cold hands? That gave her an idea... Reaching over again, she grabbed two cubes of ice. Should she? What if he didn't like it?

Taylor shook her head. He wasn't Charles. Being with Gavin was not only wonderful, but fun. Fun. And if he didn't like the ice cubes, she'd go back to the cake.

She laid her palms flat, the ice under them, on his stomach.

Gavin's quick intake of breath had her chuckling. She swirled the ice over him, followed her hands with her mouth. She kissed him all over.

She kissed her way down his stomach, stopping for just a moment, looking at his tall, proud erection. Would he like that? What if he didn't?

Gently, she took him in her hand. Smooth and hard. Contrasts just like the man. Leaning over she quickly kissed the tip of him.

He felt her warm tongue circle him. "God, Taylor."

Then she closed her mouth over him. Hot tongue and cold ice. Swirling, circling.

"Christ."

He felt the vibration of her chuckle. She loved him with her mouth, teased him with her hands, tormented him with the contrasting temperatures. She pulled him deep until he couldn't stand another moment. He wanted to be in her now. Right now.

In one deft motion he flipped her off his chest. Holding her under him, he grabbed the ice bucket and the cake.

"I said I wanted more cake. Close your eyes.... It's my turn."

His eyes were that wild blue she'd seen earlier. Staring up at him, her belly fluttered with a good dose of passion and just a bit of

DEADLY TIES

apprehension of the unknown. Taylor licked her lips and closed her eyes.

She felt him shift, felt a finger, with the icing slide over her belly, twirl around her nipples, plop against each one.

His tongue slowly, torturously removed each and every trace until all she saw were warm lights behind her eye lids.

Gavin watched her, saw her pulse beating fast already.

He'd had to reach deep to keep from coming in her mouth, but this night was more about her than him. That's the way he wanted it. He laved the icing off of her, then pressed his length against her for just a moment, kissing her.

Leaning up, she started to open her eyes, but he said, "No, keep them closed. Turn over."

For a moment, he watched the slight frown between her eyebrows, but then she turned over on her stomach.

Gavin smiled at the line of her back, the vertebrate, the dip at the base of her spine before her flare of hips.

He ran his finger from her nape, all the way down to the top of her buttocks, his hands grazing over the flair of derriere.

She sucked in her breath. He grinned and grabbed an ice cube, ran it just as he had is fingers, watching the gooseflesh prickle over her skin, the shuddering sigh as he reached the base of her spine. Leaning over, he kissed her from the top of her head to the bottom of her feet, his hands working back up, slightly spreading her legs for him. Again he reached for another cube of ice... what the hell, with one hand, he slipped his fingers in her, worked them deep and slow until she was panting, wet and incredibly hot.

"Get on your hands and knees, curl over," he said gruffly.

She shifted, doing as he asked, curling before him. He stopped, simply looked at her open, wet and waiting for him. Ice water dribbled from his hand. "Contrasts are interesting, aren't they?"

He worked his fingers deep inside her, even as he grazed the ice cube down bottom, dipped over her center, watched her shiver and pulse, his own passion at the breaking point.

He rose between her spread thighs and entered her, riding her hard and fast, her moans driving him over the edge as she screamed her climax.

CHAPTER TWELVE

Warm water lapped around them, lost under the mountain of bubbles frothed high from the jets of the Jacuzzi tub. Taylor settled back against Gavin's chest, squishing foam between them as her skin met his. The contact sent tingles along her nerve endings.

His arms wrapped around her from behind and his chin settled on her shoulder. Taylor turned her head and kissed his cheek. Their gazes locked.

"I like you wet." Hands ran up her arms and back down to lace his fingers with hers.

Taylor grinned, "Yeah, I think I've already figured that out."

Gavin laughed and the rumble vibrated against her back. That devastating smile played havoc on her heart. "Sass. You are full of sass tonight."

"Want to see what else?"

His mouth settled over hers and he kissed her so slowly, so achingly sweet that Taylor's breath caught. Gavin's tongue teased hers to play before he pulled her bottom lip between his. Her breath sighed out.

She pulled back, and saw his eyes, framed by wet spiked lashes, studied her.

"What?" she asked.

Gavin didn't answer. Instead, he settled back into the tub, untangling one of his hands to pluck a strawberry off the chilled plate set on deep ledge of the tub. He dunked it in whipped cream and offered it to her. It was hardly the first he'd fed her since they'd climbed into this monstrous bathtub. The firm fruit gave way with a soft crush beneath her teeth. Reaching out, she deftly licked the cream from his forefinger, pulling the digit into her mouth. Those eyes of his crinkled at the edges as they narrowed on her.

"None of that," he chided, and pulled his hand back. "I want to talk."

A guy wanted to talk? "I thought that was women generally, something that--rumor has it--drives men nuts. Isn't that my line?"

"Hush." He reached for a chunk of kiwi, her favorite fruit. But, instead he popped it into his own mouth.

"Hey," Taylor said, splashing him lightly, leaning to the side. "I wanted that."

"Too bad."

This time he offered her the green seeded fruit.

"So, Taylor, tell me about yourself."

She almost turned around to look at him. "What? You already know all about me."

His head moved closed to hers and she could tell it was in a negative shake. "No, I know what you do, what you want out of life, and that you were married to a completely, utterly incompetent fool."

"Ass."

"What? Oh. Fine then, an ass. Anyway, I know nothing about your family and you know all of mine."

"You know Ryan." Taylor shrugged her shoulder, and started to lean up to get another piece of something off the plate. Not that she really wanted it, but it would give her something to do with her hands. But

DEADLY TIES 121

Gavin was having none of that. He pulled her back against him and water sloshed around them and out the edge of the tub with the force of the movement.

His breath was warm against her ear. "Don't run away. Talk to me. I want to know you. Everything about you."

"Why?" she asked, resettling against him. And what was the big deal? Why couldn't she just tell him? Fear. She was scared he would think the same of her that Charles had in the end and then that would hurt. *That* realization made her angry. Gavin was not Charles.

"Because, I want to know you," he answered her after a while. Something about the answer said there was more to it, but that was all he was going to share with her.

"Fine. What do you want to know?"

"Your parents?"

One of his hands laced with hers. The other scrolled shapes on her chest and arms.

Taylor took a deep breath. "They died when I was in high school."

The finger on her shoulder stilled, then continued its meandering. "What happened?"

"I had one-act play practice that morning, so I was up and about early. Buddy Bishop and I were going over this scene that we never could seem to get right for our director and that was the only time we could all work on it. I got ready and went to school. I was running late, so I didn't eat breakfast. Never even went to the kitchen." Taylor patted one hill of bubbles down. "The sheriff and one of my dad's friends came and got me before we had even finished our first run through. There was a gas leak and when they got up and turned on the kitchen light, or whatever it just...." Taylor shrugged. "Just exploded." As though it was the most important task in the world, she scooped up bubbles, intent on making some sort of wavy sculpture.

His arm around her tightened and the hand that had been circling her shoulder now cupped it. "I'm sorry. That must have been really rough." He leaned over and kissed her jaw.

She'd never talked to anyone about it. Charles had always told her to get over it--that was life. But Gavin was not Charles. He proved that time and time again without even realizing it. Nodding, Taylor relaxed back into Gavin's embrace, her bubble sculpture forgotten.

"Yeah, it was. My entire life turned upside down and nothing was ever the same. But then, a couple of years later graduation came, and I was free to pursue life as I wanted to." She wasn't going to tell him about the foster homes, the endless round of workers that were too busy to really care. Except for one.

"Then, while working on an associates degree in human resources, I married Charles. The rest as they say, is history."

"Hmm...." He rubbed his chin against her hair, which she'd piled high up on her head. "Can I ask you another question?"

"Sure."

"How did you ever get hooked up with him? What's the story there?" He shifted behind her, straightening a little. "Not that I want every little detail, but I'm just having such a hard time picturing you with a guy that didn't care for you."

Taylor chuckled, turned a bit and cupped his cheek with her palm. "I...." Before the words were out of her mouth, she stopped them. Just like that? *I love you.* She was going to say those words to him?

Averting her gaze she looked to the right of his shoulder. Where had that come from? Taylor shook her head at herself and smiled back up at him. "I'm glad I have you in my life. You make me feel good."

"Hmm...."

Taylor wasn't about to ask what that had meant. Instead, to fill the awkward gap she could feel growing between them, or maybe just around her, she complied with his earlier question, turning back to her bubbles.

"Charles was and is Charles. He's a stockbroker and stuck on himself. It took me a long time to see that." Where to begin? With the truth? "After my parents died, I was sent to a state home."

"You had no other family?" His voice reflected his surprise.

Taylor shook her head. "No, I was adopted. Mom and Dad were older and had tried to have kids for years. They always told me I was the miracle they'd prayed for. There was a distant aunt, my father's older sister, but she was much older and wasn't able to take me in." Taylor smiled and pulled Gavin's hand holding hers out of the water.

Suds slithered down their joined fingers, palms, and wrists. "Daddy's hands were like yours."

"How so?" Both of his hands picked up water and trickled it over her. Then, putting his palms flat, he ran them from her upper arm, over the sensitive skin of her inner elbow, to her fingers, sandwiching her hand between both of his.

"You've got big strong hands. Hands that would work hard for a family, hands that are caring and gentle, but would do whatever necessary to keep those you love safe."

He was quiet for so long that Taylor started to worry. Instead of waiting longer for him to say anything she continued. "Anyway, I joined the ranks as a number and name and got shuffled and reshuffled until I was finally put with this family that dealt with kids like me. That's where I met Charles. It was at Christmas time and he came home for some sort of alumni thing this family held every year. They're really nice people, but I didn't care. I was too lost to care how nice they were."

Taylor thought back to the first time they'd met. Funny, Charles didn't seem like such a handsome man now.

"That was our first meeting. We kept in touch. After graduation he helped to a part time job with the firm he worked for. When I was

DEADLY TIES

twenty we got married. The years went by, we grew apart and then we divorced."

"No kids? I mean I know Ryan is your son, but you and Charles never had children?"

He would ask that question wouldn't he? Taylor shrugged. "I told you, you didn't have to worry about me getting pregnant."

Silence settled between them again. Then he sighed and asked, "What was the diagnosis?" All doctor now.

Though the subject still squeezed her heart, she no longer cried because she'd never conceived. Instead she laughed.

"You are the professional. Actually, they never knew. It just never worked. I never even got pregnant."

"He was tested?"

Taylor squiggled against him. "Yes, honey, he was. That was probably a lot of the strain. But in retrospect, as with most things, it all turned out for the best."

His hands cupped her knees beneath the water and the foam. Gently squeezing, he nuzzled the side of her neck. "I would have to agree there."

His hands on her knees tickled and she wiggled against him.

Warm breath heated her ear. "You know, I always knew I liked you, but the more I know you, the more I admire you."

"That's sad," she quipped.

His movements stopped, straightening, he turned her to face him, until her ankles rested on either side of his hips and her knees were tucked beneath his arms. She tried to wiggle out, this trapped feeling warming inside her, but he only clamped his arms tighter, his hands immovable at her waist. His eyes held no humor now, an intense blue, their depths unfathomable.

"You need to work on your self esteem. Taylor, you are an amazing woman. Why can't you see that?"

"That's what you see?" It truly shocked her. It was not as if she thought badly of herself, no. It was more she didn't see herself as amazing or wonderful--just normal. How did Gavin see all this other in her?

Both his hands came up to cup her face, his thumbs circling her chin. "I see this beautiful woman, who has the most heart stopping smile, a great mom, who wants the best for her son, a caring gentle soul, who cries at the pain of children. How can I not see you as an amazing woman? To know what all you've been through and that you're still...." A muscle flexed in his jaw.

If he said anymore, she'd cry. No one but her parents had ever told her anything like this.

Taylor leaned forward and kissed him. Her hands cupped the back of his head, fingers spearing through his wet, black locks. His mouth opened under hers and she poured all her heart into the mating of their tongues, of their breath. She wasn't ready to say the words to him yet. Not yet, but maybe, just maybe some part of him would know what he did to her, what he made her feel, how easily he could break her heart. Taylor knew she was heart over head in love with Mr. Gavin Kinncaid, but there was no way she was going to tell him that.

His hands--magical as they were--started their spells on her again. And wet with water and suds, there seemed to be no barriers between them. Hands slid and caressed on skin, shocking nerve endings. He touched her breasts, kneaded her stomach, her hipbones. Moving between them, his fingers found her, spread her, pierced her. Soon she was too lost in the onslaught of feelings, of emotions to think of anything but Gavin. Gavin. Gavin.

She was the most beautiful woman he'd ever seen. One hand, splayed on her back, held her up for him to see. Water and suds slid off her long body, over her breasts, down into the water. He leaned forward, pressing his hand deeper, and kissed her arched white neck. Her moan vibrated in her throat, against his mouth.

"Beautiful."

When her moans and whimpers bounced off the tiled walls, he held his hand still, waited until she looked at him. Then he slowly started to work her again. He wanted more. He wanted all. Her lips trembled, her legs shivered. Gavin shifted and in one fluid motion, filled her.

Her eyes opened and looked at him. Deep in the amber depths he sensed a change in her. One his mind didn't recognize, but some part of him did, because he felt the same way. She tried to wiggle, moved her legs, but he shook his head, keeping her legs tucked against him, keeping her open to him, vulnerable to what he wanted her to feel.

"Wonderful." He moved her up and down, keeping control of the rhythm. Water lapped between them, sloshed over the edge of the tub.

"Amazing." He pushed deeper.

Taylor never said a word, but the sounds she made in the back of her throat drove him on. Her hands slid over him like the soft wings of butterflies.

He made certain this joining was more than before, slower, fuller, complete.

Her teeth nipped his lips, before Taylor's tongue darted into his mouth, demanding more.

And more he gave.

Had he ever made love to woman and stared into her eyes the entire time, hoping she could see what he didn't understand?

Gavin pushed deeper, worked her on him until her eyes filled and she smiled on a shuddering sigh.

When he felt her tighten, knew she was cresting, Gavin jerked her head back.

Looking straight into her clouded eyes, he said, "Mine."

And followed her over the wave of passion.

DEADLY TIES   125

* * * *

Late into the night, when all that was heard was the soft sounds of appliances--the hum of the ceiling fan, the whir of the air conditioner, the tumbling of the icemaker, Gavin lay awake, lost in thought.

Taylor was snuggled up against him, her head nestled in the crook of his shoulder, her hair fanned out over his arm and the pillow and bed behind her. The coppery tresses were like soft new flames licking their way across the pristine white sheets. His fingers tangled in one long curl. Her arm draped over his chest, and her thigh was atop his.

The ceiling fan continued its slow rotation and he watched it hoping for sleep, but it alluded him.

What was he doing?

This was generally where he was either ready for the woman to leave or he was thinking how to end a relationship. Not that he'd had as much practice as was rumored--he simply avoided tangles and commitments. Kept things simple. He was busy with work, and getting his practice off the ground so that he no longer worried that he would have to join another group of doctors. He wanted his own practice. He was his own man. His own man.

Maybe not his own anymore.

Turning slightly, and tucking his chin in, he studied the woman in his arms. She was so damn beautiful his breath caught. Long lashes curled like russet crescents against her pale, freckled cheeks. He wanted to run his finger down her nose, over those full lips that were slightly parted. With one hand, he gently brushed a strand of hair back off her forehead and tucked it behind her shell shaped ears.

His? Well, that was what he'd told her.

Mine. Like some damn battle cry. Where had it come from? Gavin hadn't thought, it had simply come out. And that was not like him at all.

Wherever the hell the word had come from, he meant it.

Mine.

Taylor was his. His hand bunched in her hair and he tightened his arms around her.

Mine.

What if the woman didn't want to be his?

There was a thought. So, what of his charm? He made her laugh and she liked being with him. She cared about him. But was it more than that?

Did he want it to be?

Mine.

Yes. Damn it. Yes. She was his and surprisingly he was hers. The woman just didn't know it yet.

Gavin shifted. He had a feeling that with time Taylor would come to trust him not to hurt her and maybe come to love him.

Love?

Well, if she was his what else did he think it was?

No, he couldn't be in love. Love was … love was.… Truthfully, he had no idea what love was. He loved his parents and his brothers, his family. But he had no idea about love for a woman.

Attraction, interest, lust. Those he knew and understood, he'd experienced them enough.

But love? That emotion he didn't exactly understand, not the kind his parents had, the kind that Aiden and Jesslyn had. Is that what he felt for Taylor?

Gavin had absolutely no idea.

He did, however, know that he loved spending time with her, couldn't wait to talk to her or see her. Making love to her had been like nothing he had ever experienced in his life. The feelings just kept building, kept growing.

With Taylor, he wanted to see her smile, hear that tinkling laugh that reminded him of the stories of faeries in sunshine. He wanted to make certain she was never hurt again.

So did he love her?

Okay, he'd steer away from that question for the time being and just go with the stream of things, see how she thought about things in the morning.

This was a first. He never worried about what the woman thought. Well, he did. But this had absolutely not a damn thing to do with lust or passion. Gavin didn't want Taylor to regret any of what they shared.

Part of him wanted to wake her up and demand to know what she thought of all this, what she thought of them. But he didn't, and he was too much of a man to act like a boy.

No, he'd be patient and wait. Wait and see what she thought, how she acted, and what her feelings were, if they were the same as his.

And if they weren't?

Then he'd just have to persuade her.

Gavin smiled at the thought. He'd have to make certain she just didn't know he was persuading her, or there would be hell to pay.

But, no matter what he had to do, he wasn't letting her go. Love.… Taylor was.… Taylor was right. Simply right.

He yawned, his thoughts finally settling.

Taylor was his.

Love.

Mine

* * * *

The ringing phone jarred her awake. For several seconds Taylor had no idea where she was and panic took hold.

"Hello?"

Gavin. She was with Gavin and he was talking on the phone. They were in his hotel suite and Ryan was just down the hall with Brayden and Tori.

DEADLY TIES

Relaxing, Taylor stretched. Sunlight slanted in through the windows of the balcony doors.

"Yeah, I'll tell her," Gavin said, his voice throaty from sleep. The phone clattered back into its cradle. His eyes cut to her before he propped up on his elbow.

Taylor smiled at him, and bought her hands up to rub the dark stubble on his jaw. "What? Who was that?"

"Brayden. He wanted me to know that they were going to take the kids...." He looked away then back at her.

"Take them? Where?"

He yawned and shrugged. "I have no idea."

"Gavin!"

He pinned her down. "I don't remember that part, but they'll be back about lunch."

"Lunch? What time is it?" Taylor tried to get up.

Gavin held her down. "I have no idea. Morning."

Taylor couldn't help it, she laughed. "Yes, dear, but when in the morning is the operative thing here."

"Hmm...." He lowered his head and kissed her, a soft gentle kiss that left her yearning. "Morning, on mornings off, is only morning."

"Days off." Work! "Oh my God." Jerking out of his hold, she turned to look at the clock. It was after nine. "I have got to go. I can't believe.... Clothes? I don't have any other clothes and I can hardly wear my dress to work." Taylor shimmied out from under him and hurried to the bathroom.

"I cannot believe this. Why didn't you wake me up before now? I'm new for God's sake. I can't just miss work because I'd rather lie in bed with you all morning. I already take Friday afternoons off for Ryan's doctor appointments. I'll be lucky if I don't get fired. After the Gibbons fiasco, I've been assigned the most boring mundane cases, which is all fine and well." Taylor turned the water on in the shower, hoping it heated fast. After nine. Jenkins was going to kill her. While the water ran, Taylor went back to the bedroom intent on calling her boss because she was running late--as if the woman wouldn't have figured it out by now.

Gavin was leaning against the headboard, his arms stacked behind his head and that crooked grin on his face. "You are so sexy when you hurry around the room naked."

That grin that she'd love to kiss, but didn't have the time to, danced on his lips.

"I need to borrow your phone." He thought she was sexy.

With a smirk, he leaned over and handed the phone out to her. She snatched it away and tried to remember her new work number. It was written in her little black book at home. Lot of good it did her there. Luckily she remembered and dialed Jenkins's office.

Having accomplished that, she hurried through her shower. What was she thinking? Her wet, uncooperative hair struggled against the braid she forced it into. She wondered how to get Ryan back to Ms. Johnson's before work while she went to get clothes, which was halfway across town and in the opposite direction of her office.

She stalked into the kitchen, dressed in a robe, hoping for coffee. Gavin, dressed in a pair of black pajama bottoms, sat at the table with two cups.

"That was quick." He held one of the cups out to her.

"I have a problem."

One black brow quirked. "And that would be?"

"Can you watch Ryan for me until I get off work?" If he couldn't she would figure something else…. Damn the coffee was hotter than hell. Taylor took a deep breath and set the scalding brew on the table, pushing her burnt tongue against her teeth. "I should have thought of all this last night. I hadn't planned on staying and…."

Gavin's look made her stop. It was expectant, but daring at the same time and she didn't understand it.

Seconds stretched while they stared at each other. Finally, he cleared his throat and looked away. "I would love to watch him, if you don't think he'll have a problem with it." His blue eyes locked back to hers. "I called downstairs for some clothes for you. It's nothing fancy, some flats, and a pants suit that was in one of the shops."

He wasn't getting her clothes.

His hand shot up. "I don't want to hear it. So stuff it, Taylor."

This time he stood up and walked to her.

"You cannot buy me clothes. I know I didn't order that alarm system at the house and I want to know how much it cost."

His arm settled on her hip before his hand cupped her chin. "Yes I can, and I am not going to tell you. They are gifts, take them and don't insult me."

The man was an idiot.

"You can't just buy me things."

Oh she hated that supercilious brow of his. "Why?"

Taylor scrambled her brains. She really didn't have time for this. "Because, I can buy my own clothes and security systems."

His gaze ran over her face and settled on her lips. "So, I can buy you anything other than clothing or security systems?"

"Yes. No." The man drove her nuts. "You don't need to buy me anything."

His chuckle rumbled between them. "You're right, Gorgeous, I don't. But need and want are two very different things."

His voice could coax a moth to the flame.

"Arrrgggg…."

"I know I render you speechless. It is a charm I have."

"More like a curse."

The hand on her hip gently squeezed, and Taylor couldn't help but

DEADLY TIES

129

turn her cheek and place a kiss in his palm.

A knock at the door had them pulling apart.

Gavin opened it to reveal a uniformed woman carrying a dress bag with a copper colored pants suit that looked soft and flowy, something expensive. A sack tucked under her arm must hold the flats.

Gavin thanked the staff member and shut the door. Then, he turned and held out his gifts.

"Go put these on. I don't want you to get in trouble with your boss. What time do you have to be there?"

Taylor just looked at him. Why was he doing this? She was out of her element here. She wasn't used to gifts just because. True, both times they were things she needed, but Gavin just got them, without her even mentioning anything. He just knew.

Walking to him, she took the clothing. "I don't understand all this, but thank you."

He leaned over and kissed her, tasting of coffee. "You are welcome, now hurry."

When she turned around he slapped her bottom.

Taylor glared at the smiling man.

On a sigh, she quickly shucked the robe, tossing it to the bed. In the sack was a camisole and panties. Taylor fingered the bronze material. The flats were Italian woven leather and felt soft as butter. Shaking her head, she quickly dressed. The suit was exquisite. There were no real lines, everything just fell.

She couldn't believe she was wearing it to work. It probably cost more than she cared to think about. Even with her generous settlement she'd gotten out of the marriage and her inheritance, she still worried about money and never spent just because she could. No, all and any extra earnings went to a college fund for Ryan and another trust fund for him.

They lived extremely comfortably and she wanted to make certain they stayed that way. Which was why she never bought anything like this. The material felt like her vintage dresses, so soft as to almost not be there.

She was so busy looking at herself in the mirror she didn't see Gavin until he slipped his arms around her middle from behind.

"You look lovely."

She looked into his eyes in the mirror. "Gavin, I can't accept these things."

His sigh blew forgotten strands against her cheek. "You plan to go to work naked?"

The man could always make her laugh. "No."

"Then?"

Taylor knew she'd lost this argument. Turning the topic she asked, "Where will you and Ryan be?"

He shrugged. "I have no idea. Why don't I call you and let you know all the details when he gets back. When will you get off work?"

"Well, that depends on what happens. Hopefully, five, but I'll need to make up for the two hours I missed today, so it will probably be after six. Is that okay?"

He turned her around and kissed her like she'd wanted him to all morning.

"Fine," he said, pulling back. "Now, get to work before you get fired and find a way to blame it on me."

"I wouldn't do that," she told him, picking her evening bag up off the counter. "Oh, my dress."

His hands waved her on. "Go, don't worry about it. I'll take care of it all."

For just a moment she hesitated. The clock read fifteen till ten. Time to go. She leaned on her tiptoes and gave him a quick peck. "Okay, thanks. I'll see you both tonight."

The door shut quietly behind her and she stood in the hallway wishing she knew which suite Ryan was in so that she could tell him bye. But she had no clue and no time. She tried not to worry about that as she made her way down to the elevator.

As the doors slid home, she realized how nice that had been. How *normal*, as though it were an everyday occurrence for her to kiss the man 'bye' as she went to work knowing he was watching her son.

Taylor sighed. She was moving way too fast. Way too fast. This road could lead nowhere with a man like Gavin. Could it?

* * * *

Gavin walked back to the bedroom whistling. He thought about his afternoon appointments, the last of which was at three. If Bray and the kids were going to be later than lunch, he'd just have to let them know that Ryan needed to stay the afternoon with them, or his parents. He'd work something out. He hadn't been sure what, but he hadn't wanted Taylor to worry about it all this morning. So, Ryan could spend the morning with Bray and maybe lunch with him, then with his parents or whoever was keeping Tori this afternoon while he saw patients and made any rounds he needed to. He'd be done by four. Then he and Ryan could do whatever until Taylor got there.

A chuckle danced in the quiet air. Taylor was something he needed in the mornings. He hadn't forgotten any of his thoughts on their relationship from the night before.

Walking into the bathroom, he turned on the water in the shower.

Taylor flustered was a sight to behold. She was always so calm, so gentle, that when she was anything but, it was surprising to say the least. Her cheeks would flush and that slight frown would pull between her brows. Not to mention it threw her off and let him get his way.

This was something to remember. Maybe she wasn't as against a relationship with him as he thought. No, that wasn't it. Not a relationship with him, a commitment. That's what he wanted.

DEADLY TIES

Commitment. Gavin swiped the water off his face while the hot spray hit his body. *Commitment?*

Well, if she was his that only stood to reason. Didn't it?

The ringing phone had him turning the water off, grabbing a towel and hurrying to grab it.

"Yeah?" he asked, knotting the towel at his waist.

"Good morning, darling."

Gavin smiled. "Morning, Mom."

"Have you and Taylor eaten breakfast yet?"

Gavin licked the side of his mouth and rubbed his forehead. Subtle, very subtle. Clearing his throat, he said, "No, Mom, I haven't. Taylor had to go to work." And she hadn't eaten breakfast either. He'd make certain she ate dinner.

"How was she this morning? Ryan was chattering away about another reel he wants to learn and Tori has decided she too wants to learn the violin."

Gavin knew his mother didn't really care about the latter part of her dissertation, it was the beginning question that held all the information. "She was fine. In a hurry because she was running late."

"Hmmm.... I'm sure she was."

Before he could think of a reply to that, she continued, "Well, get on over here and have brunch with us. Aiden and Jess are here with the twins, as is Quinlan. Brayden and Christian and the kids already left for some music performance at the Smithsonian."

So that was where they had gone.

Sighing he agreed, "Fine, I'll be there as soon as I get dressed."

His mother's light laughter echoed in his ear before she hung up the phone.

* * * *

"Kaitie lass, what are you smiling at?" Jock knew that look.

"What exactly was the wager again, dear?" Without a care, she picked up a strawberry and popped it into her mouth. A mouth he'd just kissed the entire night before and one that could still work magic on him.

"You know as well as I do."

"What wager?" asked his sons.

He waved them off. "Nothing." He wasn't about to tell them that his wife, their mother, and he, their father, had a bet on one of their offspring. Jock had made the comment that Taylor and Gavin would both be coming to brunch from the same suite. Kaitlyn had said that wouldn't happen.

"Both of them, wasn't it?"

Jock didn't say anything.

Her one dimpled smile still made his lips twitch, his stomach tighten. One brow rose above her clear green eyes. "Well, dear. You owe me an entire week of gardening."

132   *Jaycee Clark*

Hell.

"I was thinking of planting lots of petunias and several other things. We also need to take out the Oleander bushes. Ryan told me they're poisonous, and he's right."

He'd just planted the damn things for her not two weeks ago.

"In fact," she said, waving her fork at him, "I think we need to go by that large nursery on the way home and pick everything out. Don't you agree?"

He hated her damn flowers, well, planting them anyway. And she knew it. The woman kept telling him it did him good, kept his blood pressure down or some such. The kids were looking from him to their mother to each other. Jock felt no compulsion to explain their conversation or their wager.

Narrowing his gaze on her he nodded, but couldn't help adding, "My turn will come."

The twinkle in her green eyes made him wonder if she didn't want him to win. Would he ever figure her out?

If his son wasn't coming with Taylor then where the hell was the girl? Surely he hadn't been that off? If he had his guess he knew they spent the night together, so why in the hell had he lost the wager?

Picking up a cube of cheese he looked again at his wife who was talking to Aiden and caught the laughter dancing just beneath the surface.

One day, one day before he died, he would understand her.

CHAPTER THIRTEEN

Taylor finished filing the last report, and looked at the legal papers sitting beside the phone. She'd just received them today, thanks to a perky clerk. Anger boiled in her. The ass.

Her phone rang and she picked it up.

"Taylor Reese."

"Oh good, I caught you."

Taylor closed her eyes and leaned back. Think of the devil and he's likely to call. Just what she needed. "Charles. What do you want?"

"Did you get the papers?"

"Papers? I assume you mean the legal notice that you are no longer responsible for child support, having terminated your rights as Ryan's father?" Amazingly she kept her voice even and calm as though discussing the weather.

He sighed. She could picture him, blond hair perfectly groomed, his suit pressed with no creases--lest it mar his gym toned five-foot-ten-inch frame--sitting behind his dark wood desk, with his elbows on the

DEADLY TIES

133

blotter.

"Taylor don't do this, it's not like your not successful enough to not to have a job." Backhanded compliments weren't anything new in dealing with Charles.

Taylor picked up a pen and tapped it.

"Fine. I got the papers. Why the phone call?"

"To explain."

He meant lecture.

"I should probably tell you this in person, and Rhonda agrees, but this wasn't a good time for me to travel and I knew you should know."

Something swirled in the pit of her stomach, tightening her already tense muscles.

"I don't think there is anything about the two of you that could possibly concern me." She tapped the pen harder.

"Your manners were always so gentle."

"And making you proud was always at the top of my list, dear." She smiled the last at him in a smirk. Looking at her watch, she told him, "I've got to get out of here. I have friends dropping by the house soon before we go out to eat, and I don't want them waiting at my house. Plus Ryan frets when I'm late."

Her gaze landed on the damn papers sitting beside her framed picture of a smiling Ryan and she wondered how this would effect Ryan emotionally. He'd lived his whole life with people not caring or giving a damn. In the last few weeks, her son had blossomed and had become more outgoing with the exception of the break in. She knew Gavin helped with that, and didn't want to see regression for any reason, especially not because of Charles.

"Yes, Ryan, how is he?" His voice held only polite interest.

Taylor ignored the question. "Charles, time is running short, so if you just called to make certain your papers arrived. They did."

"You were always different when irritated." She could all but see his hazel eyes narrow on that one. "But that's neither here nor there. I called to tell you that Rhonda is pregnant."

The words fell heavily between them. Thank God she was sitting down. If she hadn't been, she would have made a fool of herself. Was he joking? No, the serious tone was one she knew all too well, and Charles never joked.

Several moments passed, the only sound, the cars on the street and the tick of the clock. Taylor brushed a strand of hair away from her face. She stopped tapping the pen. "How far along is she?"

"Almost four months."

The math was quick. Four months went back to March. Their divorce had been final at the end of February, and a week later, the first part of March, he'd flown to Mexico and married Rhonda.

"Perfect timing, huh?" Taylor pinched the bridge of her nose. Anger rose up in her, at him for not caring to wait until the damn ink was dry, at herself for caring at all, at Fate for what she couldn't do.

All the nights she cried herself to sleep, the depression at not being able to have children, the need and urge to bear a child so strong it felt like it was clawing from her insides, all that reared its head again to sink its talons deep within her heart.

"I guess she could give you what I couldn't?" Why the hell had she said that?

A breath huffed through the line. Clearing his throat, he said, "I have something to tell you and I'd appreciate it if you listened to me, let me finish before you say anything."

There was more? What? Twins?

Taking a deep breath, she leaned up on her desk, cradling the phone between her jaw and shoulder. Why did she feel defeated? Like crying? It was stupid, she had Ryan, but the old wound opened anew, bleeding within her for what she hadn't been able to do. "What?"

"I did something when I was younger, a dumb foolish thing because I thought at twenty-one I knew it all." He paused. "I had a vasectomy."

It took several moments for his words to sink in, for their meaning to come clear.

"Excuse me?" She had not heard him right.

"Rhonda wanted to tell you all along, but I told her you wouldn't understand, but now I am telling you so that maybe you'll comprehend why I terminated my parental rights to Ryan."

The insult wasn't lost on her, but she kept her mouth shut momentarily, wanting to know what other bombshells he was about to drop.

"I was a child reared in foster and state homes. No family, no anything. I came from nothing. I decided I didn't want children, didn't want to pass that on to them, whatever had made the people whom created me to not care enough, to just leave and never look back. I didn't want to pass that on." His words were some she'd never expected to hear from him, the pain of a little lost boy. Well rehearsed in any case. "So, I had a vasectomy. I didn't want kids. Then I was worried about my career and never thought of it. Till you."

He'd never told her. No matter how lost, or what his reasons were, it was all a lie. Everything. Lies.

"At first I didn't tell you because I didn't know how, then I was afraid if I did I would lose you. So I didn't."

Taylor couldn't stand it; she pulled the mouth piece away and took a deep breath.

"I told myself so many times that you deserved to know, but I just couldn't tell you."

"Why?" she finally asked. "Don't you think I had a right to know?"

All those tear filled nights, all the self-blame and recriminations, all the worries and tensions--all for naught. And all because of him, his lies, his silence. He'd stood by and watched, had known what it did to

DEADLY TIES

her when she hadn't conceived, month after month, year after year.

This was unbelievable. Taylor rubbed her hands over her face. All the lies.

"I don't know, Taylor. The years started to pass and we grew apart and I saw how different we were, and then I didn't want to tell you."

Her hands were shaking and she had the distinct feeling she was about to lose it and cry. Damned if she would.

Licking her lips she said. "Well, if Rhonda is pregnant, then you obviously had the problem fixed. When did all this happen?" How in the hell had she missed it all?

His sigh was heavy. "About the time Rhonda and I started to seeing each other."

Almost two years ago. My God was she so stupid, so incredibly blind?

"It was around the time you started Ryan's case and wanted him to come live with us."

They had stopped sleeping together months before that momentous time. She'd written it off to the fact she couldn't give him a child and the strain was too much on them.

"Rhonda and I had been seeing each other already for several months, which you knew about."

She knew the history, but only because he'd confessed the time frame when she'd caught him. However, she knew he didn't expect her to say anything. And she couldn't think of a blessed thing even if she had wanted to.

"You and I were already having problems, and I wanted out. But then Ryan came along. You and I hadn't slept together in months. I knew where I wanted the future to go, so I found a doctor and had the reversal procedure done. You got custody, we got divorced and Rhonda and I got married."

Disbelief slowed her thoughts; shock kept her tongue stilled. Then she blinked.

"Well isn't that a tidy freaking little package. And now she's pregnant and y'all are just one big happy, soon-to-be-family." She couldn't keep the bitterness from her voice.

"I hate you. Do you have any idea...." Tears clogged her throat. "All the times...." Taylor stopped. "Thank you for calling me. At least I know it was never me. And only my coward, bastard of a husband that didn't have the balls to tell the truth."

She slammed the phone down, dropped her head in her hands and cried.

* * * *

"We can get ice cream later, can't we?" Tori asked Mrs. K.

Ryan sat in the back seat beside Tori with Mrs. K by the other door. He and Tori were going to ride in the third seat when they picked up Taylor. He hadn't seen her all day and had so much to tell her. The museum and the music. The matinee that the Kinncaids had taken him and Tori to that afternoon was so cool. They heard a symphony practicing for a Beethoven performance. It was awesome.

"I hope your mom is ready," Tori told him. "I'm starving."

"She will be," he answered.

"Doesn't take her long to get ready, does it champ?" Gavin asked him from the driver's seat.

"Nope."

"Gavin, dear, are you implying that all women take hours to get ready?" Mrs. K asked.

"No, Mom."

"Though she does." Mr. Kinncaid grumbled from the front seat. He turned a bit to look back at them. "Are you going to tell Taylor about your day?"

"Yeah, and I was.…" The mists rose in his mind, stealing his words, jerking his breath to a quicker pace.

He could see her crying, crying and crying. Yelling at a man … a man…. Charles. A phone.

"Taylor."

"Excuse me, son?" Mr. Kinncaid's voice yanked him back. Everyone was looking at him.

Mrs. Kinncaid was frowning at him as was Gavin in the mirror, and Mr. Kinncaid.

Tori leaned over. "Why'd you say Taylor?"

It was then he realized he had spoken out loud.

She was crying, he could see her crying.

"Hurry," he told Gavin, leaning up against the seat belt. "You've got to hurry. She's crying."

"What?" Gavin asked him, looking at him in the mirror.

How to explain? He'd never told anyone. No one. No one had ever known. "You've got to hurry, she's crying and it's because of him."

Ryan knew he wasn't making sense, but he didn't know how to explain.

"Who's crying Ryan?" Gavin asked him.

Ryan leaned back in his seat and looked out the window. They needed to hurry.

"Ryan?" Gavin asked him again.

"Taylor. Hurry."

Silence settled around them. He dared a glance up to the rearview mirror. Gavin was studying him with eyes as weighing as a judge.

* * * *

"Bastard. You bastard!" she whispered at the phone.

God she was pathetic. Taylor grabbed her purse, the files she needed to take with her and damn papers and hurried out of the nearly empty offices. Someone called her name, but she kept going until early evening air breathed hot in her face.

DEADLY TIES

Lies. Everything, all of it was lies.

All the tears and heartache and all of it … all of it could have been avoided.

Rage pounded hot and fast in her, so boiling, nausea greased her stomach and a headache thrummed up the back of her neck.

Damn him. Damn that selfish son of a bitch.

Taylor wiped her eyes and climbed in her car, hurrying through the early evening traffic. She needed to get home to her son.

* * * *

Gavin shut the door to Taylor's house and watched as she keyed in the code to set the system. His parents, Tori and Ryan had just left. Mom and Dad had asked if Ryan would like to stay the night at Seneca until tomorrow when he and Taylor were driving out for the family version of his dad's birthday. Intuitive parents that he was blessed with.

Taylor had reluctantly agreed. It seemed she wanted Ryan here, not that she said as much, but Gavin sensed it. However, when Tori started in on practicing a show for Pop's birthday party Saturday and Ryan had smiled and helped her pick pieces to perform, Taylor had told him to go ahead and have fun.

But the boy had still been too quiet. How had he known about Taylor crying? Let alone because of a *him*. When she'd driven up to the house, they'd all been sitting on her porch. It was as clear as the color of the sky the woman had been crying. But she'd only smiled and caught Ryan in a tight hug when he'd run to her. They'd talked quietly out on the lawn for several minutes and the strain on her face had lightened when Ryan laughed and said Reese. He was going to be Ryan Reese. But he still wondered how the boy knew she'd been crying in the first place. That was a question that still plagued Gavin. He'd ask Ryan about it later. Right now he was more concerned with the woman before him.

Leaning against the wall, he watched as she walked into the living room and stood staring into space.

Shaking his head, he wondered for the hundredth time that evening what was going on.

She'd been tense and quiet all through dinner, though she tried to hide it behind over bright smiles and forced laughter. The act being for Ryan, he supposed, who tried to cheer her up the entire time they were eating. Gavin hoped it was for Ryan and not that she thought he'd buy such a transparent façade.

He pushed away from the wall and walked to her wrapping her in his arms. She stiffened and tried to pull away, but he tightened his hold until she relaxed against him.

Gently, he rocked her. "What's wrong?"

"Nothing."

"Of course there's not a thing wrong. You're tight, tense, worried and bothered about something." Awkwardly, he walked-rocked them to the couch. Tumbling her down onto the cushions, he turned her so that she lay under and facing him.

"Tell me." He leaned down until his forehead touched hers. The dim lamplight allowed him to see her eyes. A light brown, they lightened in anger or passion to a deep amber color. Now their depths reminded him of a turbulent potion, pain and confusion shifting the color to a rich, slow roasted coffee.

Her tongue darted out to lick her lips, and he caught her chin trembling. Gently, he kissed it. "Tell me."

"I'm just being stupid and I'm still so damn pissed."

Gavin propped up on his elbow above her. Tears trailed out of the corner of her eyes to run down into her hairline. He stopped the trickle of one with his forefinger.

"What?" he asked.

"I'm not nothing."

Where in the hell did this come from? Grabbing her face between his hands, he glared down at her. "What the hell are you talking about?"

More tears fell. "I know it's stupid. But what is wrong with me? I'm not nothing. I had parents. I'm a person and deserve respect, not lies. God, the lies."

Gavin was lost.

"All those nights. All the times I cried and felt ashamed because I couldn't have a baby." Her voice wavered and cracked as she cried, but the flow of words continued. "It was just me. I mean not that I couldn't have kids, but because he didn't want *mine*."

Her eyes searched his for answers and as yet, he had none to give, leaning down he kissed her on her mouth.

"He had a vasectomy," she whispered.

"Darling, who the hell are you talking about?"

"Charles. My ex-husband. We never had kids because he had a vasectomy, he just neglected to mention that fact when I was depressed, or buying more pregnancy tests that he *knew*, knew would be negative."

He felt tremors run through her arms. Color stained her cheeks.

"I'm not following...." Children, they'd never had children and she had always said *she* hadn't been able to conceive, *she* hadn't been able to have kids.

This time he sat up and pulled to sit beside him. "Are you telling me he never told you?"

Her look clearly told him what a dumb question that was.

"Sorry. What...? Why...? I'm lost."

Taylor swiped at her eyes and tucked her leg up next to her, tilting her head to rest on her knee. "He called me today to see if I got papers and decided to inform me of his secret. He had it done when he was young, and never knew how to tell me."

"How long were you married?"

DEADLY TIES

"Eight years."

Good God. "And never in all that time, he never hinted, never said…."

"No."

Sorry sonofabitch. Gavin had no idea what to say. Looking out the window he thought about the kind of man that did such a thing, and couldn't compute it. His stubble scraped against his finger as he rubbed his jaw before turning back to her. "What exactly happened?"

Anger and hurt lacing her words, she told him about the phone call she received after being served the legal papers. The more she talked, the angrier Gavin became. "I know it shouldn't matter what he thought, or what he thinks, and it really doesn't," she told him as he wiped away another tear. She'd moved to sit closer to him and he held her against his chest. "It really doesn't. But it still hurts. All that time and energy and emotion wasted. All because he didn't tell me."

Gavin thought about that. He was pissed now that he knew all of it, enraged at the self-centered prick, yet aggravated at her too. Reigning in on his frustrations, he quietly asked her, "What were the papers he sent you?"

A harsh chuckle escaped. "I told you he stuck with me long enough for the adoption to go through and be finalized? Well even though we were divorced, Ryan still kept the Shepard name. That is the law in Texas."

"I bet you didn't like that."

She shook her head. "No. But now, I don't have to worry about child support or anything else as Charles no longer wants to claim Ryan as his child, not that he ever really did. He relinquished his rights to Ryan, probably as Ryan isn't his biological child, and as he told me before, blood tells."

Her sigh warmed his wrist as he brushed a stray tendril of copper off her forehead. For a moment he fingered the silky, reddened tresses.

Her eyes stared at his chin, then at his chest as she leaned up and picked at his button.

"I don't know if I'm more pissed at him for everything, for all the lies, for all the pointless hurt, or if I'm more mad at myself for actually letting him hurt me." Confusion warred in their depths.

"Personally, I think Charles is a royal ass." He looked back into her eyes and smiled. "But that aside, have you thought how lucky you are?"

"With Ryan?" she asked. "Yes, and the fact I don't have more little Charleses." She gave a mock shudder. "I'm just pissed and if I get really, really upset, I just cry. Not because I'm sad, I just have never been a confrontational sort of person."

"Really? That's news to me."

She lightly punched his arm.

He felt her relax against him.

"You know," he continued, "Mom always said, the Good Lord works in mysterious ways."

A smile played with her dimples. "I know. Thanks for listening."

"Hmm…." Her face was made for portraits of art. That pale smooth forehead crinkled in the center when she concentrated really hard, like she was now. Those round dark eyes with ridiculously long lashes held the secrets of her soul. A straight, freckled nose slightly notched in the center. Gavin ran his finger down the bridge of her nose, landing on her full, soft lips. His fingers spread over her pale, creamy cheeks, even as his thumb skimmed over her mouth.

Charles had had a vasectomy, which meant that Taylor could indeed get pregnant. Children. She could be pregnant even now. God knew they'd chanced it enough last night. With his child. His.

Mine.

Surprisingly the thought didn't fill him with panic. Earlier today he had thought to tell her all this some other time, some perfect time with some planned setting. But, he was learning the best things in life were never really planned or perfect. Chaos seemed to bring blessings.

"Taylor, do you remember what I told you last night?" he asked her.

"You told me lots of things last night." Long pale fingers fidgeted on his shirtfront.

"Yes, I did. But do you remember what I told you I thought of you?"

The smile reached the deepest part of her eyes. "You said you thought I was beautiful. That I was wonderful. Amazing." She pulled her hand out from under his, reaching up to cup his cheek. "How do you do that?"

"Do what?" he whispered.

"How do you just know what to tell me, what I need to hear?"

This time he turned and kissed her palm, kissed the pad of her thumb, her inner wrist, feeling the blood pump faintly against his lips. "Because I know you. I know what's in your heart."

He would tell her tonight.

"I love you," she whispered to him.

She loved him. Well, damn. She stole his thunder.

Trying not to shout and smile, he frowned and shook his head, "No you don't."

Her smile faded.

"I was all prepared to have to persuade you to love me. I love you, too, Gorgeous." He leaned towards her stopping a breath away from her mouth. "I was about to tell you those words and had my strategy all planned out for how to get you to say the words back to me."

She swallowed and her eyes swept down, the gaze stopping at his mouth. Her tongue wet her lips. "Were you now?"

"Mmm…." he said, watching her.

"How do you know you love me?"

This time he did smile. "That's easy. It just is. It's like one of those

DEADLY TIES
141

fine, soft misty rains. You hardly notice it really, but after you walk for a while in it, you realize you're wet. Simple as can be, it simply is." He cupped her face, grazing his thumbs from cheekbones, down to her chin, skimming the corners of her mouth. "I don't love you for where you came from, or where you didn't. I just love you, Taylor."

She kissed him. Their tongues met, dueled and fueled the admissions in them, the emotions and truths that became so clear here in the dim living room on a new denim couch. He turned her head to plunge deeper, blending himself with her through their breaths.

Pulling back, he looked into her eyes. "How do you know you love me?"

Her smile was soft, almost secret as she said, "You do all sorts of little things and don't even realize it, don't even really think about it. Because you are you. You make me laugh and feel special, make me believe and dream for what can be without feeling inhibited."

"And here I thought you wanted my money."

Her eyes rolled. "Of course, it's a hard won bet between your body and your money. You saw through my lie so easily."

"Sass." He pulled her into his lap. "I just love it when you're sassy."

Kissing her again, he stood, cradling her to him. Her arms wrapped around his neck as he made his way up her stairs to her bedroom.

He stopped beside her bed, setting her on her feet. He brushed her hair away from her face, then turned and pulled her to the bed. Slowly he undid her braid, running his fingers through her hair.

Her sigh moaned out. "That feels so good."

Gavin smiled. Thought about how to phrase his question. "Taylor?"

"Hmmm?" Her head leaned back into his fingers.

"I don't have any protection."

Her eyes flew open to look at him. He saw the truth finally sink home, settle and shift into place. Her shoulders lifted on a shrug even as she smiled and her dimples deepened. "I don't either."

They stared at each other in the darkened room. Streetlights streaked through her blinds, slashing across her bed, the both of them.

"I love you," he told her again.

"And I love you."

What the hell. "Wanna get married? Try for some babies?"

Several seconds passed then she finally blinked.

"What?"

His stomach muscles tightened. Gavin had no idea where the thought burst from, but it was there and he wanted it. He wanted her so bad, not just to make love to tonight, but for every night of their lives. She was his.

"I know it's sudden. But I've always known what I want. I want to marry you. I want to come home to you and Ryan, to hear about your day and his newest piece of music or some bizarre factoid he wants to share. I want to go to sleep with you in my arms after making love to you and wake up in the mornings to see you hurrying to the bathroom and complaining about gifts I get you. And if the Good Lord sees to it, I want you and only you to be the mother of our children, by blood or love."

Gavin held his breath. He'd never been surer of anything in his life. Never wanted anything as badly and never so terrified that he wouldn't get it.

Her head shook back and forth as her mouth opened then closed before opening again.

"You don't want to marry me." Though her voice told him she didn't believe him, he caught her smile.

"You don't believe me?" he asked.

"I have no idea."

Gavin chuckled. At least it wasn't a 'no'. Turning so that she was under him, he leaned down and kissed her.

In no time, their clothing lay tossed around her room. When skin met skin breaths caught and held. Passions rose to new heights as emotions flowed freely. Hands and mouths loved and cherished as moans and whispers filled the room. Their climax left him gasping for breath.

The woman was going to kill him.

"Was that some of your persuasive strategy?" she whispered in his ear.

He growled a response in the back of his throat, not moving from his current position lest he stop breathing all together.

Finally, he raised his head and looked down at her.

"You never answered me." Though he smiled at her, he hoped she saw past his light-hearted humor.

"I didn't, did I?" Her brows rose high. "I don't know, Gavin."

He released his breath slowly. She wasn't ready. Understandable. He'd rushed it. He should have waited. He should have....

"I think...." she said, grazing her fingers down his face, her voice lowering, "I need to be persuaded." Her words pierced through him.

"Really?" he asked her.

"I think so, yes." She nodded, smiling wickedly. "To get me in a better frame of mind."

Minx. He would torture her slowly. Leaning down he kissed her mouth, barely touching her at all. Shifting he felt himself filling her again. He'd get an answer out of her.

"Got your mind set now?" he asked her on a kiss.

"I'm not a good wife," she whispered.

Gavin paused and cupped her face. "Nope, not in the right frame of mind yet." Aggravation coursed through him. "I see you're lumping me with that ass again. Gonna have to fix that, Taylor."

Their lovemaking was long, deliberate in its unhurried leisure. Just as she would near the peak, he'd back off, change rhythms, simply stop. It went on for hours. He would make her beg before he had his answer.

DEADLY TIES

He touched her everywhere, branding her, claiming all of her for all of him. He loved her every way he could think of and then some.

He pulled out of her, grinning at her moan, even as she reached for him. He grabbed some pillows and pushed them under her.

"What?"

"Shhh."

Reaching down, he hooked her knees over his arms, spreading her wide as he braced his weight on his hands. She was completely open to him. Gavin surged back into her with one strong thrust.

She bowed up and he leaned down, pumping into her, taking a breast into his mouth.

"Please, Gavin, please."

He thrust shallow then deep, almost left her, then pushed back into her surrounding heat.

Licking her lips, he smiled against her mouth. "Will you marry me?"

"Please."

Gavin retreated from her, pulling completely out.

Her legs locked, vising around his arms. She was utterly exposed to him. He used one finger to graze from her pubic hair all the way down her cleft. She shuddered. Gavin flicked her clitoris, back and forth, pushing and pulling, circling it in hard small circles. Lifting her hips to him, she opened her eyes. Her arms came up and her hands clasped his face.

"Mine," she said clearly.

He thrust back into her holding her gaze captive, even as she shuddered and moaned.

"Marry me...." he whispered against her lips.

"Yes, Gavin, I'll marry you."

"Mine," he answered before he took them both spinning towards the heavens.

CHAPTER FOURTEEN

One month later

The transport bus zoomed down the road. Somehow, her name had wound up on the transfer roster. Texas prisons were full. Wasn't it a shame? And though, by any stretch of the imagination, she shouldn't have been on this bus, she was.

Nina looked up and caught Rod's look in the rearview mirror. He landed the job of driving the bus. It was only a matter of time.

She caught his barely perceptible nod.

"Shut the hell up, Dodders," an inmate said.

"You shut the hell up, bitch," Dodders answered back.

The guard stood. "Ladies, both of you shut the hell up."

A bridge was coming up. Long way down.

Rod jerked the wheel and the bus spun, a long slow snake sliding over the asphalt. They hit the guardrail, busting through. For one minute, it looked like they would stay on the bridge, but thank God, gravity kicked in. The bus tipped to one side.

Curses and yells filled the air. Nina braced.

The big tin can rolled down a steep embankment, crunching and grinding all in its way.

Glass shattered, metal groaned.

Finally, they came to a stop.

The sound of water filled the silence that thundered in her ears. Water?

She saw then that water was rising from the back of the bus. She craned her neck up and saw Rod, blood trickling from his forehead opening the cage door between the driver and the rest of the occupants. The door didn't want to give.

"Damn it." He leaned back and kicked it, once, twice, it finally bent open enough for him to get in.

"Rod, I'm pinned," someone whispered.

Nina followed the sound of the voice. The guard, she was pinned halfway under one crushed seat.

Rod licked his lips, hesitated.

"Hey baby," Nina purred.

Rod shook his head and made his way to her. As he unlocked her restraints, more yells and curses filled the air. Nina only smiled at him.

"Time to rock and roll," she said.

* * * *

Nina stuck her head out the window.

"Freeeeeee. I'm fucking freeeeeee."

"Get your ass in here before someone sees you!" Rod barked, jerking the wheel as he leaned over to pull her in.

Heavy medal screamed through the speakers as the car slid over the black asphalt of Highway 84.

"You're so damn paranoid," she told him, popping her gum and settling in the seat of his old mustang. Rod was nervous as hell, but he claimed to love her, so she played that card.

Headlights met and passed them in a whirring blur. Yellow stripes ran endlessly ahead, reflectors winking at them in the night like a line of landing strips.

"Coleman is just ahead, then it won't be long till Brownwood," he told her.

"Good." Nina leaned back, content to dive her hand against the wind through the open window.

Small things like this one took for granted.

DEADLY TIES 145

She still couldn't believe it had actually worked. The last two days were a high in and of themselves without any need for chems. She and Rod had it all planned out.

And it had worked beautifully. Of course they had had to kill the guard. Nina figured she did the bitch a favor, probably couldn't have walked again anyway, right?

They'd left the rest shackled and got the hell out of there. Rod had had a friend waiting up the road for them. Rick was the bastard's name. He helped them out for some cash and with the agreement they would deal for him. Since Rod already did this to the inmates, and would no longer have a job after his little 'love affair' with her, they readily agreed. Plus it gave them a bit of extra cash. So into Rick's car they went, where Nina and Rod changed clothes, then he dropped them off in the next town where Rod stashed a car.

Easy as that. Bam. Bam. Bam. One, two, freaking three.

Nina just knew they'd get caught. But, no. Thank whatever god watched over inmates. That and Rod's ingenuity, or Rick's, who-the-hell-ever's.

Nina reached over and lit a cigarette. The thin white paper crinkled before disintegrating as the tobacco lit. The end glowed orange in the night. Smoke rings wafted in the car before being sucked out the window.

Yeah, it had been easy.

Looking over she studied Rod's profile in the green tinged dash lights. His hair didn't really have a color. Unlike hers--thanks to Clairol, she'd gone jet black yesterday in Dallas. Clairol and a pair of scissors. Short and stylish, Rod had told her.

She ran a hand through the shortened tresses, not but a couple of inches off her bare scalp. At least it wasn't buzzed like Rod's.

He really wasn't that bad looking--in a choirboy sort of way. He was a little over weight, not much, but enough that one could tell he wasn't exactly a health nut. But then again he was stronger than most, too, with his six foot frame and extra weight.

And why in the fuck did she give a shit what he looked like? Just a means to an end. A means to an end.

On a deep drag, she closed her eyes. God, she wanted a hit. Just one. Knock the edge off this downer.

But Rod was adamant about selling the shit and getting the money back to Rick. Whatever, she had her own contacts. Which was why they were currently heading to Brownwood instead of to Austin to find Ryan and the Shepards. There was a crack house there she needed to stop at and get some personal stuff. Maybe a bit more on the side. They did need the cash. Plus she knew that for a 'service' she could get her hands on a gun. Something light. Maybe a SIG nine. Or a Glock. Probably depended on what Cal had on hand, and what he'd want her to do, and what Rod would go for.

That could be a problem. Rod didn't like to share. But it was just a lay. If she got a gun out of it and some jelly beans or rocks--blue powder would be iced, but probably too costly, and she didn't have the time to literally fuck around--then what was the damn harm?

Plus, she could find out where Johnny was. Then she would decide once and for all if she wanted to ruin the bastard for ditching her in the pen or if she'd use him. If she used him, then she'd have to dump Rod, and that was dangerous. Rod knew too much.

But there was no use worrying about any of it until she had some answers.

Her first priority was a gun, and not Rod's. He didn't have to know she had one either. After all, it wasn't as if he knew these people. They were hers, so if she needed to go talk to one of them for a few minutes then he'd have to go with it.

Crack houses weren't the safest places.

But they got her what she needed, in more ways than one.

Her plans were all rolling into play.

Air blew through the interior of the car, washing out the sound of electric guitars.

Yeah, it was all coming together. One way or another.

* * * *

Journal Entry, August 12th

Taylor's already up. I don't know what to do. Who to tell. Though I did tell Tori some of it all. And she probably thinks I'm nuts.

I 'saw' Nina the other day at school. Well, not at school, but in my mind, like I do sometimes. She was in this wreck. That doesn't make any sense does it? But then I've already written all of this over and over. I just don't know if it's real or not. I hope it's not. I mean what would she be doing in bus, in a wreck?

But last night I saw her in a car. I was getting ready to go to sleep. The house was all quiet and the adults were still all out. I couldn't stand to stay in that room. Not that it isn't a nice room. Mrs. K. told me it was Gavin's when he was a boy like me. I don't think Gavin was ever a boy like me. How could he be?

I just wanted Taylor, so I sat on the steps and waited for her and Gavin.

I'm so happy their getting married. I still can't believe Gavin asked me if it would be okay for him to marry my mom. He even wants to adopt me. I'll be a Kinncaid and everything. Though I don't think the Kinncaids ever get scared. But I was last night. So maybe I won't make a good Kinncaid.

I was scared Mr. or Mrs. K--though they want me to think about calling them Grams and Pops, don't know about that yet--would come along. I didn't want to have to explain what I was doing there. They're both really nice people, but I get nervous around Mr ... Pops.

Hmm ... that's not as weird as I thought it would be. Maybe that's

DEADLY TIES
147

what I'll do, call people things I want to in this journal even if I can't when I'm talking to them or about them.

Pops, Grams, Mom--Dad? I wonder if Gavin will want me to call him Dad. I've never had a dad before, or a grams or pops. Writing it's not so hard. Though it makes me feel funny, a tickle inside my tummy like when I have to play a piece of music for someone.

Okay, if I'm writing what I want to call them, then ... Pops makes me nervous. Not because he's bad or anything, but he sees so much. His eyes remind me of a story I read about a wizard who could just look at a person and know what was going on. Pops's eyes are like that. So, I hoped he wouldn't find me sitting on the steps last night while I waited on ... MOM and DAD. MOM. MOM. MOM. MOM.

Taylor is MY MOM. Gavin is going to be my DAD.

See, there's that funny feeling in my tummy again.

But it's a good feeling, not like it was last night after what I 'saw' with Nina. With Nina it's like a burning in my gut. That I-don't-want-to-know kinda feeling. Because if I do know, I know it will be bad. Very bad.

Like the things I'm remembering about that night in Austin when she hurt me. I don't want to remember them so I hide behind the walls in my mind. It's a game I played all the time when I lived with Nina. When things got bad, I just imagined myself in that castle, all guarded up against her. Nothing could get past the stone walls because they were magic, and wouldn't let anything bad get in. So when I start to think about that night in Austin, I just go to the center of my castle where nothing can get me. It's safe there.

I tried to get there last night, but I wanted Taylor more. Mom. I wanted my mom more. But then when she got here, I just couldn't talk to her.

I don't know how to tell her about the things I 'see', the things I know. What if she thinks I'm crazy and sends me to Dr. Petropolis? What if Dr. Petropolis wants to send me to one of those loony bin places?

It could happen. If they thought I was crazy. Nina told me all the time that was where people like me went, so I don't really believe it, but it scares me too.

Tori thinks I need to tell Tay--MOM. That I need to tell my mom about what I 'see'. I had to tell Tori when she asked me how I knew Taylor was crying the other day before we ever got there. I was afraid someone else would ask, but no one did. Mr. K--POPS kept looking at me, but he never asked.

Tori did. And I had to tell her. She thinks it's cool. If she saw the things I did, she would know it's not cool. I don't WANT TO KNOW THESE THINGS.

Half the time my 'visions' or whatever they're called aren't right. So what good is it? I mean, Nina and bus and water and a wreck? Give me a break. But when they are right, it scares me. Why can't I see anything useful? Did I know when Nina got to take me for an hour in Texas that she'd run off with me? No. I was scared she would, but no one 'showed' me ahead of time. So what good is this gift? More like a fluke or a curse.

But now I've got to tell someone else. An adult, Tori told me. She swore not to say anything, but after I told her I was worried Nina was out of prison she got all bossy. Tori can be really bossy. I have to tell Mom or Gavin--Dad? Before we leave. If not, she's going to tell her dad or her uncle Gavin. She says an adult will know who to call to see if Nina is still where she's supposed to be.

Of course, Miss Bossy wanted to know why Nina was in prison to begin with, but I didn't answer her. For a girl she is really smart. And she's right, and she knows it. Mom would know who to call to find out if Nina is where she's supposed to be.

Maybe after I write this all down, I'll go find her and tell her. Course she's probably with Gavin. They're always together. But that's what's suppose to happen--at least I think it is.

I don't know about the whole wedding thing. But Mrs. K., GRAMS and Pops are married and they're happy and they're old. So I guess it works for people. Plus Aiden and Jesslyn are happy. I think Gavin and Taylor will be too. DAD AND MOM … MOM AND DAD … I've got to get used to that. I WANT to call them that. I WANT a mom and a dad. I want to be NORMAL.

Normal is as normal does--Tori said. Whatever that means.

SHE thinks we should experiment. Tori said that I have a gift, just like my music and unless I practice and train it, it is pointless.

I do wonder if she's onto something. Though I told her to forget it. She wants to play 'mind' games where she's in a room and thinks about a shape she's drawing and I'm suppose to guess what it is from another room. Maybe Tori Bori is onto something. We'll see about her 'games' the next time I'm here.

For now, it's just a guess and I think it's a wrong guess. I mean how could Nina be out of prison. Wouldn't we know? Wouldn't someone tell us?

I'll tell Mom and Dad/Gavin … Dadgavin. Sounds like a place in Scotland or something. But I'll tell them I have something I want to talk to them about on the way home, or when we get home. Then, Tori won't tell anyone and someone can call to find out if Nina is still in prison.

That sounds like a plan. Yeah, I'll tell Mom about it all, but I don't know if I can call her MOM to her face yet. I don't think I'm ready. Not yet, but soon.

Soon.

DEADLY TIES

CHAPTER FIFTEEN

The door shut behind Gavin as they all piled bags in the entryway of the house. After spending the weekend up at Seneca, she was glad to be home. Wedding plans were in the works, thanks to Kaitlyn, Christian and Jesslyn. Gavin decided to simply wait until he was asked something.

It had been a good weekend, even if Ryan seemed to get quiet and more withdrawn. At least, until last night. Last night something had happened. When she and Gavin had returned ot the house, they'd found Ryan sitting on the stairs in his spider man pajamas, his face stark pale. He hadn't said a word, just hugged her tight and refused to let go. He never did tell them what had happened. Gavin and she worried about it all night and this morning. Ryan had hardly spoken all day today and seemed haunted.

It was later than she wished, being a school night. Ryan stood on the stairs, one hand on the smooth banister.

Looking at him, she motioned him upstairs. "Why don't you go get a shower and then you can tell us whatever it is you want to tell us? Will that work?"

For a moment he seemed undecided, then he nodded, hefted his bag on his shoulder and trudged up the steps.

"Don't be too long, honey, it's late and getting later." She watched his sneakers disappear. Gavin's arms slipped around her and pulled her back against him.

"You think he'll tell us what's bothering him?" His deep timbered voice vibrated against her back and her ear.

Taylor shrugged. "I have no idea. He just said he wanted to talk to us when we got home. And we're home."

"He's still too quiet. I didn't hear one factoid all the way home. He just stared out the window and fidgeted in the seat."

"I know."

Gavin sighed, straightened and lead her into the living room. "I have a confession to make."

"You haven't lied to me about something have you?"

His eyes narrowed on hers. "No, not really. I called Dr. Petropolis today and asked if she could see Ryan in the morning. I told her we were worried. I figured if you got too pissed or if he came around, you could always call and cancel."

That she could. The first emotion running through her was part shock, part disbelief. But she knew Gavin was as worried about Ryan as she was.

Taking a deep breath, she only said, "I wish you would have told me."

"Why? So you could say to wait till tomorrow? I didn't want to wait until in the morning and then try to get hold of her and hope for an appointment. Now, we have one at eight."

Eight? "Dr. Petropolis' office doesn't open till nine."

Gavin shook his head and walked out of the living room. She heard his footfalls echo down the hallway into the kitchen. Eight? Did it honestly matter? No.

Taylor followed Gavin. He stood by the sink, looking out into the night.

"I want to help and this was something I could easily do," he said, not turning to her. "He's my son, too. Maybe not yet, but he will be as soon as the adoption is finalized."

Yes, Ryan was his son, maybe not legally yet, not until after the wedding. But in every way that mattered Ryan was, and would be, Gavin's child.

When he turned back to her, she walked to him. Putting her hands on his chest, she leaned up on her tiptoes and gave him a kiss on his cheek. "Thank you."

A moment passed, then another. His eyes studied her, and she saw frustration in their depths. He sighed, squeezing her hands. "I'm tired of pushing against you, Taylor."

"What?"

Gavin tried to step around her, but she held onto him. He stilled and glared down at her, a muscle shifting in his jaw. "Half the time I feel like you would rather do it all alone. At least where Ryan is concerned."

He thought that?

"I'm sorry. I don't mean to hurt you. I'm just used to handling things on my own. I'm not used to sharing all this, to lean on, to expect the help."

"Well, get used to it."

He was angry and worried and she couldn't really blame him.

She sighed, and leaned into him. "I'm sorry. You're right." Taylor cupped his face between her hands. "You're right. I need to learn to lean…."

His brow cocked.

"Okay, I need to work on it quite a bit, but I'll get better. Lean, at the top of my list."

This time a grin peeked out at her. His hands covered hers and pulled them from his face. "Hmm. That was almost too easy, but I'm not going to complain." He leaned down and returned her peck.

"We just did a sorta marriage thing, didn't we?" she asked him.

"Sass," he muttered shaking his head.

This was nice. Two people, two hearts, sharing everything to become one. One. A unity. A family.

* * * *

DEADLY TIES

The music screamed through her brain. Every image was crystal clear as though someone had sharpened the world. Nina's hands were rock steady, nary a shake of a finger as she slid the lock home. She'd learned lots of stuff over the years. Never gone hungry because she knew how to get food. How to get goods to pawn. It was almost like an art, to get a lock to click open. And she was damn good at it.

That was how she'd met Johnny, rest his fucking soul. Shot through the heart down in Del Rio, Calvin had told her. At least Johnny was no longer a worry. Good 'ole Cal. He'd learned a thing or two from her when she'd 'paid' for her gun.

A sweet nine-millimeter complete with a silencer. Perfect kick-ass gun for her. Light and quick.

The house she slipped into was dark, for the most part. Little night-lights periodically glowed from wall sockets near the floor.

Rod waited in the car. She had to get out of here fast. He was already getting a conscience. While she'd given him a hell of a blowjob, she'd told him a conscience had no place in this business and would only get him killed. Course, she might be the one to kill him, but for now he was useful.

A cough sounded from down the hall. Nice big ass house. A house where her son was. Child stealers. Dammit all.

Just for a moment the world shrunk, or seemed to. Cal had given her some cosmic powder, but it was good. Some of the best she'd had in a while. She just needed some sleep. Too long on meth slowed you down even if you didn't think it did. Too high too long and your mind started playing tricks, seeing pink elephants, demons and shit.

Her black clothes swallowed the shadows, and her soft-soled shoes silently trod along the edge of the floor near the wall. The gun pressed against her abdomen, where she'd crammed it. Pulling it from her waistband she clicked the safety off. The slick of the bullet popping into the chamber echoed in the stillness.

Nina stilled, stopped breathing. She counted to ten. Nothing. Not another sound. Another ten seconds. Then another.

Finally, she crept down the hallway to the door. It stood partially open.

Focus. Music still blared in her mind, and she had to force it off, forced herself to concentrate. No distractions. No slip ups.

She'd off the couple in the bed and grab her kid. Yeah.

Easy as one.

Nina slipped through the door and hurried to the bed.

Two.

The woman first.

Three.

Nina pressed the barrel into the woman's forehead.

"Rise and shine."

The woman came up screaming and Nina laughed.

"What the hell?" a man asked, pulling her attention to him.

Nina pressed the gun harder against the woman. "Do *not* move. I have a gun." She shrugged. "And I'll use it."

The woman whimpered.

"What do you want? Take whatever you want. Just please don't hurt her," the man said.

"You mean that would matter to you?" Nina backed up a several steps. She didn't want to be in easy striking or grabbing distance, but kept the gun trained on the bed.

The woman whimpered again and tried to scoot next to her husband. "Uh-uh. Stay still."

She froze.

"Take whatever you want. What do you need?" he asked from the other side of the bed.

"Revenge," Nina said and pulled the trigger.

The silenced blast pinged in the room, momentarily flashing in the darkness.

"Nooooo. Rhonda? Rhonda?" The man was over the woman.

Rhonda? Who the fuck was Rhonda? Who the hell cared? "Where's my son?"

"What?" he bit out between a sob and a growl. "Oh, God. Baby, hang on. Hang on." He reached for the phone. Nina beat him to it and knocked it away. Framed photos and the lamp jumbled to the floor.

"My son!"

"Who the fuck are you?" he yelled at her.

"Nina Fisher and I want my son!"

"Fisher? Ryan? Sonofabitch." He picked up the woman in the bed. "They're not even here. Rhonda had nothing to do with that. With any of it. God, she's pregnant. Let me call a doctor. Please. Please."

The darkness didn't allow her to see features, though what she could see, she now registered. "Well damn."

Blonde hair glinted in the dim light.

Just goes to show. Homework was important. Very important.

Nina leveled the gun at him. "I'll let you call a doctor on one condition. Tell me where they are."

"Who?"

Nina tsked. "Mr. Shepard, stupidity doesn't become you. My son! Your WIFE! WHERE THE HELL ARE THEY?"

"Oh God, Rhonda. Rhonda. Talk to me. Please. Hang on baby. Just hang on."

"Times a wasting, Shepard."

"I don't know!" he yelled at her.

Maybe he didn't, but then again maybe he did. She looked at the woman again. The shot had caught her in the chest; blood covered him and her in the dark. Nina took two steps to the bed and pressed the barrel against the woman's head again.

DEADLY TIES
153

"Where Charles?"

"D.C. They're in Washington, D.C. I don't know the address. I swear it. I didn't care after she moved. I just know Taylor moved to D.C." He was crying. "Let me call my wife a doctor please. Please. She's pregnant."

Nina really didn't like hurting the innocent. Truly she didn't. Only those who deserved it. Like the judge she'd gotten this morning in the leg. Dammit, she would have nailed the bastard right center if Rod hadn't distracted her.

Sighing she pushed the phone towards him.

"Fine. Call."

She listened as he did. Gave the address and the crime. Gunshot. He was babbling and crying.

Nina backed up.

She saw him move on the bed.

"Damn you. Damn you!" He lunged at her.

Her finger squeezed the trigger and the second muffled explosion echoed in the room.

"Mr. Shepard? Mr. Shepard?" came a voice through the phone.

"Sorry, Charlie." Nina turned, grabbed the purse and wallet off the dresser, and ran out of the house. Sirens pierced the night as she slid into the car with Rod.

"Go! Go! Go!" He floored the mustang and swerved around the next corner.

"What the fuck did you do?" he asked her, checking the mirror.

"Tied up a mistaken loose end."

She pulled cash out of both the wallet and purse and then ditched them out the window.

They drove down streets until they hit HWY 183 going into Austin.

"Get some gas, we've got a road trip to start on."

Rod glanced at her. "Road trip?"

"Yeah, to the nation's freaking capitol. I always wanted to see the sights."

* * * *

"Aaaahhhhrrrrrrrrr," Ryan yelled, slipping on the stairs as the pain pierced his brain. He crumpled to the steps.

"No. No. No. Noooooooooo!" He shook his head back and forth. Back and forth. It wasn't real. It wasn't real. No. No. No. His fists beat on his thighs.

"Ryan?" Taylor asked him. "Ryan? Honey?"

He jerked away from her hand.

His mind screamed with what he saw, with what he suddenly remembered. And there was no place to hide. Try as he might, he couldn't get to the center of his castle. It felt as if someone had cut off his air. Gasping he tried to get his balance.

"Ryan?" Taylor asked again. He caught the concern in her voice, but he couldn't look at her yet.

Maybe if he kept his eyes tight, tight shut he wouldn't 'see' what he was shown. He wouldn't see the blood, hear the scream or the gunshots.

"Sorry, Charlie. Sorry, Charlie." Oh God. Tears plopped onto his fisted hands. No. No.

"Ryan. Look at me. Look at me, Ryan." Gavin.

Gavin was here. Taylor was here. He was with them. Not in that room. No blood, no guns, no Nina.

Carefully, he lifted his head. He still couldn't breathe, couldn't catch his breath…. The faster he tried to breathe, the tighter his chest squeezed.

"Look in my eyes. Right here." Gavin pointed with his two fingers at his own blue eyes. Ryan locked his gaze with Gavin's. "Listen to my voice. Calm down. Take a deep breath. A deep breath."

He couldn't. It was too tight.

Gavin reached up and put his hands on both sides of Ryan's face. "Breathe slowly. One deep breath. Come on. You can do it. You're scaring your mom and me."

Ryan didn't want to scare them. Closing his eyes, he took in a breath and held it. Then another. A slower, deeper one. Opening his eyes, he looked into the depths of Gavin's.

"Good," Gavin told him. "Now again."

Ryan did. Three more times until finally it felt as if maybe his heart wouldn't burst from his chest. He felt Gavin's fingers on his wrist, warm and gentle.

"Did you fall? Are you hurt?" Gavin's deep voice was calm, soothing.

Calm and soothing, not like the other…. The other. Oh God. She was coming. She shot them. She shot them because of him.

All he saw was the blue of Gavin's eyes.

"Ryan? Are you hurt? What happened?" Taylor asked, sitting beside him on the step. Her arm wrapped around him.

He stiffened, but he hoped she wouldn't let go. She didn't. Taylor never would.

Ryan closed his eyes as warm tears trailed down his cheeks. He hated to cry. Hated it. It didn't do any good. But what else could he do? Oh, his head hurt. It hurt bad.

This one was picture perfect. Never before had a vision been so clear.

He pulled his hand out of Gavin's and put it to the side of his head, and leaned into Taylor. Her other arm came around him.

"Honey, what? What is it?"

He wasn't crying. He wasn't. But he couldn't hold it in, he couldn't. It was too much, like a flood that would not be held behind sandbags.

"Are you hurt?" she asked, holding him tight.

DEADLY TIES

Ryan shook his head back and forth.

"Did you fall?" Gavin asked him.

Again all he could do was shake his head.

Minutes passed, and still he kept crying. Ryan didn't make a sound. He couldn't, if he made a sound, what little bit of himself he was holding back would go tearing out. No, the tears were bad enough.

"Come on, you two. The living room is a bit more comfortable," Gavin said.

Taylor shifted, but Ryan held on tighter. Her hands rubbed his back in circles.

"Come on, champ." Gavin's hands lifted him up. Ryan felt like a baby, but he let Gavin carry him into the living room. He wrapped his arms and legs around Gavin, burying his face in the curve of the man's neck, breathing in the spicy scent of Gavin's cologne. They both sat on the couch, Taylor sitting right beside them so that Ryan was sandwiched between the two of them.

Here he was safe.

Sorry, Charlie.... It couldn't be real. He wouldn't let it be real. Reaching up he rubbed the left side of his head, it hurt. His heart hurt.

"Ryan? Please talk to us," Taylor whispered.

What did he tell them? Would they believe him? Where did he start?

He picked on a spot on his pajama shorts. "I remember what happened in Austin," he whispered.

No one said anything. Taylor snuggled him close and Gavin put his arm around the both of them.

"Do you want to talk about it?" Taylor asked him.

Did he want to? Not only no, but--bad word or no--hell no.

The tick of the clock timed off seconds in the quiet room.

"You know, Ryan. Sometimes, there are things in life we don't want to talk about. And even though talking about them is hard, and makes us sad, scared, or angry--we feel better afterwards," Gavin told him in that voice.

He loved Gavin's voice. It would always remind him of bass notes in music. No way would Gavin yell and cuss. Ryan couldn't get such a picture to form. But though Ryan probably agreed with what Gavin was saying, he couldn't help but wonder what Gavin knew of it.

Like he'd ever heard about murdered cops, or seen people get shot just because *she* was tripping.

Taking a deep breath, Ryan said, "I don't want to talk about it. I don't want to remember any of it. But I have to. I have to tell you, and the other." Before she gets here.

Wiggling, he scooted back into the deep couch. His feet stuck out because his knees no longer hit the edge of the couch. Pulling his knees up, he wrapped his arms around them.

Neither of his parents said a word. Parents. They were his parents.

"I've always wanted a family. A mom and a dad."

His words squeezed Taylor's heart. She looked over his head to Gavin who questioned with his eyes. She smiled at him and nodded.

"Ryan," he said. "You have a family now. Taylor is a wonderful mom, and I hope I'll be half as good a dad."

Ryan shrugged. "I've never had a dad."

Gavin reached up and scratched his chin. "Well, I've never had a son, so I guess we're starting on even ground."

"Yeah," her son answered.

Taylor smoothed his hair down again. When she'd heard him yell, heard the stumble, she'd been terrified he'd broken his neck on the stairs. She still didn't know who'd left the kitchen first, her or Gavin, not that it mattered. They'd both raced down the hall to see Ryan curled up near the bottom of the steps. He hadn't fallen, thank God, but she still didn't know what happened.

Gavin cleared his throat, but before he could say anything, Taylor butted in. "Ryan, Gavin and I are worried about you. Please talk to us. We can help."

A long silence passed. Finally, very quietly, he whispered, "They killed a cop."

"What?" both she and Gavin asked at the same time.

Ryan sighed, then squirming, he explained. "You know in Austin, when she ran off with me?"

Like Taylor would ever forget those terror-filled days. "Yes," she answered, swallowing past the knot in her throat.

"Well, we were in some apartment. I don't know where. I kept trying to get away, to call the cops or you. So that night they locked me in my room."

They?

"I heard them leave. It was cold and I had to go to the bathroom. I just couldn't figure out how to get out of the room. I finally remembered a movie I saw where someone took the door off the hinges. It took forever, and I had to climb on top of this chest of drawers to get to the top hinge, but I finally got the door off just before they got home."

Her poor, smart little boy.

"I was coming back out of the bathroom and wanted a bite of something. That's when I heard their voices. He was yelling at her for not being sharp enough and that she was just as much to blame as him. Nina was burning a rock on some foil."

His nose scrunched up. "I hate that smell, like cleaners or something. That's how she'd get high sometimes. Then, she started screaming that she wasn't going down for killing a cop. She hadn't iced him. Yeah, that's what she said, 'iced.'" His small shoulders shrugged. "Anyway, they got in this argument, something about drugs and a bust and a cop they killed."

Good God. Her son's voice sounded distant, as though relating a scene from a movie.

DEADLY TIES

157

But then it wavered. "I figured I wasn't supposed to hear this story, so I tried to turn to go back down the hall but they saw me." He took in deep breath. "Johnny came flying at me. He was hitting me and kicking me. That's how my arm got broke. Then he picked me up." Ryan's hand rubbed at his throat. "But I couldn't breathe. His hands just kept squeezing. I'll never forget his eyes. They were like sharp green glass, but all red too. I know they were both tripping. I just wanted to get back to you," he said, turning to look at Taylor. His eyes darted away.

But what she'd seen in them. Oh, baby. Taylor laid her cheek on top of his head. "I was looking for you. I didn't eat or sleep. I just wanted to find you. I couldn't stand you being gone and knowing you were with her. I'm sorry, so sorry Ryan."

Tears pricked her eyes, but swallowed them back.

"She actually stopped him," he whispered. "Nina told him to stop, begged him to let me go. And he did, finally. That's the only time I'd ever been thankful to her. But it didn't last long. She picked me up and hit me, but I was already trying to jerk away. That's when I fell through the window, or maybe she pushed me. I guess someone had called the cops because the last thing I heard was the sirens."

"Christ," Gavin muttered. His hand was fisted on the back of the couch. Taylor left one arm around Ryan and with the other, reached up and rubbed Gavin's shoulder. Their eyes locked.

Taylor was taken aback by the look in his, but comforted too. Cold and sharp as a sapphire, his eyes glowed with rage. A muscle bunched in his jaw. Beneath the charm of humor lurked a warrior.

Taylor looked back at her son. Tears no longer fell from his eyes, but his hands were clasped together so tightly, the knuckles were white.

"How long have you remembered this?" Taylor asked him softly.

He shrugged. "Bits and pieces for awhile, but it all came rushing back tonight on the stairs after..."

After?

"After what?" Gavin asked, his voice tight.

Ryan shook his head.

Taylor decided on a different track, something that no one had apparently known until now. "Ryan, you said 'they' were arguing, and he--Johnny--hurt you. Who do you mean? Do you remember?"

He closed those sky-blue eyes and thought. Shaking his head he said, "I don't know. Johnny Haines, Harris, Hayes--something like that, I think."

Johnny 'H' with sharp green eyes. "Was he tall?"

Ryan turned a look on her that clearly asked what kind of question that was. "I'm nine. Everyone's tall."

Taylor found her first smile.

There had never been mention of another person. Another person who had tried to kill her son. Almost choked the life out of him. Taylor clamped down on the fear that speared through her, swallowed past the tightness. Instead, she concentrated on what he told them, the new information. "And they were arguing about killing a cop. Do you remember anything about the argument?"

His freckled forehead wrinkled in thought. "Something about a deal at a bar. I don't know where."

Taylor was impressed with what he did remember. It was months and months ago. "I'm sorry, sweetie. So sorry, I wish I could have spared you all that. I wish I could take it all away and make it better."

Ryan leaned his head over onto her shoulder.

"She's coming for me Mama."

Mama. Taylor's heart flipped, she was going to cry after all.

"What?" she asked him. He called her Mama.

"She's coming."

"Who?" Gavin asked, giving her shoulder a squeeze this time. There was a softening around his mouth. He knew. He'd noticed.

Though Taylor felt like crying and laughing and hugging Ryan to her, she figured the bigger deal she made out of it, the more likely he would get embarrassed and she wanted him to call her mama. *Mama.*

"Nina."

The name jerked her attention back to the conversation. "What?"

Ryan took another deep breath, then another. His fingers drummed on his thigh. Gavin reached a hand out and laid it on top of one of Ryan's.

"You've come this far. Don't you want to get the rest out as well?"

Ryan nodded. Looking to Gavin, he asked, "Do you remember the other day in the car when I knew Taylor was crying?"

What were they talking about? Taylor looked to Gavin's whose attention was trained on her son--their son, she corrected. Gavin's brows pulled down before he nodded.

"You never asked how I knew," Ryan said.

No, he hadn't, but he'd sure as hell wanted to. Gavin ran his tongue around his teeth. "Nope, I figured you would tell me when you were ready. Though, God knows, I wanted to ask a million times."

Ryan ducked his head down. "Sometimes--sometimes I see things, or just know things."

Gavin cut his eyes to Taylor who shook her head and shrugged. He could see the strain in her eyes, the pain and confusion.

"What do you mean, Ryan?" he asked this bright amazing boy. God, the things that had come out of his young mouth. Things no nine-year-old should know about. Rage fired through his blood. Gavin felt like hitting something, but he kept his voice steady and calm.

No wonder the kid never opened up to anyone. It was amazing he was as well adjusted as he was.

Finally, Ryan whispered, "I just see things, in my mind. Kinda like a movie or something, or like when you read a book and you get the picture in your mind. Ya know?"

DEADLY TIES   159

"Okay, you see pictures in your mind. What kind of pictures?"

Ryan's breathing started coming faster, quicker, his little chest beating out with the hurried intakes of air.

"Hey. Ryan. Deep breaths," Gavin reminded.

"You're safe here," Taylor told him. "We won't let anything happen to you."

Ryan's fisted hands thumped on his thighs, but he took several deep breaths.

"Is it about what happened?" Taylor asked him. "In Austin?"

The little head shook between them. "No, not really. Sometimes I just know when things are going to happen, or when they are happening. Not always. They're not always right, don't always make any sense. But sometimes I 'see' something and then it'll happen."

Ryan looked quickly from his mother back to him. His clear blue eyes were almost wild with panic. "It's true. I swear it. I'm not making it up. I'm not crazy."

"Of course you're not crazy, sweetie," Taylor said. "We don't think you are."

"I know you're telling us the truth Ryan. We don't expect anything else," Gavin told him.

"You believe me?" his young voice wavered. "I'm not making this up. Like in the hospital the day you two met. I knew before Taylor came home that she'd met a black-haired, blue-eyed doctor would come out and tell her the Gibbons girl didn't make it. And that day in the car. And lots of other times, too."

Gavin had no idea what to believe. But his great-grandmother believed in the Little People and that no sane person walked over a faerie ring. She was a devout Catholic. His mother believed in simply always knowing what the right thing was to do, and Jesslyn believed in the power of dreams.

Taylor laid her hand on Ryan's head. "It's okay, honey. I don't think you're making this up."

But Ryan's eyes were still locked on Gavin.

"What did you see that upset you so much?" Gavin asked him.

The boy took a deep shuddering breath. "It's not real. It can't be real," he whispered brokenly. Tears filled his eyes. "I saw her in a bus wreck so I didn't think anything of it, just a fluke, ya know?"

Actually, Gavin had no idea. Bus wreck?

"Who, Ryan?" Taylor asked.

"Nina. I saw her in a bus, with all these people around her."

Taylor was obviously as lost as he was, but they would get to the bottom of what was terrifying this child.

"Okay. Why did that scare you?" Gavin asked him.

"No, not that. That didn't scare me." Hurried now, Ryan tried to explain. But upset, his explanation was scattered at best. "I saw her at school that way, sitting in math class. The teacher thought I was sick so

160   *Jaycee Clark*

she sent me to the nurse. Sometimes when I see things, bad things, my head hurts."

Gavin looked hard at Ryan. "Does your head hurt now?"

Ryan shook his. "No, not really so much anymore. Not like it did. That's why I sat down on the stairs. It was like this white-hot pain shooting through it. It's never been like that before."

Gavin wondered at that. Was the boy psychic? And what of the pain? As a doctor he was concerned, as a father, he was worried.

"Does it just hurt your head?"

Ryan's hand waved him off. "I don't care about my head. It's what I saw. Last night, before you came in, I was getting ready for bed. I saw her again in a car on a highway. I don't know where, but she was out." Ryan turned back to Taylor. "Can she be out? Would we know? Would anyone have called us?" His questions all but tripped over each other.

"Calm down, honey," Taylor said.

Huffing out a breath, Ryan all but leapt off the couch to stand in front of them. "You don't believe me." Hurt echoed his words, as his small hands fisted at his sides. "She's out! She is. I'm not lying. I saw her. And she…. And she…. She…."

Again his breathing quickened. Gavin leaned up out of the couch and put his hands on Ryan's shoulders. Ryan's freckles stood out on his pale face. Pain, confusion and desperation warred in his eyes as he looked from Gavin to Taylor.

Gavin just looked at him.

"Deep breaths. I know." And Ryan closed his eyes.

"I didn't say I didn't believe you Ryan," Taylor tried.

"Isn't there someone you can call?"

"Yes," both he and Taylor answered.

"Then call them. She's out, Mama. She's out and she's coming here. Tonight, she…. Tonight she…." Big tears rolled down those pale cheeks to drip off his chin.

Gavin couldn't stand anymore. He pulled Ryan into his arms. "Shhhh. It's okay, champ. It's okay."

"No." Ryan pulled out of his arms. "She killed them. She--she shot them. In--in their bed. Blood was everywhere."

What was this? He looked to Taylor who was worrying her lower lip, her brow furrowed in concern and worry.

"Who?"

Ryan's chin trembled. He opened his mouth. "It wasn't real. Tell me it wasn't real."

"What did you see Ryan?" Taylor asked him gently.

"She was in a house. Our old house in Texas. I recognized the hallway." He started to tremble. "She wanted to know where we were. Nina thought the woman was you so she--she just--she just shot her. She just shot her and she didn't even care that it wasn't. But he was

DEADLY TIES   161

yelling at her, and then she shot him too. Nina just shot them. Then she ran."

He looked to Taylor who sat without color.

"Charles? Rhonda?" she asked.

A jerky nod answered her question. Ryan was still trembling and crying. "She's coming. She's coming."

CHAPTER SIXTEEN

Nina Fisher was out. Taylor called Lieutenant Morris, since he was the only cop here she knew, and he called Gatesville.

Damn it.

She'd asked him to check out Charles too, but as yet, they'd heard nothing back.

It was nearly midnight, but Taylor was not remotely tired. She felt wired, jittery and frazzled. Gavin carried Ryan up the stairs and they both tucked him in, despite his murmurs and mumbles.

Poor Ryan. He finally fell asleep, having completely worn himself out. Both she and Gavin had sat with him until he fell asleep. Gavin told them faerie stories, about the Little People.

When Ryan finally fell asleep, she heard Gavin whisper something as he touched Ryan's cheek. *This I'll defend.* What did that mean?

Taylor leaned over and brushed the hair back off his forehead. She had no idea what to think of everything she'd heard that evening. Gavin's hand on her shoulder pulled her gently back towards the door. She saw Ryan had already set his violin on its stand in the corner by his chair and music stand. The posters of faraway places and peoples should have calmed her. This was her home, her and Ryan's, but his words worked on her nerves so that everything seemed like an illusion of peace and security. A fragile shell that could easily be ripped away by the hand of a revengeful junkie. Nina shadowed a danger over their lives.

With one last look at her son, she pulled the door almost closed, but left it cracked. Just in case.

In the hallway, Gavin turned her around and pulled her to him. They just held on. Simply held, as though both needed to make certain the other was there and safe.

She felt the weight of his kiss on her head.

"Come on," he whispered, pulling her with him.

Their footsteps echoed softly on the stairs as they descended hand in hand.

"What did he mean about the car and me crying?" she finally asked him.

Gavin let go of her hand and paced the length of the room and back. His hand ran through his hair. "We were coming here to pick you up and in the middle of a sentence he starts breathing hard and goes stark pale. Tori and Mom were talking to him and he never heard them. His eyes got this faraway look in them. Then, out of the blue he whispered your name. All he said, after he looked around and seemed to realize where he was, was that you were crying; that *he* was making you cry." Gavin's mouth turned rueful. "Charles. Kid hit that one right on."

Taylor shook her head. "I had no idea. He never mentioned anything." Of course, he'd been so adamant that they believe him. Perhaps his silence stemmed from fear. What else was new? Ryan and fear were practically brothers, born of the same abusive woman.

Gavin walked over and sat down on the couch beside her. "It'll be okay," he promised, pulling her to him. "No matter what we learn or hear. It's going to be fine. I swear to you."

He couldn't promise her anything of the sort if Nina was out. But, she didn't say that. Instead, she laid her hand on his chest and her head on his shoulder.

"Well, we have more to discuss with Petropolis than we thought tomorrow, don't we?"

"Hmmm...."

His hand covered hers and squeezed before his fingers started to trace patterns on her inner wrist. Even with the gentle touch, she saw anger still fired his eyes, reminding her of the center of a flame. A muscle bunched in his jaw.

"Gavin?" she asked him.

His eyes cut to her, quickly and sharply. Where was her humorous charmer?

"Are you okay?"

"Fine."

"You don't sound fine. Do you want to talk about it?"

"No."

Taylor pursed her lips, then drew them back between her teeth. "It's hard, isn't it?" she whispered.

Gavin didn't answer her, but kept caressing the back of her hand and arm.

"Do you deal with this sort of thing day in and day out? I mean, I guess I always knew you did, and what with Amy Gibbons I knew. But my God. How can people be so...." He bit off the end on an oath.

Taylor shrugged. "If someone doesn't help them, then who will?"

"How in the hell do you keep from killing someone?"

The charmer was indeed banished. "This vengeful side of you is new."

His guttural sound might have been some sort of answer, but he helped her out. "What can I say? It's in the blood. My mother stems from rebels, my father from Highlanders way the hell back when. So

DEADLY TIES

163

there you have it. Guess I've got that feud-ideology in me after all."

Taylor didn't know what to reply to that, so she didn't. "I could use some of that tea we never got to have. Would you like some?"

"Sure."

In the kitchen Taylor kept busy, tried not to keep looking at the clock wondering if Morris would call.

She had barely walked into the living room again before Gavin said, his voice brooking no argument, "I'm staying tonight."

Did he expect her to argue?

Taylor ran her tongue around her teeth as she handed his glass to him. He took it, the intense gaze steady and daring her to object.

She sat again beside him. "I was hoping you would."

His chest fell as a sigh expelled. "Were you? I wasn't sure."

"Why not?"

"I have no idea. Maybe I'm looking for a fight." His grin was far from humorous. "I'm glad you agreed. I'd have been up half the night worrying about the two of you."

"We've already stayed up half the night," she reminded him.

"So we have. Listen, I want…."

The cordless shrilled.

They both grabbed for it; Gavin handed it off to her.

"Hello?"

The sigh on the other end had her stomach muscles tightening. "Ms. Reese? This is Morris." Like she wouldn't recognize that cigarette-gruffed voice. "We have a problem."

* * * *

The scream pulled them out of their troubled sleep. It went on and on. Taylor was up and running through the door with Gavin.

"No! No! No!" came the yell from Ryan's room.

They burst in, flicked on the light and saw the huddled form in the blankets. His young blue eyes gushing tears, reflecting the terror in his mind, in his soul.

"Ryan!" Gavin shook him. "Ryan!"

Taylor laid her hand on his muscled arm. "Here let me."

Gently, she gathered her tense son to her, rocking. "It's okay, baby. Mama's here. I'm here. It's okay." Humming she tried to calm him. When she felt him start to ease, she sang *Jesus Loves Me*. By the ending he was holding her, hiccupping, and whispering the words along with her, as though they alone would banish whatever demons plagued him.

Taylor pulled back to ask him what he'd dreamed of. But he only held on tighter, his arms vined around her.

"Ryan?" Gavin asked from the other side of the bed. Taylor felt the mattress give as he sat on it. "Ryan?"

Slowly, ever so slowly, Ryan turned his head and looked at Gavin. The man she loved reached out and rubbed Ryan's back. "You okay, champ?"

Ryan nodded. Then shook his head. Finally, he just shrugged.

They hadn't told him about his appointment with Petropolis. She figured she'd mention it this morning. The dawning sky was already heralding a new day. Taylor tried to shake off the tiredness that still pulled at her. The giant red numerals on Ryan's alarm clock said it was almost six.

This time she pulled him back and settled him on the bed between her and Gavin. All of them leaned back against the headboard. Sheets with sailboats on them lay bunched at the foot of the bed, along with the colorful patchwork quilt Ryan used as a blanket.

"Ryan, we have something to tell you."

Actually, they had a hell of a lot to tell him. The things Morris told her… Shaking off the black, horrid thoughts, she said, "Yesterday you were so quiet and we were very worried about you. We called and made an appointment for you this morning." He remained very still between them.

"Is this because of what I told you last night?" he whispered. "About 'seeing' things?"

"No, but I would like for you to talk about that with Dr. Petropolis. I'd…." She looked at Gavin. "*We'd* like to discuss that with her too. You shouldn't feel bad for having such a gift, Ryan. But seeing as how affected you were by the things you saw, and what you remembered, we want to keep the appointment this morning."

Taylor didn't think he would argue, and he didn't. "What time? Will I miss school?"

"Actually, it's at eight."

He only nodded.

Gavin raised his brows at her, and she could only shake her head.

"I'll tell you what." She gave Ryan a squeeze. "Why don't you start to get ready, or just lay up here and rest a bit. I'll go down and start on breakfast. Waffles."

Finally, he moved. Raising his head, he looked at her out of bright eyes. "Homemade ones? From scratch?" His dimples lazily winked at her.

Feigning offense, she gasped. "Do I make any other kind?"

"Not unless you're in a hurry," he answered.

"Well, I'm not in a hurry this morning. We've got plenty of time." She made to get off the bed.

Ryan grabbed her back in a hug. "I love you, Tay--Mama."

This morning's dark cloud did have a ray of sunshine bursting through it.

Taylor smiled. "I love you too, sweetie."

* * * *

Dr. Petropolis folded her hands on her desk and leaned onto her elbows. A classy woman, in Taylor's opinion, always wearing suits

DEADLY TIES

with the perfectly groomed hair. She was middle aged, fit and trim, but her sharp, intuitive mind was what interested Taylor right now.

"I'm glad you brought him in this morning, Ms. Reese." She nodded to Gavin. "And Mr. Kinncaid. I must say I have seen a vast improvement in that child since he first came to see me."

Her smile was soft as she looked at Gavin. "He's crazy about you and the idea of having a real mom and a dad. he told me this morning that he called you Mom, last night--to your face. An idea that has worried him some. As he put it, it felt good, like when you dive into a swimming pool and end up flipping underwater. You're tummy gets all jumbled, but in a good way."

Taylor smiled back. She liked that analogy and knew exactly what he meant.

"Did it bother you at all that he called you mom?" she asked.

Taylor shook her head. "No, the feeling was quite mutual."

"I thought it might be." She turned back to Gavin. "He's still not quite there yet to call you dad."

Gavin nodded. He was drumming his fingers on the arms of the chair, and jiggling his foot that was propped by his ankle on his knee.

"Do you wish to share something, Mr. Kinncaid?" Dr. Petropolis's blonde brows rose above her eyes.

Immediately, he quit the tell-tale signs of nervousness. Then, he leaned up and looked to her.

"I get the impression you both would like to tell me something? Usually the best way is to just get it said."

"I know you can't actually tell me what you and Ryan talked about. But I have to ask if he mentioned 'seeing' things."

The psychologist got up from behind her desk, walked over and sat on the corner of it. "Yes, he did."

Taylor expelled a breath. How to say the next bit? "The thing is, he was upset enough, and with the type of person Nina Fisher is, we called an acquaintance last evening. He found out several interesting things."

The doctor's sharp gray eyes narrowed fractionally.

Taylor hurried through the rest of it. "It seems there was a prison break. And Ms. Fisher has indeed escaped."

Petropolis stood and walked to her window. Turning back to them she said. "Ryan believes what he sees. He knows his 'visions'--for lack of a better term--are not always right, but he believes in them. I've seen many cases in my career that do indeed back parapsychology." Her elegant hand waved. "But that is neither here nor there."

Gavin spoke up. "he told us several things last night. Nina being out was only one of them. There was the night in Austin when she beat him because he'd over heard about a murder. Then there was his....." He gestured to the doctor. "Visions. He was upset over the fact she could be out and coming for him. But he said he saw her kill two people, shoot them in their bed."

"Yes, I know, he told me. A gift or a curse." This time she sat again behind her desk. Giving them a level look, she asked, "Are you telling me that is true as well?"

Yes. Oh, God, yes. Taylor could only nod.

"My, God."

It seemed everyone took a deep breath at the same time and then let it out.

"They're not dead," Taylor clarified. "Well, not exactly. The woman is on life support in hopes to keep the baby alive. Charles, my-ex," she explained, "he's in the hospital but seems to be doing fine. The bullet caught him in the upper shoulder."

"Have you told Ryan?" Dr. Petropolis asked.

"That's what we wanted to talk to you about," Gavin said, reaching out to take Taylor's hand. She grasped it tight.

The doctor looked down at her desktop. Finally, she faced them. "I think you should tell him. One, he needs to know. Two, the longer you wait, the more he may feel betrayed that you didn't trust him enough to tell him what he would consider something he should know. Plus, I believe he needs to be on his guard. However, having said that I think I should warn you. Ryan has been very worried since he thought his biological mother was out of prison. The fact that she is could easily send him into regression. He may not talk at all, retreating into his own little world. Might even pull away from comfort offered. Things you saw in the beginning with him."

This was what she was afraid of. Taylor knew all about regression. She nodded, the calming music playing in the back ground not soothing her at all.

"But, then again, he might surprise you and go the other way, acting as if none of this bothers him. I don't see that happening, but it could. I do know that this will bother him a great deal, be extremely stressful for him, make him question his environment and the stability he's come to know with you two."

Taylor looked to Gavin. A muscle bunched in his jaw.

"That makes you angry, Mr. Kinncaid."

"Hell, yes."

"And me as well. The advice I give you is to tell him. Do not lie, be straightforward and honest. Then be there for him. Don't push him too hard, but don't let him completely shut himself off either."

"How do we know if it's too much or not enough?" Taylor asked.

The doctor smiled again. "You've done an excellent job so far, Ms. Reese. Just do what you've been doing. Mother him. That's all you need to do." She looked at Gavin. "And father him as well. Ryan might even turn to you more during all this. You're distanced from his life before. Though Taylor saved him, so to speak, previously, you've completed a circle in his dreams for a family. You weren't there, so as an outlet, a sort of denial that this could all be happening again, he

DEADLY TIES

167

could turn to you, connect more with you. Though, in actuality, it would be because of the security and safety, the comfort and peace he's learned with you since you've come into their lives. Plus, you are the prominent male figure in his life, and no matter the times, children generally feel better, in a healthy environment, if the male is there to scare away the monsters. Mom can do it, just as well," she added, turning back to Taylor, "but we are still a very sexists society despite all our p.c. tags."

Gavin sat stunned at the doctor's words. Ryan turn to him? Trust in him for safety? And why in the hell wouldn't he? Gavin would do everything in his power to protect the boy. But it was almost terrifying hearing it the way the doctor put it.

He turned to look at Taylor to get her reaction to this. Her eyes were worried, but she gave him half a smile.

"You both have to be there for him in different ways at this time," Dr. Petropolis gently said. "Another thing, I have a feeling Ryan could blame himself after you tell him about the shootings. Make certain you clarify that is not the case."

What? "Do you honestly think, we wouldn't?" Gavin asked her.

A rueful smile passed her lips. "You'd be surprised what I have to explain to some people. I meant no offense." She checked her watch. "I hate to do this because you probably have more questions, but I have a nine fifteen appointment."

So she did. Gavin understood schedules and patients. Trying to juggle time, seemingly personal, caring visits, and the constraint of knowing another patient waited. He rose, pulling Taylor with him.

Dr. Petropolis scribbled a number on her card and handed it to Taylor. "You're fiancé already knows my home number, but here is my mobile. Feel free to call me anytime if things become too … intense. And if Ryan needs to, or wants to, call and schedule another appointment in the morning. I would like to see him in the next couple of days to see how he deals with the news you're about to tell him."

She walked them to the door. "Oh, and though I'm not suppose to break patient/doctor confidentiality, I think I can tell you this. I have no idea what your living arrangements are in regards to a yard, but after all this is over, Ryan really like puppies. Yellow ones."

With that, they walked out of the office smiling and into the waiting room to see Ryan gently kicking his feet off the couch. He stood up when he saw them, apprehension in his eyes.

It was clear even to Gavin that the boy wanted to know what was going on. How to tell him? When to tell him? He'd talk to Taylor about that.

They both had work. He'd already pushed his rounds and appointments back a couple of hours. He needed to get going.

Stopping, he turned Taylor to him and asked her quietly. "Do you think it's okay to send him to school?"

"I don't want to, but I don't want to mess up what he's used to either. I actually wish, for the first time, that I didn't have a job. I want to take him home and keep him safe."

Gavin agreed with her, but knew Ryan wouldn't. "Do you want to take a bit more time off work and tell him now? Or wait until this afternoon. Depending on babies, I should be off my around five." Unless one or two of his patients went into labor. He had several that were close to their due dates.

"That's fine. I'll pick him up after school and just take him to work with me for a couple of hours. When I explained things to Jenkins this morning, she was very understanding. I may have to take off tomorrow after we tell him today, and I'd rather not take off any more days than I absolutely have to."

"We also need to talk to Morris. Do you think we could get Ryan to talk to him? To tell him what he remembered." Taylor only shook her head and shrugged at his question.

Apparently her ex had been coherent enough to tell the police who had shot him and why. A fact that chilled Gavin's blood. Nina Fisher didn't seem to care whom she harmed or killed as long as she got what she wanted. And Gavin knew what she wanted was Ryan.

He walked them both to their car and got into his, giving Ryan a tight hug and promising pizza for supper. Instead of the smile he'd hoped for, Ryan only raised his brows, got into the back seat and buckled his belt.

Taylor hugged and kissed him. Gavin held her longer than necessary, but he didn't want to let her go.

Finally, he pulled back long enough to kiss her again on the forehead. "Be careful."

"I will."

"I know, I just worry." And would keep worrying. "Do you care if I call you during the day? To make sure everything's okay?" Generally, they left the other alone at work, but a few times they had swapped phone messages.

Her smile didn't reach her eyes. "Of course, why wouldn't it be?"

Stupid he supposed. "I don't know. I don't want to bother you, but I'd worry all day. Hell, I will worry all day."

"I know. I will too." Her hand smoothed down his chest. "Tell you what--why don't we make plans for six at the house. I'll order a pizza, since you've already mentioned it to him."

Damn, he forgot. Taylor liked to cook food, so she knew what was in it. She hated preservatives unless occasionally. "Sorry," he said. "I just thought it would be easy and stress free."

"It's fine. Really. He loves pizza."

Ryan opened the door up. "He'd like Chinese. If that's okay?" he asked.

Gavin smiled. Kids heard everything. Looking into Taylor's eyes, he

DEADLY TIES   169

saw some of the tension in them easing. "Sounds good to me. You?" he asked her.

"Fine."

"Then it's settled." Gavin opened her door. He liked this car and it had fewer miles on it than her old one. Maybe he'd get it for her as a wedding present. What to get his son was still a mystery. Actually, come to think of it, maybe the puppy wasn't such a bad idea.

Shaking off the thought, Gavin leaned down into Ryan's still-opened door. "You have fun at school. Don't let any of this bother you, okay? We'll see you this evening."

His palm slapped with Ryan's as the boy's small hand high-fived his. Gavin shut the door again and turned to see Taylor sitting behind the wheel.

"All in?" he asked her.

"Yeah. You be careful, too," she told him.

"Always. I'll talk to you later." He watched her drive out of the parking lot before he walked to his car.

Time to fill his family in on the latest events. When one came after one Kinncaid, they came after them all. Kinncaids stuck together. Though maybe he'd wait. With Dad's blood pressure he didn't need to be worrying. Yeah, maybe he'd wait.

Gavin just hoped all this was for naught, that they'd catch the psychotic woman before she got to D.C., but something told him that wouldn't be the case.

* * * *

Nina took a drag of her cigarette. Rod paced down the side of the car. The Mississippi slugged by, its muddy waters lazily flowing across all that space.

Memphis. She was in Memphis, Tennessee. If she weren't so damn pressed for time, she'd stay and see some of the sights.

The King's Mansion. Freaking Elvis Presley and his Blue Suede Shoes. What-the-hell-ever. She'd just like to ride that riverboat across the way. That might be cool. Boring, but probably cool, like some old western or something.

"I can't believe you shot them!" Rod turned on her again, stalking up to her. "Where the hell did you get a damn gun? You're not supposed to have a fire arm!" A vein ticked in his forehead and his meaty fists rested on his lean hips.

He got so damn worked up over things. "Rod, I'm not supposed to be out of prison either."

"You never told me you were going to kill anyone," he accused. "I thought you were wronged. I thought you were innocent."

She was innocent of lots of things, just not what he thought. Nina shrugged.

"I was wronged." She glared up at him. "They stole my son from me. My flesh and blood."

170   *Jaycee Clark*

His eyelids slowly lowered. "I know, babe. I know. But this is just wrong. That woman was pregnant. You shot her."

Yeah, that had been a mistake. "I didn't mean to. I thought she was Shepard. No one told me they got divorced."

"That doesn't excuse a damn thing, and you know it." His finger pointed at her chest. "You swore after the judge you wouldn't shoot anyone again. You swore."

Nina blew smoke in his face. "So? I lied."

She walked past him, jerked the driver's door open, and slid behind the wheel of the old beat-up convertible they purchased. They stashed his car in an alley in Austin behind the Social Services' office. This one they traded some goods for. It paid to know people.

Rod glared at her, then turned and glared at the river.

Nina almost felt sorry for him. Almost, but not quite.

"Are you coming or not?" she asked. Lots of road to cover. She had wanted to be in D.C. tonight, but it looked more like it would be in the wee hours of the morning. Or maybe not. Maybe they'd stop off in Nashville. She always wanted to see the Music City.

"They'll be expecting us, you know," he finally said, turning to her.

"Yeah, I know. I thought instead of heading straight there, we could stop at a couple of places on the way. Give things some time to settle."

"We could be recognized."

Nina snorted. Was he kidding? Rod looked like a foxy albino with his pale golden eyes and almost-white locks. They were looking for a brown haired clean-cut man. She had chopped and colored her hair.

"Rod," she said, patiently. "That isn't likely to happen."

"Why the hell not?" He strode around the front of the car, jerked his door open and hurled into the seat, slamming the door shut behind him. "That Shepard man you tried to kill saw you."

"It was dark. And besides, I had on a cap." Nina reached up and patted his cheek. "You worry too much."

She cranked on the old engine. "So where do you want to go? See Elvis' home? Or head to Nashville? Or that Music Hall of Fame place?"

Come to think of it, she didn't really know any of the new country artists. She hadn't listened to those twanging songs in years. Metal was more her style. Maybe she'd just stop by a few bars instead.

"I don't really give a flying rat's ass what the hell you want to do." Rod slunked down in his seat, laying his head back against the headrest. "This is a bad idea. A very bad idea."

"What's bad about it?" Nina took her eyes off the road for a second to light another stogie up. "I've got a plan."

"Care to share it?"

"Nope, not yet. I want them to wonder, to worry first. Then, when they start to relax, just a bit, we hit 'em." Her pad of her thumb rapped against the steering wheel.

DEADLY TIES
171

"Hit them? As in kill them?" Rod sat straight up.

Damn straight. Instead, she laughed. "No, just that's when we strike." She gave him a brief glance. "You watch too many movies."

What he didn't know would obviously not hurt him. The question now in her mind was what she would do with Mr. Rod Thomas after she had her use of him. Just leave him somewhere? That wasn't so bad, he could take a lot of the heat off finding her. But he might remember something, and Rod was the type to turn over on his cronies to save his own ass.

Yeah, Rod would have to die later. She looked at him again. A shame really. He was kinda cute in a weird sort of way. But she'd wait and see what happened. Just wait and see.

What to do once they reach D.C.?

Nina, thanks to files on hand at the Social Services's office, knew where Ms. Taylor Reese now worked. Same job, different scenery. Homewrecking families in a different part of the country.

Well, wreck away Ms. Reese. Wreck, away. The day of reckoning is coming.

Nina laughed and drummed her fingers to the song blasting from the radio.

* * * *

Journal Entry

I hate it when I'm right! Hate it. HATE IT! Gavin and Tay--MOM just told me that SHE's out of prison.

I knew she was. I just knew it. But I guess they must have believed me, because they called to find out for me. Then there was the shooting.

I never liked Charles. He was a jerk and he made Taylor cry. But I don't like it that he got shot because of me. And it was because of me. I know, I know. It's not me that shot them, and I didn't make Nina do it. But she wouldn't have gone there if she hadn't been looking for me. But I know it's not really my fault. I do. I just feel really, really bad. Like I should have been able to stop it or something, but I didn't. And that poor little baby. I hope it lives.

Mom called the hospital where Charles is to talk to him, but she wasn't on the phone long and was crying when she got off. Gavin was mad 'cause he thought Charles had said something to make her cry, but she said that wasn't it at all. Charles did hold her partly to blame, or she said that he wanted to. But he also told her to be careful, to make sure I was safe. And because he was nice and he started to cry, Mom started to cry too.

Gavin settled down after that.

After they told me all that, they called Lieutenant Morris again, since he knows what's going on and all. They didn't tell him anything about me 'knowing' things. They lied. Though Mom said it wasn't exactly lying.

Whatever. They told him I had a bad dream and was upset that she

172   *Jaycee Clark*

was out. That was it. They also told him about Charles calling and what had happened. Then I had to talk to him about what happened in Austin. Morris wrote lots of stuff down. He let me look in his little notebook, but he writes kinda like Gavin and I couldn't really read it. But it's still cool that he writes everything down in it.

I asked him what happens if he ever lost it.

He just grinned and said not to say that. I might jinx--isn't that a weird word--him. He hadn't lost it yet, and didn't have a clue what would happen then. Morris asked all sorts of questions. Questions I really didn't like. I had to remember all that stuff I don't want to remember. Finally, he was done and said he'd make some calls and find out something and get back to us, or have someone from Texas get back to us.

I don't know what difference all that made. Morris said that cop might have had a family that wanted answers and now they'll have some. That I was helping. I don't know about all that. I just wish it would all go away.

I wish things were like they used to, before I started to remember all this stuff. Before Nina broke out.

We were planning the wedding. I want to think about the wedding. I think that is cool.

Gavin and I are wearing tuxedoes that are just alike. I get to walk Taylor down the aisle, and get to stand beside Gavin all through the ceremony. I hope I don't have to stand up there too long, but if I do, I guess I'll have to.

Yeah, I'll think about the wedding and my music and not worry about the other. I won't worry about HER. I won't.

I have a REAL family now. Or almost. I almost wish the wedding were already over and that I was really a Kinncaid. I can't wait to be Ryan Kinncaid.

Gavin told me the family mottto. It's: This I'll Defend.

Isn't that cool? I think it's really neat.

I practice writing my new name today. I'm going to show Tori when I see her next time. It's kinda weird, us having the same last name.

Ryan Kinncaid.

David Ryan Kinncaid. I hate my first name. I like Ryan. Guess 'cause I've always been Ryan. Only my Granny ever called me David Ryan. I don't remember her much, I just know I lived with her for a while. But, then she died and I had to live with Nina. Granny smelled like soap and cookies. That's all I really remember about her.

Ryan Kinncaid.

CHAPTER SEVENTEEN

DEADLY TIES
173

"What else do you have on your mind?" Gavin asked her. His fingers tapped on his laptop.

How to tell him? She wasn't sure how he would react. Part of it, she knew he'd probably get mad at her, but that was part of it. The other idea, he might be shocked.

Well, it would *probably* shock him. She never really knew with Gavin. It was more daring than anything she'd ever thought up or dreamed of. But since Rhonda had gotten shot, Taylor realized just what lengths Nina would go to in order to get her flesh and blood. The boundaries she would cross to make Taylor pay. The thought of anyone getting caught in the crossfire again, this time someone who meant the world to her, gave her courage.

"Gavin?"

He was busy typing notes into files. Oval, silver rimmed reading glasses sat his nose. She vaguely wondered if she had ever seen him wear the spectacles before and couldn't remember. No, this was the first time. His dark hair glinted in the lamplight. Tonight, in his rumpled clothes sitting in the corner of her couch, he looked very homey with his shirt unbuttoned and his sleeves rolled up to his elbows.

"Yeah? I'm waiting." The blue tinge of the notebook's screen reflected off the glasses covering his eyes.

Taylor took a deep breath. "What would you say if I called the wedding off?"

For the barest of moments his fingers paused over the keys and then quickly clicked again. "Might I ask why you would wish to do so?"

This wasn't the reaction she had envisioned. It threw her off. "Because."

"That's not an answer." He looked at her over the edge of the silver rims. Something shifted in the depths of his eyes.

"Well, that is...." Taylor sighed. "I just think it would be better if we waited to get married." What if he was here when Nina found them? What if he or a member of his family was killed because of the vendetta this woman had with her? She'd never forgive herself.

"Why?"

Taylor propped her elbow on the back of the couch, resting her temple against her fisted hand. How in could she get him to understand? He kept typing. "I simply think it would be better for the both of us, for everyone if we waited."

"Until?" His thumb hit the space bar twice.

Could the man not stop and look at her?

"Until Nina is caught! Until this is over!" Taylor made to get off the couch.

He moved so quickly, she never saw it coming. His hand manacled her wrist. "Sit down."

Looking down into his eyes, she saw she was off--way off. The blue of his eyes was turbulent, stormy. The skin across his face was tight.

Taylor sat.

"Do you mind explaining all this to me?"

Her chapped lips were rough under the tip of her tongue. "I just...."

"Do *not* insult me by pushing me away." He leaned closer to her, his other hand snaking up around her neck. "If you think I'm just walking away from all this, from you and Ryan, especially now, think again, woman."

"I've upset you," she whispered.

"No, you pissed the hell out of me." His normal smiling mouth, was thinned, the corners tense.

"I'm sorry." She reached up and cupped his cheek. "I just--She'll do anything Gavin. Anything. I don't want to see you get hurt because of me."

His eyes narrowed. "Do you honestly think I'd walk away to let you and Ryan fend for yourselves?" The deep baritone of voice heralded thunder, daring her to agree.

It was ridiculous. Shaking her head, she said, "No, I just thought I'd try to see what happened. And if you wouldn't leave then...."

One black brow arched sardonically. "Then?"

Deep breath. "Then." Taylor lowered her hand, following it with her eyes as it slid it along his corded neck, down to the open collar of his shirt. "Then, I was going to ask you to marry me." Her eyes looked back to his. "This weekend, in Gatlinburg or Vegas or somewhere." Quickly she rushed on. "I know it's sudden. I know it doesn't make sense."

His expression gave nothing away, his brow still lifted above his eye.

"I don't want you hurt. I said that already...." God she was making a muck of this. "She, Nina, shot without thought, without thinking. She was aiming for me. That's what Charles told me. Nina thought Rhonda was me."

The skin on his face was still taut, pulled over his rugged features. The carefree charmer was gone, and in his place the highland warrior half his family lineage told of. "And what? You expected me to turn away from that? You think I haven't realized this?" Both his hands gripped her shoulders. "God Taylor. I don't.... What would.... Damn it." Gavin stood, raking a hand through his hair. The echoes of his footfalls bounced in the quiet room. He whirled to face her, his hands on his hips.

"She is not going to ruin our lives. I'll be damned if she will. We're taking precautions, we've talked to the cops." His finger pointed outside. "There is a patrolman driving by outside every half hour. I'll talk to Aiden about a bodyguard. He got one for Jesslyn last year. Yeah. I realize you're scared, but...."

"Would you just be quiet!" Taylor didn't know who was more

DEADLY TIES
175

shocked, him or her.

He stopped and tilted his head to her. Like a damn lord or something allowing her to speak. Oh! This was all wrong! They were fighting, not that she hadn't thought they might, but....

"I want Ryan to have the Kinncaid name," she blurted out.

"Taylor," Gavin's voice was calm now, as though explaining something for a child. "He will." Gavin walked over and sat beside her again. His hands clasped between his knees.

"No." She turned to him. "Just hear me out please. I'm bad at explanations and I've already screwed this one up." On a sigh, she tried again. "The thing is, with Rhonda I realized how serious this all is. Nina wants my blood, I know that. She swore it to me time and again."

Looking into his eyes, she took a deep breath and said, "If something were to happen to me I want to know that Ryan will be safe. That he won't be bounced back into the system." The thunder was building again. She could all but see the lightning in his sharp eyes. "I want our son to have a family to go to. It might not just be me she attacks or kills."

Taylor laid her hand over his joined ones. "That terrifies me, and makes me want to do something, anything to make you leave. I don't want to see you hurt. But I know you, and I'm selfish enough to want you with me. To help me through this. At least if we were married and you adopted Ryan, he would have you. And if something happened to the both of us--then I know your family wouldn't think twice about taking him in." Would they?

The storm still raged in him, she could see it in his eyes, in the hardened lines of his body, as though he were ready to spring. But his voice was calm. "No, they wouldn't think twice about it."

His sigh blew against their hands. "I see your point." The clock ticked the seconds off.

After several moments she finally asked, "Well?"

When he looked back at her, her heart rolled. That crooked smile would always and forever cause the butterflies to riot in her stomach. Or she hoped it would.

"First, nothing, and I repeat nothing is going to happen to you or Ryan. But other than that, there is one problem with your plan," he said, pulling her towards him as he settled back into the corner of the couch. "Actually, several."

Taylor rolled her eyes. "Forget the problems."

"I can't. There is no way I can take off this weekend to go to Vegas or even Gatlinburg, as much as I want to. I've already swapped weekends and days with doctors for our honeymoon in a few weeks. So the next three weekends, I'm on call."

Well hell. "Oh." Taylor propped her chin on her stacked hands resting on his chest.

"But, I guess we could do the Justice of the Peace thing." The rueful tilt of his lips, and scrunched nose told her what he thought of that one.

"We don't have…."

"Now we do." His arms wrapped around her. "Never thought I was the type for elopement."

"We're not eloping."

"Aren't we? Mom will be so disappointed."

Now she started to see his problems. "Just forget it."

"No." His arms tightened. "The more I think of it, the more I like it. I just wanted to give you a special day, one with flowers, and your dress, and music and an aisle."

It was his wedding day as well. Taylor looked down at his chin.

"I've got an idea," he said. Gavin's arms squeezed her tighter. "I'll go by the courthouse tomorrow and see what we need to do to get married by this weekend. Though, I don't think it'll be a problem. We already planned on a ceremony at Mom and Dad's, so we've got the Maryland marriage license. We can probably get married tomorrow. We'll just have to drive up to Rockville so the judge can do the deed. I guess we should tell Ryan and the rest of the family. And if everyone seems upset, or if you still want to, we can still go ahead and have a big flashy ceremony in four weeks." His breath blew against her hair. "What do you think?"

"I don't know. It seems like a lot of trouble. Maybe we can just have a big reception later. I don't think we have to do the ceremony over do we? Or I guess we can. Whatever."

One side of his mouth lifted in a half-grin. "We'll see."

"So we're getting married?" she asked him.

"Looks like."

Mrs. Gavin Kinncaid, she liked the idea.

Gavin hooked his finger beneath her chin and lifted it to his mouth as he leaned up to meet her.

"You don't mind do you?" she asked him against his lips.

She felt his smile, saw the corners of his eyes crease with amusement. "Mind? That you'll be mine totally, completely and forever by the end of the week? Maybe even by tomorrow night? I hardly think so."

* * * *

Gavin made a few phone calls. They could get married that very day. Since this was a big day for Ryan, they told him and Brayden, but that was it. Gavin gave Taylor a song and dance about it being easier this way. And it would. Mom would probably not speak to him for a week when she found out, but they could still do that big ceremony thing later.

Taylor's chilled fingers cooled his palm. Holding hands, they stood before the desk in Judge Robert McAffery's office.

When they walked out of here, Taylor would be his wife. His. He looked again at her. Coppery strands of hair trailed down from her

DEADLY TIES

French twist. Her gaze was locked on the judge and there was that slight crease on her forehead, but her dimples faintly peeked out.

Everything would be fine.

Out of the corner of her eye, she cut her gaze to him, and her dimples deepened as a pale blush stained her cheeks. He couldn't help it, he smiled. Rushed or not, this was the happiest day of his life.

Gavin called her at work and told her to meet him at her house at eleven-thirty. Since they were both pressed for time, they quickly changed. She wore one of her antique dresses in ivory. It was all silky and cut just like the blue one she'd worn for the ball. Taylor was absolutely beautiful. He called three flower shops that morning to find the bouquet of honeysuckle and roses she held.

Ryan was dressed in pressed chinos, a shirt and tie. Brayden stood to the side clicking pictures from a disposable camera.

"By the power vested in me, and the state of Maryland, I now pronounce you husband and wife." Judge McAffery clasped his hands in front of his waist. "You may kiss the bride."

Gavin looked down into her over-bright eyes and wished this wasn't so damn rushed. Cupping her face, he brushed his thumbs across her lips. Just a breath away, he whispered, "I love you."

Her lips smiled under his as he gave her an open mouth kiss. When her tongue danced with his, Gavin almost forgot where they were.

Brayden's voice brought him back. "Could you put your hand up again? I missed that shot."

Click.

They pulled away laughing.

"I present to you, Mr. and Mrs. Gavin Kinncaid." McAffery shook his hand, and kissed the back of Taylor's. "I still can't believe you tied yourself to this one. Never thought I'd see the day when he settled down."

Gavin rolled his eyes. "Yeah, well, it just took the right woman."

"It always does, son. It always does, with everything in life."

Brayden strolled up and gave her a hug. "All right, now can we really get married, Gorgeous?"

Taylor looked from one to the other.

His brother continued. "Brayden here…" He jerked his thumb towards Gavin. "And I thought we'd pull one last twin prank. You married Brayden. I'm Gavin."

The smile on McAffery's face fell. "Excuse me?"

Gavin punched his brother in the arm.

"No, I married the right one," Taylor said, sliding her arm around his waist. "You're Brayden. And this, is my husband, Gavin." Her hand, holding her bouquet of honeysuckles and roses patted his chest.

"Well," Brayden said on a smile, "it was worth a shot."

"Do you honestly think I wouldn't know?" she drawled.

"Brayden Kinncaid, that was not amusing. Though I'm sure your father would think so," McAffery said, waggling a finger.

"Indeed sir, indeed." Grinning wickedly, Brayden said, "I think you should call Pop now and tell him *all* about it."

A twinkle lit the judge's eyes. "I would dearly love to, but I promised I wouldn't. Now," he said taking a deep breath and turning to Ryan, "I think we have some other business to discuss."

Ryan fidgeted, looking around the room, until he noticed all of them staring at him.

"What?"

Gavin held Taylor's hand and squatted down so that he was eye level with Ryan. "Well, Taylor and I wanted to surprise you. We put a rush on those adoption papers and since this man is a judge, I had him look over everything. Instead of waiting, we thought we would go ahead and sign the adoption papers today. What do you say? You want to become a bona fide Kinncaid today?"

They hadn't told him anything until they picked him up from school. And then he'd only said, he still wanted to walk Taylor down an aisle.

Ryan looked from Gavin, to Taylor, to the judge. "Really?"

Gavin made an 'x' over his chest. "Cross my heart."

He seemed to think about it for a few seconds. Then he looked to the judge. "It'll be legal and everything. She won't ever be able to un-Kinncaid me?"

No one needed to ask who 'she' was. Gavin's heart squeezed.

The judge shook his head. "No, son. Your mom here and the Kinncaids have explained everything to me. I see no reason why you can't become a Kinncaid today, granted you want to. And as for her, she'll never have another thing to do with you."

Finally, Ryan's face lit up, breaking into a huge grin that seemed too big for his nine-year-old face. "Wow."

Taylor hand tightened on his. "Wow," she laughingly said.

For several minutes, Gavin, Taylor and Brayden waited outside. The judge was in his chambers talking to Ryan. After what seemed an eternity, the door opened. Both McAffery and Ryan were smiling.

Papers were signed. The camera kept clicking along with mutters, "Mom's just going to *love* these pictures."

Gavin turned and glared at his brother just as Brayden, grinning, took one more shot. His brother would get his just rewards.

When everyone filed out of the office and into the bright afternoon sun, Brayden held up a hand. "Okay, stop you three. You need a first family picture."

Under the big old sycamore trees, Gavin put his arm around Taylor and they both put their hands on Ryan's shoulders.

Brayden yelled, "Cheese!"

Two more pictures later, they all climbed into the Navigator. Gavin turned to his brother. "Thanks, Bray."

"Mom and Dad are going to strangle you and I'll get in trouble just

DEADLY TIES

for knowing."

Gavin smiled and chuckled. That brought back too many memories to count. "Just like the old days."

Brayden slapped his back as he hugged him. "You take care of them."

Gavin nodded "I will." Hell, he'd have to tell them all sooner or later. "Do you think Mom and Dad would come into town for dinner?"

They could all go to the hotel to eat. Not exactly the way to start a honeymoon, but that was later. Now, was what Gavin worried about. Looking at his watch, he saw it was approaching one. Hell, he had to be at the office at one-thirty.

"Yeah, they probably would." Bray ran his tongue around his top teeth, propping his hands on his hips. Black brows, identical to his own, rose above his shades. "I guess I get to call and ask?"

Gavin only smiled.

"Shit. Yeah, I'm sure they will. Depends on what I tell them though."

True. "Tell them to meet us at *Heather's* in the hotel at seven." Seven should work.

"I doubt Tori and Christian will come, it's a school night. Quinlan's in Ireland and Aiden and Jesslyn flew out to Colorado."

The less the better in Gavin's opinion.

"Fine, but if Christian and Tori can come, make it a family thing and if not, that's fine too."

"Mom's going to grill me."

Gavin smiled. "Of course she will, why do you think I'm having you call her? Tell them it's about the wedding, something's come up.… No, don't tell her that either. Hell, I don't care what you tell her, just get them here."

"I can handle it." Brayden checked the time. "As much as I'd love to stay and chat with you, I need to get to the shop. I have several clients coming this afternoon, and since this was sorta last minute, I couldn't reschedule."

"Yeah, me too. We're both going back to work and dropping Ryan off at school."

Brayden shook his head. "You know if you lived closer to Seneca you could send him to that private school where Tori goes and.…"

"Good-bye Bray. I'll talk to you later." With that, Gavin climbed behind the wheel. "What a day, huh?"

"I'm hungry," Ryan said.

Of course the kid was hungry. It was lunch and he and Taylor were both pressed for time.

"Hey, can we eat at McDonald's?" Ryan asked.

Gavin looked at Taylor. Pathetic. Their first dinner as a family. He felt like he was sliding down on his ratings of suave. She seemed to read his mind.

Grinning she said, "I think that would be a great idea. How about drive through?"

He laughed. Justice of the Peace and McDonald's. "McDonald's it is."

"Memorable." Taylor chuckled.

"Never forget it."

"All right!" Ryan said from the back seat. "Does this mean that this afternoon when I sign my name, I can write Ryan Kinncaid?"

* * * *

Jock listened to his wife's mutters and worries for the last hour. All damn afternoon truth be known. It was beyond him why women talked things to death. 'Course he wasn't the one who talked to Brayden. Or was it Gavin that had called?

Hell if he knew. It was one about the other. But then why in the hell would Brayden have called for Gavin? Weren't his sons grown men?

"You could say something," Kaitlyn said as he pulled under the entrance of the hotel. The valet came running and opened his door.

"I could, yes. But why? When I can't get a word in edge wise." He grabbed hold of the handle above the door to heft himself out of the car. Damn his aging body. But, Kaitlyn leaned over and grabbed his arm.

"I'm worried, Jock. Something is going on. I just know it and it's not good. Not good at all."

Jock sighed and closed his eyes. "What did the boy say when he called?"

"Not a damn useful thing." Her green eyes flashed.

He'd have to have a talk with the twins--those two did nothing but worry their blessed mother since the day they were conceived. Sighing, he took her hand. "I'm sure everything's fine," he lied.

One russet brow cocked. "Jock, Brayden said we had to come to town for dinner at seven. That Gavin had some news to tell us."

"She's probably pregnant or something and they want to move the wedding up," Jock said, patting her hand. This time he got out of the car as she huffed out her side. He tapped the circular hood ornament.

Damn boys. You'd think at least one of them could conceive a child within the sanctity of marriage. Couldn't a bloody one of them keep their blasted zippers shut? Ian--well he wouldn't think about that. But Brayden, then Aiden and now--damned if he wouldn't be right--Gavin.

He nodded to the valet. Kaitie's arm fit into the crook of his arm, and as it always had, it gave him a faint jolt to feel like his arm was made especially for hers to fit into, like an interlocking puzzle.

"We should have had girls," he muttered. "Less trouble."

"Of course, Jock dear. I had such control over the sex of our children." Her heels clicked on the cobbled stones. "And if we had had girls, you'd be going off after some man with your shotgun ready to do him bodily harm when she came and told us she was pregnant before the wedding. It works both ways, dear."

Kaitie had him there. If they had daughters he would have been one

DEADLY TIES

of those over-protective fathers. But that was who he was.

"Still I would have liked to have walked a daughter down the aisle." That old twinge pricked at his heart as it always did when he thought of having a daughter.

But life was life. And he was dealt a herd of roughhousing boys. Boys that seemed to give him lots of grandchildren. Jock smiled at that.

"You'll get to when Christian decides to marry someone."

That caught him off guard. The girl who had shown up on their doorstep so many years ago was not the starving teenager she had been then. She was a grown woman. There was a thought. And God knew he loved her like a daughter. She'd been a part of their family for so long, he took her for granted. He'd never thought of the day Christian Bills might not be around mothering Tori, or helping Brayden.

Maybe the walking down the aisle bit was overrated. Come to think of it, he didn't much care for the thought of giving her to another man, or another family. He liked her just where she was. A Kinncaid. He scowled at his wife, and she only grinned back and patted his arm.

Kaitie went before him when the doorman opened the door for them. His gaze roamed over her. She was over sixty and built like a thirty-year-old--at least to him. Sculpted muscled calves flexed as she walked in her dark emerald silk suite. Her hips might be a bit rounded after bearing five sons, but he liked her ass just the way it was, even when she constantly complained it was too wide. His fingers itched to rub the silk of her suit over her....

"What are you looking at?" she asked him, jerking him out of his fantasy.

Grinning widely, he told her the truth. "You. And how I still think you're the best looking woman God ever put on the earth."

Her eyes rolled. "Honestly, Jock. Can't you keep your mind on matters at hand for more than two seconds?" But he caught the faint blush and the twinkle of her eye.

"Kaitie lass, why worry over something until we know about it. Seems kinda rushing things a bit." They walked to the restaurant.

"Mr. Kinncaid. Mrs. Kinncaid." The *maitre d'* smiled at them. "The rest of your party has been seated." He led them through the restaurant to the back alcove that was reserved for family only.

Gavin, Taylor, Ryan and Brayden were sitting at the round table.

They saw them coming. Everyone stood up. "Dad, Mom, we wondered when you would get here," Gavin said.

"Did you think we weren't coming?" Kaitie asked. He caught the edge to her voice, and he noticed the boys straighten.

This should be fun. The curve of his wife's back stiffened as he guided her around the table to the chair Gavin pulled out for her.

"All right. I want to know right now, what is going on." Kaitie always cut right through the chase when she wanted to.

And something sure as hell was. Brayden was grinning like a damn loon, Gavin wouldn't look either of them in the eye and Taylor was fidgeting. Only Ryan seemed normal.

The boy's grin was so wide; Jock couldn't help but smile back. "Hi, Mr. K."

"Hello, Ryan. You look happy." Jock settled into his chair between his wife and Brayden.

Ryan nodded. "I am." Blue eyes twinkled.

The last time Jock saw the boy, he was quiet and withdrawn.

"Mind if I ask why?" Jock leaned back as the waiter set a glass of water in front of him. He saw the man start to get out his pad, but Jock waved him off.

"Well." Those blue eyes were guileless. "I can't tell you. It's a secret."

Bloody hell. Turning to Taylor he asked, "Are you pregnant?"

Taylor flushed to her hairline.

Brayden started laughing but cut it off soon enough when Jock turned and glared at him.

Gavin started in, "For the love of God, Dad."

"It's a legitimate question," Kaitie said.

"Taylor can't have kids, that why she adopted me," Ryan said.

Well, that was definitely news. And some Jock wished he would have known ahead of time. He hated making an ass of himself.

Looking at Taylor he said, "I do apologize. With this family, that's usually what it is. Sorry."

If that wasn't bad enough, the woman smiled at him, a real smile with joy in her eyes. "No, Mr. Kinncaid. It's okay. Actually…" She looked at Ryan.

Brayden stood. "I need to go check something. How 'bout you come and help me, Ryan?"

The two were barely out of earshot when Kaitie leaned over Gavin and patted Taylor's hand.

"I'm so sorry honey. But, you have a wonderful son in Ryan, and I'm certain you'll find other children to adopt." Kaitie tended to chatter sometimes. "Why between Gavin in obstetrics and my friends still in pediatrics, we're bound to come across plenty of kids that need a good and loving home."

"Kaitie, if they want to adopt, I'm sure they'll go through one of those adoption agencies or Taylor's job."

His wife turned a looked at him. "What's wrong with finding a baby through Gavin's job."

"Did I say a single blessed damn thing was wrong with it?"

Her mouth thinned and those green eyes, the color of expensive emeralds, narrowed.

"Mom, Dad. Stop. Good God," Gavin interrupted.

Jock looked from his wife to his son at Gavin's voice. His son and his soon-to-be daughter-in-law were holding hands and grinning.

DEADLY TIES

Gavin continued, "Actually, it seems Taylor can have kids. But that's not what we have to tell you."

"What do you mean she can?" Jock was getting confused.

"It's a long story, Mr. K.," Taylor told him.

"And it doesn't have a damn thing to do with what we want to tell you," Gavin said.

"Watch your mouth, young man," Kaitie admonished.

"Yes, Mom, sorry." Gavin looked at Taylor. "What we want to tell you will come as a shock, but we have our reasons," Gavin said, exhaling heavily. "It fact, it's pretty bad, or it could be, but we won't let it." Turning back to them, his mouth was tense at the corners, and something shifted in his eyes.

It was the seriousness that had Jock straightening in his chair. Out of all his children, Gavin was the most laid back, the most relaxed.

"Honey, what is it?" His wife's hand reached out and covered her son's, the other seeking his under the table and squeezing tight. "Are you sick?"

"Kaitie, let the boy tell us."

His wife's shoulders rose on her inhale.

"We got married today."

Someone dropped a tray, dishes broke, silverware clattered and glasses tinkled. Jock couldn't have cared less, didn't even turn to look.

"And?" Hell, he thought it was something drastic like cancer or some other disease.

"You did what?" Kaitie asked in that tone he knew all too well.

"No, I'm not sick. It's not what we've done that's got us so worried. We got married, today. It's the reason behind it that has us all walking a proverbial tight rope."

Jock stuck his tongue in his cheek and leaned back. Better the boy handle this one on his own.

"Mom, I know you're disappointed, what with all the plans you've put into the wedding at the house and all." Gavin swallowed.

"And all?" Then she turned on Taylor. "And you went along with this? What of the invitations, the flowers, your dress? It won't matter if you're pregnant or not, that's what everyone will think. 'Oh, it's another Kinncaid, hurried wedding. Wonder how *early* this baby will be born.'" Yes, Kaitie chattered when she was worried, and she'd been damn worried all afternoon.

To be told it was only marriage should have relieved her, and Jock was certain it did, but she needed an outlet--thus the complaints over the *when* of the deed.

"Mrs. Kinncaid, we still want to either have a big ceremony or just a reception in four weeks," Taylor tried. Jock had to give her points. His wife was going to be pissed for a good week over this. Not that Gavin lived at home--no, he'd be the one that had to hear it all.

On a sigh, he sat back up.

"Why? Today?" she asked. "And what? You couldn't call us? Your own parents?" Kaitie did have a point.

"No, Mom. I should have, but it all happened so fast."

Her titian head shook, catching and spinning the lights. "Why?"

Gavin took a deep breath, his eyes narrowing. "It's a long story. Please listen patiently."

"I just can't believe…. At least we were *invited* and *included* in Aiden and Jesslyn's rushed wedding."

Jock rolled his eyes. Maybe longer than a week. Maybe more like a month.

"Mom."

"Don't you 'mom' me. I can understand hurrying through things. Fine, but we raised you better, you could have picked up the damn phone and called."

Yeah, probably a month, at least.

"Why?" she asked again.

Jock squeezed her hand.

She turned on him, her eyes flashing. "What? Are you going to sit there and tell me this doesn't upset you? Our own child.…"

"Kaitie, let them explain."

"It's my fault." Ryan hopped up into his chair.

"Sorry, I kept him busy as long as I could," Brayden dropped down into his seat.

"Did you know of this?" His mother asked him.

"Of?"

"Don't you pull that act with me,"

"Mrs. K?" Ryan started again. "It's my fault. The reason they got married."

That statement shut her up. Jock breathed a sigh of relief.

Gavin turned to Ryan and pointed a finger. "Do *not* say that again. You're mother and I did what we thought was best. None of this is in anyway your fault."

This conversation was getting dizzy.

"Will someone please explain?" Jock asked, leaning up and taking a drink of the water sitting in front of him.

"Taylor and I got married today at the Justice of the Peace. Judge McAffery."

"Robbie?" Jock asked, nodding.

"Yeah, Dad, Robbie. Anyway, there's a reason we needed to get married so quickly."

"Me," Ryan interrupted.

"No, to keep you safe," Gavin countered.

Brayden leaned up. "If I may? The short version is that the woman who gave birth to Ryan has escaped from prison. Not only did Gavin and Taylor get married today, but Ryan is now officially a Kinncaid."

Prison? What the hell was this? Ryan looked down at the tabletop.

DEADLY TIES   185

"Ryan?" Jock asked the boy.

"Dad.…" Gavin started, but Jock cut him off by raising his hand.

"Welcome to the family, son." He stuck his hand across the table and Ryan gingerly shook it. "And Taylor too," he added looking at her.

"I'm sorry, Mrs. K. I know you were all excited about flowers and stuff, and I wanted to walk down the aisle beside Taylor in my tux like Gavin's." His face pulled tight. "But she's out, and she wants me back."

Silence descended.

"I can't go back to her. I just--I just can't. She's not nice. Not nice at all." Blue eyes normally as clear and guileless as a summer sky were shadowed by phantoms Jock couldn't see. Ryan's voice quieted, and his finger traced his scar. "She gave me this, when she threw me or I fell cause she hit me, through a window. I almost died that night."

Kaitie's hand flew to her mouth.

Taylor's hand rested on Ryan's shoulder, rubbing gently. "Honey, you don't have to go into all this."

"Yes, I do. They should know, in case she comes up. What if she goes to their house?" His chin trembled. "What if--what if she thinks I'm there and does the same thing to them she did in Austin because she wants me?"

Ryan's young jaw firmed. Determined eyes turned back to look straight into his. What Jock saw there, caught him off guard. These were not the eyes of a child, but one of a man who had seen too much.

"She – she--Nina just shot them because of me."

What? Turning to Gavin he started to ask whom the boy was talking about.

But again, Gavin was pointing his finger at Ryan. Jock could see the tick in the corner of his son's mouth. "Ryan. I said, I don't want to hear you say that again. Did you pull the trigger?"

Ryan's head shook. "No, sir."

"Did you give her the gun?"

"No, sir, but…."

"Did you help her escape or supply the … woman with drugs?" Now Gavin was leaning low over the table, his voice no more than a whisper, but all the same effective.

"No."

"Okay then."

"Gavin, lay off," Brayden said.

"I will not. I'm sick and tired of the two of them blaming themselves for what this.…" His mouth clamped shut, biting the rest out. "Incubus does. Ryan for not stopping her, for her doing anything bad, and Taylor for feeling guilty that she's not the one on life support."

"Life support?" Kaitie asked.

Taylor swallowed. "Charles and his wife were attacked in their home two nights ago. She broke in and shot them, the woman, thinking I was still Mrs. Charles Shepard. Charles and Rhonda's parents are keeping her on life support in hopes that she'll carry the baby to term."

Holy Mother of God.

Several moments passed in silence. The murmurs filled the air with whitewashing sounds.

Finally, Kaitie leaned over and kissed Gavin's cheek. "You could have just explained," she offered.

Jock couldn't hold the chuckle in. "What in the blessed hell do think he's been trying to do since you laid into him?"

"What's incubus?" Ryan asked.

"It's a sort of demon, or evil person that hurts other people, a nightmare," Brayden offered. "Though I can't remember if it's the female or male version of it."

"Oh." Then Ryan grinned like the little boy he was. "Incubus," he repeated. "Yeah, that's a good description. Cool word too."

"What other words do you like?" Brayden asked him, keeping the conversation light while Jock and Kaitie tried to comprehend everything they'd just learned.

"Oh, lots and lots of words."

"Such as?" Brayden asked, signaling to a waiter who stood holding a tray with a bucketed bottle of champagne. The foiled wrapper glinting in the light. Flutes stood at empty attention.

As Bob, the lucky waiter of the evening, opened the bottle of bubbly and poured the glasses, Jock realized the boy still called them Mr. and Mrs. K. When everyone had a glass of golden sparkles, and Ryan a glass of ginger ale, Bob excused himself.

Ryan, wiggling in his seat, finally answered Brayden. "I like succeed. And conundrum--that's problem. Learned that one in math the other day."

Jock leaned up on his elbows. "Succeed and conundrum, huh? Well, Mr. Ryan Kinncaid. Kaitie here and I have a conundrum you can help us succeed in solving."

Both Kaitie and Ryan looked at him. He continued, looking straight into Ryan's eyes. "We like our grandkids to call us Grams and Pops. Not Mr. and Mrs. K."

"He's right," Kaitie agreed.

Ryan's face lit up with his smile. "Okay. Grams and Pops."

Jock grinned.

Then, he looked at Gavin and nodded to his son, holding his glass up.

Gavin stood. "There's a tradition we Kinncaids hold to. On special days, days of weddings, and births, the men of our family make a solemn vow before his clansmen. Supposedly this goes way back to when we all wore blue paint and lived to fight off the English." His son's gaze scanned the table. "Since we're so few in numbers I guess I'll get to do this again."

Emotion swelled in Jock's chest. His son had become a man. He

DEADLY TIES

187

shook off the thought.

Gavin raised his glass to both Taylor and Ryan and swore, "As those before me have done, and those after will follow, I pledge my love to you, wife of mine. For on this day, you become my helpmeet, my other half. And to my son, a child of heart and love," he added to Ryan. "You both become Kinncaids. And as tradition holds, I swear before all those here: *This I'll defend*."

* * * *

Nina's focus tightened to one sharp point. She'd done a line back at that last rest stop and she was ready to go. Go for fucking ever.

Damn straight.

Damn straight.

Someone screamed on the stereo about drugs and hate. The words stabbed her mind. Kept her seeing the road, what was in front of her, what was behind and where the fuck she was going.

A semi blew past her, the suck of wind tossing into the old convertible they were in. Rod snored in the passenger seat. How in the hell he could sleep with all they had to do was freaking beyond her. Nina patted her thigh as she cruised down I-66. No stopping tonight, no stopping. No way.

They'd finally reached Virginia, big damn state. She had hoped it didn't take nearly as long to drive across as Tennessee did. Nina hated that redneck, hillbilly state. And people thought Texas was bad. Texas was freaking normal. These people were weird.

A sign quickly approached. Zooming past, she caught the words. *Arlington National Cemetery next two exits*.

In the nation's fucking capital. Not long now. She sniffed.

Ryan was here some-damn-where and she'd find him. Him and that Shepard bitch and who-the-hell-ever else was with them.

Have to drive all this damn way for her own freaking kid. The idea that someone had already tipped them off to her escape rushed the blood through her veins. Rush.

She was on a fucking high!

The paper with Taylor Shepard's--no wait. Reese. Like the candy cups. Peanut butter and chocolate. Whatever. Reese? Who the hell was named Reese?

Nina squinted at the next sign. Now which fucking way? Grabbing the map, she tried to see her highlights.

"Wake the hell up and be useful, why don'tchya?" Shoving Rod, his head whipped up.

"Huh?"

"The map. Read the damn map. What's the exit?"

Cars whizzed by. Three o'clock in the morning and people had nothing better to do than drive? Why the hell weren't they at home in bed?

"Where are we?"

"D.C., honey. We're in Washington, D-fucking-C.

CHAPTER EIGHTEEN

Liquid gold surrounded her, flowed through her veins, made her want to weep with its suffocating beauty. Taylor lifted a hand to touch the sun, bright, powerful.

Roughened skin scraped her palm, pulling her from the iridescent dream into the pale dawn of reality. But the wonderful feelings, gossamer in their tangibility, sharp as talons in their intensity, still soared through her.

She felt him shift and thrust within her, and shuddered as heat and need pulsed through her system.

He leaned down, kissed her mouth, his tongue as deft at stroking her to passion as him inside her.

Gavin rose above her, his muscles corded as he braced on his arms. He rocked against her and she rose up to meet him as his grin crooked his mouth.

"Morning, wife."

Taylor could only moan.

"I wondered when you were going to wake up and join me," he said as he leaned down, warm breath whispered against her ear, chills shivered down her spine.

The joining, gentle in its rousing suddenly awoke in a storm of emotion. Wave after wave crashed through Taylor, and all she could do was accept.

He rolled to his side, and pulled her with him, still joined. They lay and touched, caressed and kissed, until she only felt him.

Gavin pulled her leg up to hang over his hip, thrusting deeper, always deeper....

Taylor watched him, the tension in him building, building. Her nerves coiling with each measured stroke.

They rocked together until he reached between them and Taylor gasped as the orgasm all but blindsided her.

Gavin stiffened, the blue of his eyes going opaque as he whispered her name with so much tenderness, her eyes stung.

"I love you," she whispered as his eyes slid closed. His hair was wet through her fingers; water still pearled on his shoulder and back. The fresh scent of soap and mint from toothpaste tickled her nose.

"Love you, more." He grinned. Reaching out, he caressed her breast, his finger drawing circles and shapes on it. She sighed and wiggled. He dropped his hand to her waist. A glance at the clock told her they still

DEADLY TIES

had a couple of hours anyway.

"When did you get in?" The last two words were stretched by her yawn.

Black spiky lashes lay on his cheeks. "A little while ago."

"Was it a boy or a girl?" He'd gotten called out a little after midnight.

"Two boys and two girls," he mumbled.

She watched as he drifted to sleep. The rugged curve of his jaw, the straight line of his nose begged her finger to run over and down them. Taylor simply watched.

Wife. Gavin was always calling her wife. Husband. He was hers and it terrified and thrilled her and calmed her as nothing else in her life ever had. She still couldn't believe she was actually Mrs. Gavin Kinncaid. The ceremony might have been rushed, but she didn't care. Husband, wife, father, mother, son.

Family.

The entire newness of it could almost be overwhelming.

Her head fit perfectly in the crook of his shoulder as his arm curved around her, keeping her close.

"Any more phone calls?"

She barely suppressed the yelp that lodged in her throat at the sound of his voice. "I thought you were asleep," she whispered. "You should be. You're tired, and who knows when your pager will go off again."

His shoulder barely moved under her head with his faint shrug.

The phone calls. She didn't care to get into that right now. Patting his chest, she said, "Go to sleep."

"With all that thinking you're doing?" He opened his eyes, skewering her. "Calls?"

"Only a couple."

"Did they say anything?"

Taylor shook her head. "Do they ever?"

For the last couple of days they got several hang-ups. Or maybe breathing. Once, she could have sworn someone chuckled Ryan, but she couldn't be sure. No caller I.D. It was always unknown.

But she knew, as did Ryan who it was leaving messages and calling all hours of the day and night.

"What aren't you telling me? Is it Ryan?" He started to sit up, but she tightened her arm across him and he stilled.

"No. He's upset, as he has been, and he's not really eating, not like normal. He's gotten so quiet. Last night he had a nightmare."

His screams had brought her awake instantly. She'd been trying to calm him when someone knocked--the patrolman. Seeing her light he'd come up to the door at three a.m. and heard the screams. She assured him everything was fine, that it was a nightmare. What a mess. Damn Nina Fisher.

"What was it about?"

Taylor shook her head. "I have no idea, he wouldn't tell me.

Wouldn't even mutter a word about it, just wanted me to sleep with him. I did." That's what was wrong. "I did. I fell asleep in his room."

"I carried you into this one. You were about to fall off that little bed of his."

"Hmm… That's the only reason you wanted me here?"

His grin was tired and faded slowly. Taylor settled against him, listening to the strong thump of his heart, she too fell asleep.

* * * *

It was noon when a knock echoed through the entryway and into the living area.

Taylor got up to answer it, but Gavin stayed her with his hand on her shoulder. "I'll get it."

Settling back on the couch, she watched the movie and grabbed another handful of popcorn from the coffee table.

"I probably should have called first," Christian's voice said from the front door.

"No, come on in," Gavin offered.

Taylor flicked the television off and walked out of the living room to see Christian and Tori coming through the door.

"Hi," Taylor said.

"Sorry, I have a huge favor to ask."

"Well, I won't do it, unless you come in and sit down," Gavin told Christian.

"Where's Ryan?" Tori asked.

"Upstairs." Taylor jerked her thumb towards the ceiling. "Follow me and I'll show you to his room."

The little girl, dressed in khaki shorts and a blue tank top, started to follow her, carrying a long black case.

"Not so fast, Tori Bori. Where is my hug?" Gavin crossed his arms over his chest.

A single dimple winked in the little girl's cheek as she smiled up at her uncle. Setting the case on the floor, she hurried over and let Gavin lift her up.

"I've missed you squirt." He pulled back a bit. "Have you grown on me? Got an extra rib? I think I should count them."

"No, Uncle Gavin!" She started to squirm even before he started to tickle her.

"One, yeah, you still have that one." His finger squiggled in her side and laughter rang out. "Two. Three. Four."

"Stop. Stop." Her giggles ceased as Gavin set her on the floor. "Really, Uncle Gavin. You just saw me last weekend." She straightened her shirt.

"Well, a lot's happened since then."

Tori turned back to Taylor. "Can I see Ryan now?"

"Sure, come on." Taylor saw Christian and Gavin go into the living room. She and Tori went upstairs and down the hallway. "Here it is."

DEADLY TIES 191

Knocking quickly, she turned the handle. Ryan was looking out the window.

"Ryan? There's someone here to see you." That got his attention.

"Ryan!"

"Tori!" There was that freckled smile Taylor loved so much. "What are you doing here?"

"I brought my keyboard," she said, lifting her black case. "I thought we could play some songs together."

"That'd be cool."

Taylor walked back downstairs, leaving the two kids to their mini-performances.

"You really think she'll try something?" Christian asked.

"We don't know, but we're not taking any chances," Gavin answered as he paced down the length of the living room.

Christian sighed. "Look, I don't want to add to your worry, but I don't know what else to do. Bray's in a meeting till three, it's Becky's day off, and Grams and Pops are playing golf. I got the call a little while ago and these clients are big with a capital 'b'. Really important. They stopped in D.C. for the day but are booked later. This is the only time I can meet them."

"Today is Saturday, can't you wait till Monday?"

"They won't be here. It should only take an hour or so. I'm supposed to meet them for lunch at the Four Seasons."

Gavin's sigh huffed through the room. "Fine. We'll order pizza in or something. I'll call my brother and let him know what's going on." His frown tensed his face.

"I'm sure it'll be okay, Gavin," Taylor offered.

His glare shot arrows across the room as he turned it onto her. "I don't want you or Ryan hurt. And I'll be damned if I drag anymore of my family into this."

Like she dragged him. "I'm sorry," she said.

A muttered oath whispered out as he waved her off. "I didn't mean you were to blame, for God's sake." His cheeks puffed out on his exhale.

"Never mind," Christian said. "You're right. She can go with me and sit in the lobby or I'll get her room or something. I'll figure something out."

Gavin's glare told them both what he thought of that. "Nina Fisher isn't the only crazy nut out there. And that would hardly make a decent impression." One large hand raked through his hair. "Don't worry about it. I'm just testy from lack of sleep. Everyone's right. It's fine. You go to your meeting. We'll take care of the kids. I'll call Bray and let him know what's going on. Besides, we've got a cop sitting outside the house."

The drive by had become a sitting surveillance after Lieutenant Morris, working with the Austin P.D. and the Texas Rangers, realized that Nina had indeed killed a cop, a guard, besides the shooting of the Shepards. A judge's shooting was also linked to her. When the phone calls started two days ago, an unmarked car was always sitting across the street. Though their presence was a relief, it was also stressful. Taylor wasn't used to people always watching her, but with Gavin on call, it was nice to know that the good guys were sitting outside, keeping their eyes open.

Christian looked at her watch. "Okay, I'm supposed to meet them at one, and it's after twelve, so I'm going to get going." Walking up to Gavin, she leaned up on her toes and made him lean down so she could kiss his cheek. "Thanks. I owe you one."

"Just make certain you remember that when I come and ask you to baby-sit."

"Yes, sir." As she reached the doorway where Taylor stood, she reached out and gave Taylor a hug. "You hang in there. This will all be over before you know it, and that woman will be behind bars where she belongs."

"Yeah, but will she stay there, this time?"

In a hurry, Christian swirled out the door. Music drifted down the stairs, a piano mixing with the strains of a violin. Gavin pulled her against him, wrapping his arms around her.

"Why does it seem like I'm over reacting, but I know that I'm not?" His voice whispered into her ear.

This was where she loved to be more than anywhere. Right here in his arms.

"You're not over reacting. I don't think we should let our guard down, or underestimate Ms. Fisher," Taylor mumbled against his shirt. "But, I think one hour will be fine. Besides, you should have seen Ryan's face when he saw Tori. Those two are as tight as thieves."

"Let's go order some food."

"You know, since you've moved in, we've eaten out more than in. It's really not all that healthy."

* * * *

Nina Fisher watched from the minivan--which they'd traded the old car for--parked down the street as the woman climbed back into her silver Volkswagen Bug. Money that one. Where in the hell was the little girl she'd had with her? Didn't matter.

"Where's the girl?" Rod asked.

Maybe he was a bit smarter than she gave him credit for. "Well, I guess she's still inside."

"I don't know about this, Neen."

She hated his nickname for her. Neen. Bean. Clean. Then again she'd always hated her freaking name too.

"Don't know about what?" She straightened her crisp blue shirt. "We've watched them for two days. The SPOC up there in that unmarked." Like the damn cops were so smart. Idiots. "The rich doctor

DEADLY TIES

leaves at all hours to deliver babies." Good looking doctor too. Ms. Reese remarried, another rich man, this one a baby doctor. Nina would bet he knew how to really please a woman.

Her glance shifted over to Rod with his bleached hair. Unlike some people. Not that Rod was completely incompetent, she'd had worse, but then again, she'd also had a hell of a lot better.

"Look, just stick to what we talked about okay?"

His head shook. "I don't know."

"Dammit Rod, I want my kid back. We hope the doc's out, but if he isn't, then we still hit them." It was a good plan. Nina was rather impressed with herself. She wouldn't be breaking and entering. No, the door would easily be opened for her by the very people she was plotting against.

Costumes were wonderful things. She buckled the belt on, replacing the fake gun, with her own nine millimeter. The world was a strange place. Yeah, this plan would work.

Easy as one, two, three. Not that she really *wanted* the brat. It was the principle of the thing. And from what she had seen of the doctor, the newest sucker of one Taylor Reese, he came from money. If he was at home, she'd have to make certain they didn't kill him. After she acted out her little fantasy against the new Mrs. Doctor, perhaps he'd pay to have the little bastard back. Not that she'd give the kid over.

"What about the cop?" Rod asked.

What happened to the days of working with smart people? "You think he'll think twice when I walk up to him? You let me worry about Mr. Bodyguard." Nina climbed from the back into the driver's seat, her uniform completed. "You just get dressed, pull the car around and wait for me. If you see I need some help, then get off your ass and help me. Got it? Just don't screw it up. They *have* to open the door for us, or it's all lost." The alarm she didn't know how to work around, or have the time to find out.

Her gaze was pulled to the house. One happy freaking Brady Bunch. Probably made certain the kids' seat belts were buckled and all that shit. She started the engine and took the next block, driving over three and parking the van. In this neighborhood, a dumb-assed minivan would look as at home as a daisy in a flower bed.

"And we know when to hit 'em. Timing is everything." She flicked the lid of the console and got out her bag of stash. It glinted pale blue in the sunlight, pure as new-fallen snow.

"You really need that?" Rod nagged.

"I say we get ready. Ready to rock-and-freaking-roll."

The powder hit her nose, tingling, stinging until it numbed. When it dropped, she felt the constant irritation she felt towards Rod start to fade.

Rock and Roll. 'Bout damn time.

The waiting was the hard part, but wait she would. Half an hour later, she climbed out and shut the door. Rod wore his old uniform, close enough for the neighborly glances.

"Give me five minutes, then pull around to the front of the house," she told him.

Nina walked quickly down the sidewalk.

"Afternoon," a woman waved from her porch.

Nina stopped, put a finger to her hat. "Afternoon. Have you seen any unusual people hanging around the neighborhood, ma'am?"

"Why, not that I can think of. What's happened?" the woman asked, all full of concern.

"Not a thing, ma'am. Not a thing. If you happen to see anything unusual, please let us know." It was all she could do not to laugh.

"Okay, I will."

Nina walked on down the sidewalk and turned the corner. There was the unmarked sedan. Carefully, she unclipped the gun. Walking up, she planned to tap on the window, but realized the man inside had already rolled it down.

"What's going on?" he asked, his gaze raking over her.

"Just a patrol of the neighborhood. No one's seen anything out of the ordinary, sir," she told him companionably.

"I didn't know about any canvass of the neighborhood."

Nina smiled sweetly and brought the gun up into the window. The two silenced pings were lost in the interior of the car.

The man slumped in the seat.

"That's because there isn't one." She carefully shifted and put the gun back in her holster. Scanning the neighborhood all was quiet. As if she had every right to be there, Nina walked across the street towards the house.

* * * *

Gavin dug around in the pantry looking for plates.

"I like the princess one," Tori said.

There they were. Paper plates were one of man's greatest inventions in his opinion.

"That's a girl's movie. How about the other one with the underworld guys?" Ryan tried yet again.

They were still arguing over what movie to watch. Taylor was upstairs. Gavin tossed the plates to the table and watched as the two kids left the kitchen.

"How 'bout the one with the girl warrior? I like that one," Tori compromised, her voice fading as she and Ryan walked down the hallway.

Okay, plates. Gavin shook his head. He turned back to the pantry. They needed cups and paper towels. The pizza should be here any minute.

The doorbell rang.

"Pizza!" The kids yelled.

DEADLY TIES

195

Gavin leaned into the hallway. "Wait, I'll get it."

A uniformed blue shirt shifted through the glass top of the door. Gavin tossed the cups on the table and started down the hallway.

"Ryan, wait," Taylor said coming down the steps.

But, Ryan had already unlocked the door and started to open it. Suddenly, he went white, gasped and froze. Gavin had seen that look before. In the car when he'd 'seen' something, the night on the stairs when he'd 'seen' something, and the night he 'saw' the Shepard shooting.

"What's wrong?" Tori asked Ryan.

Gavin started running. The door flew open, knocking Tori back.

A uniformed officer grabbed Ryan and pressed a gun to his head. "Stay back."

Gavin skidded to a halt.

A woman. The officer was a woman. Dark short hair. Nina. God help them and she had a gun.

Her eyes flashed at him, Ryan squirmed in her grasp. "Be still." She tightened her hold on his son.

His.

"Let my son go," he told the woman.

Her head tilted. "Your son?"

She tsked and Gavin saw her arm squeeze tighter. Ryan twisted and turned.

"Don't hurt him. Please, don't hurt him," Taylor pleaded, from the stairs.

Damn it, why couldn't Taylor just be quiet. Gavin couldn't see her, but he knew she was above him.

The woman's eyes swiveled at the sound of his wife's voice, and her mouth lifted in a grin.

"Ms. Reese. Long time no see." Nina pulled Ryan harder against her. The long black silencer too damn close to Ryan's head. "I'm just retrieving some stolen property." She glanced at him, then back to Taylor. "You don't mind, do you?"

"Please," Taylor begged. Gavin saw her pale hand on the banister. "Please just let him go. Don't hurt him."

Again, the woman smiled and it was far from pleasant. "Now, why would I hurt him? He's my flesh and blood. Mine." Her eyes pierced them both. "Mine." She shrugged and looked to Taylor. "But he's not the one I *want* to hurt, is he?" She brought the gun up and aimed it at Taylor. He could see the intention in her eyes.

"No!" Gavin shouted.

Two short pings shot through the air.

"Mama!" Ryan screamed.

Gavin heard Taylor fall down the stairs. Oh, Jesus. He took three steps forward.

"Stay."

Her gun leveled back at Ryan. Gavin stopped. Taylor lay on the floor, blood pooling around her. Her eyes stared at him, blinking and unfocused.

Oh God, baby. Hang on.

He looked back up to see Ryan still squirming in her grasp as she inched closer to the open door. He could rush her, but what if she did hurt Ryan? What if she just shot him? He couldn't chance that. God, what the hell was he supposed to do?

"Let him, go," Gavin rasped.

Her throaty chuckle answered him. "Not a chance. He's my ticket to better things in life, doc. You, know, I was going to leave you alive, but...." She started to bring the gun around.

Ryan leaned down and bit Nina's arm.

"You little shit!" Her hold slackened and Ryan wiggled free.

Gavin flew at her, slamming her back against the wall. Another ping sounded and ice burned across his upper arm. Gavin knocked the gun away. It clattered into the living room.

"Run, Ryan! Run!" God the woman was strong.

"Mama." Ryan just stood there.

He heard a whimper from behind the door. Tori!

Nina Fisher was much stronger than she looked.

Her eyes flashed an evil fire at him. "You're pissed cause I did your wife? Trust me, you were wasting yourself on her," she spit out. Her nails raked down his face.

They grappled and wrestled. Pictures flew off the walls as they stumbled into the living room.

Her fingers clawed down his neck.

Gavin hooked his leg around her knees and pulled them both down.

Bitch.

"Run! Ryan!" Gavin glanced over his shoulder to see Ryan holding Tori and pulling her towards the door. Taylor lay still on the floor.

The alarm shrilled out.

Gavin didn't care. A red storm raged through him. He squeezed her throat. "You're not getting your hands on him."

"No!" Ryan yelled.

Nina slapped her fist against his ear right before something crashed into the side of his head and the world grayed and blackened.

* * * *

" 'Bout damn time," Nina told the man who hit Gavin over the head with the little round entry table.

Ryan tried to push Tori back behind the door. They'd set off the alarm. Gavin lay on the floor, not moving. His arm and face bleeding. Was he dead? Had they killed his dad too?

Taylor. Taylor. His mama.... Blood seeped slowly across the floor.

"Get the kids," Nina said, her voice raw.

Ryan tried to make himself move, but he couldn't. He couldn't leave

DEADLY TIES 197

Gavin, and Taylor and Tori.

The man's hands closed around his arm. The contact broke him out of his stupor. Ryan fought against the hold. "Let go! Let me go!"

"Help! HELP!" Tori screamed. "Help!"

"Be still." Nina stumbled into the entry, grabbed Tori, and hit her. "Shut up. You," she pointed to Ryan. "You do what you're supposed to and I won't have to hurt your little playmate here."

"Just leave her here," Ryan tried. Please let her leave Tori.

"No."

They all stumbled into the harsh light.

"But you don't need her," Ryan tried again. "She's just scared. Leave her here."

The man picked him up. "Be quiet kid."

A van waited out by the curb, the back door open.

Where were the cops? Why wasn't anyone helping them.

"Goddammit Rod, move your ass!"

Ryan was tossed into the van, Tori was thrown in after him.

"Down. Get down on the fucking floor, now!" Nina hopped in after them, aiming the gun in their direction and sliding the door shut.

Tori crawled to him, wrapping her arms around him. He held her and prayed that they'd both be safe.

He'd been right all along, happy endings never happened.

* * * *

Someone kept screaming. Why wouldn't they stop?

"Ryan?" Taylor croaked out. "Gavin?"

It felt like someone lit a fire in her chest. Taylor licked the side of her mouth. The coppery taste of blood thick on her tongue.

Someone was screaming. Weren't they?

What was she doing down here? She didn't remember falling, didn't remember tumbling down the steps.

The world grayed around her.

Nina!

No. The kids. Oh, God, please protect the children.

Gavin?

Taylor lay on the floor. She could feel the blood seeping out of her, could see the smear of it across the wall above her.

Her chest no longer burned. It was cold, so cold. As though death breathed over her and sat waiting in her living room.

Ryan. Her poor little boy. She didn't protect him, and Tori. Oh, God.

She turned her head. Gavin. No. His eyes were closed and blood slithered down from his hairline. Please God, let him be alive. Please.

Something ... she had to help. Help. Get help. Taylor tried to move her hand. Tried to move....

The ceiling pitched and rolled above her, the walls tilted.

Someone help. Please, God help my child, protect them both....

The world went black.

198   *Jaycee Clark*

* * * *

Gavin heard voices.

"Check out back. Where the hell's the goddamn ambulance?"

He opened his eyes. A cold fire burned across his arm, and it felt like someone took a sledgehammer to his....

The kids!

Gavin rolled over to his knees.

"Mr. Kinncaid?" Someone squatted down beside him.

He tried to focus on them as nausea rolled up his throat. Gavin swallowed, shut his eyes, then opened them trying to ignore the pain screaming through his head.

Him. Morris.

Taylor! Gavin pushed himself to his feet and stumbled to his wife. Oh, Christ.

No. He shook his head, clearing his vision, shoving the nausea down. "Taylor?"

Gavin fell to his knees beside her, her blood soaked into the trousers of his knees. He felt for a pulse, her fingers like ice.

"Kinncaid? The ambulance is on the way."

Please, by the Grace of God, please. Her head lolled as he tried again to find a heartbeat, the flesh of her neck warm. Barely, it was barely there, and too damn fast. Blood loss. "Hang on, baby. Just hang on." A gurgling sound came from Taylor. He ripped her shirt open. Dammit. She caught a bullet in the lung.

Think, he had to think. Gavin stood and stumbled to the kitchen, tearing a drawer open, jerking out the Saran Wrap. His fingers left a trail of blood on the doorframe as he hurried back to Taylor. On a muttered oath, he fumbled and ripped a long sheet of the clear plastic and covered the wound to keep the air from escaping.

"Give me your phone," he told Morris. He grabbed it and dialed, his hand shaking so bad he could barely punch the damn buttons.

"This is Dr. Kinncaid. I've got a sucking chest wound from a gunshot at…" He rattled off the address. Pain shot through his head. Morris had told him the EMTs were on their way. Think, he had to think, for Taylor. "Ambulance is en route. She's got a pulse, low BP. I need a crash cart and at least four units of blood ready at Sibly. And make damn certain there's a vascular surgeon standing by ready to take her to the O.R. or I'll have someone's fucking head." He threw the phone to Morris. People moved and rushed around him.

Looking up he saw Morris' serious face. Oh, God, the kids. "Ryan?" he croaked out. Tori? What if they were dead upstairs? He started to stand.

Morris shook his buzzed head. "No one else is here, Mr. Kinncaid." He pointed to Taylor. "Is she alive?"

"Barely." Sirens blared.

"Gavin?" Christian stood in the doorway, with another policeman,

DEADLY TIES

her face stark white. "Oh, God. Oh, my God." Her eyes flew up to catch his.

"She's alive for now, and by Christ, she's staying that way."

"The kids?" Christian asked.

"Kids? Plural?" Morris asked, grabbing his phone back.

"Yeah, my son Ryan Kinncaid, and my niece Victoria Kinncaid." He wiped blood out of his eye. "She took them."

* * * *

Please, God, just don't let her die. Just don't let her die.

They pulled up at the hospital, the sirens pierced the air. Gavin ran beside the gurney, latched onto it near the head. Taylor was lost beneath a mound of blankets and machines. The hose leading into her mouth obscene to him, even as he knew the intubation helped save her life.

She'd probably need a chest tube, and if the bleeding didn't stop.... He couldn't think of that. Gently he leaned over and kissed her forehead, "I'm sorry, I'm so damn sorry."

One of the EMTs put her hand on his arm.

"BP's dropping." Machine's whined and blipped. They raced her through the ER doors and down a hallway.

"She's coding," someone said.

Damned if she would. "You are not going to die on me. We've got to get our son back and you've got to help me. Don't you dare die on me."

"BP's fifty over forty. Gave her two units of O-neg, one unit saline...." The shouted words stabbed at him.

"Trauma one." Another voice yelled.

Gavin started to follow them into the crash room, but a nurse shot an arm up to stop him. "You can't go in there."

"The hell I can't. That's my wife. I'm a doctor."

"Be that as it may, you know the rules."

"Fuck the rules."

"Gavin."

He turned at the new voice. Dr. Joseph Ellis stood there in scrubs. Gavin fisted his hands.

"Look, I won't say I know what you're going through, but we've got to stabilize her and get her into surgery. You'll do us no good in there." He laid a hand on Gavin's shoulder and it was all Gavin could do not to throw him off. "You'll be more help to her, to us, if you stay out here, answer questions and talk to the cops."

Through the glass panels he could see them working on her, her head lolling on the gurney, blood soaking her bra. Sweet Jesus Christ. Gavin knew the man was right. But he felt so helpless. Closing his eyes, he nodded.

"Fine, I'll stay out of your way. But I'm not moving from here. I've a right to stand here." He opened his eyes, daring the other doctor to argue.

Ellis didn't. "I'll hold you to that and keep you updated. I'll let you know when we take her up to surgery. Get someone to look at that laceration on your arm and head. You look like you have a concussion." The door swung shut behind the doctor.

Gavin didn't give a damn about his arm or his head. All he cared about was his wife.

Masks moved as orders were barked, instruments used, people in green and blue scrubs hurrying around.

He had no idea how long he stood there, how much time passed. All he saw, all he thought about was Taylor, her pale bleeding body lying on that table, as he trusted others to save her.

* * * *

Nina grinned over at Rod as they drove down the highway. "Fucking-A we pulled it off." She glanced in the back and saw the kids holding onto each other. This was something she hadn't expected.

"Why in the hell did you bring the girl? We're kidnapping. That's a serious crime. And at gunpoint. Shit."

Rod could be as dumb as a box of damn rocks. Like kidnapping was a major thing to worry about, he'd better worry a bit more about his accomplice to murder.

"You'd rather I put a bullet in her?" Nina asked him sweetly.

His glare told her what he thought of that. "You could have left her there."

"I could have, but it was easier to get Ryan to go with us if I used her. Want the kid to do anything, just use the girl. Don't know where he gets it." Soft hearts got you nowhere. Blood and adrenaline raced through her system.

"I've got a bad feeling about this, Neen." Traffic whizzed by them as he kept to the speed limit. "I was reading the paper while you went to the house. These Kinncaids are rich and powerful. I don't think we should have nabbed their kids."

"Ryan is mine. MINE! He's not a fucking Kinncaid!"

Rod took a deep breath. "Fine, I don't think we should have taken the girl."

"Well, you're not along to think are you?" she spat at him. Idiot, damned idiot! But something he said, clicked. "Look, we knew the doc was loaded."

Rod shook his head. "No, I mean more than loaded."

"Rich? How rich?"

He shrugged. "I don't know, they own a hotel here in D.C. or something."

Nina turned in her seat to look at the kids. "Is this true?" Neither of them answered her.

"Is this true?" she shouted.

Ryan nodded, and the girl followed, jerking her head up and down.

DEADLY TIES

Rich, huh? Hot damn

"This might just work even better." She had been thinking she could knock the girl out and just leave her somewhere and take Ryan with her. After all, she knew Mr. Doctor would probably pay to *think* he was getting the boy back. But lots of money changed things. Money with a capital 'M' changed everything. If these were really wealthy people, they'd pay to have both kids back. And probably meet any price she asked for. Yeah, for enough dough, Nina would happily hand Ryan over. Not that she cared either way. Nina didn't think she had the stomach to kill her own flesh and blood, if it ever came to that.... But she could sure as hell use him to get ahead in this world. Fucking-A-Right, she could. She might just let the doc pay to have the little shit back for real.

"You talking a flea trap, regular motels, or a bonified, ritzy thing?"

Rod looked into the mirror. "I don't know, ask them."

"You're family own, like Holiday Inn, or Motel 6?" she asked.

The girl raised one brow, "Hardly." And that was all she said in her perfectly cultured young voice that pissed the hell out of Nina.

Feeling daring, she grabbed Ryan and hauled him to her to get the girl to answer. "Hardly what?"

The girl's chin trembled. "We own five star hotels and resorts."

"So, your family is really rich, kid?"

The girl looked away and shrugged, "I guess so, I don't really know."

Well, there was a way to find out. How did a kid know how much they had if they'd been spoiled all their little pampered lives?

"What kind of house do you live in? Is it big?"

"Yes, I live with my grandparents, unless I stay at the hotel with Daddy."

"Don't tell her another thing, Tori." Ryan said.

"Shut the hell up, brat." Nina hit him upside the head with the gun. It was time he remembered who his mother was.

"Lots of cars? Been many places?" she fished.

Looking at Ryan, then back at her, the girl told Nina she could use Ryan as a lever just like she used the girl. "Yes."

Hot damn.

"You're daddy would pay lots of money to get a pretty little thing like you back wouldn't he?" Nina asked. She wouldn't say she'd kill the girl in the ransom note, or call. No, she had something better. Sure to make any daddy's heart fill with terror and rage at the very idea.

Nina had a plan.

CHAPTER NINETEEN

Gavin moved to the side so that the hallway was clear. The familiar hospital noises around him were now foreign, piercing his soul with every squeak, clatter, yell or cry.

A nurse had finally pulled him away long enough to stitch his arm where the bullet grazed, a dose of antibiotics, and put a butterfly bandage on his head. He'd declined the pain meds. She'd wanted him to stay in bed, he had a concussion. Gavin couldn't have cared less. Someone had come in to try and ask them questions and he'd answered what he could.

He turned back to look in the trauma room. The doctors and nurses worked furiously on Taylor, their hands covered with her blood, he couldn't leave. God he couldn't leave. His eyes stung and he swiped viciously at them.

When he spotted the saw, he knew what was coming and God, there was just no way he could watch that. Closing his eyes, he leaned his head back against the wall, felt another useless tear slide down his cheek.

God forgive him, he hadn't kept her safe, didn't protect her like he was suppose to. Didn't protect Ryan ... or Tori.... Shit. It felt as if someone reached in his chest and squeezed his heart until he couldn't breathe.

"Gavin?"

He opened his eyes to see Brayden standing there. His brother's face pulled pale and taut. Oh, shit. The kids.

"Bray ... I'm--I'm sorry. I'm so damn...."

"Don't." The word lashed out. His brother stood with his hands on his hips. "Just don't."

He couldn't very well blame his brother. Brayden looked past him into the trauma room. Taking two steps, he looked through the glass and what color was left in his face fled. "Christ."

Gavin glanced into the room to see someone straddling his wife, using the rib spreader to crack her chest open. Bile rose in the back of his throat.

They had to stop the bleeding. They had to stop the bleeding. In order to save her life, they had to stop the bleeding.

Knowing the medical reason for what they were doing was completely different when it was someone you loved in there. Moaning a curse, he wiped his eyes again and forced himself to look back at his brother.

Bray turned on him. "How in the ever living hell can you stand here and watch that?"

Gavin bit down till until pain radiated up his jaw. "I can't leave. I just can't leave her," he finally managed.

Something shifted in his twin's face. Bray reached up and grabbed his arm. "Come on."

With one look over his shoulder, Gavin followed his brother around

DEADLY TIES

the corner and into the waiting room. Christian sat crying in one of the chairs, Morris sitting beside her, other uniformed and plain-clothes policemen stood by talking quietly.

Before they reached the group, Gavin slowed. "I know you're pissed at me. I don't blame you."

Brayden stopped, his arm dropping to his side, and his chin hitting his chest. When he looked back up, fury shot from his eyes. "It would be easy to blame you, or to blame Christian for dropping Tori off. But it could have been any of us. Any of us. What if the kids had been with Mom and Dad? What if they had been with me? My God, you both could have been killed. You're my damn brother, I don't...." Bray trailed off.

When he continued, it was softer. "It's bad enough that we have to tell Mom and Dad about the kids. I'm just glad I don't have to tell them their son is fighting for his life, along with his new wife. You could easily be in there too!" His hand jabbed at the air in the direction of the trauma room.

"None of it makes a shit, Gav. The point is the woman who put your wife in that trauma room is the same one who has our kids. Don't blame yourself, not right now. We've got to think, to call everyone, figure out what the hell to do. Besides, Christian is blaming herself enough for the both of us."

Bray's gaze studied him. "What the hell happened to you? You really look like you should be in one of those rooms."

"I'm fine," Gavin brushed his brother off. He rubbed his hands over his face, the coppery scent of blood filled his nostrils. His hands were streaked rust, and he realized his clothes were bloody. "Oh God."

For the first time since med school he felt lightheaded at the sight of blood. Taylor's blood, his head swam and his knees weakened. He didn't have time for this. Clamping down, he swallowed past the knot in his throat. Taking a deep breath, he asked. "How did you get here so quick?"

"Broke several speeding laws." Bray looked at him again. "Are you sure you're okay?"

"A bullet grazed my arm. Something hit my head. Someone else must have been with her."

He tried to remember exactly what happened.

"Come on, let's talk to Morris."

Bray led him over to the chairs and the cops. Gavin couldn't sit. He paced.

Morris cleared his throat. "I can't image what all you are going through, but I need you're help right now. First off, I need a picture of both the kids."

"Fine," both he and Brayden answered.

Then something that had been bothering him registered. "Where in the hell was the guy who was supposed to be watching our house?"

Gavin asked, furious that the police hadn't done their jobs. Raging at himself for failing to protect his own damn family.

Morris's dark eyes sharpened. "Sergeant Rivers is dead, Mr. Kinncaid. Murdered while sitting in the car. After I finish here, I get to go tell his wife that he's not coming home."

Shit.

Morris's phone rang. "Excuse me."

When he walked away, Gavin turned to Brayden. "Have you called Mom and Dad yet?"

Bray shook his head. "No, but Quinlan's at home. I'll give him a call and tell him to go out to the Country Club and get them."

Gavin said, "Tell him--Tell him not to tell them until they get here, or.... Hell, I don't know. This could easily send Dad back into the hospital."

"Just what we need, a cardiac arrest. I'll tell him to do what he thinks is best. You give Aiden and Jess a call, they'll want to know." Brayden walked out the hospital doors. Gavin walked to the nearest line based phone.

He got off the phone with his brother, knowing Aiden and Jess were leaving immediately for home. And they'd keep calling to find out what was going on.

As he turned around, Dr. Ellis strode towards him, and he saw a gurney come out of the trauma room and head towards the staff elevators. "We've managed to stabilize her, and finally to stop the bleeding. It's time to get her to the OR."

He held out his hand. "Thanks, Joseph. I--Thanks."

The short doctor only raised his brow before he turned and jogged to catch the elevator.

Relief slowly trickled through Gavin. Not that surgery was without its complications and risks, but it was a step up from where they had been.

By God, he might be a doctor, for all the damn good it was doing him right now, but if saw the woman who did this.... He'd rip her apart with his bare hands and leave the pieces for someone else to deal with.

Healer or no, Taylor and Ryan were his and Nina Fisher had dared to harm that. If it was the last thing he ever did, Gavin vowed he'd find Nina Fisher and make her pay.

* * * *

Aiden hung up the phone, striding to their bedroom and grabbing a small bag. They could leave the rest and take only what they needed.

"What's going on?" Jessie asked.

He held up a finger and dialed the Gunnison airport, arranging for the jet to be ready in half an hour.

"What Aiden? What's happened?" She held one the twins on her shoulder, concern clear in her eyes.

"Taylor's been shot and the kids have been kidnapped." Aiden raked their toiletries into an overnight. "Pack only what we need. We're

DEADLY TIES   205

leaving in fifteen minutes."

"Oh, my God. Aiden."

Just for a moment, he pulled her close, breathed in her light airy scent that mixed with the powder and milk of his infant son. Thank God his family was safe. But his brothers. The kids.

"Kids?" she asked, pulling away from him.

"Yeah, both Ryan and Tori. We're going home." He patted her back and she pulled away.

"Of course. I'll go tell Anna and we'll get the boys' things together." She stopped at the door. "Are you going to call him?"

He didn't need to ask who 'him' was. No one in the family talked to their other brother, Ian, but Aiden. Then again, no one knew he talked to the elusive black sheep of the family. No one, but Jessie. Nodding, he got the phone back out and dialed a sequence of numbers he received on a postcard a couple of weeks ago. he said what he always did then hung up.

They were walking out the door and piling into the leased SUV when his phone rang.

"All right, I'm secure but time's short. What's up?" his brother's gravelly voice said.

"We've got a hell of a problem," he answered, filling in the information. Finally he said, "I don't know if you can help, but I knew you'd want to know."

"Who the hell is it again?"

"Fisher, we think. Nina Fisher. Look, the boys are going to be going out of their minds. Do you want me to mention this--mention you--to them?"

A long pause answered him. Aiden knew the dynamics of the knowledge he held. He, and only he, knew of Ian keeping in touch with the family. Aiden also knew that whatever his brother was into was not the average job. He didn't ask, but had his suspicions.

"Let me think on it. Is this the phone you'll be on? Where are you now?"

"Colorado, but I'm about to get on the jet and head home." Doors shut and still he waited for his brother's reply.

"Keep your phone charged. I'll call you."

And that was that.

In no time, Aiden and his crew were flying home. Who in the hell would risk taking one of theirs?

* * * *

"What in the hell is going on?" Jock asked again. They were speeding towards town. Kaitie sat in the back seat. Quinlan whizzed them in and out of traffic. Jock grabbed the handle above the door. "You trying to kill us?"

"No."

"Then answer the damn question. What the hell's happened?" Jock wanted answers.

His son sighed, checked his mirror before swerving over into the other lane, passing yet another car. Quinlan's fingers drummed on the steering wheel.

Jock wondered if his child thought he was stupid. First off, the boy never did a blessed thing but work. When they'd seen him at the clubhouse they knew something was up. He'd only told them to come on, they had to get to town now, and they'd left without a question. But they'd questioned the hell out of him since then, little damn good it did.

"Quinlan, darling, your father and I are worried. It would be better if you just told us," Kaitie said gently from the back seat.

Quinlan's gaze flicked to the mirror. "Do you have his nitro pills?"

That did it. "I am a grown man, I think…."

"Jock." Kaitie had a voice you didn't argue with.

Fine.

"Quinlan, tell us now. The not knowing is worse." Her hand reached out and grabbed his. Jock gave it a squeeze.

Quinlan licked his lips. "There was…. Someone…."

"Just spit it out, damn it." The boy would send his blood pressure soaring just by stuttering around.

"Taylor's in the hospital, and the boys wanted me to bring you to the hospital so you wouldn't worry."

"What's wrong with her?"

A pause. "I'm not exactly sure."

"Quinlan," Kaitie said from the back seat.

His son sighed again, apparently he recognized the voice too. "Brayden said she'd been shot."

"Shot? Oh my. Oh no." Kaitie's hand squeezed his.

"Is she okay?" Jock asked.

Quinlan's lips compressed.

"Is she okay?" he asked again.

"I don't know," Quinlan admitted. "Honest. All I know is that she was shot and they were working on her."

Why? "Who on earth would shoot that woman?" Even as he asked it, he knew.

"We've got to get there. Poor Gavin, and little Ryan. That child will be utterly distraught," Kaitie mumbled.

Since Jock was watching his youngest son, he saw the narrow of the eyes, the tightening of his son's grip on the wheel until his knuckles were white.

"Quinlan? What else?" he asked.

They stopped at a red light and Quinlan turned from it to look at him. The green of his eyes, so like his mother's, was furious and worried. He cleared his throat. "I might as well tell you. Now. So you'll know when we get there." He took a deep breath, checked the light. "Whoever shot Taylor, took the kids."

DEADLY TIES

"Oh my God," Kaitie's hand vised on his.

"Kids?" he asked.

"Ryan and Tori."

"No. No," Kaitie said.

Jock turned in his seat, grabbed her other fist. The bastards, who ever the hell they were, would pay.

He didn't come this far in life, to create the family they had, to build the empire he had to see some two-bit whore bring it all down.

"Kaitie." Her glistening eyes rose to his. Tears trickled down her pale, freckled cheeks. "Kaitlyn lass, we'll find them. We'll find them, I promise you."

And when they did....

Dammit, there was the damn tightness. Fumbling, he reached into his pocket and pulled out the little pill bottle. Kaitie still had hold of one of his hands, but he didn't care. Laying one powdery white pill under his tongue, he cursed his age and health, and cursed whoever was stupid enough to steal his grandkids.

* * * *

Gavin paced the waiting room. He'd changed out of his bloody clothes and wore scrubs. Everyone was there except Aiden and Jesslyn. They were waiting on Taylor to get out of surgery. He stopped again and looked at the clock. Four hours. It had been four damn hours and not a word. Not a single word.

At least the waiting room was empty except for his family.

Gavin rubbed his hands over his face and tried not to think what the time meant, what was happening with the kids, what could still go wrong....

"Honey, come sit down," his mother said, handing him a cup of water.

"I don't want to sit, Mom. I can't sit." He took a sip of water and set the cup aside, pacing again.

Whispers and quiet voices drifted around him. All he could think about was the look in Nina's eyes. How she hadn't thought twice about using Ryan, threatening Ryan, and some part of him knew, she could easily kill his son. Just as easily as she'd shot Taylor.

God.

The door squeaked open.

Gavin whirled.

Joseph stood there, in bloody scrubs, looking exhausted.

The silence was so loud, it breathed.

"Joseph?"

The doctor ran his hand over his face. "Gavin, let's sit down."

"Oh, Jesus."

Someone helped him into a chair.

Joseph sat in the one next to him and faced him.

Gavin couldn't take his eyes from Joseph's hazel ones. "She's still alive, but barely."

All Gavin heard was that she was alive. Alive. "Thank God."

Joseph sighed again. "Gavin, I'm not certain if she'll make it through the night, it's going to be touch and go."

She was going to live. She was too much of a fighter.

His mother rubbed his shoulder. "Taylor will make it, doctor. I don't doubt it."

Wrinkles creased around Joseph's eyes. He licked his lips.

There was something else.

"Something happened in the surgery. What?" Gavin asked.

Joseph opened his mouth, closed it, then looked away. Finally, he said, "We lost her twice, got her back. You're right in that fact she's a fighter. But her body can only sustain so much shock. With the shooting, blood loss, surgery and…." He trailed off.

"And?" Gavin asked, his gut tightening.

Joseph put his hand on Gavin's arm. "She was pregnant. I'm sorry."

Was. She was pregnant. A baby. His baby. Their baby. God. Gavin's eyes slid closed.

Sickness rose up in him. He nodded.

"There was nothing we could do."

Again Gavin nodded.

"I'm sorry," Joseph added standing.

"When --" Gavin cleared his throat. "When can I see her?" He took a deep breath. All that mattered right now was her and finding the kids.

"We're getting her set up in S.I.C.U. You can see her as soon as she's settled."

Gavin stood. "Thanks, Joseph."

With that the man walked out of the room.

Gavin stared at the closed door. His wife, his son, his niece, his baby. He couldn't breathe. Tears pricked the backs of his eyes and he swallowed.

"Sit down," Brayden said, taking his arm.

Gavin sat, buried his face in his hands.

Someone sat beside him.

"It'll be okay, honey," his mother said, rubbing his back. "It's all going to be okay." Her voice wavered on the end.

Tears leaked, fell into his hands. Looking at his mother he said. "My kids, she's taken my kids from me, and Taylor.… How can.… What am…." He swallowed, felt the trickle down his cheek. "Taylor wanted a baby, Mom. She really, really wanted a baby." And now she was fighting for her life.

"I know. I know she did." His mother pulled him to her, wrapped her arms around him.

Gavin squeezed the tears back and hugged his mother.

* * * *

Taylor was on a respirator and had so damned many tubes and wires

DEADLY TIES
209

hooked to her, Gavin had to take a break. He couldn't stand to see her like that. Not Taylor, not his wife.

So now, he was here, pacing with his family and the cops. For the first time in his life, he was glad, truly happy he lived so close to those he loved. Maybe living outside the city, closer to home wasn't such a damn bad idea after all. Right now he'd give his life for simple little league, Taylor cooking supper and the idea of his parents popping over whenever the hell they wanted.

Wish in one hand....

"Mr. Kinncaid," said Lt. Morris, pulling his attention back. "I think it would be better if someone were at the command post. Since Ms. Fisher knew your phone number, and obviously your address, then she'll more than likely call that residence."

The man was right, but Gavin couldn't leave Taylor here and be there at the same time. He didn't know what the hell to do.

"We'll go to the house," Brayden said, his hand on Christian's shoulder.

"We'll go with you," his mom added.

"I'll take the hotel," Quinlan offered.

It was soon decided where everyone would be. Jess and Quinlan at the hotel, just in case someone called there, while Aiden stayed at the hospital. Brayden and his parents were going to the house. Where apparently, the mobile crime team had finished. Thank God.

"We've printed the house," Morris said.

"Why?" Gavin asked, stopping his trek across the room. "I saw Nina Fisher. She was screaming about Ryan being hers."

"We want to see who else was with her. I want every 'I' dotted and 'T' crossed," Morris answered.

All anyone seemed to know was that a white minivan had been parked in front of his house and a boy, a man, a girl and a woman all climbed in the back. Several neighbors had come out when the alarm went off.

Gavin rubbed his face, the stubble on his jaw scraping his hands. He called and made arrangements for someone to cover his patients. Everyone knew what happened and all were more than willing to help. God, he'd--they'd all--answered so many questions he could hardly think.

Gavin tried not to guess how many white minivans there were in the metropolitan area alone. God, why hadn't they heard anything yet?

Everyone started to file out of the waiting room, but Aiden called Brayden back and shut the door.

The three of them stood alone near windows that looked out over the street. Gavin saw Aiden's reflection check around the waiting room. What was he up to?

When it was empty, Aiden said, "I need to ask you both something." He leaned back against the window, facing the room, Gavin on one side and Bray on the other.

In a low voice Aiden asked, "How far are you willing to go to get the kids back?"

"You need to ask?" Brayden whispered furiously.

"What exactly are you asking?" Gavin wanted to know.

Aiden pursed his lips and said, "I think I might know someone who could help. Someone who has ways of finding things out."

"Who?" Brayden asked.

The corner of Aiden's mouth lifted. "He won't let me say just yet. But if you're interested, meet back here at three."

"Tomorrow?" Gavin asked. By tomorrow he wanted Ryan and Tori home. By tomorrow he wanted Taylor awake and well. Why tomorrow?

"No. Three a.m." Aiden checked his watch. "In about five hours."

Brayden shook his head and walked away, saying over his shoulder, "Whatever. Why the hell in the middle of the damn night?"

Aiden shrugged. "Have no idea. Maybe his flight won't get him here until then."

"I'll see." And Brayden was gone.

Silence settled in the room around them. Gavin walked to the door and looked down the hall to see the armed guard stationed outside one of the SICU desks. The other right outside Taylor's door.

Walking back into the waiting room, he looked at Aiden still leaning against the wall.

The irony of it struck him. A year ago their roles were reversed. He'd had no idea what his brother had been going through. Not really. Not then. But now?

"How in the hell did you not want to deck me last year in Colorado?"

Aiden flashed a smile. "Who said I didn't want to?" Then the humor faded. "That was the worst time of my life. I wouldn't wish it on anyone. Not anyone." Aiden pushed off from the wall and wrapped Gavin in a tight hug. "I can't promise it's going to be okay, but we're all going to do the best we can. And we're all here for you."

Gavin could only nod. "I failed them, Aiden."

His brother pulled back and shoved him into the chair behind him. "Let me guess. The whole motto thing?"

"It's not funny."

Aiden held up a hand. "I never said it was. Believe me." He plopped into the chair next to Gavin's, huffing out a sigh. "I'll tell you what Dad told me then. It's not your fault." Giving his best--and all too close in Gavin's opinion--imitation of their father's voice, Aiden continued, "I didn't raise stupid sons. So, be there for Taylor. That's what's important now."

Gavin gave a small smile. Empty words. "Bet I wasn't the only one you felt like decking then, huh?"

Aiden only grinned in turn. "Go, sit and hold her hand. It helps."

DEADLY TIES   211

Yeah, it did. And it was past time to get back to her. "I not only failed to keep her and Ryan safe, but the baby. I can't help her, Aiden. I've never felt this…."

"Useless? Incompetent? Better yet, impotent."

"Bite your tongue."

"If you need someone to beat up on you instead of yourself, you'll know where to find me. I'll be right here. Now go." Aiden settled back in his chair.

Gavin slapped Aiden's back, and walked down the hallway to his wife's room. What the hell was happening with the kids? Were they okay? Were they hurt, hungry, scared? What if Nina had already shot them and just left them in some damn alley to bleed to death like she'd left Taylor on the floor.

Or what if she just locked them somewhere, in a closet or something and….

Gavin stopped in the middle of the hallway, and planted his hands on his hips. Stop. He had to stop it! This was the road to utter madness. The fear was like a snake pit, just waiting to strike and devour. Barely nodding to the security guards, he shoved open the door and strode into her room. An I.C.U. nurse was checking vitals.

She only raised her brow. "You're not supposed to be in here."

He checked her I.D. tag. "You going to try to throw me out, Leah?"

She smiled softly. "No, but you are going to sit here quietly, and not tell her anything you shouldn't."

Did the woman think he was born yesterday?

He pulled the chair closer to the bed. The door closed softly. Gently, he picked up Taylor's hand, noting the I.V. tapped into her vein, hadn't bruised the back of her pale, translucent hand. The cardiac monitor rhythmed her heart rate, the soft whoosh of the respirator reminding him how fragile her situation still was.

As though he could forget. She had more tubes, wires, and machines attached to her than he cared to see. Laying his head on the rail, he prayed. Prayed for God to heal her, prayed for the kids to be safe, prayed as he never had in his life.

The tears he'd been fighting all day tore through him. Tears of anger, fear and hope. Love and hate. Terror and heartache. Everything collided together in a smashing coalescence of helpless rage. He bit down past it, shut it off. This was helping no one. No one.

Finally he lifted his head. Taylor was still unconscious, and so pale she faded into the white of the pillowcase. A faint light above glowed down on her. The blue plastic tubing running into the side of her mouth obscene even as it kept her alive.

"I'm sorry, Taylor. I'm so sorry." Gavin sighed. "I feel like that's all I've said to anyone today." He'd apologized to her, to his brother, to Christian, hell to his parents. To God.

He reached up and brushed a strand of hair away from her forehead.

"Did I…." He cleared his throat past the lump lodged there. "Did I ever tell you what I first noticed about you?"

The inhalation of the respirator answered him. "It was your dimples."

He touched the spot on her cheek where, if she moved her mouth just so, they appeared. They didn't now. "And your freckles." His fingers trailed over the bridge of her nose. "You weren't wearing any make-up that day, and you were still the most beautiful woman I'd ever seen."

God, how had this happened? Why had it happened?

"You still are, Gorgeous." He swallowed again, but it did no good. "You can't leave me." Her hand was cold in his.

"I don't know what … I can't imagine life without you in it. I couldn't go on."

What a horrifying thought. But it plagued him all day. Whispering a chill down his spine, icing the blood in his veins. "You have to hang on, to fight. You've got to wake up." But not too soon. He'd have to answer questions and he just couldn't bring himself to tell her that their son was missing. Taken by a mad woman at gunpoint.

"Soon. But right now, I know you need to rest. To build your strength." He tried to put some humor in his voice. "After all we've got a honeymoon in three weeks."

He'd planned to take her to Tahiti--private beaches, wonderful scenery, lots of time just for them. But now?

"I want to take you to Ireland to meet Gammy." Gavin settled in his chair, kept her hand in his. "She's ninety-five and still spry as can be. She's this little bitty woman who believes in the Fair Folk, and is full of stories. God, I love her stories. You and Ryan will love her, and she'll love the both of you."

Gavin told her about Gammy, his mother's grandmother. Then, that turned into a faerie story, which turned into another and another. He couldn't stop talking, so he didn't. He would have talked all night if a knock on the door hadn't interrupted his quiet revelation about the man who'd shown back up to his village years after he left only thinking it was the next day.

Leah peeked her head in. "Your brothers are asking for you."

A glance at his watch told him it was after three. Hell. He'd forgotten. Rubbing his face, he stood, then leaned over and placed a soft kiss on Taylor's brow. "I'll be back in a minute. Don't want to leave you hanging, wondering what happened to Mr. Flaherty."

Leah came in and jotted down her information on chart as he left.

The hallway looked the same as it had when he'd gone into her room, if not a little quieter. Five rooms semi-circled around this nurse's station. He saw more movement down the hall at the next station. For the most part, the hospital and the surgical I.C.U. rooms settled into the stillness of the nightshift.

He rounded the corner to see Aiden and Bray sitting in chairs facing a man in a ball cap, pulled so low, his features were indiscernible.

DEADLY TIES   213

"It's about damn time. Never change," said the man in the cap.

Who the hell was Mr. Caps?

Something about the voice tickled Gavin's memory, but he was too damned tired to try and figure out what it was.

"I'm here aren't I?" Ignoring the visitor, he looked at Bray, who looked as worn and haggard as Gavin felt. "Anything?"

"Fuck no." Bray stood and started to pace. "I'm going half out of my damn mind. Mom had to give Christian a sedative. She's still convinced it's her fault for dropping Tori off. Mom had to call in a prescription for Christian's inhaler. She had an asthma attack. Hasn't had one in years. All because she blames herself." The disbelief in his voice, told Gavin that Bray no more blamed Christian than he did Gavin. It was heartening and humbling. "Dad's stretched out on the couch complaining, but Mom told him he was staying right there or he could check into the hospital because his blood pressure was just too damned high and she didn't have time to fret over him." Bray smiled wickedly. "He shut up and propped his feet up."

"Hmph." Gavin crossed his arms.

"Shut the door, Gav," Aiden said.

Without thinking, he did, and then wondered at it.

Aiden motioned for Gavin to sit. Too tired to make an issue out of his brother telling him what to do, he did it. Aiden took up a post by the door. Bray fell into a chair a few feet across from Gavin. Mr. Caps sat, his elbows on his knees, a couple of chairs down.

"God, it's nice to see you guys."

Gavin looked at Brayden, who shrugged his shoulders. Aiden muttered something about idiots, and Mr. Caps laughed.

Clearing his throat, Gavin said, "Look, Aiden said you'd help us, and I appreciate it, but I don't have time to sit here all night, and neither does Bray. So can we get on with why we're here?"

Silence settled around them, and though Gavin couldn't see the man's eyes, he could feel them on him. "Your charm always did mask that strip of seriousness in you."

Gavin frowned. What in the hell was that suppose to mean? And how did the guy know him?

"I've already run several searches since I got word what happened." The man's voice was roughed as though he might smoke.

"What searches?" Bray asked.

"All kinds. Suffice it to say, anything can be found if you know where to look." He shifted, glanced towards Aiden. "I don't have a lot of time here, but I'll give you what I've got. Ms. Fisher has a rap sheet a mile long. That is one mean woman there."

And this was news how? Gavin gave him a level look.

Mr. Caps ignored it and continued. "It seems Ryan was raised by his maternal grandmother the first three years. She fought for custody and when she finally won, she died suddenly in a freak accident. Custody went back to his mom."

"How did the grandmother die?"

The man waved his hand. "That's not important. Patterns, gentlemen, patterns. The point to this is the woman has been killing for quite some time. Not really serial, in the textbook fashion, but there is a pattern. Those who wrong her tend to meet their end suddenly."

"I tracked her through her guard at Gatesville. Seems he helped her escape by wrecking the transport van and killing another guard."

A wreck? Ryan had seen a wreck. "How the hell do you know all this?" Gavin asked.

Mr. Caps didn't even pause, but kept going. "By following their car, gas stations and whatnots, we traced them to a crack house in Brownwood, Texas, where it's believed she obtained the nine-millimeter she's currently carrying." The man leaned back. "After that, we go to Austin where the judge who worked her case was the target of a drive-by. Got hit in the leg. The office where Ms. Reese--excuse me--Mrs. Kinncaid, used to work was broken into and the grand finale was, of course, her attack at the Shepards. That was all before her debut here in D.C."

"I'm betting they ditched the white minivan for something faster, before word got out. From things I've gathered in various files, it seems Ms. Fisher and her sidekick, Rod, have enough powdered meth on them to make a little nest egg. That is if they don't use it all first."

This just kept getting worse.

"Following her patterns, I would have to say she's probably got the kids here in town. It would up the ante so to speak. And she has no use for them. Though most of her good fortune has been pure luck thus far, the woman you're dealing with is not your average jeb head. She's shrewd."

Bray's sigh huffed out. "So, you think she'll call?"

The blue cap nodded. "Definitely. The media this case is producing, she'll know the worth of the kids."

Kids. "You think she'll let Ryan go?"

The ball cap tilted. "For enough money, yeah. But having said that, he's also her 'flesh and blood' as she's been known to refer to him. So, that puts him at a greater risk. They're both used to him being her punching bag." He looked at Brayden. "Are Ryan and Tori close?"

Bray was looking at the newcomer hard, as though trying to figure something out. "Yeah."

"He's protective of her?"

Bray nodded.

Mr. Caps looked back to Gavin. "That could be a serious problem. Nina Fisher exploits weaknesses. She'll use Tori as a lever against Ryan and if he thinks Tori's in danger, he'll turn Nina's anger onto him."

The words hit Gavin like needle sharp rain. And the man was right,

DEADLY TIES

that's exactly what Ryan would do.

Then the names hit. Ryan and Tori. Not Victoria as the news broadcasts said. Few, other than family, called her Tori.

For the first time, Gavin got a good look at the face. A slightly familiar face, hardened through the years, sharpened around the edges, but something in it was the same. Or was it? "I'll be damned."

A smile, lightening quick, flashed before it was gone. "Wondered how long it would take you."

Bray caught on. "No. Ian?"

Their brother held up a finger. "No, names. And while we're at it, swear to me now on both your families that you will tell no one of me, of this meeting. You know nothing."

"Why?" they both asked.

Aiden's chuckle mixed with Ian's.

"They're still Tweedle-Dee, and Tweedle-Dumb," Ian said, using the childhood names both he and Bray hated.

"But…" Bray started.

"Forget it, put any questions you have to Aiden. He'll answer what he can. Right now we don't have time to get into it. Just know, I've missed the hell out of you guys."

"No one? Not even Mom?" Brayden asked.

"No one." The words lashed out. "It's for everyone's safety. If I've learned you have told anyone, and I'll find out, you will not see or hear from me again. I'll get the kids back, or do what I can to help, but that's it."

Gavin didn't care presently what promises he had to make. He'd have dealt with Satan if he could get Ryan and Tori back.

"What do you want us to do?" he asked.

There was that grin he hadn't seen in more than twelve years and it was flashing for the second time. Surreal. This whole damn day was surreal.

"Still the peacemaker. Actually, the question is what do you want me to do? As I said, my bet is the city. A person can get lost in a city a hell of a lot easier than some back woods hillbilly town. And the city allows them cash for their drugs. Right now I'm checking all the two-bit motels."

Gavin didn't want to think of the number of those.

"What's your question?" Gavin asked, Ian had never gotten to that.

Ian ran his tongue around his teeth. "When I find them, I'll get them back."

Gavin nodded. "And?" He could tell there was an 'and'.

Ian seemed to weigh his words. "On second thought, never mind. But I will tell you this. The police are going to be asking you questions, you know nothing about me. And since you know nothing about me, this meeting never took place. You will have no idea how in the hell your kids wound up safe and sound at a local ER or on the nearest police department steps. Got it?"

Loud and clear.

Bray still sat staring at Ian.

"What?" Ian asked, turning to look at Bray.

"You've changed."

Ian stood, slapped Bray on the back, shook Gavin's hand and said, "In more ways than you care to know." He hugged Aiden, then looked back at them. "I'll be in touch."

And with that, he opened the door and walked away.

CHAPTER TWENTY

"Ryan," Tori whispered, "I need to go to the bathroom."

"Can you hold it?" he asked her.

"I'll try." Her sigh blew against his cheek as she settled beside him again. Ryan was sitting on the floor, leaning against the wall, tied to the bedframe. One of Tori's hands was tied to his. Neither of them could get out, and Nina was passed out in a chair. He didn't know when she'd wake up. Ryan really hoped this wasn't one of those times where she slept for days. He remembered those from before.

It was dark outside again. Another entire day.

This morning--barely at dawn--Nina untied Tori and jerked her out the door. Telling Tori all the while that if she tried to pull any tricks, they'd disappear and leave Ryan tied to the bed. He couldn't do anything as Nina dragged and shoved his friend towards the door, all the while stuffing Tori's black hair up in a cap and telling her to keep her head down.

Nina said they had to make a call. She'd turned to him then, yelling that if he tried to escape, if they got back and he was gone, she'd kill his friend.

Ryan prayed the entire time they were gone. Scared to death Tori would do something to flip Nina into a rage. But Tori said they walked several blocks, got on a bus and got off several stops later to make a phone call. Nina asked someone on the phone about a meeting with half-a-million dollars for each kid. Nina was supposed to have met the Kinncaids at the train station at noon. He and Tori knew it was Gavin and Brayden because Tori got to tell her dad hi.

But, noon had come and gone with Nina in the chair she'd occupied since early that morning. Maybe she was dead. What was it called when someone died because of drugs? A.D.? It was a vowel and D. E.D.? No. O.D.! Over dose. Duh. Maybe she overdosed--O.D.-ed.

And where was that guy they'd been with? He'd come in and left, then come in again and left. Ryan knew he was gone when she made

DEADLY TIES
217

the call, and Ryan never heard her tell him about it later when he came in. Rod. That was his name.

"I want to go home," Tori said.

"I know you do, Tori Bori. But we can't yet." He rubbed his cheek against her hair and pulled at his hands again, trying to work the bindings looser. There was a nail or screw that was kinda loose. He kept trying to rub the layers of tape against it to get it to snag or cut. But, he'd had no luck. At least Nina hadn't taped their mouths shut.

"I wanted to talk to Daddy longer this morning too. I wanted to, but she only let me say, 'Daddy'." Tori sniffled. "She told him if he didn't send the money, she was going to sell me. That some man would pay a high price for me. Do you know what she meant? I don't want to go anywhere."

Ryan's blood chilled at Tori's words. He knew what Nina had meant--well, sort of. Nina had turned tricks before. He remembered the boyfriends she took money from. She'd been a whore. He learned that in one of the foster homes.

"You won't go anywhere," he vowed. "At least not anywhere that she would send you, unless it's home. I promise."

"Is she gonna kill us?"

Like she almost did Taylor?

Ryan grinned at the memory of how Nina yelled and screamed when the T.V. said Mrs. Kinncaid was listed in critical condition at some hospital. Boy, had Nina been mad. He'd gotten hit for it, but he didn't care. His mom was alive. Finally, he answered Tori, "No. She might get mad and hit me, but she won't kill us. She needs us to get the money."

"I don't like it when she hits you." Tori's hand came up and traced his busted lip. "You didn't talk back to her, like she said. You were only asking a question."

Yeah, he only asked a question. He knew asking if Nina had heard anything about his 'mom' would set her off and turn her anger away from Tori. Tori had asked for something to drink. Since Nina had been coming down off a high--he remembered the mood swings--she wasn't in the mood for a 'mewling brat.' When she'd started towards Tori with that look in her eyes he'd seen too many times before, he'd quickly asked if his mom was still alive. Thank goodness she hit him instead of Tori. He couldn't stand it if she hit Tori again.

"I know that. Nina is Nina." Ryan shrugged. He'd spent all day thinking. Rod wasn't really into this thing, or from what Ryan had been able to tell. One of them needed to get away and get help. His wrists were raw from working them all day. "Listen, I've been thinking."

"About what?"

Ryan bit down at the sight of the bruise on her cheek where Nina hit her yesterday. "I'm sorry," he said. Not that he'd meant to say that. It just slipped out.

She cocked her brow. "For what?"

Ryan sighed. "I never wanted you to know what this was like." Ratty, dingy rooms that smelled bad, getting hit and ducking blows. He wanted to cry too, like Tori, but he couldn't. He didn't want her to be too scared.

"She gave you that scar didn't she?"

Ryan nodded looking straight into her eyes, expecting to see that pitying look people always gave him. The one he hated. Instead, her eyes lit like a blue flame, burning with anger.

"Ohhhh ... I hate her. I just hate that mean old woman." Tori was mad.

Ryan grinned. "I do, too." Scooting closer he whispered, "Now, listen. I've been thinking. One of us needs to get away. You've got one hand free and your tape isn't as thick as mine. First, we'll get yours off...."

"Then I'll untie you."

If there was time.

"Then you make a run for it and I'll stay here so she won't go after you."

"What? Are you out of your mind?" she whispered. "I'm not gonna leave you. I can't."

"Yes you can."

"Why don't I stay?"

Ryan rolled his eyes. " 'Cause I'm the boy."

"So?"

"So, that's what the Kinncaid men do." At least he thought that was what the motto was.

"That is such a dumb thing to say. When we get home, I'm gonna tell Grams the women need to say it too. Not just the dumb boys."

"Whatever, now come on."

* * * *

Gavin stood next to Bray at the train station. Not a single blessed person fitting the description the caller had given them had shown up all damn day.

Another train rumbled out of the station, the noise faded to a groan at this level, though he again felt the floor's faint vibration. People hurried and shuffled along trying to get to where they wanted to go. Everything had a kaleidoscope view to it. He saw it all, but it was distorted, shifting.

Bray cussed again. "I'm going to kill that woman. When I get my hands on her, I'm going to wring her junky neck."

Gavin was exhausted, and Bray looked the same. A vein throbbed near his brother's temple, a telltale sign of trouble.

"They--she--who-the-hell-ever, isn't coming," Gavin said. "They'd have been here by now."

"We think so too," a voice said in their ear. They were both wired,

DEADLY TIES   219

per police instructions, and both carried black duffel bags with unmarked, non-sequential bills for half a mill' each.

Something must have happened. Gavin prayed it wasn't bad. He'd called Aiden all day to see how things were at the hospital. None of them mentioned the *other*. Especially not with mikes taped to their chests. Taylor was improving and holding her own, thank God.

"What if she's just detained?" Bray asked. The hopefulness in his voice not lost on Gavin.

"Look, as much as she wanted this, all the trouble she went to, she'd have been here, Bray."

Still his brother's gaze scanned the crowd. "You didn't hear her, Gav. Tori was scared and crying. I want my daughter. Now." His eyes mirrored Gavin's rage, flaming to a burning September stone. "Here's the damn money. Does the bitch want more?"

"Settle down, Mr. Kinncaid. Go to your car." Morris' voice echoed in the earpiece.

"I bet she made the cops. She said 'no cops', she'd spot them." Bray was on a rampage as he turned and stalked to the doors. "Next time, no bloody ass cops."

As the humid evening air hit them, Gavin changed the duffel bag to his other hand. He didn't have any words for his brother. He felt the same exact way and anything Gavin said would be empty and probably a lie.

What he wouldn't give to hear Ryan's voice again. Just for a minute.

"Did she say why she didn't let Ryan say anything?" he asked yet again.

Bray stopped. "I told you, I only talked to Tori for a few seconds. All the woman let her say was 'Daddy.' That was it. Nothing else but her demands. And her fucking threats." He ran a frustrated hand through his hair. They both strode to their car, got in and sat there.

"Now what?" Gavin asked.

"Don't have a fucking clue."

"Drive to the hotel. A task team is assembled in one of the suites there. We'll escort you when you get there." With that, a click sounded in their ears.

Gavin jerked the tiny earpiece out and tossed it into the slot in the console. In no time they pulled up in front of *The Highland Hotel*. He just wanted to get this over with and get back to the hospital. Aiden assured him that nothing had changed, that Taylor hadn't awakened yet, but he didn't like being away from her.

He looked across the seat at his twin as Brayden got out and shoved his way through the throng of press outside the hotel. Damn vultures. Gavin got out and followed. In the lobby a policeman put them on an elevator and they went straight to the top, to the family suites. Gavin brooded.

"I swore I'd never let this woman get close to them, never let her hurt them." Damn it.

"Will you shut the hell up?" Bray lashed. "Do you think this is your fault? Do you think I don't feel bad as well? I'm her damn father. I'm supposed to protect my little girl, make certain nothing bad ever happens to her!" Bray looked at the numbers atop the doors as they rose, his jaw working back and forth. "Do you know what that woman said to me?"

Gavin had heard most of it, dozens of times, the ransom, the demands. The sick threats. He silently waited on his brother.

"She said," Bray's voice cracked. "She said, I had a pretty little girl. And if I couldn't pay for her, someone else would. A pretty little thing like her would have no trouble being bought."

Gavin couldn't say a word. Not a fucking word.

"Oh, Christ Jesus." Bray slumped back against the wall of the elevator.

A tear trailed over his brother's cheek. Gavin felt his own eyes sting. Reaching across the small space, he pulled his brother into a hug.

"We're going to get them back. We are. Come hell or high water we will."

The doors pulled apart and they stepped out. The hallway here was a mass of people who all quit talking the minute they walked off the elevator.

Gavin opened his shirt, ripped the taped mike off and threw it to Morris. "Here, for all the damn good it did."

Bray did the same and they both strode into their parents' suite, tossing the money bags on the table. All calls from the house were being routed to here. Jesslyn stepped up and motioned for them to follow her. Gavin grabbed Bray's arm and did as she asked.

"Aiden wanted me to tell you something." She pushed the door shut behind her. "he said a lead is being followed. Something about dingy motels in certain parts of town."

"Where?" They both asked.

She shook her head and shrugged. "I have no idea. That's all he said."

To hell with this. He wasn't doing a damn bit of good here. "I'm going back to the hospital."

"Wait." She grabbed his arm again.

Gavin looked at her, really looked. Shadows circled her eyes, and she was pale. "This must bring back things for you."

He knew she'd gone through what no parent ever should. Now he understood what a degree of pain his sister-in-law must have suffered when she'd lost her family.

She shook her head. "Don't worry about me. I need ... I don't know ... Aiden said to tell you."

"Tell me what?" Gavin asked her.

She pulled her bottom lip between her teeth. Finally, she said, "I took a nap with the twins earlier. I had a dream."

DEADLY TIES

Gavin knew she believed in her dreams, and with good reason.

She smiled. "They're alive. A little bruised, but alive."

"Where?" Bray asked.

"I don't know." She shook her head again. "I'm sorry. It was dark all around them and they were sitting on a floor by a bed. Tori had a bruise on her cheek. Ryan had a cut in his eyebrow, a black eye and busted lip."

Gavin took a deep breath.

"They're alive. I know it. They are. I heard my little girl's voice tell me, 'He'll find them.'"

Her eyes bore into his. "*He'll* find them. Bruises disappear, time fades and love heals. Remember that."

Brayden looked at Jesslyn, then at him. And nodded. "Let's go."

Gavin hugged her and whispered, "Thanks." Kissing the top of her head, he let her go, then followed his brother out.

* * * *

Tori finally managed to work her hand free. Ryan saw her wrist was red from the adhesive of the tape, raw from where she'd pulled and jerked to loosen the binding.

"Here, let me get you out." She leaned down and worked on his hand with her teeth. Her short, sharp teeth scraped against the outside of his thumbs as she bit into the tape. Sitting back and glancing over her shoulder she said, "Try it now. Pull them like this." She twisted her wrists in different directions. Ryan did and the tape tore more. Again and it pulled almost in two. Rubbing the last of it against the edge of the bed frame frayed it enough he could bust the silver tape apart.

Grinning he looked at her. "Thanks." He grabbed her hand. "Come on, let's go."

"You mean you're going with me?" she asked.

Ryan looked at Nina; she was still out cold. They could run and find the police, or just a phone. He had a quarter in his pocket.

"Yeah. Come on." They started tiptoeing across the room. Glancing over, he saw Nina shift. Please, please let this work. He wanted out of here. He wanted to get Tori out.

The gun was stuck in Nina's pants. As quietly as possible, they made it to the door. Ryan reached for the chain bolt, looking out a crack in the curtains. No. No. Not now.

Rod was walking down the corridor. Ryan leaned over and looked out the window.

"Hurry up," Tori whispered.

"We can't."

"Why not?" She was pressing against his back.

"Rod's coming."

"Oh, no."

"Hey, what the hell are you two doing?"

Ryan spun around at the sound of Nina's voice. Gruff and all but growling.

"What the hell are you doing?" She rushed to them and jerked Tori away from him.

"It's my fault!" Ryan shouted.

Nina had hold of Tori by her hair. "Is that right? Well, from now on, I'll just punish your little friend here every time you piss me off." Her eyes glared at him. "How do you like that?"

Her hand rose, pulling Tori up on her toes. Tori whimpered, her hands holding the top of her head.

He didn't hear the door.

"Nina? What the hell are you doing to that girl?" Rod asked, dropping a bag on the table.

"What the fuck does it look like I'm doing? I'm sick and damn tired of them not listening. They're going to learn." She brought her hand back.

"No!" Ryan rushed her, knocking her hand back.

He didn't know who was more shocked, him or Nina. She let go of Tori, grabbing him by his throat. The door! The door was open!

She flung him off and turned on Rod. "Where the hell have you been? Oh shit. What the fuck time is it?" She glanced at her watch. "Fucking-A. NO!"

"What?" Rod asked her.

Tori stood by the door, behind Rod, where she'd scampered after Nina dropped her. He caught her eye and jerked his head to the door. "Go!" he mouthed.

Her head shook.

"Go."

Rod and Nina were arguing.

"What have you done now, Neen?"

"Don't call me that stupid, sonofabitchin' name!"

"Go," he told Tori again. Her eyes filled with tears. "It's our only chance. Go!"

She turned and rushed out the door.

"You idiot!" Nina yelled, bringing the gun up and getting a shot off, the bullet biting and spitting wood from the doorframe.

"God, Nina." Rod moved in front of her as she rushed to the door. Ryan stood up. "We've still got the other one. I'm not letting you shoot some innocent, little girl."

Nina slapped him and stepped back. "What do you care?" She paced back and forth. Ryan tried to fade into the wallpaper.

* * * *

Tori hurried down the steps, rubbing her arm where a piece of wood hit her. She had to hurry. Had to hurry. She had to find someone to help her, to help Ryan before it was too late.

She hit the bottom and ran. Stopping outside the front office she tried to think of what to do. What had Nina told the owners? What if they

DEADLY TIES

didn't help her, but took her back?

What to do? Tori swiped at her eyes. She walked away from the door. They might help her. She walked back and straight into someone.

"I'm sorry," she mumbled. "I'm sorry." She followed the jean legs up, all the way up to his face, which she couldn't see behind the cap and the shades. Why was he wearing a cap and shades in the dark?

What if he hurt her? Ryan!

"Pl--Please, can you help me?"

His hands grabbed her shoulders and she winced. They still hurt from when Nina had shaken her.

"Tori?" His voice was deep.

"How, how do you know my name?"

He looked around. "Everyone knows your name kid. You're all over the news. Where's Ryan?"

"You'll help me?" She could have cried harder.

"Where's Ryan?"

Tori pointed up the steps. "The last room around the corner. She was mad and has a gun, but Ryan told me to run. So I did."

She couldn't stop crying. "Go inside and stay there. Right there inside the door and wait for me." His hand pushed her towards the opening even as he was turning and running up the steps. When he was nearly at the top, she lost sight of him, his black clothes blending into the darkness.

Who was he? Tori didn't know, and didn't care. He was helping. She turned and walked to stand just inside the door, her eyes trained on the upper level.

* * * *

"I can't believe this!" Nina screamed. Turning, her gaze on him. "This is all your damn fault!"

She charged at him. Ryan tried to dodge away, but her first hit caught him in the ribs, stealing his breath. Her next one, busted his lips and he went down hard, grabbing the door.

"Nina, good God. Stop." Rod stood in front of him.

Ryan pulled himself up.

Nina glared at Rod, aiming her gun. "I should have done this a long time ago."

Ryan watched as she squeezed the trigger. Rod staggered back, trying to get his own gun out of his waistband.

As quietly as possible, Ryan inched towards the opening. Nina's eyes zeroed in on him. "Where are you going?"

The gun came up and Ryan dove through the door, wood chipping off as a bullet hit the frame.

Ryan slid across the cement, into the iron railing, hitting his forehead and slamming his shoulder.

"Nina, let him go!" Rod yelled.

Ryan scrambled up. He shook his head as the landing tilted. His head hurt.

He had to move, had to get away. Before she came.

"Go to hell," Nina screamed from the room. Two shots echoed.

Run. Run. Run.

Ryan ran. He heard the door bang and looked over his shoulder.

Someone picked him up and clamped a hand over his mouth. Ryan squirmed. The leather glove was cool against his mouth and chin.

"Ryan. You're safe. You're safe." The man held him tight against him, but Ryan couldn't see him. It was dark and they were inside a doorway.

"When I tell you, run. Run to the bottom of the stairs, Tori's there. Wait for me. Got it?"

Ryan nodded. The gloved hand moved from his mouth. The man sat him on his feet.

"Now, go!"

Ryan tore off down the corridor. Tori was at the bottom. She was safe. They were going home.

* * * *

Ian watched as the small shadow started down the stairs. He'd have to hurry. In silence, he made his way to the doorway of the room the kids came out of.

As quietly as night shaded day, Ian looked into the room. A man lay dead, his eyes staring sightlessly up at the ceiling. Ian's prey leaned against the wall, close to the door, holding her leg. Blood slowly oozed out of it as she inched towards the door. He waited till she got to the doorway.

"Shit," she muttered. "Damn kids."

Just as she stepped out, he smashed the back of his fist into her face. She staggered back, tripping over her accomplice, and dropped her nine millimeter. A silencer, that must have cost her.

Ian stepped into the room. He noticed the wood chips missing from the doorframe. Just the height to hit a kid dead center. Rage rolled through him, but he'd learned long ago to coat it with deadly ice.

Reaching down, he grabbed Rod's gun.

"Who the fuck are you?" She scooted back, but he followed, and picked up her discarded nine millimeter.

"I'm the Reaper. I could make your death quick with a bullet through your brain or maybe the heart." He leveled his gun at her. Her tripping eyes rounded.

No. Ian stood. Too many questions, and there would already be plenty of those. But he didn't want to leave her mobile either.

"I think I have something better in mind." He smiled, aimed at her kneecap and pulled the trigger. Amid her screams, he dropped the gun he used back near the dead man's hand. Quickly, he chopped down on the side of her neck, the room silenced. Ian dropped her gun a good ways away from her.

DEADLY TIES

225

Scanning the room, all was as it should be.

He pulled the door halfway to. Taking out his phone, he hurried along the corridor, down the stairs and to the kids as he told the dispatcher he'd heard gunshots and screams coming from a certain motel room, if someone hadn't already called it in.

The kids were both huddled just inside the door. The night manager was nowhere around.

"Come on. Let's get you home."

The kids looked undecided, but finally conceded.

He got them in the rental car he was using.

The boy was favoring his right arm. "Ryan?"

"Yes, sir?"

"You okay?" His eyes were round and bright, as were Tori's. Shock more than likely.

"My shoulder hurts," Ryan admitted.

Ian ran his hand over it. Dislocated from what he could tell. There were scrapes along his forearm and hands.

"Just hang on. I'll have you at the hospital in no time."

Ian climbed behind the wheel.

"You helped us," Tori said.

"Yes." He pulled out of the parking lot and onto the highway.

"Why?" Ryan asked.

Because Kinncaids stick together. Ian shook his head, he couldn't very well tell them that.

Cop cars pulled up to the hotel. Ian looked in the rearview mirror. Spotlights shone on the correct door.

Smart men.

"Who are you?" Tori asked.

"You both ready to see your dads?" he deflected the question.

"Yes," they both answered.

"Good. They can't wait to see you. They're waiting for us at Sibly." Or they should be by now.

"Thank you for helping us," Ryan said. "What's your name? We need to tell our parents your name."

Ian laughed. "Rob Roy."

" 'kay." Ryan settled back into the seat.

Ian saw him reach over and take Tori's hand.

Quickly, he maneuvered through the traffic to the hospital. When he pulled up at the ER, he saw all the media vans. Damn. He turned the car around and found a quiet side entrance. Scanning the area he saw, amazingly, no reporters.

Ian put the car in park and got his phone back out. "Can you two get inside okay?" he asked them.

Ryan and Tori nodded.

Ian dialed Morris's number. On the second ring it was answered.

"Lt. Morris. There's two kids on their way to the ER I think you'll be interested in." Ian flipped the phone back closed.

"Come on, you two." He helped them out of the car. Yeah, definitely shock. Tori was shivering. Dammit he wished he at least had a blanket.

"You two, take care," he told them both, walking them across the street.

"Thanks," they mumbled.

"Go on, I'll watch you from here."

Ryan stopped and looked back at him.

Ian met his gaze and said, "I promise you, you will never have to worry about that woman, ever again."

Ryan held his stare a moment longer, then he turned and took Tori's arm. The two walked side by side along the sidewalk. Ryan was one great boy.

Ian wished he could walk them inside and make certain they were all right, but that was out of the question.

He watched until they disappeared into the side door, then he slid back into his car, started it and drove away.

The buttons were smooth on his phone as he dialed Aiden's number.

* * * *

Gavin, Brayden and Aiden were in the I.C.U. waiting room again. And like before it was deserted.

"Does he ever tell you anything?" Bray asked. "The man never did. What damn lead?"

Taylor was doing better, thank God. He and Bray had arrived half an hour ago. Gavin had been in Taylor's room until the nurses came in to check vitals and change the bag of fluids hanging from the I.V. stand. He passed Morris in the hallway. The man followed them around like the plague.

When he arrived from Taylor's room, Aiden was lounged in a chair, letting Bray spit and stew.

Gavin knew Aiden wasn't nearly as blasé about the entire event as he played. One only had to look into those eyes to see the banked worry and fury.

"he said he'd call as soon as he found something."

Bray continued to mumble and pace.

Aiden looked up at him. "How's Taylor?" he asked.

Gavin nodded and took a deep breath. "It looks like she's really going to make it, probably even a full recovery, all things considered." He rubbed the back of his neck. He'd grilled her doctors and the nursing staff and felt a small weight finally lift from his chest. But even then the fury he'd felt for the last two days only grew, and roared to life again. "We just need to get the kids, and I've never felt more helpless, more useless in my entire damned life."

The chair he kicked went flying. Both his brothers looked at him, their expressions all too alike.

Aiden opened his mouth to say something but the ring of his mobile

DEADLY TIES

cut him off. All he said was hello and yes, then handed the phone to Bray.

Gavin stared as his twin blew out a breath he'd been holding. Smiling, Bray covered his eyes with his hand, and fell into the chair behind him. "Oh, Thank God. Thank you God."

Bray nodded a couple of times, choked out a 'thanks, bro' and then handed the phone to Gavin.

"Yeah?"

"The kids should be arriving in the ER there at Sibly now." Ian's voice slid a large part of the weight on his chest off.

All Gavin could do was nod. "How are they? Are they okay? What of Nina?"

A sigh huffed through the phone. "The cops should be taking her into custody as we speak. She's a little worse for wear. Tori had a few bruises, and she'll probably be in shock. But she's fine." The pause stretched.

Gavin swallowed. "Ryan? Is he okay?"

The silence stretched.

"Answer me, dammit."

"Ryan is pretty beat up. I'm sorry, Gav. I hurried, but I wasn't in time to stop her from laying into him. He saved himself more or less. Dove out of the door like he was sliding into home. Banged his head and shoulder pretty bad."

Gavin felt his knees weaken. Walking to the nearest chair, he dropped into it.

"How bad is he?" Gavin closed his eyes. His breath stopping in his lungs.

"It could have been worse. Lots of bruising, and from his breathing, I would have to say he probably has a couple of bruised if not cracked ribs. I think he dislocated his shoulder and got a concussion when he dove through the door."

Gavin looked up at the ceiling trying to catch his breath. Squeezing his eyes shut he tried to block the black visions that danced in his head.

"I'm sorry, I wasn't sooner, Gav. But he is fine."

What had Jesslyn said? Bruises fade and love heals?

Forcing air into his lungs and past the lump in his throat, he managed to answer his brother. "Don't apologize to me. If not for you, they might not even be coming here. I owe you. If you ever need anything. Anything.…"

He heard the smile in his brother's voice. "I'll know where to find you. Now get downstairs. They should be there by now, if someone hasn't way laid them in the hallways."

The line went dead in his ear.

Gavin tossed the phone back to Aiden just as the door burst open. Morris stood there and motioned them to follow.

"The kids might be downstairs. We got a call earlier saying they were

228   *Jaycee Clark*

here." The man checked his watch. "We've also found Fisher and her accomplice."

Gavin saw his brothers' smiles and felt a small one turn up the corner of his mouth.

CHAPTER TWENTY-ONE

Gavin and Bray rushed to the ER, along with several policeman, doctors and pediatric specialists. Everyone was notified and paged.

Where the hell were the kids? Gavin looked around.

An ambulance pulled up. Media vans still camped outside. The doors whooshed open.

"Daddy!" Tori yelled from behind them. Everyone turned to see Tori rush to get to her father. Bray caught her up and held her tight. Gavin heard her crying, saw his brother's tears. Thank, God.

He looked back down the hallway to see Ryan leaning against the wall, a nurse beside him. Chills raced through him as he looked at his son.

Gavin shoved several people out of the way.

"Ryan?" He wanted to grab him up in hug, but Gavin was afraid he'd hurt him. Damn Nina Fisher to hell.

"Ryan?" he asked again.

His son blinked as if trying to focus. His pupils were dilated. Shock. "Dad?"

Gavin didn't know if he sobbed or laughed and he didn't care. He reached out and gently gathered his son to him. "Yeah, Ryan." *Dad.* "It's me. I'm here."

Bruises fade…. Love heals. Gavin stood and cradled Ryan against his chest.

Ryan's lips were busted. "Where's Mom?"

"She's upstairs."

"Dr. Kinncaid."

Gavin followed a nurse to an exam room. He didn't want to let Ryan go, but they needed to check him out. Gavin could see a bruised bump forming on Ryan's forehead above his eyebrow. His cut eyebrow.

Carefully, he laid Ryan on the bed. Gavin held his hand. Wires were attached and X-rays were quickly taken.

Thank God, he had his child back. That his brother had his child back. That was all that mattered. That was all that mattered.

If he could take away all the pain, change it all, Gavin would, but he couldn't.

"Where's Tori?" Ryan looked around. "Tori? Where's Tori?"

"Shh…." Gavin grabbed his hand, held it between the both of his.

DEADLY TIES

229

"She's with her dad. She's fine."

Ryan nodded and closed his eyes. "My shoulder hurts."

"I know, we'll give you some medicine to take the pain away then we'll fix it."

Gavin just watched him, couldn't take his eyes off of this brave, amazing boy. People worked around him, orders were given and followed. Minutes passed.

"Where the hell's my grandson?" Gavin turned as the curtain was jerked back. His parents stood there.

Gavin could only shake his head at his dad as tears filled his eyes. His parents walked to the bed.

His mother's hand squeezed his arm, and his father nodded. For the first time in years, Gavin felt like sobbing like a baby. Taking an enormous breath, he quelled the emotions running through him by swallowing hard.

"Oh, poor, baby," his mom said, reaching a hand out towards Ryan.

"Look, just look what she did to him, Mom," Gavin said. The tears fell anyway. "I didn't stop her. I promised him he would always be safe. I swore to protect him and that she'd never hurt him again. And look…."

Gavin bit down until he was sure his teeth would shatter.

His mom wrapped her arm around his waist, hugging him. She whispered, "It's going to be fine. He's a strong little boy, incredibly strong, and so is his mother. This is just a dark time for your family right now, but it's going to pass." She leaned up on tip-toe and brushed a tear away. "It'll pass."

"Right, she's right. My Kaitie lass has always known what she was about."

Gavin nodded at his father's words, not looking up when he heard his father clear his throat.

"Pops?" Ryan opened his eyes.

Jock moved to the other side of the bed. "Yes, Ryan, it's me."

"Thought I heard your bark."

They all grinned at that, except for Jock. The old man's jaw muscle worked, and he only patted Ryan's hand. Gavin noticed his father's eyebrow were doing the 'v' thing they did when he was trying not to cry.

Jock turned his attention to his wife. "Kaitie, can't you talk to someone to get him moved to a private room? Too much damn noise down here."

She nodded, rubbed Gavin's back and turned to walk away. Gavin grabbed her hand. "I've already got rooms for both him and Tori on the fourth floor. As soon as they're finished down here, they'll be moved. We're waiting for the pain meds to kick in. He's got a dislocated shoulder," Gavin told them.

"Is Tori okay?" Ryan asked.

"Yes, Ryan. She's fine," Gavin told him again.

"She tried to shoot her, but she missed. Missed me too. I dove into the railing." He gave a small smile. "Those baseball guys make it look easy."

Gavin didn't want to think about that--what it meant. Instead, he said, "You did great."

"Is Tori really okay? You're not lying to me are you? Where is she?" Ryan's eyes were glazed, probably from a concussion, but still they searched frantically around.

Gavin laid his hand on Ryan's chest. "She's fine, Ryan. She's with her father."

Ryan looked as if he were trying to compute that, when another doctor came up. Gavin's parents stepped outside to the waiting room. He stayed by Ryan's side while the doctor went through the run down of his son's injuries. Concussion, contusions, abrasions, two bruised ribs and one dislocated shoulder.

Gavin bit back the oath on the end of his tongue.

Dr. Lopez was a nice pediatrician. She talked to Ryan about what hurt, what procedures she would take and how bad it might hurt. Not hiding anything, she told him what meds she was going to give him and that the first batch would make him relax. They couldn't let him sleep just yet because of the concussion. Ryan listened to every word.

When she was finished, she said, "We'll relocate your shoulder, just pop it back into place, and then we'll move you to a room upstairs. Any questions?"

Ryan nodded. "Where's Tori? Is she okay?"

Dr. Lopez smiled. "You know, she asked me the same thing about you. I'll be right back."

Ryan turned to him. "What did she mean by that? Is Tori okay or not?"

This was going to be a problem. Again he assured his son. "Ryan she's…"

"Ryan!"

Gavin glanced up to see his brother holding Tori. She squirmed out of Bray's arms and hurried to the bedside. Giving a sidelong glance at Gavin, she climbed up onto the bed to sit beside Ryan.

"Are you okay?" she asked. "Oh, look at you! She is just mean. Mean! I should have stayed. I never should have…."

"You still talk too much," Ryan muttered. But he'd relaxed Gavin noticed. "Are you all right? They never told me."

Her smile was hollow. "Of course. I'm fine. Though Daddy says I have to spend the night here in the hospital."

"Yeah, me too."

"I hate hospitals," she leaned over and touched his cheek.

"Yeah, me too."

Gavin noticed Ryan's breathing was easier and the lines around his

DEADLY TIES
231

mouth weren't so tight. The pain meds they'd fed into Ryan's I.V. were starting to work, thank God. About damn time.

Looking to his twin, Gavin started to ask....

Bray answered Gavin's unspoken question. "She wouldn't calm down. I finally had to bring her down here to see that he was okay."

* * * *

The next day, Gavin wheeled Ryan into the I.C.U. room. He'd told him that Taylor was still sick, hooked up to monitors and machines so that the doctors would know immediately if anything needed to be done.

Gavin himself wasn't sure this was such a good idea, but Dr. Petropolis had come at midnight to talk to the kids and again at eight this morning. Between talking to the police, the doctors and their parents, the kids detailed everything that happened in the last couple of days. Every time Gavin so much as thought about it, or heard another word uttered about it, he was so pissed off he couldn't see. In any case, Dr. Petropolis now had one new patient and had recommended for the kids to spend time together. They needed the reassurance, and Ryan and Tori both needed to see Taylor was alive. They'd been through several traumatic experiences.

Traumatic. That sounded so damned tidy. Traumatic. She also recommended family counseling once Taylor was up and about. Gavin figured they would all need it and vowed to do whatever he had to make certain his family healed.

"Is she going to wake up?" Ryan asked.

"Sure she is. They're keeping her medicated right now so that she'll get plenty of rest. She needs to sleep."

And he needed to see her light brown eyes again. Gavin needed to see those dimples peek at him from the corners of her mouth.

He sat back as Ryan started talking to her, much as he had that first night. Their son told her story after story. Gavin would let him talk for a while, but not too long. Ryan needed his rest too.

"And then this horse came and...." Ryan stopped.

"What?" Gavin asked him, brushing a strand of hair back off his wife's forehead.

"She squeezed my hand, Dad." Ryan smiled. "She squeezed my hand. Mom's gonna be okay."

Gavin looked down at her, the hand holding his faintly tightened. He looked at his son. "Yes, she is, Ryan. Yes, she is."

EPILOGUE

232   *Jaycee Clark*

Three months later

Nina Fisher sat in a jail in D.C. It was the same as all the other damn cells she'd been in, though maybe there were more guards. She was still waiting on transport back to Texas where she was now incarcerated for life.

Yippi-fucking-who. Endless days of monotony and submission. Anger burned bright in her for the injustice of it all.

The slot in her door opened and her meal tray came in. Solitary sucked. Eat and breathe in this freegin' cement hole. Every damn thing was made out of cement.

Made it hard to find readily available metal objects.

Sighing, she got off the mattress and limped over to the door. Her knee, or what was left of it, hurt like a bitch. Damn the sonofabitch who pulled that trigger. On a muttered oath, Nina grabbed her tray off the small ledge.

Sludge. It was all sludge. No damned variety. Nina tossed it on the small outcropping that was supposed to be a mini table or desk or some such shit. She wasn't hungry, not really.

Not there was anything else to do. Hell, might as well. Nina dug in. All of it finger food, not even a freaking fork. Like she'd stab herself with a fork.

No thank you. She'd find another way.

Halfway through the meal, she realized there was something in the salad, something under the lettuce. Picking it up, she carefully shifted her body to block the camera's view.

A plastic bag.

Hot Damn! She could see the pale blue powder. Oh, thank you God. Someone loved her after all. As naturally as possible, she slipped the bag out from under the lettuce and dropped it down the front of her jumpsuit.

* * * *

Later that night, in the dark, she pulled the package out. With the tip of her finger, she tasted it. Ambrosia. Sweet.

Since she'd spent the last few months in this hellhole, she knew it like the back of her hand. Carefully, she turned over and shook some of the powder out onto the ledge by the wall. The darkness hid her, or the guards would be in confiscating it.

Reaching gingerly around, she found her one book she was allowed. Ripping out a random page, she rolled it up.

For a split second she wondered where this came from.

Who the hell cared? When would she get any more?

After the first line dropped, she railed another. Hell, they'd search her cell in the morning, might as well enjoy the shit.

Halfway through her fourth line, she knew something was wrong.

Pink dots danced in front of her, shaping, shifting. They changed

DEADLY TIES

233

green and blue....

Something wasn't right....

Before she could figure out what it was, it was too late.

* * * *

A man sat back in his hotel room, a glass of orange juice at the side of the plate of fruit. The paper told him nothing as yet. With one hand he flipped through the channels on the TV with the remote. He was waiting on the news.

It seemed Notre Dame was on a winning streak. Never much of a sports fan, he turned to the business section of the paper and checked his stocks.

"....On a local interest this morning. Nina Fisher, the woman charged with kidnapping Ryan and Victoria Kinncaid, the children of prominent D.C. brothers, Dr. and Mrs. Gavin Kinncaid and Brayden Kinncaid, was found dead this morning in her cell. Authorities say she died of an overdose.

The search for Hammal...."

Overdose. He folded his paper and picked up his fork, spearing a strawberry. It crunched in his mouth.

Yeah, pure blue crystal meth laced with a little J.C. acid would do that to a person.

He finished eating his breakfast, thinking of the day ahead.

Ryan would never again have to worry. After all, he'd given the boy his word. He might be a lot of things, but if gave his word, he kept it.

The man packed his bags, and cleaned the room, wiping it of prints. Once outside, he disappeared into the crowd.

* * * *

"Ryan!" Taylor yelled from the kitchen. Her chest still pulled, but that was normal they told her and it would fade. She lifted her foot from the mess in the floor.

The music from the living room continued to drift on the air as Ryan kept playing.

"Ryan!"

"Ma'am?"

"Come here!"

"In a minute."

"Now, young man."

She heard his sigh here in the kitchen.

"Can't I finish playing that piece, Mama?" he asked, coming to a halt in the doorway.

She only pointed to the mess on the floor.

"Oh, man!" he complained.

"Your puppy didn't make it outside."

"Sorry." Ryan hurried to the paper towels and ripped several off. "I thought I got Luna out in time."

Taylor retrieved a plastic grocery bag. "It's fine. That's what puppies are known for. Is Luna out back?" She looked out the window to the back yard scattered with fallen leaves. Autumn hung crisp in the air; its presence sang in muted tones of gold, orange, reds and browns.

Thanksgiving was in two weeks. And she was excited about celebrating it in their new home. After D.C., Gavin asked her if she minded moving closer to Seneca. He started talking little league this and little league that. Taylor didn't care where they lived as long as one Nina Fisher left them alone.

Now, they lived half an hour from D.C. and about twenty minutes from Gavin's parents.

"When's Dad gonna be home?" Ryan asked, tossing the soiled paper towels in a sack she held. He took the bag and tied it off to take outside.

Taylor checked the clock. Should be anytime. The rumble of the garage door had her grinning at Ryan. "Looks like he's here."

Gavin walked into the kitchen through the side door, tossing his jacket over a chair. Smiling that crooked grin that would for always cause her heart to race, he strode to her and wrapped her in his arms. She felt his inhale against her chest, against her hair.

"How was your day, dear?" Taylor asked him in her best Carol Brady voice. Personally, she missed the office, missed the people and the work. But as yet, she just wasn't up for it. Maybe after Christmas. She still tired easily, still hurt, though she tried to hide it from Gavin, and for the most part he let her.

"Fine, and yours?" he asked, leaning down and kissing her.

"Gross," Ryan muttered.

Taylor's chuckle mixed with Gavin's. He looked at Ryan. "Go take your mess out to the cans."

Ryan rolled his eyes, and walked out the door grinning.

Never, in all her dreams, did Taylor think it would be this simple. And it hadn't been. After she'd finally woken up, there were days and weeks of hospital or therapy, both physical and psychological. Some sessions were private; some were with Gavin and Ryan.

The road hadn't been easy by any means, and it still had its bumps, but over all things were better than they'd ever been.

"How long do you think he'll be out there?" Gavin asked, tucking a strand of hair behind her ear, his thumb trailing the edge, down to her lobe. Shivers danced down her spine.

"Not long enough for what you're thinking, I assure you." She traced his lips with her finger. God, he still caused her heart to flip over.

"Well, then, we'll have to get him busy on homework or something. I need to take a shower and tell you about my day. Delivering babies and dealing with pregnant women makes me want to see your belly all round." His eyes twinkled down at her as his hand rubbed low on her stomach. The intention was clear in his eyes before his mouth lowered and kissed her with all the love she felt mirrored her own.

Pulling back, she looked at him. She'd often wondered if his hadn't

DEADLY TIES   235

been the hardest road of all. She knew Gavin still blamed himself, and probably always would for what happened to them. And he was forever trying to make it up to them.

Taylor sighed. Life would work it all out. In time, in time.

Walking to the door, she opened it up. "Ryan! Time for homework!"

Turning back to Gavin she grinned. "Didn't you say something about a shower? And working on babies?"

* * * *

Journal Entry

I haven't written in a long while. I still can't believe it, Nina is dead. It reminds me of that weird movie Mama likes so much. Ding dong the witch is dead.

That sounds really bad I know. Truthfully, I'm glad she's dead. I just don't know how I should feel because of that. Is it bad that I'm glad?

But enough of HER. I'm writing cause I had another vision. A good one. A really, really good one.

Yesterday evening I walked into the living room. Dad and Mama were snuggled up on the couch. They do that a lot. They were watching some movie back when people drove funny looking cars that looks like they have bicycle wheels--I can't remember the name, something about tomatoes--that's another one of Mama's favorite movies. I think it's the clothes in it, cause they're like the clothes she wears.

Anyway, I saw something that I should probably tell them about, but I don't want to. I want to wait and let them tell me. And since I can't tell them, I'll just write it.

I'm going to be a big BROTHER!

I'm going to have a baby sister. I'm not sure when, but isn't that cool? I wonder what we'll call her?

I can't wait till the day she's born. I'm going to teach her all sorts of stuff. I'll teach her about puppies and my violin. I can teach her about music. But I think the most important thing I'll teach her, will be about family. Yeah, I'm going to tell her that no matter what, love always tells. And of course I'm going to swear the Kinncaid motto to her: This I'll defend.

THE END

Printed in the United States
33282LVS00003B/1-63